PENGUIN BOOK

SAFE IN THE KITCHEN

Aisling Foster grew up in Ireland where she attended the National College of Art and University College, Dublin. After writing for advertising and fashion she became a freelance journalist and broadcaster. She has written plays for Radio 4 and *The First Time*, a story for young adults. *Safe in the Kitchen* is her first novel. She lives in London with her husband and two children.

AISLING FOSTER

SAFE IN THE KITCHEN

PENGUIN BOOKS

For Roy

PENGUIN BOOKS

Published by the Penguin Group
Penguin Books Ltd, 27 Wrights Lane, London W8 5TZ, England
Penguin Books USA Inc., 375 Hudson Street, New York, New York 10014, USA
Penguin Books Australia Ltd, Ringwood, Victoria, Australia
Penguin Books Canada Ltd, 10 Alcorn Avenue, Toronto, Ontario, Canada M4V 3B2
Penguin Books (NZ) Ltd, 182–190 Wairau Road, Auckland 10, New Zealand

Penguin Books Ltd, Registered Offices: Harmondsworth, Middlesex, England

First published by Hamish Hamilton 1993
Published in Penguin Books 1994
1 3 5 7 9 10 8 6 4 2

Printed in England by Clays Ltd, St Ives plc

I

A Political Funeral: Dublin, 1970

* * *

She was glad of the mink. She had put it on for the first time yesterday and already its soft folds felt like a second skin, the wrappings of a well-groomed, more comfortable person than those other old women standing around the grave in dull tweeds and dreadful man-made fibres.

They were all looking at her, of course, the political wives, pricing the fur, strand by strand. Pattie MacNally in a mildewed astrakhan, too old and bulky for today's requirements. Beside her, Molly Nolan standing firm in the mud, her brown boots mismatching a high-waisted blue serge like something from the maid's day off.

Rita lifted her eyes to the sky. This was no time for pettiness, no time to consider the virgin widow with a face like a bag of hammers and the same black weeds she had worn since the day after she married the Hayden boy in his condemned cell in 1921. With so many photographers one must not get pinched around the mouth and spoil the lines Mary's make-up girl had drawn only a few hours ago.

No need to check Mary's get-up. She looked marvellous, almost young, if you did not inquire too closely beneath the netting. The way she stood, so tall and straight with tragedy, collapsing afterwards on Liam's arm as the mourners drifted back towards the cars. Anyone might think it was her own husband they were putting in the ground.

'Dear lady.'

He was large, this stranger who had stood waiting for her to turn from the grave, a squat, square bluebottle. The fist holding her hand seemed too big, the face squashed and full cheeked as an infant Eskimo beaming into her

3

eyes. When he leant towards her, she had a momentary fear that he expected to rub noses.

'Fabulous, Mrs O'Fiaich, beautiful as ever!'

It was most awkward. She did not know this man from Adam, yet here he was making personal and quite inappropriate remarks. To compound the sin, he did not move on, nor offer the usual decencies. Only stood there, rooted like a deformed oak, staring not exactly at her but at her ears.

The accent was foreign. If he were a diplomat or some visiting dignitary, he should say his piece and go. She looked down at his bear-sized brogues with the mud of Frank's grave clinging to the soles and her memory was washed by a wave of cinnamon, the hot sweet spicy smells of New York, Boston, the Midwest, scents of hotel suites, railway carriages, private dining-rooms, and Nina.

'Sergei! Sergei Grigoryev! What on earth are you doing here?'

As if she did not know.

'Surely, in your country, you not forget old friends?'

So it had finally happened. They had followed her here, to Frank's funeral, to claim what was theirs.

She wanted to pull herself free from his big bear paws, to reach for the diamonds at her ears, feel the glow of rubies and the cool strength of each pearl point. But the Russian was holding both her hands, and for the first time that day she could feel the chill frisson of wind about her neck.

II

Coming Out in 1916

* * *

For as long as Rita could remember her favourite dress had been the white muslin with the seed-pearl bodice. Mama had had it cut down from one of her own, and when people admired Rita in it, Mama would look at her sadly and sigh, 'I know, isn't the threadwork wonderful!'

Mama loved clothes. They were her passion, her moral standard. Apart from bridge and the way her face went when she ate the skin off the custard (her hand a beaky seagull darting to the jug, her head tipping back to gulp the slippery membrane), Rita had first associated that word, passion, with Mama's feeling for clothes. Long before Rita had ever even heard of S.E.X.

Mama dressed up for everything. She noticed what people wore, even the maids. To her, new inventions like the zipper or permanent pleats were the cleverest thing, far more admirable than refrigerators or the motor car, and she would go on and on about them most amusingly until everyone was laughing and Papa would tell her to concentrate on her cards.

Mama had worn the muslin dress when she was a débutante. Mrs Roche adjusted it for Rita every year. And each year, as the dressmaker struggled to accommodate the maddening new dimensions of Rita's body, Mama told the story of the night of her presentation at Dublin Castle. Rita could only stand like a statue, pierced by pins as Mrs Roche became absorbed in the tale, waiting for the moment when the Lord Lieutenant crossed the room to put his name in Mama's dance book.

Then Mama and the old seamstress frowned at the

7

short, solid Rita. Mrs Roche whispered, 'God, but you must have been only gorgeous, Mrs Fitzgerald!'

Papa said that Mama could have married anyone. She was the toast of Dublin. It was funny to see how pleased and proud Papa still was that she had chosen him, a doctor, a younger son of the Tuam Fitzgeralds. Mama seemed to find their union strange too. She was forever making it clear that living in a big Victorian house in hospital grounds had taken some getting used to. Her own home in Westmeath was a ruin. She had brought them to see it once when returning from a house party in the west. She wept, standing amongst brambles and wild buddleia, describing lost gardens, averting her eyes from Queen Anne chimneys arranged above crumbling walls like the broken teeth of a beggarwoman. Papa said later that when Mama was a girl the house had been so riddled with dry rot she had had to hold on to a safety rope to go downstairs.

Rita was sixteen when Mrs Roche came to the house to work on a new ballgown. Rita begged Mama for white muslin and pearls like that first dress, but Mama thought that with the way the war was dragging on and the disturbances around the country they should choose something to last. It was she who picked out the cream grosgrain with pink lace for the sleeves; she insisted it would look perfect when Mrs Roche had finished with it. So, that season of 1916 and the three years before her marriage Rita danced in a dress which always made her feel like one of her stiff little nursery dolls, never a fairy-tale princess.

Not that there ever was a proper season for Rita Fitzgerald. People tried, of course, but somehow Dublin didn't have the heart for it. It was impossible to be happy when the boys she should have been dancing with were away at the front. Or, worse, had become faded sepia faces frowning from the tops of pianos. There was a gloom about home too. Even the beloved kitchen was no longer a place of sanctuary. Black armbands appeared as if part of the

8

uniform, harbingers of the sudden weeping storms which could shatter the easy chat around the big pine table. Then, of course, there was the uprising.

The whole thing was quite incredible. Mama and Papa had set off for Easter Monday at Fairyhouse in their usual high spirits, leaving Rita and Anne Marie to prepare for the Shackletons' tennis party. Driving there with Mlle Peirrot, the dogcart was halted by boys in army uniforms. A fear rose from the youths like an invisible steam, mingling with the fug of incomprehensible English accents. They looked so out of place on familiar suburban roads, the emptiness of street and pavement made sinister in the early afternoon sun. When they turned suddenly from demands for proof of identity to shoot the small tan mongrel trotting purposefully down the carriageway, only Anne Marie cried. Mlle Peirrot screamed in French for someone to take hold of the pony's head as the little dog jerked and whimpered and went still.

Its death was a sort of release. The young men laughed then and allowed Rita to take the reins from the governess's limp hands and turn the trap for home.

The strangest thing about that day was its silence. Apart from the echoing thud of shells like far-off fireworks, Rita felt as if all Dublin were holding its breath, listening for some whispered message. The only movement on the road came from armoured vehicles labouring up the hill outside or speeding down again. No chance of escape. All amusements had been cancelled, including a daffodil ball for which Mrs Roche had trimmed Rita's dress with silk flowers. Rita didn't know what to think. It did seem a bit mean that Pearse and Connolly should stab the British in the back when everyone was away at the front. But it was exciting to have a revolution only a mile or two down the road. Mary thought so too. She got through on the telephone to say there was a barricade outside the house in Merrion Square and her mother had refused tea to the rebels. Rita and she were laughing when the line went dead.

Wandering into the kitchen to forget the tension upstairs created the most terrible silence. They turned from their work to stare at Rita as if she were a stranger. Christine put on her most businesslike manner, treating Rita like a customer in Mitchell's, not someone she had sat on her knee and fed soda bread and jam from the time Rita was big enough to push her way through the double door.

'Well now, Miss Fitzgerald, what can we do for you?' There was no welcoming smile as Rita sat herself at the familiar table, no offers of the cook's best china for a pour of the tea.

Rita stayed anyway. There was nowhere else to go. 'Oh, Christine, isn't it horrible about the Post Office?'

The cook looked shifty then, rubbing at her shining black hob as, one by one, the other servants slipped away. When she spoke, her voice was a spoon too sweet. 'Don't I know it, miss, isn't it shocking altogether.'

That was when Rita understood, from the mocking triumph in the woman's voice, that it was not shocking at all. For Christine, or Mrs Kelleher (who looked after the household) and Mr Simmonds (who drove Papa and was in charge of the garden) and even young Eily, the general recently arrived from Longford and what Christine called 'a right eejit', something extraordinary was happening, a momentous, once-in-a-lifetime something which was tossing the pieces of their lives high into the air, so high that when they fell, the bits of the puzzle would never again be made to fit like before. Even one of Papa's mild mongols from the hospital across the field seemed to sniff with more assurance over the silver polish.

It was what made the people at this side of the kitchen door, and the ordinary people in the street and in the countryside beyond, suddenly different, set apart from Mama, Papa, Anne Marie, Rita, Mlle Peirrot and perhaps Mrs Roche − or perhaps not. As far as Mlle P. was concerned, the French Revolution was happening right outside the gates; it was only a matter of time before the mob would stream up the North Circular Road from the river like a pack of rats and drag the entire household to the guillotine.

'They make us to stand in carts – in the open horse carts!' The governess rocked and moaned in the little nursing chair. She looked dreadful, her olive skin paled to a dim green and her brown eyes bloodshot with weeping. Scrunched up like that with her faded gold hair clashing where it fell on her old plum-coloured dress, she reminded Rita of a flag abandoned on the field of battle.

'Oh the shame! This country, it is disgrace! It could not happen in France!'

Mr Simmonds told her there was no chance of flight. The ports were closed and a general curfew had been ordered. By nightfall, when Mama and Papa had not returned from the races, even the stolid Christine grew agitated. She sent Mr Simmonds out to get news of happenings in town, but he returned quickly to report roadblocks in both directions and a guard on the hospital gate. 'We'll get no help from the hospital neither. Didn't Matron tell me the poor creatures are in a terrible state, and them addled soldiers only demented with the explosions!'

Christine took off her apron then. 'We'll say a prayer, so.' She had the whole household kneeling with her in the sitting-room, including the stricken governess, when Mama walked in.

'What in Heaven's name are you doing, Rita? Has someone died?'

She looked like a ghost, or not like Mama at all. Her hat and veil were gone, so that her hair hung about her face like cobwebs. The new spring coat had a rip on the sleeve and one shoe was missing. She was quite delighted by her reception.

'Tea, Christine, please, and some sandwiches! I haven't had a thing since we celebrated a win on the four-thirty!

'But where's Papa? How did you get home?'

'I walked, darlings, absolute miles. I got so tired of your father driving from pillar to post, stop here, turn around there; hours it took us, with guns waved under our noses by every little butty in a uniform. I finally told him to let me out at the Mahons' crossroads. Then I had to navigate a pile of milk drays to get here!'

'Oh, ma'am, we were dreadful worried! But where's the Doctor?'

'The silly man wouldn't leave the car. Says it'll be used to block the roads. He's right, of course, they kept trying to take it from us.'

She too seemed changed by events, so charged with the strangeness of what she had seen she even laughed when Mlle Peirrot moaned like a barn door and Anne Marie whispered, 'Guns, Mama? Do the rebels have guns?'

'Of course, darling. They took pot-shots at us on Bolton Street. Papa said the paintwork is ruined!'

Papa looked most peculiar when he walked in. His top hat was still on his head, continuing the white line of dust which plastered his front as neat and thick as a fresh marker on the tennis court. He had been all around the city, attempting approaches from every side. The last successful run from Dolphin's Barn had left him with front lights shot out and a leaking carburettor. All he would say before ordering a bath was 'Idiots!', a word he went on repeating for some days.

His mood was not improved the next morning. He was particularly upset by a telephone call he managed to make to Colonel Fitch of the 3rd Battalion, Kilmainham. The Colonel had been very rude, even though, as Papa said, 'That fella has played bridge in this house – by God, he's dined at my table!'

It hurt Papa deeply that the caller implied blame for what was going on, even hinted that Papa, as a doctor, might give medical attention to the rebels, whom he called 'your compatriots'. When Papa mentioned the Hippocratic oath, Colonel Fitch slammed down the phone and Papa shouted 'Ignoramus!' to the empty hall. There was nowhere for him to go except the hospital, which was now stiff with the military guarding their shell-shocked patients. The Stephen's Green Club was closed because of snipers in the park. Papa attacked the spring lamb at luncheon as if it were the enemy of the people.

What most maddened Papa that Easter week was Constance Markievicz. Hers was the part in the business which he could not understand. As he told everyone when her name was mentioned, 'Know the family well, the Gore-Booths. A fine house in Sligo. Decent people.' All through those days of uncertainty and through the following years of upheaval Papa would stare at her face in his newspaper and mumble 'decent people' with a bewildered shake of his head.

Nobody else shared Rita's wonder at how a lovely girl like that could have married a foreign bear like Markievicz, even if he were a count. Yet Mama rather approved of her. Perhaps it was the wide-brimmed hats she liked, or the stylish way she wore her revolutionary uniform. For such panache, Mama could forgive anything.

Loving Ireland

* * *

'Dreary!' Mary kept hissing loudly, trying to get Rita to stand up and walk out in front of everybody. 'Will you listen to the blather!'

Certainly the talk on pre-Christian Ireland had been a little disappointing, but Rita was not bored. She was watching Frank Fee in the front row, liking the way his ears fitted so closely to his head, his wonderful stillness in an audience which shifted and coughed irritably as the learned professor mumbled on and on into his beard.

She knew Frank was pleased to see her there. He positively beamed at her, as if she were the only person in the room, making no attempt to hand out his leaflets or take up a collection for the cause.

When Mary said, much too loudly, 'For God's sake, let's get out before we have to take tea with these fogies!', he had taken control. They thought he was leading them downstairs to the hotel reception rooms, but he carried on out the front door, bringing them along Merrion Row to a public house. There were a lot of rough men inside with the smell of porter, and a singing woman with swollen feet who was thrown out soon after, cackling and cursing.

Confusion broke over Rita's head like a wave. Of course, such places were not entirely unknown to her. She couldn't help glancing at open doors as she walked past, and, like that woman who continued her aria from the gutter, there was often some human spillage on the street over which you had to step. But this was hardly the place for a man to bring ladies. Perhaps he should be told. In a way, though, she thought there was something rather thrilling about someone so unfettered by etiquette. He looked the

14

most relaxed she had yet seen him, leaning on the bar talking confidentially to the barman. Odder still, Mary was in her element.

'This is the queerest cup of tea I've ever seen, Mr Fee!'

She made him laugh, saying '*Sláinte!*' as he watched Mary take a sip of the sweet port he had brought. A most unsuitable drink so early in the evening, but Rita had to admit the lava flow of the stuff slipping into her empty stomach was very pleasant indeed. His eyes were on her face when she glanced up. A clear blue stare, the way judges in the Horse Show examined Papa's hunters, thoughtful, considering.

'I hope this is all right for you, Miss Fitzgerald?'

'So tell us, would you describe this as your club, Mr Fee?' Mary's laugh was always a bit loud. Her glass was almost empty. With her chin on her hands she was perusing him in that languid way of hers.

'You wouldn't catch me spending money in a club or hotel, Miss Kelly, full as they are with English blackguards holding on to the last rags of the Empire.'

Mary shook a finger at him; she was openly flirting. 'Don't say that to Rita! Isn't her father a member of a gentlemen's club! Which one is it, Rita – the Stephen's Green or Kildare Street?'

The shame of it! Frank was regarding her as if she had just pulled off a false beard. The downright dishonesty of the girl! Hadn't Mary's father only applied for membership of the Stephen's Green last year and been refused? Rita had heard Papa tell Mama that the trouble with Mr Kelly was all spit and no polish.

'Papa's a doctor – chief registrar of Mount Clonkee, the lunatic asylum. It wouldn't do for him to be in public houses – but he *is* Irish.'

Frank smiled kindly at her as though she were an innocent child who had just claimed Jesus was a cousin of the King. 'Well, this club is good enough for this Irishman!'

Mary laughed. 'I wouldn't have thought you a drinking man!'

'Indeed and I'm not' – he nodded at the glass of red lemonade as he whispered – 'but, do you see, these are great places for leaving things – to collect or pick up.'

For all her knowing nods, Rita could tell that her friend had no more idea what the man was talking about than she did.

'Well, all I know is this place is a thousand times better than where we've just been. Honestly, Rita, if that old fuddy-duddy hadn't stopped when he did, I might have thrown my shoe at him. I was that bored!'

Frank seemed disappointed. 'He was a bad speaker, all right, but some of it was very interesting.'

'Interesting? I'd find a list of war dead more interesting than all that stuff about bits of old pots and flint stones!'

'And what did you think, Miss Fitzgerald?'

His smiling intensity reminded her of the way Sister Pauline would will her to reach the top note in a choir solo.

'Dull in patches, I suppose, but I thought it rather wonderful to realize that we had an advanced civilization so long ago. I must have assumed our culture was imported by some invader or other; that the Irish themselves were pretty much a blank sheet.'

Mary was laughing at her now. 'God, you're a scream, Rita – a typical Dubliner! Honestly, Mr Fee, I don't think she knew a word of Irish or a note of her own music before she met me!'

His smile was beautiful when he turned it on Rita, a break of hawthorn blossom against a clear sky. 'What is it Our Lord said? "Better we bring one sinner to God than all the good men in the kingdom"?'

She could feel herself blushing. 'Oh, I'm converted all right!'

When he looked at her like that, she understood the romance of Ireland, the richness which for almost a year now she had struggled so hard to uncover. Nothing Mr Hyde had told them about the western isles, or Mr Yeats on folklore or Mrs Comisky about the ancient roots of

Irish grammar, nothing in intense study or regular attendance at all those meetings of the Gaelic League could bring such a rush of excitement to the whole subject of her country as this person, Frank Fee. What was it about him, a thirty-year-old County Clare man with a long, narrow face, the red hair giving poor protection to the high brow from which two points protruded like a bullock whose horns had been cut? She wanted to reach forward and touch the boniness there, to find some secret switch which would release all the knowledge within.

It was at one of the League's musical evenings they had first met, or, she liked to say afterwards, bumped into one another when dancing the Walls of Limerick. She noticed him before their dance. He was different to the others, gangly and unkempt beside the eager students, professional men and girls from good families for whom the discovery of Gaelic Ireland had become fashionable lately. Mr Fee was different in other ways too. He had been pointed out to Rita as a man to watch, a friend of Eamon de Valera since their stand together in 1916, a rising star in the nationalist movement. Odd, in such genteel company, to realize that Frank Fee had come from a place where reels were danced every Saturday night, yet was as awkward as she. But whereas he was stiff and forgetful of the moves, she found it difficult to control her body, to contradict years of childhood ballet, willing herself ramrod straight, allowing only her feet to tap out the rhythms.

He seemed quite dazed when they stopped, still holding out her hands in front of him, their arms crossed. They laughed as they disentangled themselves.

'Thank you, Mr Fee, but I've simply got to sit down!'

She had not expected him to accompany her. He had seated her far away from the samovar where the others were gathered for tea and biscuits. She tried not to look across the room at them, avoiding the tiny winks and waves from Mary, who stood in the group around Mr Russell, their speaker for the evening.

'*Tá an bhrón orm. Níl aon mhaith ionam chun rinnce.*'

'I'm sorry' – shaming to have to say it, she knew he'd think the less of her – 'but I'm only a poor beginner at the language; you'll have to translate.'

'I was only saying you must forgive me, I'm no hand at the dancing!'

'And I'm no feet!' she joked, but he was looking at her so seriously she felt the heat rise again in her face.

'You know enough, anyhow, to realize it's time we learned new steps.'

She loved his voice, so soft yet certain. And the clear light of belief shining from his eyes.

'It won't be long now before we're all of us dancing to a different tune. It'll be an Irish one, and sure then, won't all our feet move as one?'

'I'm trying, but there's so much to do.'

'Ireland will be great again when we have all learned our lessons. We can work together for that.'

As he spoke he gathered her in. She wanted to reach across and touch the scarred knuckles, to pull down his scant sleeves over the delicate whiteness of his wrists. Sitting talking to him like this, listening to his ideas about a new, self-reliant Ireland, he was like some exotic creature, another species to the usual smooth-cheeked young men with their braying, English-educated accents. You would not find Frank Fee at tennis clubs and garden parties. He was a beautiful jewel, an uncut diamond which, she realized suddenly, she wanted more than anything in the world.

Dinner at Clonkee, 1918

* * *

They could not see what she saw. The way Anne Marie
sat there staring at him, anyone might think him a new
arrival at the zoo. To Mama and Papa he was a country
bumpkin, an upstart. The stiffness of his manner, the
slight hesitation before he spoke, the apparent simplicity
of what he said in that gentle, musical voice of his: none of
it was beautiful to them. He was a symptom of Rita's little
hobby, a blow-in from her interest in Irish culture, in the
language and music and fable which Mama, Papa and
stupid, childish Anne Marie pretended to find so peculiar.

But they could not shake him. When Papa first stared
at Frank's hands reddened by a summer on the farm,
Frank made no move to hide them. Over dinner he
seemed to use them more, pushing them into the pooled
arena of light which bounced on to the French polish from
the huge fringed shade above, sweeping aside the glitter of
silver and crystal to make his point, to describe an Ireland
loosed of England's yoke, a chrysalis cracked open from
which a new form of beauty would surely emerge, a
nation shaped of small farms and helpful neighbours,
where luxury would be a lump of bacon in the pot and all
posturing excess thrown back across the sea.

'Explain your plans for trade, Mr Fee. Surely you'd
concede that trade is a two-way business, would you not?'
There was a patronizing tone in Papa's voice. He was
peeling an orange, one circular mushroom eased off the
top, five equal triangles pulled smoothly away between
thumb and blade to be stacked neatly on the plate.

Frank sawed into his fruit, the blunted silver of the little
knife making no impression until a sudden spurt of juice

stained his hands. Everyone had stopped eating. Anne Marie giggled into her lap. Honestly, when would the girl ever grow up? Frank wiped his fingers slowly and rolled the napkin into its silver ring. He had been thinking about Papa's question, had not noticed the incident with the orange, abandoned now like a punctured corpse.

'Self-sufficiency, Mr Fitzgerald, that's our aim. Remove excess, opportunities for greed, possession of one man over another, and what would any fellow need? – only a cow or a pig and maybe a few spuds.'

Her father smiled as he looked around his table, at the candlelight playing on the pierced brass firescreen, the glint of swords and scabbards on the walls, the Egyptian tapestries stretching to where two skins, a black bear and a leopard, hung snarling in the gloom. Papa's ancestors might have been disturbed by the conversation, staring down in amazement amidst so much gilded booty borne home from the colonies.

Rita had always loved this room; she supposed Frank could not. To him everything here would represent the burden of the past, useless objects testifying to a time which the future would rewrite, would smash and trample like something so contaminated it would be better to scrap it and begin again.

'I don't think you'll find many Dublin men who'd agree with you, Mr Fee. We're not too *au fait* with keeping cows or growing potatoes on the North Circular Road, nor many other places in this great city of ours!'

Mama's tinkly laugh joined Anne Marie's titter. Rita almost hated them. It was horrible what they were doing, casting Frank as a bear she saw in Munich once which a man had prodded and prodded until it danced.

Yet, to look at him, it was as if Frank did not even feel the tug on the chain. He smiled back. 'As you know, Mr Fitzgerald, Dublin is the Pale. As such, some may come to view it as an anachronism, an irrelevance to the new nation.'

'And what exactly do you mean by an irrelevance, Mr Fee?'

'I mean that after we have dismantled the machinery of imperialism, we will be looking outside the boundaries of the Pale for the *real* Irish people. Oh yes, you may smile, but when the days of our liberation come, it will be in the fields and mountains we will look for Ireland's inspiration, to the empty landscapes which this city, like too many across the water, has drained of people, our one great resource; and which, God willing, we will fill again with new hope and productivity.'

He spoke like that, like a missionary, no, a visionary. Tears pricked her eyes. He was so right, so perfect in his perceptions of how it must be, that it was impossible to understand how Anne Marie could splutter into her napkin like a hen with a fit. Mama was whispering at Eily to clear, and Rita could see she too was trying not to smile. Papa seemed rooted to his chair, pulling hard on his moustache.

'So, you're one of these fellas who wants to send our workmen back to the fields?'

'Indeed, they might be glad of some employment, not to mention a release from Dublin's slums, which some say are the worst in Europe!'

'What if they don't want to go? Let us suppose they prefer their tenements to the mud cabin and an acre of land you might offer them? What then?'

Mama was standing now.

Frank made no attempt to rise. Rita could hear Anne Marie give an offended sniff through her silly little nose. It was wrong to hate your sister, but watching her whisper into Mama's ear, Rita despised Anne Marie's dainty neatness, her pointy little face pulled back to smooth brown hair, her tiny wrists and ankles, her sharp-angled body which let her childish velvet dress hang in smooth lines, never inclined to bunch and lump as clothes did on Rita unless she counted every crust which went into her mouth. It was so unfair. Her sister with all of Mama's delicate features while she, Rita, was fashioned like Papa: broad faced, short legged, rugged, as different as a Connemara pony to a racehorse.

Yet Frank had hardly noticed Anne Marie. That was one of the things Rita loved about him, the unwavering quality which kept him doggedly pursuing what he wanted, never distracted by a prettier face like other men.

He walked back into the sitting-room with Papa and she could hardly take her eyes off him. She watched him as Papa droned on about war reparations and the Irish debt, saw him look across at her and smile. His mouth, in repose, was like one of Botticelli's angels, a witty squiggle which, when drawn back to expose his crooked teeth, suggested something more dangerous, even cruel. Yes, no matter what Mama and Papa said, she was in love with Frank Fee.

'Are you planning to settle in Dublin, Mr Fee?'

There was a mocking note in Anne Marie's voice. Rita knew what was implied.

'Don't be silly, Anne Marie. Won't this be the centre for the new parliament when we get it?'

Anne Marie laughed. 'Oh, I can think of plenty of places I'd want to set up a parliament if I could choose – and it wouldn't be in dirty old Dublin!'

'Nor anywhere in Ireland, if I had the choice!' Mama added.

His eyes, when he caught hers, were kind. He gave a tiny wink and everything was all right. Frank Fee understood her difference, her apartness from this ridiculous, impossible family. She had dreaded bringing him here, letting him see. But he had understood.

Mama and Papa looked worried. They had become dull, two dressmaker's dummies waiting to be stowed in the attic. As for Anne Marie, she was a stupid doll.

A Celtic Tableau

* * *

Mrs Roche had copied the costume for her from an illustration by Maud Gonne in the new collection of heroic legends published by Maunsel's. It was indeed the perfect image for Cathleen ni Houlihan. The compliments from the other members at the League's Christmas party confirmed what the mirror at home had told her: the gold threadwork edging the green silk shift lightened the brown of her long hair and the leather thonging on her bare arms and legs emphasized the whiteness of skin.

'To the life, Miss Fitzgerald!'

'An inspiration to us all!'

The struggle it had been! Finding all the props and getting Papa to lend Mr Simmonds to drive her to this house in Sandymount. Then arranging the whole thing, the other contestants struggling with their swords and animal skins in a space already much reduced by Mary's golden chariot. Young Mr Orr had seemed particularly affected by Rita's tableau, shouting 'Bravo! Bravo!' only seconds after the curtains opened, causing the silly wolf-hound to forget its careful tuition and try to slip its leash.

Afterwards everyone said it was the best portrayal they had seen, better than Mr and Mrs Simms as Diarmuid and Grainne or, indeed, Mary as a fearsome Queen Maeve. Mr Russell had asked if Rita might sit for him in his studio one day and all agreed with Mrs Ormond's remark that Rita was an inspiration to young nationhood. Mr Orr brought Rita some tea and held the dog for her. They had been discussing the origins of fairy rings when Frank Fee had appeared, out of place in his tight suit amongst the roomful of heroic figures. She was so glad to

23

see him there she almost jumped up and kissed him, but the way he glared at herself and Mr Orr anyone might think it was they who were the odd ones out.

'Mr Fee, Frank, you came! Do you know Mr Orr?'

The expression on Frank's face when he looked at Charlie Orr's Finn McCool costume was almost sneering.

'You missed Miss Fitzgerald's finest hour, Mr Fee. Young Ireland herself in living tableau!'

'Is that what it is?'

Was he displeased? He stared at Rita's bare limbs so that even in the hot room she felt compelled to pull the velvet cape around her shoulders.

'It'll take more than fancy dress to get the Irish people behind our struggle. And more than these airy-fairy myths.'

He disapproved of her. If she could have torn off the silly costume there and then, she would have. Why was it always like this, the awful, stomach-lurching uncertainty, wanting to please him, never knowing how? She had hoped he would be here tonight, had put off her appearance until the last possible moment just in case he was delayed. Success meant nothing in his absence. Now he was here and it was as if this man who had forgiven her so much was finally seeing her for what she was: a silly, empty-headed socialite, no more serious about the fight for nationhood than all these chattering members of the Gaelic League with their jolly suburban voices and fancy dress.

'I say, Miss Fitzgerald, I've just had the most splendid idea!'

Charlie Orr beamed with excitement. He was quite sweet, really, just too young, a cardboard cut-out of a man compared with Frank Fee.

'Why don't you and I do "The Marriage of Strongbow and Aoife" next time? I'll get some of the fellows from Trinity dressed up as slain warriors. I think I could locate some chain mail and you could wear that outfit! What do you say?'

'Miss Fitzgerald has no intention of playing the bartered bride, Mr Orr.'

It must have appeared rude, drawing her across the room like that, abandoning Mr Orr with the wolfhound and her empty teacup. There was nothing she could do. The way Frank gripped her elbow anyone might think she was a dangerous prisoner who would try to flee at any moment. When they reached the door, she realized he intended removing her from the party. He didn't understand how impolite that would be, or about the dog which must be returned to Mama's friends in Clonsilla.

'You mean you'd rather stay here, with this crowd of gawms?'

He made it difficult to think, his urgency, his presumption that she would do his bidding. Yet he had said nothing to win such a commitment. He had only danced with her, sat with her, sought her out in gatherings such as these. They had never been alone, not entirely. Why, even after that visit home, he had not bothered his head to write a note of thanks or telephone Mama.

'I can't leave now, Mr Fee. There are prizes, and Miss Cunningham has brought her harp.'

'You want me away, so? Only there's a meeting I thought might interest you, in Rutland Square, for a new publication they're planning to support the Irish Volunteers. I was wrong.'

He had grown hot and breathless. Papa got angry like that sometimes, behaving as if he had been personally slighted by a messy dish of butter or the failure of the car to start. Perhaps all men were like that. Frank had his hand on the doorknob when he muttered, 'I suppose the next time I see you you'll be marrying that Sassenach student?'

'Only as Aoife, I assure you!'

'Well, it's foolishness, so it is, this play-acting. Even fellas like Hyde or MacNeill would tell you the same: the road to freedom is a harder one.'

'Aren't you being a little over-serious, Mr Fee? What's

wrong with making Irish things fashionable for a change, even if it is only make-believe? Doesn't it help your party funds, and give people a bit of fun?'

'Is it fun you're after, Rita Fitzgerald? Or are you serious about wanting to turn this country into a nation?'

'Of course I want to help the Irish struggle. I only wish I knew how.'

It was the right answer. He almost smiled. 'I could show you, if it's what you want.'

'I should like that.'

She had to look away, his gaze was so intense. A maid pushed through the door between them bearing a green shamrock Christmas cake so that Rita almost missed his whisper. 'We should maybe get married, so, Rita Fitzgerald, and join our lives for the struggle.'

Everything was right. All she had hardly dared pray for, would never have whispered out loud even to Mary, was coming true: Frank Fee had asked her to marry him. This fine, sharp-faced countryman who knew so much, could see so far with those sea-blue eyes, wanted her to share in the making of Ireland's future.

'If that is what you want, Frank, then yes, I should like it very much.'

'That's fixed, so.' He blew on his right hand then, a mock spit, and shook her own. Two farmers making a bargain. '*Is tú plúr na mban*, there isn't a woman could beat you.'

It was only when he was slipping out the door that he smiled at her properly, and the warm pleasure of it touched her like a blessing or a kiss.

Waiting at the Crossroads

* * *

Nothing. For two weeks she had rushed to answer the phone, hurried to meet the postman, searched Papa's face for some hint that Frank had been in touch. But there was nothing, no communication from Frank Fee, no word or sign which might calm this madness in her, this fluttering, lurching sickness which addled her brain and reduced her appetite: which she recognized as love.

Mary's telephone voice sounded mocking. 'Any word from your man?'

'Not yet.'

'Probably for the best. Don't you think he's a bit intense, Rita, the way he goes on, as if saving Ireland was a sort of religion or something? And I've heard since that he's up to his neck in some Fenian organization. Now that I come to think of it, somebody told me he got a knock on the head in 1916. It can turn people mad, you know – ask your daddy.'

If only she hadn't told Mary. She couldn't stop herself, she had to tell someone. She knew she hadn't imagined those words, the straight look in his eyes when he spoke them. It had filled her with such happiness that by the time she returned to the company she feared the pleasure must already be radiating out of her eyes, seeping through every pore so that she shone like an icon or one of those Italian glass statues of the Virgin which light from inside.

She had blurted it out in the car going home, whispered it to Mary over the wolfhound and the collapsed cardboard of her chariot, and Mary had screeched so that Mr Simmonds nearly crashed, roaring it out all wrong and upside down.

'Let me guess, it's Charlie Orr! God, and there was I thinking he was paying you all that attention because he liked dogs!'

'Don't be silly, Mary, it was Frank asked me, Frank Fee!'

'You can't be serious? Sure nobody marries a fella like that!'

The back of Mr Simmonds's closely shaven head seemed to bristle more than usual as the gears slipped and clashed. Now everyone in the kitchen would know.

If only he would telephone. The sound of his voice, always so clear and certain, might silence the whispers in her brain, the doubts asking who she thought she was, how she could imagine she might interest a man like Frank Fee, could ever marry him. They were laughing about it in the kitchen, she could tell, smiling and nudging each other when she came through the swing door, going quiet when she answered Christine's inquiries about the possibilities of a finishing school now the war looked like it was finally over. She could swear the little maid from Monaghan had giggled when the cook remarked on Rita's lack of appetite. 'What's wrong with my cake, Miss Fitzgerald, is it in love you are or what?'

Christine must have told Mama too. They were all looking at her strangely, exchanging glances when she asked about the post or stiffened when the doorbell rang. Each morning they tried to get her out of the house, but she refused to help Mama with her charities, or Papa with the bills and medical correspondence he so hated. Anne Marie even suggested games of tennis, but Rita stayed firm: Frank would come back to her; he was a man of his word. Meanwhile, as the cook had noticed, her appetite was rather poor. Perhaps when she married Mr Fee, her love would turn her slim and beautiful, and keep her that way.

Papa held the letter in front of him before he opened it. 'His Majesty's Prisons Service. Bet this one is about that fellow I discharged last year. Still thinks he's at the Somme.'

Mama sighed. 'Why these people write to your home address I'll never understand. Hardly a fit subject for breakfast!'

'Wait now, it's from Saunders. Remember that army fellow who oversaw the conversion of the north wing a few years ago?'

'Oh yes, funny little fat man. Wasn't it he who got the bee in his bonnet about putting you into uniform to treat his soldiers?'

'Big shot in a prison in Armagh now ... Great God Almighty!' There was a queer pallor to Papa's face as he handed the letter to Rita. He suddenly looked very old. 'Perhaps Rita can explain what this means?'

Beneath the grimly headed notepaper Rita read:

Dear Doctor

Please excuse the intrusion over what may very well turn out to be something and nothing, but I felt I should draw your attention to a tricky question which has arisen here. It's an odd business, but from our time together in Dublin I know you will want to take swift action. The facts are as follows: almost two weeks ago a man by the name of Francis Xavier Fee was arrested for attempting to cause a public affray (the Intelligence people tell me they think he was planning to assist in a prison break-out, but that is harder to support) and is here at His Majesty's pleasure (chances are there will not be a trial, but this sort of action keeps unsavoury elements off the streets). Now this is the difficulty, and I feel sure there has been some mistake, but the fact is, the prisoner has stated he is affianced to your daughter, Margarita, and named you as a possible source of bail.

I should appreciate your prompt response to this matter. As you can understand, Mr Fee's connection with your family makes decisions about how to proceed rather more delicate than usual.

Best wishes
Godfrey Saunders, DSO
Acting Head of Security, Ulster Section

The relief! He loved her. Frank Fee intended to marry her. He would open the door of her cage and she would escape into a new world, a country of their own making.

They were all staring at her, Papa leaning back in his chair as if he had been shot. Mama broke the silence. 'How dare you smile like that, you silly, silly child!' Anne Marie sniffed and giggled like a demented sheep. None of it mattered. Everything would be all right now. This happiness: it was hard to come back to earth, to remember how far she had to go to explain their plans for their life together and for Ireland.

'I'm sorry. I'm just glad he's all right. I've been so worried!'

'But the man says he's going to marry you, Rita! Surely there's no substance in that?'

Sometimes parents could be almost stupid. When would they realize it was time to throw away the old ways, foolish conventions like requesting a girl's hand or an official announcement? Frank had said they must forge a new way. And the sooner the better.

The Marriage of Margarita to Francis Xavier,

1919

* * *

'You're far too young!'

Everyone knew that Mama had married at nineteen. Rita had grown up on the story of her whirlwind romance: met and married to Papa in three months flat and never a single regret. It made her opposition all the more ridiculous. The weeping rows with Papa were worse, with his threats of parental law and enforced exile. Only when the Jesuit priest began his daily visits did Rita feel sure of winning. At other times Mama would have called his little talks about personal sacrifice and God's will 'Irish toshery', the sort of stuff she blamed the priests for using to keep simple people simple. But now she was silent.

It was Christine who said what they all thought. 'He's wrong for you.'

That hurt, to realize how fiercely against the marriage Christine was. She, of all people, should be in favour of their alliance. After all, Frank was working so hard to liberate people like Christine, to give them back what had been stolen from them: property, as Frank often said, which was more than land; their culture and their national pride too. Rita had tried to explain that and had been dismayed how bothered Christine had got, shouting that the Easter revolutionaries had gone too far with talk of cutting off Ireland altogether and sending the people back to the land.

'It's all very well for some poor eejits to live on a bog, but what about me? And what about the gentry? Where are they supposed to go when our gunmen are running the country? Dead in a cellar, I suppose, like that Russian crowd?'

She got so agitated she dropped the china cup reserved for Rita's visits to the kitchen. It was smashed beyond repair, which appeared to bother her more than anything. Her voice was hoarse when she banged down the servants' white mug full of tea. 'Well, miss, you might as well get used it!'

Rita's tea had tasted different in the thick delft, bitter and not so nice.

Mama finally agreed to a September date, with the proviso that Rita should spend the summer months travelling on the Continent with Mama's sister, Dot, who lived in Paris. Papa said it would give Rita 'a little finish', but she knew both parents hoped she would forget what they called 'la romance Celtique'.

She would miss Frank, but it was one way of getting out of the house, away from Mama's moans about 'The waste!' and Papa's baffled stare. When Mama offered to do her portrait in watercolours, it felt like a reconciliation. Mama was usually in such a good mood with a paintbrush in her hand. But Rita tried to have a little chat about Mama's own marriage and Mama got into a furious temper. She screamed about the Fitzgeralds being Old Irish, listed in *Burke's Landed Gentry*, whereas 'The only place you'll find that jumped-up gombeenman of yours is in the criminal files!' She took herself off to her darkened bedroom. On the abandoned canvas there was only a lumpy outline on a background the colour of a bruise.

Everything had become waiting-for-Frank time, lying on her bed dreaming, or meeting Mary to make plans. Anyone could see Mary was jealous the way she said, 'Do you not think, maybe, you *are* a bit young?' and 'One good thing, I suppose, at least you'll get away from home.' Rita felt sorry for her sometimes, stuck in Merrion Square with no sign of a man.

It was hard to imagine the exact shape of their married life. In daydreams she could only see herself at Frank's side, working with him late into the night, writing speeches, ordering little refreshments, glowing under his proud look as they entered important meetings with party chiefs (she was on another diet, and once she got away from Christine's sulks she would stick to it always), supporting him while he delivered their cures for Ireland's pain, for eradicating the illness he called 'the English disease'.

'And where are you planning to live, Mr Fee, when Rita and you are married?'

Anne Marie had been asking silly questions all afternoon. She was supposed to be helping Mama in the garden, but kept flopping back into their window-seat in the drawing-room where they were trying to compose a speech about Ireland's right to nation status at Versailles. It was most intrusive. He had returned to Dublin only a few days ago and Rita cherished every moment they spent alone. And then he had seen the male patients getting off the hospital lorry and made a mild remark about the exploitation of labour, which made Anne Marie even worse, almost patronizing. As if Rita hadn't explained about Papa's attempts to open up the asylum to the outside world, how he had lowered the high walls around the grounds and was trying to help some of the long-term inmates with simple employment.

'Are you planning to live on the north side or the south, Mr Fee?'

Frank seemed unprepared for such questions. He shrugged, staring with a sort of disbelief at three simpletons pulling the huge roller over the lawn.

'We'll rent a flat somewhere, I suppose. Our needs will not be great anyhow, will they, Rita? Just a bit of an old place for herself to cook the dinner and the two of us to lay our heads.' He blushed then and went silent, concentrating on the notes Rita had typed.

Disappointing to realize that he had not made any plans. But Mama had often remarked how Papa would live in a stable if he was let; men were like that the way they would never notice the details.

Later that day Papa dropped in unexpectedly for tea and called Frank into his study. There was a frightful row. At least, Rita heard Papa shouting a lot and Frank emerged looking baffled to say that Papa was insisting on buying them a house, which he, Frank, thought quite unnecessary. If Rita needed one, she had better go and choose it herself.

Yet, when she found the new detached residence in Terenure, he reared up against it. 'What would we want with a place this size?'

Compared with home, it wasn't large at all. Red brick, double fronted, the stained glass and granite sills still a bit raw, it stood behind a railed front garden in a quiet cul-de-sac. The three main bedrooms were spacious enough and three small ones scattered from kitchen level to the attic would do for servants and, Mama had remarked tartly, for Frank's dressing-room if he ever owned more than the one suit. Rita would have preferred Rathgar, only two tram stops nearer town, but Papa's ideas of house prices had turned out to be rather pre-war. Still, with three quarters of an acre, the back garden carved from an old estate was the largest on the road.

'We may not need this space now, Frank, but in a few years wouldn't it be nice to be settled, not to have to move again?'

'Why would we?'

The house agent gave a knowing smile. Rita felt shy having to say, 'You know, when children come . . .'

'Oh.' He looked up the staircase into the echoing vault of upstairs. 'Meantime, are you thinking to fill it up with lodgers?'

Best not to dwell on what the agent made of them. How was he to know that Frank was not like other people? She had laughed at the idea of herself as a concierge and taken him about the house again, pointing out the broad landings, the big folding doors between sitting-room and dining-room which would make a fine space for parties, the study across the hall in which she and Frank would work together late into the night, the kitchen and scullery down five more steps with a little bedroom off it where a cook might be housed.

There was so much to arrange. She found it hard to impress on Frank the extent of furniture, rugs and curtains needed for a house that size, so she and Mary simply scoured auction houses on the quays. A large number of good pieces turned up there. Mary said they found their way out the back doors of big country houses abandoned by their owners.

Rita had just got home from an auction in Ranelagh when Frank appeared in the sitting-room. He carried a flimsy blue envelope before him like a bomb.

'Darling! What a surprise! Would you believe I got an antique French bed for five shillings?'

'Read this.'

'Can you stay for dinner? Is that all right, Mama?'

'Good evening, Mr Fee.'

Why must her family always pretend amazement at Frank? It was a good thing he wasn't over-sensitive.

'I beg your pardon, Mrs Fitzgerald, but I have a letter from Mr de Valera. He's leaving Versailles for the States, Rita, planning a big tour, you see, and he wants me over there in a month.'

There it was, written in a strange, bare style with no how-are-yous or small talk, demanding Frank across the Atlantic as soon as possible.

'Imagine! You in America and me in France! But for how long?'

'I don't know.'

'Doesn't he know you're getting married?'

'Maybe we'd have to postpone that.'

Tears. Then a sort of weeping hysteria. No surprise to see her parents pleased with the delay, but the way Frank had accepted it was horrible. 'Believe me, Rita, there's no way of knowing how long it'll take. It depends on the reception we get and how much money we can collect. Besides, he's a wanted man, so he can't come back here until the British grant him a pardon.'

She had held on to the letter, reading it and rereading it in her room, with Frank eventually allowed to visit her there, increasingly worried, like everyone in the house, by

35

her fury. It wasn't until the third day of sobbing and refusing to eat that she noticed how it began.

'"Dear O'Fiaich"? Look what it says, this isn't your letter, it's addressed to a Mr O'Fiaich, not Frank Fee!'

'That's my name, Rita: the Irish for Fee. Didn't you know we're all adopting the Irish forms, to set the agenda, the Chief says? It's the start, don't you see, of getting the language into everyday speech.'

So, it had begun: changes were already under way in which she was to be allowed no part. Frank had run downstairs for Papa. The sedative helped her say what she wanted, what she was not prepared to trade. 'I'm going with you. We'll have to get married now.'

She slept then, dreamlessly. The next morning it was arranged that she should become Mrs Frank O'Fiaich in three weeks' time and they would sail to the United States the next day. Frank appeared happy enough, though he said he'd have to get the nod from the Chief who was on a boat somewhere. He paid no heed to Anne Marie's sniggering renditions of what she called 'Mr Fee's new name', pronouncing it always with a harsh, hawking K on the last syllable so that it was almost an insult. Rita ignored her too. Soon Frank and she would be thousands of miles from this tiresome child, away from the despairing lift of Mama's eyebrows or Papa's glares. There could be no society wedding, but it was the one Rita wanted: a true marriage of minds.

III

At Sea

* * *

Rita was ill on the voyage. Probably all the fuss of the last few hurried weeks catching up with her, and that little twinge of disappointment afterwards, the first morning she woke beside her husband in the hotel in Cork. Alone together at last, she had expected him to be like he was with other people, easy, full of plans and enthusiasms, the man at the centre to whom everyone turned. She had not expected his constraint, a shy, fumbling awkwardness which made things complicated and uncertain, even when they were up and dressed. Still, they had managed it somehow, though the act they shared was painful and peculiarly discordant. She wanted to ask Frank if the principle was the same as for breaking in a young horse. If so, she should accept the chafing and unpleasantness, though she did think that if she had had four legs Frank might have used a more gradual approach. She wanted to ask all sorts of things, but apart from some groaning at the end, he was so silent that questions seemed inappropriate. If she had been an animal, though, surely he would have tried soothing her with words and praising her?

Frank must have felt strained too. Mr Blythe and Mr O'Connor, who had joined them on the ship at Cobh, acted quite uninterested in her stories of the wedding. As far as they were concerned, Frank's time was their own, even when they weren't trying to plan strategies or compose speeches for their arrival in America. But it was just as well he had something to occupy him. The tiny window-less cabin and rough seas soon left Rita prostrate on her bed. After their first evening on the ocean, when illness projected her from the dinner table in some disarray, she did not see the Russian woman or her two amusing companions until a night's sailing from New York. Frank saw her, though. He took quite a shine to the Russian party, joining their table each night with his colleagues for intense political discussion and, she suspected, a fair amount of drink.

He had nicknamed this strange Russian woman 'The Liberties'. He couldn't get over the way she enjoyed male company, matching each philosophical theory or bawdy story with a more extreme or shocking one of her own.

She came scuttling now between crowded tables like a harbour tug, her voice shrieking with laughter, her thick hair streeling loose pins, the big flannel skirt puffed like a sail. 'Rita!? We miss you, *chérie*! You are well?' There was a rust line of gravy down her shirt front and her round yellowish face could have done with some rouge. 'Such talk you miss, yes, fighting talk, you know!'

She threw her head back and shrieked with laughter, causing a number of heads to turn in their direction. Frank was deep in conversation with the men. He did not turn around at the sound of Nina's voice, but Rita could see his narrow back stiffen slightly.

'Yes, Meester Frank Ofay, I talking about you-hoo-hoo!'

It was hardly the time, but Rita would have liked to inquire why he had not returned below as arranged to escort her to dinner, why she was forced to enter the saloon alone like this, in front of the whole ship, on the arm of a highly eccentric Russian female.

He rose, half standing, his long thumb tracing the warp in the pink linen tablecloth, head hanging like a cab horse waiting for the off. He was wishing Nina away. That was why he did not shift himself to find her a seat, why it was left to the other gentlemen.

Not that Nina could be bothered to wait. Before Mr Blythe had placed Rita, Nina grabbed a chair from another table without a by-your-leave and plonked herself down. She looked so jolly, almost carefree, as she tapped out a cigarette on a long amber holder, gazing about the room as if this were a grand ball. It did feel exciting, all the talk and smoke and crush of waiters and colourful dresses. Though judging by the passenger list, there was nobody at all interesting in second class.

'I tell you, Rita, is same thing all place – Irish mans, Russian mans . . .' Nina waved a dismissive hand at their friends across the table, three Irishmen and Mr Pokrovsky and Mr Grigoryev, the youthful Russians who reminded Rita of Don Quixote and Sancho Panza. 'Ignorant donkeys – how you call it? Peasants!'

When the word struck home, all the music from the orchestra, the warm mix of laughter and glass were suddenly muffled inside Rita's head. She must smile. And it was important to keep the voice light when your husband was being criticized so dreadfully. 'Come now, Nina, hardly peasants! Frank grew up in the country, of course, but –'

'You understand me, Rita, you same, like me, educated woman, cultured woman. So, me, I speak dialectic. Your mans say me potatoes, my mans say dead souls! Then I speak new society. Your mans say me poets. Hah! And my mans tell me Marx and Engels – which they not read – never! I tell you truth, *chérie*, such mans is peasants, ignorant fools!'

As Nina rocked forward on her chair, Rita could not help noting little splatters of spittle escaping about her lips. She had what Mama referred to as a 'homely' face. The mole near her nose recalled Angela MacNamara, a girl who had surprised everyone last year by landing herself a perfectly sweet accountant at the tennis club. Mama said it was because she was a good listener.

Nina was unmarried. Surely, in her late twenties, she was cutting it a bit fine even for Russia, even if she had been busy with a revolution? From what Rita could gather, the woman came from a distinguished family in St Petersburg, even if on their first evening at sea she had referred confusingly to that life as 'Bourgeois!' She appeared quite content with her single status. Perhaps there were no accountants left in Russia who wanted to be listened to. Or maybe, like Irishmen, Russians liked a little finish.

'Are bubbles, you know, waste from bones. So, to make soup good, Rita, womans, what you say, wipe off scum? If no, we regret glorious revolutions, your 1916, Russian 1917!'

Rita laughed, although it was somewhat impolite to describe a person's husband, sitting right across a table from her, as some sort of waste product. Not that Frank seemed bothered. He was ignoring them again, everything but his body sitting in on the intense discussion of the men. Suddenly she understood Nina's hostility. Really, she blushed with the shame of it, of how rude Frank could be, remembering the look on Anne Marie's face when Frank had buttered his bread with the fish knife, remembering Papa's remark afterwards: 'The fella's a bogman, my dear, interesting and bright, I grant you, but at thirty years old, well . . . If he were a dog, I'd say quite untrainable.'

'Frank, darling, you haven't forgotten us?'

He turned when she touched his sleeve, with that special shy smile of a little boy called away from his toys. She felt the tiny bird flutter inside her again, a fearful excitement at loving this strange creature with the long earnest face and beautiful eyes. So what if he reddened a bit when he failed to attract the bar boy's attention? Such things were of no importance to him.

She loved to look at her husband. There was no waste on him, a small, fine-boned man, the milky skin thickly freckled over flat cheekbones, the nose long and bony, mouth wide and thin. It was the face of rural Ireland. A good face. If only Nina had not said 'Peasants!'

It was she who grabbed a passing waiter, 'Whiskey, yes, I have Irish whiskey! And Comrade O'Fiaich? She, I think, takes English lady drink, sherry from Spain?'

Rita saw the little pucker of Frank's disapproval as he signed for the drinks, the startled way he watched Nina toss hers down like pure well water.

'At last are better, *milaia*. Tonight, tomorrow, we go movies, yes? You know is theatre here? Every day I am going – twice, three times! Lillian Gish? You know this woman? So beautiful!'

Be calm, Rita told herself, he will learn. It just took time. Soon their life together would be like childhood, with that same carefree feel of summers on the Continent with Mama. The restless excitement of limitless travel, collecting highest mountains, crescent-shaped beaches, islands, aqueducts, whatever Mama had decreed for each long summer, with Papa in charge and every station porter, waiter and boatman so charming – and God help them if they were not.

She had tried to describe those times to Frank, to suggest that some day they might travel in Europe together. But his first trip outside Ireland had been to Versailles and he had not enjoyed it. As he said, what time had he for foreignness when he had to turn Ireland into a nation, and re-establish Irish as the first language of its citizens? Yes, that was a task. He must complete it first, breathe life into the dying beauty of their mother tongue and with it bring back the culture and tradition which three hundred years of English rule had tried to eradicate. Then he would be ready to look outwards, and she would show him so much more: wilder, more extraordinary places than he had ever imagined in his simple country life.

She must try not to judge her new husband like this, through Papa's eyes – or Nina's. America would be different, a land where the rules were not so strictly applied. Funny to think it the country which Papa always claimed he had no wish to see. 'Far too new!' he would say when someone expressed an interest, as if the place were a passing dance craze. Well, that was poor old Papa. For the present it would suit herself and Frank very well indeed.

The Big Country

* * *

She had become a clockwork doll wound to its limit. It was wonderful to feel so alive to this peculiar, never-ending country, in which every sight, taste and sound was bigger, sweeter, more clamorous for her attention than she had thought possible. Of course, she had anticipated skyscrapers, she had seen them in pictures and books; she had known there would be open plains and wide panoramas, the landscape of cowboys. But it was the scale of everything she had not expected, the unmapped tracts of tenements around every city, the huge, uncounted population of Negroes and foreigners who filled the wide boulevards yet appeared invisible to her American hosts, the gigantic plates of food which those booming Americans could consume without a flutter of guilt. From the moment the boat docked she felt she could be a million miles from Dublin's polite squares, a time traveller released from all the petty constraints of home.

Mr de Valera met them at the port. After all she had read and heard about the man, she had imagined him to be rude, even uncouth, but she was pleasantly surprised. The manner was that of a headmaster, quietly judicious, making acceptable the way he left her standing to one side while he exchanged information with the rest of her party. When the introductions were finally made, anyone might think he was glad to see her. 'You came, so.'

Here the lack of charm was unimportant. Similarly the stiff formality of the man, the refusal to loosen a thread of his high shirt collar or tight, priestly suit, as if to do so might allow weakness into such a very male place. This was his country, of course, the land where he was born.

44

His mother hadn't sent him back to be raised in Clare until he was three years old. There had been some dubious rumours about the circumstances of his birth, the sort of remarks which caused Mama to observe that for such keen Christians, the Irish were surprisingly unkind.

'Believe me, Chief, there was no stopping her!'

He barely smiled, but there may have been a flash of humour behind the polished glasses. 'Ah, Frank, you're a novice where the women are concerned. You'll soon learn!' Mr de Valera had left his own wife at home. Rita had invited her to the wedding, but she had not come. Poor lady. It must be like being married to the Scarlet Pimpernel.

His secretary appeared delighted with her. 'It's great to see you, Mrs O'Fiaich! Now we can go to the sodality together. I'm scared stiff on my own!'

The woman could turn out a nuisance. Having won her place in the delegation, it would not serve any purpose to be lumped in with the mousy Kathleen Napoli Mac-Kenna.

'Thank you, but I'm afraid I can't make any commitments just yet. Mr O'Fiaich may require my services from time to time.'

Miss MacKenna gave her a funny look, but she did not make any suggestions of that nature again as they travelled about the country, their world the insides of trains, sports stadiums and hotels like this one in Chicago, a cathedral-like place heavy with modern flowing foliage and elongated angels, the gold paint hardly dry on the walls. So many cities, so many banquets, monster meetings, rallies. So many smiling faces and firm handshakes that afterwards Rita found it difficult to recall exactly where they first ran across the Russians again.

The men were signing the register when she saw Sergei. He reminded her of an empty suitcase, a small block of a man built to be fat, sitting alone at the centre of the vast lobby, his heavy suit more creased then ever, oversized brown shoes greyed by summer pavements.

'Mr Grigoryev, how marvellous! Are you staying here too?'

'Mrs Frank! Good, good!'

His face was rubbed and blotchy, the eyes red. For a moment she wondered if he had been crying.

'Is Nina with you?'

'Yes, Madam Comrade, but not in this place, another, how is it, better price? We are hoping Chicago is listening to us.'

'Of course they will! The Americans seem quite fascinated by revolutions – they can't get enough of ours! You may have heard we had numbers touching fifty thousand in Detroit, and more again in Cincinnati.'

Sergei looked doubtful.

'I can't wait to see Nina. She'd be amused to hear I've started speaking to ladies' groups, you know, luncheon clubs and so on? And all those women want is more stories about Easter Week. I often have to make them up!'

'In my country peoples are hungry for bread. Here we feed stupid stories to fools!'

'Don't I know! Can you imagine the whole of Easter 1916, minute by minute! Sometimes I'm almost convinced I was locked into the Post Office myself!'

The man appeared more depressed than amused, only brightening when Frank and the others joined them. 'Comrades! My friends! At last is true revolutionaries. Tonight we eat together, yes?'

Frank and Ernest Blythe tolerated the bear hugs and the kissing. Mr de Valera grew taller and stiffer so that Sergei only managed a mouthful of waistcoat buttons. He had picked up a strange American accent. 'What country, no? Crazy land, my friends, I not understand. Liberty, justice, fraternity, what is this, please? I say them, you need revolution, we show how you find justice. We take liberty to masses. But they not like, they not listen. Is bad, comrades, because to Russian peoples they give nothing!'

The Irishmen had the good grace to look embarrassed.

'But do not grow sad, my friends. No. Today I sit, I

46

wait rich émigré, but no show. Do I despair? No, soon glorious revolution comes here also. So, tonight we drink, yes? Russian vodka and Irish whiskey. Make plan for national partnership!'

How shabby Sergei looked, weaving his way out of the huge swing doors, solid and unremarkable as a statue in some foreign square. She appraised Frank as the lift creaked upwards to their room. America had been good for him. The months had polished him a little, put iron into his voice. He seemed to fill his suits now, to walk with his shoulders back, and put a firmer grip in his handshake. The change in him had altered things between them too. He had caught the hunger of the place, a restless, driven quality, so that he no longer lay in the darkness beside her, listening to her breathing, waiting for the slightest stir from herself before reaching out in the darkness. His early awkward shyness had been replaced by a sort of urgency, as if tenderness were a luxury his schedule could not afford. Nor did he hold her afterwards as he had in their first weeks of marriage, stroking her gently in a kind of gratitude.

It worried her, this change, but it would be unfair to upset him by mentioning it. Such subjects were not to his liking. Besides, the Chief's new bonds scheme was getting some unpleasant resistance from Irish-American politicians, keeping Frank on the go almost round the clock. And even if they could talk, Rita and he were rarely alone. Every waking minute seemed dedicated to cultural groups and millionaires. And always there were the journalists. Of course, their circumstances were special, but married life was not as she had imagined. Nor did that thing, that happening between them in the darkness, feel quite right. Long after it had stopped hurting she suspected that it did not please Frank either.

It was probably the same for all women. Those chance remarks between her mother's friends made sense now. The raised eyebrows over the teacups, 'Don't talk to me about men, the brutes!', the dark side of the marriage contract, something to balance the happiness of sitting beside Frank at a reception or watching him hush the huge crowds before Mr de Valera appeared on a platform. They were the moments she was proudest of him, certain that no matter what Mama and Papa thought, Frank had been the right choice. It was a privilege to be there by his side, sharing his Irish name, raising funds for the great country they were going to make.

Speaking at ladies' luncheon groups had been her idea. As she said to Frank, 'Remember, I talked you into taking me here. I bet I could get American wives to talk their husbands into supporting us!'

The Chief had been dead against it, but then, she had noticed he did not welcome new ideas from others. She had seen him looking at her narrowly sometimes. Perhaps he preferred women to be kept like suits, hanging about in wardrobes to be brushed down and used as required.

But even he should have admitted it by now: Rita's contributions were turning into an asset. The ladies of the Shamrock Society or the Green Ribbon Sorority could not get enough stories about Countess Markievicz toting a gun in St Stephen's Green, or of the women of Gardiner Street carrying supplies to the rebels beneath their skirts.

To begin with, when Frank was writing her talks, Rita sandwiched such excitement between leaden facts about the Irish economy or emigration. In the early mornings Frank sometimes lay by her side and schooled her on milk quotas from good and poor land, the relative value of a pig and the various means of harvesting wheat in each county. She didn't interrupt. It was one of the few occasions when he could give her his full attention. But after a while he lost interest, leaving her alone to embroider her speeches to her heart's content, adding a romantic twist of newlyweds falling together under a hail of bullets on the steps of the church, a story of a lost child, of a faithful dog shot by an English bullet as it dragged news of reinforcements through the lines. There was nothing those ladies liked more than a tear and a smile.

She wished she could tell her husband her thoughts, the little things which occurred to her as they travelled about, like the differences between city people and country folk. He would not want to listen. He would never believe that the women of the American cities' grim, man-made landscapes had no interest in cows or crop values except as a recipe for cottage cheese and soda bread. Frank and Mr de Valera's plan to re-establish the rural idyll for the Irish family was irrelevant. The suggestion that anyone could live happily ever after in a mud cabin on an acre of land would have been greeted by Rita's audiences with laughter and offers of boat tickets to the good life of the United States.

To the women she met Ireland was somewhere else, as remote as history. If people chose to live there, then the ladies were prepared to give their support. They liked the idea of keeping brave puppy dogs fed and cocking a snook, or a gun, at the English. Rita sometimes suspected that those good women thought Frank, herself and the de Valera party quite mad to try.

That night in Chicago, as Frank described an extraordinary Kansas mayor in a lime-green suit and shillelagh and Dev laughed for the first time in weeks, Rita realized that in this vast country of many millions of friendly faces, only the little band of Russians, Sergei, Piotr and Nina, truly understood the Irish. Peculiar as they were, Piotr and Sergei could talk about their country without the sentiment which tended to clog conversation here. Also, it was nice to be taken seriously for once, to hear Nina tell again how Ireland's revolution had been such an inspiration for her own. Was that why, at the end of the evening, when Nina kissed her on the lips, Rita did not pull away?

A Letter from New York, September 1919

* * *

Dearest Mary

Wonderful to find your letter waiting here! Please don't complain about mine. You have no idea how busy life is, nor how little time of her own a wife has. With all this hopping about the country I have only unpacked our trunks and found a nice place to take coffee before it's up with us and off on the road again. The amount of laundry left behind is horrifying. Most of my correspondence is expended on hotel housekeepers in hopes of picking things up on our return! And I can't tell them when that will be; as far as schedules are concerned, Mr de Valera is a law unto himself.

You said 'big' wasn't a good enough description of this country, but it's not unlike the steaks they serve which overflow their plates, bigger, wider, higher than anything at home and raw around the edges, except for the countryside, which is all the above and also wild and endless.

The people we meet are like that too! With the exception of those Russians I told you about (whom we bump into in the strangest places), everyone seems quite happy to do and say whatever comes into their heads. It was no surprise to read about the first marriage in the sky (was it reported at home?), a Lieutenant J. Ellwood Bouwin? I doubt if he'd have persuaded an Irish priest to get into an aeroplane to do the honours!

We're back here because of the transport strike, which has rather scuppered the Chief's plans for the moment. My Russian lady friend, Nina, took me to *Oh What a Girl!*, which was wonderful but so hot they gave the whole audience fans. They're threatening a theatre strike next, so I saw Broadway just in time!

You wouldn't believe it in the boiling weather we've been having, but the newspapers are full of advertisements for furs. I have my eye on a Hudson Bay seal with skunk trim for when Frank strikes gold! Meanwhile I sidetracked him into Greenbergs this morning and talked him into buying me a rose poplin suit just like one I'd seen in *Vogue*. The jacket is pin-tucked, with some lovely embroidery on the belt and collar. Frank likes it, though he thought sixteen dollars very high!

I enclose a photo from a Cleveland newspaper. That's me on the left of the platform looking like I'm asleep, but I was listening really. I see there was a huge Victory Parade in London – was there anything in Dublin? I do miss you and the old country more than I can say. Do write again soon.

All my love

Rita

Treasures

* * *

Mama had some lovely jewellery. There was an opal and sapphire ring which she blamed for all the good and bad luck in her life, and pearl drops suspended in silver filigree which tickled Rita's face when she kissed her goodnight. Most of all, Rita prized Mama's bow and arrow brooch, the shaft shot with diamonds, the sharp tip ruby-flecked like blood.

There had been some fine jewellery at the reception. Rita admired it all, but Nina reacted as if it were a personal offence. 'Hah, those jerks! Stupid womans, covered in sparkle, how they say me "freedom", hah? Or "God"!'

Rita didn't mind when she insisted they leave. Frank didn't need her. It was just one more gathering before a public meeting in Madison Square Garden, the usual chat about saving Ireland and a catalogue of English wrongdoing. Also, some of the guests had objected to Nina and her colleagues.

'What in heck's name are those Reds doing here?'

Nina and Piotr stood abandoned at the edge of the crowded room.

'The Russian party? But they're so nice! Let me introduce you.'

The American benefactor looked startled, pulling her into a huddle with his wife. 'This is an unfortunate thing, Mrs O'Fiaich. I know those people, and it would not look good for you to fraternize with them.'

'Oh, but they're charming! They've had such a difficult time. I thought it might be nice if they came tonight and met some people –'

'Are you a Christian, Mrs O'Fiaich?'

The question was ridiculous. The man was a bore. So many Americans one met seemed extraordinarily religious; Mr Blythe had remarked once that they made him feel like a heathen. Yet to look at this rich man with the long, flat face and deep lines fanning from his eyes like the sun in a child's painting he might be mistaken for an Achill boatman.

'Then you must beware of such people. They are the anti-Christ, ma'am, and they would strip us bare!'

His wife put her hands to the emerald necklace at her throat. 'I'm sure Mrs O'Fiaich couldn't imagine such a thing, coming from the Island of Saints and Scholars!'

'My apologies, ma'am, but it's true. They would plunder us, that is their plan. And they're not going to stop at revolution in their own country, no sir! Those Reds are the same everyplace – bad news for God Almighty and worse for business!'

Rita had been looking forward to asking his wife about her hair combs, but there was no chance of that now. 'I'm sorry you think that, Mr Caffrey. But here's Miss Nanovich. I'm sure she could set your mind at rest.'

Nina came surging across the room, people rippling away on either side. She grasped Rita's hand like a drowning swimmer. '*Chérie!* You I save from terrible peoples!'

'Nonsense, Nina, let me introduce you to Mr and Mrs Caffrey –'

They had gone. A space had formed around Nina and herself, a bulwark of backs of heads. Nina was glaring about the room. Surely her background told her that even if she despised such occasions, they could be useful; or perhaps she thought a graceful smile would compromise her ideals.

'Are pigs, these peoples! Look! Fat, stupid pigs!'

'Oh, Nina, the way you exaggerate! Isn't it fun to see everyone dressed up to the nines? Look at that woman over there! Could all those diamonds be real?'

Nina stared rather rudely at a tall woman in evening dress, flaring her nostrils as if trying to catch her scent. When she turned back to Rita, her eyes were narrowed and.calculating. 'Is real, I think. So, my little Ritushka, you like such things?'

'What woman doesn't? But what I can never get over is how so many women can afford to dress like that. You wouldn't see dresses and jewels of that quality at home, or not outside Dublin Castle.'

'Decadence also in my country. Not now.'

'I know you had to stop it, but doesn't it give you the tiniest thrill?'

'You find such things beautiful?'

'Well, yes.'

'So, you come with me, my friend. I show best.'

It was only polite to go with her, to cheer her up. But it was a worry the way she grew more agitated as they travelled south in the cab, complaining about America, the mean-mindedness of its citizens and their wastefulness. Rita tried to calm her with tales of her own group's problems with Judge Cohalan, but the Russian wasn't really listening. She had produced a silver flask of brandy and insisted Rita share it with her; probably not a wise mixture after sherry.

There was no lift in the dusty hotel. Nina ran up the stairs two at a time, complaining now about Sergei and Piotr. 'Always, they say I take care! I, because am woman!'

Her little room was surprisingly bare, the huge bed taking up most of the space. Apart from a few papers and notebooks, everything was cleared away, no stray clothing, no beads or boxes, and none of those little creams or powders on the dressing-table which might offer aid to a blotchy complexion.

'What a nice room.'

Nina ignored her. She dragged the threadbare curtains against the night and strode to the far side of the bed. 'Do with me, please.'

Rita realized that she was helping to strip back the bedclothes one by one. Was this a Russian custom?

'Ah!' Nina's hand pounced on something in a fold of blanket. A huge amethyst pendant framed by ribbons of red and blue stones. The uncut rock gleamed sulkily in the light of the single bulb as Nina pushed it across the sheets.

'Take this!'

The heavy chain felt warm, something that had languished in bed all evening. Each link was beaten so fine and smooth it might almost melt, the gold as soft and rich as ancient honey.

'Also this!'

Fat pearls clunked against the pendant. The longest string of the biggest, most perfectly matched pearls Rita had ever seen dangled from her hands. The clasp was gold, snakes' heads with green jewelled eyes.

'What a tease you are! I thought you said you hated jewellery!'

It felt good to laugh, but Nina was too intent on her hunt to pay any attention. She was on her knees now, running her hands under the bed and beneath corners of the tattered rugs, gathering an armful of diamond tiaras, necklaces, brooches, bracelets, hair ornaments and pieces for which Rita could not think of a use but could only gape at in amazement. This cornucopia of metal and precious stone was unreal, unnatural, breathtaking.

'Is disgusting, no?' Nina dumped her haul on the battered dressing-table and stood puffing for a moment. 'And more bad, insulting I think, I must care these things. I, who give blood from body to throw this garbage!'

'But they're real, aren't they? I mean, they're rather good?'

'Good? Hah! Is joke! No, Rita, is necessary we must cut this, destroy, for good health of Motherland!' She picked up a handful of the hated objects and let them fall. They clattered back together, shimmering, indifferent, radiating the confidence of unassailable beauty. Nina was sorting

55

them, pushing them about, grunting angrily when faience beads refused to release a filigree and sapphire butterfly. 'Stupids!' She pushed the pile together and stamped over to the single picture on the wall, a drab reproduction of a goddess. From behind she unhooked a small velvet bag. 'These I forget I think, because I want forget!' She pushed the bag at Rita. 'You count, my friend. Am sick. I cannot look more.' She stretched out on the creaking bed, muttering angry Russian words.

Rita didn't understand, didn't care to think about anything but her need to touch all this raw, naked excess. When earrings and rings tumbled out over her hands, she could not resist a cry of pleasure.

This was perfection. Here, repeated in miniature, a fusion of flawless gems and great craftsmanship. 'Do you think I might possibly try on one or two?' Her voice was husky with wanting. If only Mama were here, she would love this. She might appreciate at last the thrill of Rita's new life. Nina shrugged indifferently and closed her eyes. Rita blocked her mind to what she might think. All she wanted was to push the sapphires into her ears, to slip the fabulous chunks of emeralds, rubies, diamonds, tourmalines, and goodness knew what else on to her fingers.

Nina was watching through half-closed lids. 'You also, my little sister? Like greedy empresses, like womans.' Her voice was merely the dull burbling of the streets below the window, sounds hushed by a soft curtain of excitement as Rita removed the little pearl earrings which Papa had given her for her wedding and shakily pushed the confection into her lobes. It seemed important to wait, not to look until she had fumbled a selection of rings on to every finger, a kaleidoscope of shape and colour.

Mama always claimed that Rita's ears were her best feature. Gazing into the mirror in this cheap hotel room, she had to admit she may have been right. Even in the flat electric light she knew she looked quite extraordinary. Sparked by such stones and so much artistry, her hands had become fine and narrow, paling to resemble those of a saint in an icon. Her face was angelic, a heart repeated in the lozenge outline of diamonds, the blue sapphire centre picking up the surprise of her eyes, a tail of white and rose diamonds repeating the curves of stray curls which had fallen from her hair.

Nina had appeared behind her chair, bending down to help tug off the tighter rings, trying more exquisite combinations of colour and pattern. 'Womans are fools, Rita.' The voice was softer. She smoothed back the loose hair and pinned it behind Rita's ear. 'Beautiful fools. For such stupids, they give much, yes?'

Her gentleness was surprising, massaging Rita's lobes after the heavy weight of the sapphires. The long, pale fingers felt cool as she deftly replaced the first stones with emerald drops and slipped a matching necklace around her throat. Its jealous stones felt dry and hot, like the snakes Papa had once talked a keeper into draping about her shoulders on a visit to the Zoo. She had enjoyed that, watching Anne Marie scream. The closeness of Nina standing behind was another reminder: of Christine in the old kitchen at home; a sharp body odour mingled with cloves. Just thinking of home, of sitting at the table in the kitchen watching the cook beat and roll away childish problems, brought a gust of happiness to mingle with the present, quite bizarre delights.

'Head back, *kroshka moia*.'

She allowed her head to tip backwards against the soft bulge of Nina's stomach. Her friend was smiling down at her.

'Oh, Nina, why didn't you show me these before?'

'I show many things, Ritushka.' She leant over Rita to pick up the smallest pair of earrings, a cluster of diamonds from which hung a single ruby cut like a tear and tipped with a tiny pearl. The breasts against Rita's head felt like downy pillows. 'You have not tried these, I think?'

'There's so much!'

Once again Nina had replaced the earrings, pushing

the new posts into the ears, smoothing each one as if it were a piece of rumpled silk. She was so close now, as familiar as another pair of hands, or a mother. Holding Rita's head back against her so that it was difficult to see in the mirror.

'Wait, wait, is more you discover!' Somehow, she had removed every ring. 'This also pleases hand.'

Someone else in the mirror. No longer a woman dressed for make-believe, not Rita Fitzgerald from the North Circular Road nor Mrs Frank O'Fiaich from the red-brick house in Terenure. The woman who smiled back at her was exquisite, a Dresden figurine, a porcelain face flushed with the heat of rubies, cooled by the high collar of pearls, made playful by a diamond cherub clasp. She raised her right hand to touch an ear and saw the matching ruby ring.

'You like wedding ring of old Empress?'

'It's lovely, but I wear mine on my other hand.'

'In Russia, is so.'

Nina spoke with the smooth, measured tones of a nanny. Her voice, the mesmerizing vision of the jewellery and the tiny shivers of her fingers on Rita's bare shoulders were both calming and exciting. In this unpromising room Nina had woven a spell. Rita's mind skittered between questions about what time it could be, how the big meeting in the sports stadium had gone, whether Frank had been given an opportunity to speak, how it was that hands like Nina's could send bolts of pleasure to her stomach and beyond. She looked in the mirror to see what on earth Nina could be doing, but somehow her eyes always halted at the latest splendid jewel with which the Russian woman had decorated her.

Her breast was exposed. As if in a dream she could see the right one in the mirror, freed somehow from her gown. She had never seen it like that, all alone, with someone's hand kneading, stroking, pinching the nipple, sending waves of pleasure through her whole self. Breasts reminded her of Our Lady, the virgin mother. Sin.

'Oh dear, I'm afraid I feel rather faint!'

The strange sensations stopped. Nina had produced another flask and was holding it under Rita's nose. A deep breath drew only a chill emptiness to her nostrils, an absence of the expected spice and salted flowers.

'Drink! Drink, *milaia*!'

The flask was pressed to her lips. It seemed bad manners to refuse, to question, at this point in the evening, the practice of drinking from the neck, or of mixing this rather tasteless liquid with what had gone before.

'More! Is good – is Russian!'

Glowing tongues fanned out from inside, becoming indistinguishable from the other feelings which had returned as Nina's hand caressed under her dress, moving always downwards. Rita closed her eyes, shutting out the image of the bejewelled madonna before her, the statue of a virgin she had seen once when she was small, carried through a Corsican street. In the darkness an extraordinary convulsion flooded through her. Then everything was still.

'I'm afraid I absolutely must go. Frank will be worried!'

Their eyes met in the mirror. Nina's had become huge black pools. Her breathing was laboured, as if she had climbed many flights of stairs.

'Frank? Huh! Same like all mans, fusspot for stupid things, not womans. I tell him, good comrade wife is jewel!' She was removing the pieces from neck and ears and hand and hair, tossing them back amongst their fellows, deftly readjusting the front of Rita's dress as she unpinned an enamelled brooch. 'No, such mans do not value womans. You will see, Ritushka. To us they not give power – babies only!'

Rita shivered. She was cold suddenly, and very tired. The jewellery still winked and burned before them. Many of the stones were uncut, in settings made almost crude by their generosity of lumped gold and beaded frames.

'All this, these things, they're very old, aren't they?'

'Pouf! Are blood of oppression. Greed and cruelty of tsars!'

'Surely this isn't from the Russian royal collection . . .?'

'No more! My peoples take power from Romanovs, shoot and strip stupid bodies! For such baubles many die. Many, many! And now I leave work to make guard such stinks. I say Sergei, I throw all into sea. But no! New rulers of my country say take, sell! Is stupids. In America nobody want!'

Romanovs. Rita felt quite faint again. The family joke rang in her ears, the phrase Papa always shouted upstairs when he grew impatient with Mama's missing earring: 'For Heaven's sake, wear something else! They're hardly the Russian crown jewels!' Nina had said 'Romanov'. The most precious jewellery in the world.

'But why?'

'"No authority," they say us – we, comrades of revolution! So, because am woman, I travel like this. I carry in clothes, hide in room like squirrel. And now I think I do this until return to motherland! And for *rien*!'

Nina was laughing, her mood quite changed. It *was* funny, what she said, in a macabre sort of way, and nice to laugh together like this. Wonderful, too, to realize that Nina trusted her enough to share such a secret.

No matter what Nina said, the heap of metal and stone on the dressing-table was breathtaking. How could she speak of blood and cruelty? Jewels of this quality and antiquity were above such grossness. They were only themselves, absolutes, as perfect as any work of art. In them still glowed the magic of grand occasions, the throb of great music, the swish of silks, memories of powerful women, queens, empresses and wives of great men who had assumed so much beauty always to be theirs. A succession of women, until it had come to her turn to wear them, in this dim, brown room in a foreign city.

'So, *dorogaia*, I have jewels. And we have fun, huh?' She stroked Rita's cheek as she helped her with her cloak.

Just for a moment the memory of fingers on more intimate areas returned like a whisper from a dream. 'I can't thank you enough, Nina, for letting me see – for taking me into your confidence.'

'I tell you, *chérie*, you and me, is true revolutionaries. Understand what is pleasure, yes? So, you play jewels again?'

'Oh, I should love that!'

'I am hoping this, Ritushka. We are different, no? Not frightened to break rules – stupid mans' rules!'

Rita remembered Frank again and moved towards the door. 'I must go. Thank you so much for a, a splendid evening.' Their embrace was long and warm, with the smell of Christine again, soda bread and the kitchen.

'Thank you, *milaia*. We play soon?'

Rita touched Papa's tiny pearls and glanced down at the claddagh ring of which Frank was so fond. Papa, Frank, they really had a very limited conception of what was truly beautiful.

A Revolutionary Wife

* * *

The streets were on fire, or perhaps it was herself. Her whole body glowed, hands and ears felt singed. Such excitement might flare her secret into the night sky, scattering it like fireworks over the frantic city.

Frank hardly looked up when she came in. He had dragged two trunks out of the dressing-room and was flinging clothes and underwear about the bed. '*Dia duit* and thank God you're back! Will you tell me where are my brown braces? We've another breakfast meeting in the morning and no sign of a collar stiffener.'

She wanted to run to him, to hold him and share her heat. To tell him that it need not be a shy and silent fumbling in the darkness, two sticks rubbing together in a cold grate.

'And another bloody party tomorrow night. It beats me where the Chief is getting the energy.'

She put her arms around his waist before he could pull away. Oh, the sharp white bones of him, the cool of his shirt on her cheek.

'Will you whisht, girl, can't you see I'm looking for something?'

How to tell him everything? She lay on the bed and examined this man she had married. He was so innocent. Eleven years older, yet tonight he seemed far younger than herself. He had no idea how big the world was.

'I've had such a time!'

'I saw you went off with that quare Bolshie woman. Don't tell me she's good for the crack?'

'I've never met anyone quite like her.'

'Nor will again, God willing! So listen, if you're such

pals, would you ever tell her to do something about that tache? It's not right on a female!'

'Oh, don't be so mean!'

'Isn't it the truth? Doesn't she know a blind man wouldn't get past those whiskers!'

It *was* mean, laughing with him like that. But she wanted to laugh all night, to dance in his arms. He hoicked the trunks off the bed as if they were bales of straw, then lay beside her with that shy, blurry-faced look of his.

'Sometimes, Frank, you're so provincial! When you get to know Nina you'll realize that sort of thing doesn't matter a bit.'

'And sometimes, my little lady of the Pale, I wonder are you Irish at all. What are you doing palling up with her anyhow? Haven't you got a husband here who's only dying to get to know you?'

He was stroking her face. Usually when he did that, running his finger down her nose, smoothing her forehead, she had to suppress the image of a horse being calmed as it is backed between the shafts. Tonight, after Nina, there was still so much sensation in her she could think only of the ribbon of pleasure winding down to her toes.

'If you want a girlfriend, why not pal up with Miss MacKenna? She's got Dev's ear, that one, it would do me no harm.'

She kept her peace. An evening with that vestal virgin would mean an earful of Dev's *bons mots* and a lot of sanctimonious chat about Ireland and the faith. But there was no point saying any of that to Frank. The last time Rita had expressed an opinion about a colleague's wife he had given her a lecture on how the woman came from a great rebel family and was so devout, which had nothing to do with anything. Just sometimes Frank made her feel like the bad fairy at Sleeping Beauty's christening party.

She moved his hand to her breast. He hesitated for a moment, surprised. His face flushed as she slipped off her evening dress and unhooked the garments beneath. At last he let his gaze move from her face to her breasts. They looked surprisingly white and small, less grandiose than the earlier glimpse in Nina's dingy mirror. She wanted him to touch her there. A memory of Nina drove her to pull at Frank's shirt to reach the warm skin of his ribcage.

'*M'anam istigh tú . . .*'

With a groan he pressed his mouth to her breasts, sucking and licking there like a calf, his hands pulling at the petticoats still trapped beneath her. She arched her back to release them, allowing his hand to slide up between her thighs.

At last Frank was no longer the shy husband or preoccupied politician. Tonight he was loud and fervent as her body twisted and rolled upon socks and vests and rustling tissue paper. The end, when it came, was so intense that afterwards they lay together for a long time, panting into one another's faces. Half an hour, at least, before the old politeness slid back between them like a thin sheet of glass.

A Letter from Dublin, November 1919

* * *

Dear Miss High and Mighty

If you write to me again demanding letters, I swear I'll put myself in an envelope and land in on the two of you! What kind of a country is it that can't manage to forward a person's post? I must have written to you half a dozen times since the summer, big newsy ones which you say you never got. All right, so, I'll give you a quick catch-up, but I'm telling you now, this is the last. Just because you're so busy with a husband and all his important doings, you needn't think I haven't got plenty to do. I love your descriptions of the clothes and the hair. And where was it you said you had oysters boiled in cream? I haven't felt well since you told me that! The Daddy has put a curfew on dining out, so afternoon tea in Robert Roberts is becoming quite the event. Weather upside down too, unbelievably warm, so that just as I was planning to make my entrance into Grafton Street with my yellow umbrella (have you got coloured ones over there yet?), I find I'd be better off with a coolie and a big palm leaf. I could have done with the umbrella in the summer. The poor nags at the Horse Show did more swimming than jumping, but everyone was so glad to be back they went anyway. The smell of wet rubber and manure in the main hall was nose stopping! I wore a new cream piqué, ruined of course.

I've been taking dancing lessons with Miss Haines to pass the time. You should see my quarter-turns! All done, actually, for a dance in Kingstown Town Hall in aid of the fallen girls, but Daddy and Mammy pulled out at the last minute; said there were a lot of army boys invited which might be dangerous, what with the goings-on at the moment. To 'make up for the disappointment' Mammy took me off to the first meeting of the

Catholic Truth Society! Give me the Gaelic League any day (though they've gone awfully political lately). Imagine! Lord Killanin on 'The Beautiful, its quest and significance'! When Mrs Mary Maher started on about 'St Brigid and Her Teachings to the Women of Erin', I thought I might burst. I missed you then, Rita Fitzgerald. Mammy sat rapt through it all, but I think she would listen to the Hail Mary backwards if she thought it was Culture.

I suppose Frank knows about the McCabe trial? Three months with hard labour for trying to sell those bonds for funding a government here. Isn't that the sort of thing your fine husband is at? We have a rail strike too. Have you read *The Moon and Sixpence* by Somerset Maugham? I hear it's racy. Bring it back with you soon – and bring me some true stories about married life!

From your best friend on the shelf

Mary

A Comradely Dinner in New York, 1920

* * *

Afterwards Rita could not remember who thought up their little scheme. At the time she believed it was herself. But years later when she looked back, she used to wonder had Nina planted the seeds of the idea, like so much else.

'Hey-mon! Eat, eat! You must be big, yes, for fights!'

Not much chance of turning Mr de Valera into a glutton. He looked pained as he watched Piotr noisily spoon up the last grains of sugar from his coffee-cup. Nina wiped her mouth with a flourish. 'Only persons which know hunger can revolt – *c'est vrai, mes amis?*'

Mr de Valera gave her one of his rare smiles. 'I believe they apply a similar philosophy to pugilists in this country; you may have heard it, Miss Nanovich? – "Stay hungry".'

They were all able to laugh then, the Russian party perhaps a touch too uproariously. Sergei thumped the table with his great fist. 'Stay hungry!' His laughter filled the room. When he heaved back into his chair with a belch, even Rita could not help smiling.

The Chief's nostrils tightened slightly. It had been hard enough to talk Frank and himself into accepting the invitation to this florid private room above a restaurant, and to keep Dev's latest recruit from Dublin out of it. Mr de Valera had grown a little wary of the Russians lately, and now the meal was over Rita could feel his impatience to make a speech or leave. She wished Nina's people would hurry up with their proposal.

'Ding, ding, ding!'

Extraordinarily, it was Nina who was standing, banging a spoon on her wine glass so that spots of cream smeared the crystal.

67

'Lady and gentlemans!'

The Irishmen were exchanging glances. They feared the worst: 'The Liberties' might soon dance upon the table.

'Comrades. Our friendship in United States is historic moment of revolutionary struggle – friendship of great, free motherland and little serfdom of English imperialists . . .'

Rita could almost hear Frank's hackles rise.

'Many months, *mes amis*, wandering capitalist desert, when hearts of two nations are beaten together . . .!'

Mr de Valera had relaxed into his usual speech-listening stance, back perfectly straight, face blank, fingers joined as if in silent contemplation. He was probably rehearsing a reply. Only his eyes behind the gold-rimmed spectacles swivelled upwards sometimes to engage the speaker with the messages of caution and disapproval he could not quite suppress. Nina ignored him. She was in full flow, addressing the gods and satyrs daubed upon the ceiling as if they were a rabble, her face shining like armour, a faint sweat breaking out across the thick brows.

'Same as you, we travel. But payment for labour is not equal. No, American peoples turn behinds to us. So, what we care? Pouf! . . .'

She was taking an awfully long time to get to the point, explaining that revolution was something called a 'dialectic', a beautiful child which would grow and change and eventually become mother to all nations. As far as Rita knew, the two Irishmen present had never expressed much interest in other nations, nor would they welcome a mother for what Nina called 'our common cause'. Both parties enjoyed their political discussions. But they had always agreed by avoiding the big issues, their differences, like Mr de Valera's plans for small family farms and the Russians' dream of vast state collectives.

Frank began to shuffle his feet and for a moment Rita was afraid he might put up his hand. What was the phrase from his school-days? '*An bfvil cead agam dul amach*

68

más é do thoil é'? He had told her once how tempted he was to use it when the Chief went on too long. Nina's sudden look must have reminded him of a teacher. He sat back again, defeated.

'To make child grow, we need money. Much money put food in mouth, feed ideas of glorious leaders, do works of comrades, Marx and Lenin, and revolutionary committee. As they say in movies – make dreams come true! But in this place, what they know of Russia? Dead ones of terrible war? What you can know, little Irish, of my blood-letting?'

Frank and the Chief woke up for a moment.

'You, you lose few, few peoples in "Easter Rising". Is tiny, nothing! But always, in my country, we say is great, this thing you do.'

Mr de Valera seemed to have moved his mind back on to a higher plane. He stared impassively at Nina, politely indifferent. Frank was examining his fingernails. The daily visits to the barber-shop and the new suit from Park-Taylor had added polish.

'Are stupids, these Americans, hating English, helping little Ireland . . .'

A pulse on Mr de Valera's forehead had begun to throb. He pressed his fingers to the spot as if seeking peace through prayer. Nina was breathing heavily, blackbird eyes now stabbing around the table, pinning each man to his chair with every pointed word. She was not conventionally beautiful. Yet Rita only had to look at the hair straying down upon the neck, at the unkempt clothes, to feel a cold tide of longing rise over her body, an appetite which each snatched moment with her after their first jewelled night had somehow only sharpened.

'Together, my friends, in comradeship, we go forward.'

The Chief half rose to reply, but Nina waved him down.

'So, I make proposition, yes? Is this: you raise much, much money, yes? Irish bonds, Comrade de Valera, give big fights with American friends, but are good. Maybe too much success, yes? Maybe three million dollars, maybe more?'

Frank glared at Rita across the table. Surely he knew that anyone who could read a newspaper could have worked out that sum for themselves?

Nina still held the floor. 'Big moneys makes problem, yes? Is too much now? I have solution . . .'

Nina had begun slowly unbuttoning her jacket. Dev twitched and swivelled, seeking escape. She had started at the waist and was working her way upwards, quick fingers slipping loops over rough fabric buttons to reveal, at first, a rather crumpled expanse of greyed blouse. Her male companions seemed indifferent to the show, refilling their glasses, Piotr occasionally winking at Frank or Mr de Valera, Sergei busily scribbling something on a white napkin with a stumpy pencil.

When the first jewels shimmered on to the table, Rita heard Frank breathe, 'Jaysus!' She looked at Dev. Nothing showed except a sudden patch of colour on his cheeks.

Nina had removed her jacket now, deftly pulling heavy necklaces from the lining around the collar, unpinning brooches from interfacings, unbuckling a pouched belt, spilling out velvet sacks, plundering hidden pockets and false padding until the tiaras, pendants, necklaces, brooches, rings and a large jewel-encrusted cross came dumping and clunking upon the tablecloth. A magician spinning handkerchiefs into precious metal and stone.

When she sat down, the silence was total. Frank and Mr de Valera stared, mesmerized, at this heap of showiness. The stones seemed the only creatures left alive in the room, their lights beneath the low shades like distress cries, rescue flares from this loveless trade.

Nobody wanted to make the first move. Mr de Valera gave a dry cough and Frank swallowed loudly, his Adam's apple working furiously beneath the starched white collar. Sergei poured himself another glass of port. Someone had to push things along or the head waiter would be knocking at the door wondering were they all dead. Rita took a deep breath.

'These, Eamon, Frank, are the Russian crown jewels. Or, at any rate, a small part of them.' With men like Frank and Mr de Valera there was always the danger they might mistake such treasures for baubles from Switzer's. 'And what Nina is proposing is that we bank some of our excess funds with her country – in the form of a loan – and take the jewels as security.'

All eyes were on her now, Frank's wide in amazement, Nina's smiling encouragement, Mr de Valera's narrowed with amusement or disgust. There was no going back.

'As Nina says, this may be the answer to our own problem. I mean, bringing all that money back with us, while things remain unresolved with the unrest and so on, could be a mistake. There is always the chance of the wrong people getting their hands on it, of it being used for evil. On the other hand, if we bank too much money here, it may lead to awkward questions.' She had to stop then. It was the way the Chief's eyebrows twitched every time she said 'our' or 'we'.

He rolled a pearl between his fingers. Rita could almost feel its voluptuous roundness, still warm from Nina's body. For a moment she feared he might put one between his teeth to check its authenticity. It was a surprise to find that the thought of his mouth upon such perfection made her slightly ill. The long rope slid coyly away from him across the table. He reached out again to prod apart emerald and ruby pieces as if they were a heap of dried leaves.

Somehow she stumbled on. 'Obviously, as Nina and her comrades have found, such a historic collection cannot be sold on the open market. The new Russian nation must first establish rights of ownership, which may take time.'

Frank had picked up a diamond bracelet. It flashed a message across the room, a silent scream against the hands of ignorant foreigners. The way Frank dropped it he might have been touched by fire.

Nina's voice sounded almost caressing in the silence. 'For success, arrangement is secret. Absolute. Nobody know nothing. So, here is deal.'

Sergei surrendered the crumpled linen napkin on which he had been writing.

The fussy way Mr de Valera studied the few smudged lines there, slowly reading and rereading, pointing up an occasional word or phrase to Frank, he might have been sitting at Versailles. Again, the heavy silence, only Sergei's occasional little belches and the angry crunching of Nina's raspberry lozenges.

Mr de Valera pushed back his chair and stood up. Frank was caught on the hop, hurriedly dropping a small tiara beside his plate. Rita noticed that Dev had folded Mr Grigoryev's napkin and was pushing it into his pocket. 'A most interesting evening. I shall need time, of course, to consider your proposal.' As he bowed his goodnight, the clamour from the Russian men began. All that had been unsaid came tumbling out in broken sentences, following Dev and Frank to the door, helping them with coats and hats as they continued to babble on about comradeship, the combined strength of two emergent nations, the revolutionary struggle.

The women remained seated, jewels burning between them. Nina smiled and stretched out a hand to Rita, too far to reach. 'This I fix for you. Is what you want, yes?'

'Thank you.'

'Me, also, you make free.'

'Rita! Are you coming or what?'

Frank, expecting her to get up from the table any old how, to be ready for him at the door. It was Nina who pulled back her chair and led her to him.

IV

Home to Dublin, 1920

* * *

'You've got fat!'

Trust Mary! No wonder Mama always called her 'your wild Irish friend', as if Mama weren't Irish herself.

'I have not – it's this dress!'

The way Mary walked around her in the hotel drawing-room you'd think she was examining a cow at a mart.

'Well, it doesn't do a thing for you!'

Agony to keep anything from Mary. But on the voyage home Rita had made a vow to herself: she would prove as trusty a soldier as any man, even under Mary's interrogation. The trouble was that she had not considered the complication of a swelling stomach. Her clothes were getting tighter, so that sometimes, if she didn't battle with a needle and thread, the jewels sewn into undergarments and wrapped around her waist prodded painfully at her skin.

'Goodness, Mary, to think I actually missed you!'

'Take no notice of me, girleen, I'm jealous. It's been deadly without you. Hardly a decent man left after the war and now the whole country up in arms.'

'I even missed your moaning in America – everyone was so polite!'

'Listen to herself! You, who's only been in the most exciting country in the world, a married woman, travelling with one of the most famous Irishmen since Parnell!'

It had felt nice to be back, walking down Grafton Street with Frank's ring on her finger, grown up at last, so that even the beggar children called you 'Missus!' when they tugged at your sleeve.

'You sound like Sister Immaculata! Remember the way she'd tell us to count our blessings just when we were ready to jump from the chapel roof!'

'That old crone! I'm surprised at you, Mrs Frank O'Fiaich, still harking back to the dark ages!'

Away less than a year, yet in her few days home Dublin was making her feel like Rip Van Winkle. On the telephone yesterday Mama's voice had sounded quite chill. 'It's about time you woke up!' Simply because Rita had suggested Frank and herself for a bridge evening at Clonkee.

'Don't you dare clam up on me, Rita. I want to hear *everything* – and I'm not just talking about America!'

Mary screamed with laughter, throwing back her head on its strong neck, her big eyes rolling. It was a pity she was so highly strung – she could be good-looking, beautiful even in a long-stemmed sort of way. But, as Mama said, anything Mary did, she did with too much brio. Fine men like Frank had a tendency to hesitate and turn away, unnerved by the unpredictable shouts and whispers, the way she ate and drank as if she could still remember the Famine.

'You turn Miss Prim on me now and I'll never speak to you again!'

Rita looked around the public room, clusters of comfortable armchairs bobbing across an expanse of sea-green carpet. Dublin felt so quiet after the cities she had seen, a murmuring backwater stirred only by the clink of spoons on china, sounds of hooves and tram bells on Dawson Street mingling with the strains of violin and piano. America had been exciting, yet somehow it was here, back home again, that life had become complicated.

On domestic matters, Frank and she turned out to have totally different ideas. How on earth had he expected her to manage the house without staff? He seemed genuinely surprised when she told him she was interviewing a cook, even became angry when he learned the annual wage, talking about how his mother had managed with no help

76

at all and how Irish women must no longer ape the dilettante lives of the English. It was all Rita could do not to remind her husband of what that hard life had done to his mother. One of Rita's little cousins at the wedding had whispered that she looked like the witch from under the sea, to which Mama had responded, 'Out of the mouths of babes!' The very thought of turning into such a husk helped Rita to weep. Then Frank relented about a cook, though the low wage he offered had brought only one respondent.

Mary had no interest in such issues. Rita knew what it was she wanted to know, questions they had whispered and giggled about after lights out. But how could you describe those nights in hotel bedrooms, the strange feel of a husband pressing down on top of you, the thing he poked into her, into that secret place which she couldn't even have put a name on, until Nina? Russian women appeared to be able to name names. But for all Rita knew, they might have been the wrong ones. Besides, many of the terms she had used were not even English.

'We will talk, Mary, but I'm interviewing a cook this evening and I have so many things to pick up for the house!'

'All right, why don't I help you shop and then come home with you? God knows, I've little else to do!'

'Sorry, but we have builders starting and everything is in such a mess.'

'I thought you'd got the house straight before you went away?'

She had to be so careful or Mary would ferret it out of her. 'Just one or two improvements in the kitchen.'

Mary was so full of life, so sure, she made Rita feel as old as Mama. Though these days Mama got about more than she did. Rita had hardly seen her since they got back. On the telephone, when Rita told her about the small wage Frank was prepared to pay a cook, Mama had only sniffed, 'What did you expect?' Rita had hoped she might ask Papa to help, but they had both become rather distant, implying their foolish daughter had made her bed and must now lie on it.

'So tell us what you *do*, Rita, you and Frank.' Mary's voice was the familiar schoolgirl whisper. 'What does it feel like to be alone with a man all the time? Is he always wanting to, you know . . .? Or do you just sit and hold hands?'

Her ability to embarrass had not changed. It was fortunate the orchestra was playing 'The Blue Danube' quite loudly. A waiter rushed forward to help Rita with her coat.

'Oh my God, I'm so stupid! I've just realized!' Mary grabbed her arm. 'You are, aren't you? Oh I could kick myself, calling you fat when all the time the obvious was staring me in the face. You're going to have a baby!' She was bent over Rita, long arms wrapped fiercely about her so that the larger diamonds of a floral wreath bracelet pressed into the flesh beneath Rita's arm. 'Imagine you, you poor lovey – a squealing babbie!'

The lady on the violin gave Rita a smile. Had she heard? Rita wanted to cry. Her friend's suddenly soft voice, her fragrant soapiness, the cool of her cheek brought a wave of regret for the schoolgirls they had been.

And then they laughed, as they always had, at their despair. At how, up to now, they had believed one day they would be free, that they would escape into somewhere far stranger and more dangerous than the place which the nuns had called 'The World', out into something much more exciting than the convent, or matrimony.

The Stars in Their Courses

* * *

Unmarried people had no idea of married life, of how little of one's time was one's own. Quite apart from the fact that Frank disliked theatres and concerts, he seemed to want to socialize less than ever now they were home.

'*Níl aon tintán mar do thintán féin*,' he'd say, night after night as he stretched his stockinged feet to the fire. She'd given up asking to be taken out, or even reminding him to put on slippers. There was so much politics about these days she was glad to have him stop home for an evening, whatever he did. He had been annoyed the time she replied, 'Roughly translated, I suppose you're saying there's no place like home. But I wouldn't mind seeing a little less of it!'

Mrs O'Reilly had entered their lives as if the interview for the post of cook-housekeeper was a mere formality. A large Dublin woman whose teeth were the only clue she might be younger than her camel-like frame suggested.

'Perhaps you could give me some idea of your repertoire, one or two special dishes?'

The woman had become quite agitated, her long upper lip curling back in disgust over the strong teeth. 'What do you mean, dishes? Amn't I here to cook, and maybe do the odd bit of clearing up? You'll be engaging a girl, I suppose, for the heavy duties?'

'I'm not sure about a girl. My husband is not keen on a large staff.'

'I'd expect a girl. Fifteen years I was with Mrs Cullen – and it wasn't my cooking killed her!'

It was so difficult to judge people. 'Indeed, but I only wanted some idea, you know, of the sort of things you like to prepare ...' Mama had always appeared to blossom when interviewing domestics.

'*I'd* like? Isn't it what youse like I have to know? What's your birth date?'

The woman's skin looked boiled.

'Em, September the tenth.'

'Virgo. Right, so, I'll have no bother there. And the master?'

'January the seventeenth, though I don't quite see why –?'

'Why? Are you joking me, missus? Why are the stars fixed in the sky? Why does the moon come out at night and us women do funny things? But Virgo and Capricorn, we should be all right in that department. So, how soon do you want me?'

A routine had somehow been established, of herself sitting with her embroidery in the drawing-room, the clatter and smells of Mrs O'Reilly and the evening meal rising up the five steps from the kitchen.

'*Conas tá tú?*' He would pat her shoulder on his way to his place at the other side of the fire and she would answer, '*Tá mé go maith. Dia is muire duit*', always with that question niggling in her head of what she would say if she had taken ill that day. What was the Irish for 'I have had a miscarriage, I may die'?

Her study of the language had not progressed past what she had picked up in the Gaelic League. It seemed beyond her, an oral tradition, they said, no need for the sort of school textbooks she had used to learn Latin and French. There was so much dreary stuff to read too, a lot of rather adolescent poetry and stories about rowing across lakes and driving cows. She had complained about them to Frank once and he claimed the new writing was perfectly good; that anyway old Irish literature was not the sort of thing a lady should be exposed to.

Such conversation disturbed her. It was wrong, of course, but in the short time they had been home she had come to dread their evening ritual, the long sigh as he eased himself into his chair, that polite smile which re-minded her of reverend mothers, army generals, the rictus of powerful people behind desks at custom posts.

'*Go maith.*' He would repeat it like a response to a prayer before he slipped into English. 'And how was your day?' His voice sounded false, put on to appease the listeners hidden behind the furniture, seeking forgiveness for communion with this English-tongued wife.

And so she offered news of Papa's new motor which had bolted on the North Circular and nearly hit a coal dray, further plans for the kitchen, a disagreement with the laundry man. He nodded benignly, a priest hearing con-fession. They did not touch him, those domestic problems. He was even unbothered by the burnt offerings which, despite all Rita's hints for improvement, their new cook slapped down each night: good fish and beef and fresh vegetables frazzled to kingdom come. He munched through them contentedly enough before his next set of rituals: the move to the drawing-room for a last cigarette of the evening, a close scrutiny of the newspapers, the household rosary and bed.

Sometimes when Rita looked up from her accounts to suggest she book for the new Yeats play or invite some people for dinner, he would get suddenly rattled, behaving as if the listeners, those purists safeguarding their textbook Irish lives, might step out from behind the curtains and handcuff Frank for treason.

'We've no need of that sort of carry-on.'

'It's just that I'm home all day. I suppose I haven't enough to do. Isn't there any way I could help you more?'

He put his paper down and considered her rather seriously. 'Haven't I said it often, you should get more involved in local events? Aren't there lots of clubs and sodalities a woman in your position could be at?'

'Well, yes, I've been thinking about that. I was wonder-ing about writing up a few little talks, you know, to give to local groups. There are so many amusing stories I could tell, like the Irish-Americans and the problems we had with them, or the rows between President Wilson and Mr de Valera, and maybe the fund-raising difficulties of our Russian friends?'

Frank's voice shocked her with its urgent, angry growl. 'No! Absolutely not! Not here. And for Jesus' sake, Rita, don't you know not to mention the Bolsheviks?'

She hadn't meant to upset him. She fought back tears. 'I just want to help, to be of some use −'

He took her hands then, gripping them more tightly than he realized. 'Listen, why don't you ask Mrs Kennedy to bring you into one of her church groups? Father Leonard was telling me only the other day there's so much chatter over the vestments he's surprised anything gets done!'

Mama always claimed church activities were for the maids, to keep them out of harm's way. Rita tried, but she could not settle to Mrs Kennedy singsonging about Father Dineen's cold or the shame that Mrs So-and-so's son hadn't taken the Sacrament since Easter because of his involvement with the rebels. Rita didn't want to be sewing garish surplices between the little spontaneous prayers with which Mrs Gorman would punctuate her conversation and the knowing nods and winks from the vast Mrs Reynolds (swollen legged mother of thirteen) when it would inevitably be revealed that she, Rita, was expecting.

Rita dreaded the reaction of these good people, a mixture of embarrassment and innuendo. She dreaded the scrutiny, the eyes, as if what Frank and she did in bed − or, more precisely, the passion which had been released between them during her magical months in America − was flickering like a film on the presbytery wallpaper. For those church ladies the marriage act was a guilty secret, the one stain on spotless lives.

Frank admired such women, which was why, at first, Rita had tried to be like them. But she worried that church societies and sodalities would make her less available for Ireland. She went to mass with Frank, of course, on the Sundays when he was at home – the long twelve o'clock with all the trimmings – then stood by his side on the steps afterwards as he shook hands with all and sundry. She might have been one of those political wives she had met in America, but somehow Terenure was not quite the same. Nobody asked her about the political situation, never mentioned the nasty troubles about the countryside which seemed to get worse with every passing week. People rarely thought to shake her hand, nor expected her to contribute with anything more than a smile.

Safe in the Kitchen

*   *   *

She hated the safe. She didn't mind that the workmen appeared to have been in the kitchen for ever, so that every one of Mrs O'Reilly's meals came seasoned with a sprinkle of soot and plaster. What she could not bear to think about was the potential power of that intruder. When the safe was finally concealed behind a sliding panel above the range, the jewels, her precious life and blood darlings, would be torn from her body, stripped from the pockets sewn into her underwear, unwound from the wide elastic belt around her waist, unpicked from the hollow place where her back curved into her hips. She would shed all their gorgeous bulk and she would be reduced to Rita O'Fiaich again, wife, pregnant woman, ordinary.

'I've been wondering, Frank, what makes you think those things will be safe in the kitchen?'

They could never call them 'jewels' in case Mrs O'Reilly overheard, or the new little girl from the country. He looked up at her from his paper with that cool, schoolmasterly way which had become his lately; a look which went with the emergent politician's voice, spelling things out, simple and slow.

'Because, woman dear, won't the safe be well hidden there, and sure if it is found, what good would it do a thief? Amn't I the only one who'll know the combination?'

That was the moment when she realized the full extent of her loss. He had ordered one of those new safes he had seen in the American hotels. She felt faint, almost panicked. The precious stones and metals became molten lumps around her body, pressure points which cleaved suddenly to her skin like children clutching their mother, screaming in fear of being dragged away. She knew how they felt. Sometimes, when their discomfort and the noise from the kitchen drove her upstairs to rest, she removed some of the jewels from their secret hiding places. At first she had enjoyed only looking at them, playing with them in her hands or feeling the slide of them across her skin. More recently, though, she had begun to try on one or two pieces, to dress up for them, even fantasize a little. All perfectly harmless, of course.

Her voice was hard to find, buried somewhere at the bottom of her chest, but she forced it to be light and teasing, the way Frank liked. 'Mightn't that prove a little dangerous?'

His eyes appeared puzzled over the half-moon spectacles. Could he tell how much she cared?

'I mean, the way things are at the moment, I get the feeling that anything might happen. Not that it would, of course, but with going off to those little trips of yours to Heaven knows where . . . As I say, if anything were to happen, at a time when, you know, certain persons from overseas could turn up looking for their property, well, it could prove awkward . . .'

'You may have a point there.'

She tried to smile bravely, with enough due *gravitas*. Her voice sounded admirably steady. 'I would be proud to keep that secret, Frank, so we'd not let it out of the house.'

This time he looked irritated, folding a fresh page of his newspaper with studied precision. 'So that any one of my enemies could walk in here and do God knows what to get that number out of you?'

'Oh, honestly darling, as if!'

'All the same, I'm glad you're taking the situation seriously. So, why don't I put the details in a letter and give it to old Joe O'Brien? He'd pass it on to Dev, if, as you insist on saying, anything should happen to me.'

There was no arguing with the man, but what more could she do? He was condemning the jewels, her jewels, to be sealed away in darkness, never allowed to sparkle, never set free again to play on an occasional secret Sunday afternoon.

Waiting for those rare interludes, those shadowy hours when she could be sure the servants were out and Frank engaged elsewhere, was like being a child again, waiting for a birthday. The anticipation was part of the pleasure. And now Frank was going to take that from her. He would dim those few fabulous moments in her humdrum days as surely as fire and death in the countryside were putting out the cultural light of the city.

'I must say I'm disappointed, darling, that you don't trust me to share this responsibility. After all, I was involved from the start.'

'Amn't I only thinking of you? Knowledge is a dangerous thing. Anyway, why would a woman of the new Irish nation be bothering with that rubbish? Won't you soon have something much more important to take care of?'

He put his hand on her stomach and she slapped it away. She couldn't help herself. He had been feeling for their baby. She, like a bitch with pups, was protecting the jewels.

'You're a strange girl, Rita.'

He had gone from the room before she could make it right. Maybe she was strange, but wasn't he even more so? The front door slammed. He would break the glass one of these days.

A Dinner Party in Terenure

* * *

'Aren't you a princess!'

Trust Maura Regan to put her finger on it. A woman who wouldn't know a Fortuny from a crushed dishcloth.

'Will you look at the dress, Con, and the headdress! Sure it's a princess from the royal family Frank has for himself and no mistake!'

Frank had been handing out drinks, rather slowly, Rita thought. He looked up sharply. 'We're all Republicans in this house, Mrs Regan, I can assure you!'

'Listen to the man, Con – mesmerized by his own wife!'

Con Regan shrugged and gulped his whiskey. 'Do you think you can get Dev to bridge on the taxation levies, Frank? We could have a bit of trouble in that area, if the English ever talk to us.'

'Men!' Mrs Regan settled herself by the fire. 'Blind bowsies, the lot of them. Tell me, Rita, is it their mothers we should blame?'

'Mothers seem to get blamed for every male failing. I'm praying for a girl!'

Mrs Regan shot up in her chair. 'Oh saints above, don't say that now! Doesn't everyone want a boy, especially these times with all the fine lads lost to the Boche and in our own fight.' She blessed herself fervently. 'Don't go calling down bad luck on the whole shooting match, and you looking so grand!'

Rita felt strangely detached. It couldn't be right for someone giving her first dinner party, but she felt as if none of it really mattered. Perhaps it was the fault of the guests. Mama would never have approved of such blatant displays of religiosity in her own drawing-room, nor of

Maura's seamless drone about the qualities of her large brood.

Rita had gone to so much trouble to make tonight a success. It hadn't been easy to create an effect without the silver, crystal, and even flowers from the greenhouse which Mama could call upon. Perhaps that was why, at the last minute, she had put on the tiara. Wearing it gave her grace, a certain assurance, and drew eyes away from her ballooning stomach. Besides, she owed it to the jewels to share a little enjoyment before their incarceration in the kitchen. She only hoped they approved her poor attempts at decoration. The battered pod dining-table looked quite dignified beneath two layers of damask, and anyone would think the honey jars were made for candles, draped so artfully with ivy and honeysuckle. Candlelight, too, from the brass on the mantelpiece threw a kinder radiance upon the worn patches of the Indian rug and softened the ugly varnished boards around the edges of the room. Odd to realize that apart from her own family and Mary, everyone she knew nowadays seemed to think she was living in the lap of luxury. When she had complained about the awful décor of the dining-room to Mrs O'Reilly, the woman had given her a look of pure scorn. 'Sure who in the name of Jaysus would be interested in that class of carry-on? You and that gentleman of yours have better things to do!'

Rita had seen Mama entertain often enough; seen all the fuss and the panics beforehand and then the charm with the first guest, as if a curtain had gone up. Here, with Frank, it wasn't like that. Why, the occasional time they went out together, did the men he introduced her to seem to shy away? Did she look so awful, full blown like this? Or was it sometimes as she suspected, that to Frank's country friends she appeared too bright, overdressed, citified, the way Frank had made her feel when he walked into the bedroom just as she was fixing the tiara in her hair.

'Putting on a bit of a show, aren't you?'

'Don't you like it?'

'It's grand, but you can hardly pretend this place is Buckingham Palace.'

Papa always complimented Mama on her appearance. It was good manners. Nor would he have allowed his guests to behave like Con Regan, locked in political chat so early in the evening. On the other hand, he might have inquired about the provenance of his wife's jewellery. But then, Frank had no interest in such things. Her remarks about women they met made her realize that her husband lacked a visual sense; he could not afterwards recall a detail of their dress nor even the colour of their hair.

Putting a shine on her husband's rough and ready manners was proving more difficult than she had expected. He ignored her complaints about the new beard. When others remarked on his changed appearance, he winked. 'Sure it's handy when you're in a hurry!' People always laughed as if congratulating him about something. Well, it was only a little thing, but as his wife she didn't like the way it scratched.

Maura Regan looked impressed by the sitting-room anyway. She had commented favourably on the huge religious picture which Frank's mother had given them for their wedding. Con Regan had blessed himself. Rita hated it. It was Frank who insisted it be hung there, taking up almost a whole wall. Still, as a compromise, he had agreed to some redecorations. The red and gold wallpaper from Walpole's heightened the rich blue of the Virgin's robes and the pink and gold of her attendants. With the faded velvet chair covers and art silk curtains made up from Clery's coat lining, the effect was quite sumptuous.

Ellen had her raw face round the sitting-room door. 'There's more company, ma'am!'

Mary walked in like a fawn stepping into a forest clearing. Over beige drop-waisted chiffon she wore a long string of amber stones, large and lustrous, enough to remind Frank and Mr Regan to stand up. Kissing her cheek, Rita could smell her warm French perfume. Rita had asked Frank to buy her some scent for this party and

89

he had come home empty-handed, laughing at the prices they were asking in town, saying she smelt sweet enough. Perhaps he was right. Mary knew nothing of such constraints, living with adoring parents in their big house in Merrion Square. They could afford such luxuries with the Kelly stores nearly as common as pubs all over Ireland.

Maybe Frank and she *were* as poor as he made out. How could she tell? He said money was a man's business, although at home Mama had always handled the domestic expenses.

Someone else had entered the room, a big rugby-playing type with a bluff sense of himself rare in Frank's circle.

'Ah, Dermot, you found us all right!'

So this was Dermot Quinn, some minor factotum in Mr de Valera's entourage, the young bachelor invited for a pair with Mary. He was beaming into Rita's face as if he were a rugby coach encouraging a player to score a try.

'Mrs O'Fiaich, I can't tell you how pleased I am to be here tonight!'

His accent was Dublin, which made a nice change from the bulk of Frank's political friends. Rather common, though, reminding Rita of the young patient of Papa whom Mama had taken on to do some gardening years ago. He had been so nice one afternoon, showing her how to plant lettuce seeds, and was gone the next day. Papa said he needed more treatment.

'It's a dull time the rest of us are having, with the city going dark with curfews. And looking about me now, isn't it how I've always suspected: it's you married couples doing the gallivanting!'

'Enough of the old *blague*, Dermot, and come over here and explain these new levies to Con. He thinks I'm making them up!'

Really, Frank was the limit. 'Just a moment, darling, we must introduce our guests. Mr Quinn, do you know Mr and Mrs Conor Regan, and my friend, Miss Mary Kelly?'

'Not to worry, Rita dear, Mr Quinn and myself met on the front steps!'

'And didn't I tell you to call me Dermot?'

They seemed to have made quite an acquaintance in such a short time. Dermot Quinn wore a smile like a horse putting his nose in a bucket full of oats. He sat himself beside Mary, ignoring the calls from the men. Despite the accent, he had a better idea than some of how to behave in company.

'Have you come far, Mr Quinn?'

'Clontarf, Mrs O'Fiaich. No distance these days with the trains and the trams.'

Mary laughed. 'Don't cod yourself, Mr Quinn. The north side is another country altogether! In fact, the way it's filling up with blow-ins you might think you were still in the country!'

'Don't listen to Miss Kelly, Mr Quinn. I am from the north side, the North Circular Road, and a very respectable place it is.'

'Is that right, Mrs O'Fiaich? Then you forgot to give me the secret handshake!'

The way everyone laughed made Rita feel quite silly. There was too much of the play-actor about this fellow. Maybe that was why Frank had been reluctant to invite him.

'What's that on your head? It's divine!'

Mary was reaching across at her, trying to touch the precious tiara. Maybe it was the jokes at her expense and now this plunder, but Rita couldn't help herself. She leapt backwards, clutching the decoration, feeling its diamond hardness chill her fingertips.

'Don't, Mary, please, it's only held on with a few pins!'

Too late, Rita saw the wondering in Mary's face, the glimmer of suspicion.

Frank too was looking at her, alerted by the thrill in Mary's loud whispered, 'Did you get it in the States, darling?' From his baffled expression, she could see Frank had not a clue what the fuss was about. Brought up in a home where clothes remained unchanged and jewellery was almost unknown, he was oblivious to Rita's adornments: trivial and incomprehensible souvenirs from another world.

Mary had to be silenced. A foxhound on the scent, eyes bulging, her voice rising to a triumphant bay as she called back to the others, 'Don't tell us, Frank, you've been buying your wife expensive jewellery! It'll be frocks in Paris next!'

Frank was only insulted by Mary's suggestion. He was soon in full flow about the corruption of 'English tastes' and an Irishwoman's needs being as simple and inexpensive as a wool shawl, which got everyone, except Mary, nodding piously. She appeared unimpressed too by Rita's murmured explanation. 'Can't you see it's only a joke of a thing, a cheap little trinket?'

Dealing with Tradesmen

＊ ＊ ＊

Frank had selected Mr Noone. He insisted he was the man for the job, but then, for all his political expertise, Rita sometimes wondered if Frank was such a great judge of people. She had taken an instant dislike to the builder, from his dusty boots to the lack of a bowler hat. But there was no point in complaining. Mr Noone was chosen because he was a party man. And certainly, to find someone who would secrete a safe in a kitchen chimney-piece without telling the world and his wife did require a measure of loyalty and discretion.

But there was no getting away from the fact that Mr Noone was proving unreliable. For ages now it had seemed there would be no let-up on the dirt, grime and noise gusting up the kitchen steps and around the house. Yet, to begin with, the task had looked simple enough. All Mr Noone had to do, as he said to Rita himself, was to 'knock an old space' into the huge chimney which projected out above the range and insert the small safe. After weeks of banging and dirt, and worse days in which nothing happened at all because nobody turned up for work, something had gone frightfully wrong. Mr Noone blamed his little apprentice for cracking the flue, but really, as Rita couldn't help remarking, if this was such a fiddly job, Mr Noone should have done it himself.

There was a squalid scene in the kitchen that day. Everything was coated in a veil of fine plaster, recalling how Clonkee used to look shrouded in sheets when the family returned from long summers abroad. The red and black tiles were whitened with dust, as was the dresser with its green and red Chinese tree dinner service. Even the carpeting on Mrs O'Reilly's armchair beside the range looked spongy with the stuff. The cook and the workmen had become moving statues, faces hewn like figureheads on Mount Rushmore.

'The moon is in Mercury, missus. Didn't I tell you this morning about the magpies? Three of them *and* a black cat! Sure we're lucky the sky didn't fall in!'

It was quite awful the way Mr Noone roared at the lad and Mrs O'Reilly shouted at all of them. Rita tried to introduce some fairness, but it was no use. Mr Noone fired the boy on the spot, sending him home to Gardiner Street without a penny in wages. Rita saw him out the side gate and gave him ten shillings for the big family he supported, a sum which she was to regret as more weeks passed and the house remained filled with dust and workmen.

'It's bollixed, missus. Pardon my French, but this eejit took a terrible whack at the chisel and we're into the main flue.'

'It wasn't my fault, Mr Noone!' The boy was dancing about, ashen faced beneath the grime, with the shocked, guilty look of someone who had just murdered his mother. 'He tole me knock it there. "Knock away," he says. "Sure it's as solid as Pharaoh's tomb."'

Mrs O'Reilly was pummelling dough on the table, snorting. So that was why the woman's soda bread turned out like bricks. 'It's a disgrace, Mrs O'Fiaich, letting a wild creature like himself loose in a respectable household!'

'Well, I'm sure it can all be rectified, if we calm down and discuss this rationally.'

'Oh, it'll be fixed all right, missus, I can promise you that. I'll get my best workman over here as quickly as possible.'

The dough took another header on to the scrubbed boards.

'Why didn't yez have yer best workmen hammering me head off all along? Why didn't he listen this morning when I read the lad his stars out of the newspaper? Ask him that, Mrs O'Fiaich! And inquire what I'm supposed to do in the meantime with no range!'

'You can't expect a man to work miracles, isn't that right, missus? Didn't Mr O'Fiaich know it was a tricky one? It's not everyone would be able to fit a thing into a little space like that.'

'No, and you haven't done it yet, have yez?'

Rita could feel the jewels growing sharper and heavier. With every day now, as her body expanded, even the child inside her seemed to resent the precious lumps and bumps strapped around it.

It was hard to decide what to feel about this delay. It was an extension of the time in which she could keep the jewels near her. But as she stood there in the kitchen feeling tight and uncomfortable, she had a sudden realization that she could not harbour them for much longer. Supposing something happened to her, that she fell ill, developed complications in the pregnancy? Would Frank be prepared to carry jewels in his combinations?

Mr Noone was struggling to regain lost ground. 'Not that I ever liked that old range. As I said to myself when I walked into this kitchen, Mrs O'Fiaich, I'm surprised at the likes of you people being so old-fashioned. Isn't the man of the house leading the nation forward, out of the past? And isn't the gas all the rage now? I know there's many a professional cook wouldn't take a job without it.'

Frank had been away on one of his mysterious trips, so she had had to make the decision herself. Mr Noone promised her the choice of a new gas cooker would speed up the fitting of the safe. An untruth. Somehow, in all the mess and muddle, his attention switched from the chimney-piece to the gas pipeline coming in from the road. Thus, as Rita expanded and the baby kicked harder each day against jewelled walls, the safe gathered dust on the scullery floor. Meals came lukewarm, cooked at awkward hours in neighbours' ovens.

For Rita, time inched forward like a snail. She wondered about such creatures when she went out in the evenings to pick flowers for the table. There was something brave and innocent about the tiny questing horns stretching on to the paths, something admirable about the glossy line from head to tail interrupted only by the security of its shell. Here was a house from which its occupant could never be released. She wondered did the snail treasure its burden as she did, hugging her bulk to herself? Was there a special place within its shell, like the kitchen, in which the snail felt secure?

Frank crushed snails when he saw them. He had planned a vegetable patch when they returned from America, but it had slipped his mind. He rarely went into the garden, there wasn't time in the short periods he was at home, and he took no interest in the problems of the kitchen. 'Important business' was the most information Rita could extract about where he was going or when he might be back. It was Mrs O'Reilly who was able to anticipate his movements, though Rita could only suppose she read them in the tea-leaves.

She had stopped him one morning on the way out, prodded by the way Mrs O'Reilly had casually handed her master a large packet of sandwiches and a flask of tea on a day when Rita had expected to see her husband home for luncheon.

'Just a moment, Frank, I'm rather worried. I need to know more.'

'You what?'

'I met Mrs Gorman on the road this morning, she was asking if things are getting worse. She said she'd heard the politicians can't control the Volunteers any more.'

'Dangerous talk, Rita. You should put a stop to that.'

'I know, but I didn't know what to reply. It made me feel stupid.'

'Ah, haven't you enough to think about? Preparing to rear the future generation in an Irish Catholic home?'

In the mornings, there were thin lines of silver glinting across the garden path, the only proof for Rita that time had gone by at all.

Things did seem to be getting worse. She wrote a letter of condolence to Mrs MacSwiney after her husband died on hunger strike and didn't hear a word back. The widow was from a very good family in Cork. And only the other day, when she had commented to Mrs O'Reilly on a newspaper report of an ambush, the woman had looked amazed by her sentiments, going on and on about the English having executed the poor Barry boy. As if that were an excuse.

It was ridiculous, of course, to find oneself so often reduced to the companionship of a cook. But apart from the church flowers, which Rita did enjoy, and an occasional coffee with Mary, there were few alternatives. Once, when Rita suggested herself for tea, Mama had been quite unkind. 'No, Lady Conlan and the Bowe-Whites are coming. They're upset enough by the situation without meeting *you*!'

Just because she was Frank's wife. But of course, so many people like Mama and her friends might as well be living with their heads in the sand, refusing to agree that the English had to be thrown out, that Ireland must be set free. When Frank had finished the struggle, they could begin an ordinary married life. She would be useful to him then, with a new nation to establish. Perhaps Frank and she would travel to represent Ireland abroad, might even set up an embassy, somewhere nice like Paris or Rome. She would be good at that. Frank was not interested in such speculations. He could think only of today. Sometimes, when she tried to talk about the future, she suspected he viewed her as a task completed, as if she were a point of order or a law on the statute book which he had fought for and won and could place in a file, expecting no further trouble.

Bloody Sunday

* * *

It was how it should be, this family outing. Rita and Frank walking down the road together like any married couple, even if it was Sunday and everything in town would be shut, even if they were only going to mass in St Stephen's Green.

A pity it was so early. An hour or so later and people might have passed them by as they stood at the tram stop, seen them together, Frank in his brown worsted, she in her velvet cloche with a veil and the big camel coat Mama had reluctantly lent her for the pregnancy. Her ankles were swollen this morning, but you couldn't have everything.

It had been quite a business getting ready on time. She thought she heard the telephone ring at some still dark hour, but the first she really knew was Frank's face bending over, shaking her. He had to repeat himself two or three times before she was properly awake. 'I said to get yourself up now and we'll catch an early mass in town.'

She was always a bit slow in the mornings. It was hard to shake off the dream still playing in her head. Frank had been there, in the garden at Clonkee, with Carl and PJ, two middle-aged depressives scratching the gravel around the house as usual, and Mama's greedy little Cuddles jumping up at her the way he always did when the maids banged the gong.

'It's not teatime yet, is it?' Her voice sounded odd and fluting, an echo half forgotten.

He tried to smile, repeating slowly and carefully that it was half past six and she must get up.

She put out a hand to smooth the tension lines from his cheek, but he jerked away.

98

'You've shaved off your beard!'

That was what was different. He made her think of their courtship days, with that exposed look about him as he entered Mama's drawing-room, timid yet determined. 'Foxy,' Papa used to mumble, whatever that meant. Without the grizzled jaw he looked almost the old Frank again, though the eyes were more wary now.

'I'm glad. You know I never liked it. I've just been dreaming you were Cuddles. What a silly creature he was – a hunt terrier, of course!'

The linoleum was freezing when she stepped off the bedside rug. The landing would be cold. Oh for a cup of tea in the warm bed, just the two of them. No chance of that at this hour. You were lucky to see Mrs O'Reilly by ten on a Sunday morning, and if you complained, the woman had a tendency to quote some illiterate socialist slogan by Connolly or his ilk and have Frank nodding agreement to the final 'Amn't I right, Mr O'Fiaich?' and a triumphant shake of the head at her mistress.

Surely, though, they had deserved a lie-in?

'But why? It's so horribly early. And what's wrong with St Joseph's?'

He had shouted at her then. 'The plan is for nine o'clock at the Green! And I need you there!'

'Goodness!' was all she said when she looked into his eyes. They seemed jerkily excited this morning, bright with the look Cuddles gave when alerting you to the cake.

'I'm sorry, *alannah*.' He touched her shoulder briefly. 'You know how it is, we're all a bit stretched these days.'

He must be tired because of the late hour he had come to bed last night. She would have liked to inquire why she was needed at a mass in town when there was a perfectly good church just around the corner. She knew better than to ask. Frank expected her to predict his wishes as easily as the cook, insights which apparently excused the way the woman would walk into the sitting-room with only a cursory knock to demonstrate some hidden significance in a playing-card. Frank encouraged her. No wonder Mrs

99

O'Reilly was beginning to establish herself as the household's resident seer. Frank liked her mawkish mumblings about death and enemies. But then, he was much more superstitious than Rita. Something to do with growing up in the country.

She had meant it as a joke – 'The family that prays together, stays together' – but Frank hadn't even smiled. Funny the things one noticed: the loss of beard made Frank's ears look more weatherbeaten than she remembered.

'Well, aren't you the early birds!'

They hadn't noticed Mrs Winn's black eminence until she was upon them on the main road. Her nipped-in serge and the shiny feathered hat gave the impression of a large crow skidding down in a field.

'Like yourself, Mrs Winn.' Rita smiled gaily, as if it were the most ordinary thing in the world to be standing at a tram stop on the Terenure Road East at five minutes to eight on a Sunday morning. Times like these she wished Frank would agree to getting a motor. At least he had the wit to doff his hat.

'Duty calls.' Mrs Winn gave a nod across at the church as if she were answering a summons from God himself. 'There's no one else would get me out, I can tell you!'

A screech of metal from inside the terminus gave hope that deliverance was at hand. If only it would hurry up. The tension of her husband's determined silence, or light rain gusting from the crossroads, made Rita careless. 'Oh, we're off to mass too, Mrs Winn! Mr O'Fiaich has taken it into his head to go to Stephen's Green for a change –'

The look on Frank's face was like a fist. He might as well have grabbed her by the scruff of the neck and shaken her. She felt her jaw lock. It hurt, that silent snarl, and the shame at her own lapse, a betrayal.

Through the pounding in her ears she heard Mrs Winn's creaking laugh, sounds of the locks and bolts with which her late husband had made his fortune. 'Stephen's Green, is it? Don't let Father Michael hear you're too grand for us, Mr O'Fiaich, just because they're printing your name in the newspapers!'

The woman was nothing but a common gossip. What was she doing living in Terenure anyway? Someone on her income should be in Rathgar or Donnybrook. Obviously an eccentric. Frank was right to mistrust Dubliners like this, 'Palers' he called them, cushioned by their money and their certainties.

Frank hurried her on to the tram, the day spoiled before it had even begun. She could see he was furious, sitting there smoking edgily, staring out the window, ignoring her.

When she tried to slip her hand in his at Rathmines, he nearly shot from the seat.

'I'm sorry.'

By the time they were getting off the tram she was wondering if a suggestion of coffee in the Russell later might save the day. 'Heavens, Frank, it's only twenty minutes past eight! Perhaps we should take a turn about the Green?'

'Go ahead, so. I'll stop here if it's all the same to you.'

It was not all the same to her. They were ridiculously early for mass because of Frank's fussing and now he was suggesting his pregnant wife should walk alone in a city park. 'We could just go in for a sit-down. There's over half an hour to kill.'

The way he stared at her then you'd think he hadn't ever noticed her before. A carriage had stopped at Number Eighty-six and disgorged a group of students in evening dress. The army had raided the National University earlier that month and caused a lot of resentment, but those boys looked peaceful enough. The horse broke wind noisily as the cabbie whipped it out into the street.

He was trying to smile, but something wild and frightened scurried about in the back of Frank's eyes. 'We're attracting attention, Rita. Now will you please do as I ask?'

The pain of his rejection made her want to sink down like a common streetwalker on the cold pavement. How had it come about? He had asked her here and now he wanted her gone, wished it so hard she felt that if she had been a cat he would have lifted her with his boot and kicked her across the wide road and over the railings. Yet to see them there anyone would think they were a husband and wife having a quiet conversation.

'Please, come with me.'

He was lighting a cigarette, refusing to look at her. 'Go on, so. With that belly you'll need to get the weight off your feet.'

He didn't watch her go. His sights had been over her shoulder, down the road towards the Winter Palace Tea Rooms. Turning to cross the street, she noticed two men in long raincoats trudging slowly towards the church. When she looked back, Frank was grinding his cigarette under his heel as if preparing to greet them.

The child kicked when she stepped off the pavement. She pressed her hands to it, feeling the knobbly hardness of jewels there. Why couldn't Frank see that she was carrying so much for him, would take on any burden if only he would include her in his plans? She did not look back. The park opened up to her, a happy pungency of damp earth, laurel and the shivering lake. Perfection would be having him here to share its winter prettiness, but then, wasn't she lucky enough already? She would be his trusty soldier, must not be selfish like Mama, who would have sulked if Papa said one cross word. Frank O'Fiaich was special, and he was her husband. As the nuns had so often said, you couldn't have everything.

Lying In

* * *

When her mother telephoned the next day, Mrs O'Reilly had instructions to say her mistress was indisposed. There was no need to be told about that treacherous insertion in the *Irish Times*. Hard enough to hush the voices inside Rita's own head, spelling out the facts, arranging everything into a sequence as they must have happened after she left Frank at the church, after he had disappeared. A litany of awfulness, useful only for quelling another sound which threatened to break loose from her lips and roar about the darkened bedroom: a scream of horror, anger, humiliation, betrayal.

Despite the uncertainties of the day before, the morning had begun quite promisingly. Mrs O'Reilly came striding in like Cromwell at an unprecedented seven a.m. 'Jesus and Mary, missus, but aren't you the cool one!' Dumping down the breakfast tray (properly laid for once), fetching her wrap, letting in the sunlight with a pull at the curtains that nearly had them on the floor, rattling on about 'Wasn't that a great day's work!' and 'I'd never have credited it, though I've heard tell you Virgos can be very steady.'

Usually on mornings when Frank was away, Rita was lucky if the woman had sidled in with her sniffs and her sighs by nine o'clock. And it would be all Rita could do to get her to draw the curtains before she was off out the door with a disapproving 'it's all right for some' look.

This was a most welcome change; one which might be encouraged. 'How clever of you, Mrs O'Reilly, to serve the one breakfast! Mr O'Fiaich never did turn up yesterday. I have a bone to pick with him over that, leaving me high and dry!'

Mrs O'Reilly gave one of her whoops. 'Huh! I'd say the army lads will be picking a few bones when himself gets back!'

She stood by the bed, arms akimbo, waiting for Rita to look at the newspapers, fanning them out over the eiderdown around the blue china and the tea cosy with the cottage garden scene which Sister Louise had made Rita unpick and re-embroider only a few years ago. Rita tried to focus on the headlines. Better to concentrate on their dreary news than dwell on yesterday, on the hurt she felt at Frank's abandonment, the peculiar sense of loss as she knelt in the pew and wondered where he had gone, then boarded the tram alone. Worse, his husky, almost inaudible instructions down the telephone last night, 'You're to say I was with you, at the mass!', only reiterated each time she begged to know where he had gone or what had happened; shouted loudly, angrily, when she tried to tell him how worried she had been, 'Listen, woman, will you ever shut up and listen!', until the line went dead.

EXECUTION
MURDER
BLOODY SUNDAY
14 DEAD
REVENGE

The words jostled before her eyes, repeating their bloody message in letters huge and piercingly small. It was hard to think why Mrs O'Reilly had taken such liberties, why she had turned back the pages on such unpleasantness. But there it all was: murky pictures of a house in Earlsfort Terrace; the interior of some rented room off the South Circular Road; lines of faces, men and boys; the same story everywhere.

NATIONALIST EXECUTION SQUAD MURDERS
14 UNARMED MEN IN CITY CENTRE RAIDS

And always beside that, another story.

'I sent the lad back for them other ones, missus. I knew you'd want to see the lot!' That was another peculiar thing this Monday morning, the hush of respect in the cook's voice. 'I said to myself when I saw it, she'll be expecting more than a mention in the *Times* for this!'

'Thank you, Mrs O'Reilly, but there was no need to take it upon yourself to get more than the two papers. They add up to a tidy sum, you know!'

All those people killed and maimed, on a Sunday too. The nationalist papers were claiming that the men shot yesterday morning had been British agents, planning some coup against republicans. A nasty business, whatever the truth. All the same, just for once, it would be so nice to take breakfast without quite so much unpleasantness.

Lying in the darkened room afterwards, watching a spider spin a web from picture rail to curtain, she felt silly, ashamed. The way Mrs O'Reilly had cackled with glee as she pointed a finger at the relevant passages in the *Irish Times*, then led her through the pieces in the other papers, all listing Frank's name alongside Richard Mulcahy and Cathal Brugha; implicated in the day which everyone seemed to be calling Bloody Sunday.

It had been bloody all right. She could taste the gore, the smell of the butcher's shop mingling with the cleansing spiciness of the incense she had breathed so innocently as she waited on after mass, trying to concentrate on the Benediction, to forgive Frank for failing her. Asking God to banish a tiny twinge of anger and foreboding.

Bloody Sunday. Why did that name ring a bell, remind her of something she wished to forget?

Her tea was cold by the time she had consumed every word. She knew it all now. The exact thirty minutes after nine when 14 men around Dublin were simultaneously murdered in their lodgings, the suggestion that some of the assassins had attended eight o'clock mass at St Stephen's Green before going about their work.

Then in the afternoon, the 12 dead and 107 wounded when the British forces took their revenge on spectators at Croke Park. And finally, suggestions in the Stop Press sections of last night's torture and death under interrogation of David McKee and someone called Clancy in Dublin Castle. Mr McKee sounded familiar: Rita thought she might have met him at some reception or other; was he the quietly spoken young man with a pleasant smile?

Over the second cup of tea, when she turned back to the *Irish Times* in hopes of balance, she found her own name:

Francis Xavier O'Fiaich, the well-known Republican agitator, was reported to have attended nine o'clock mass with his wife, Margarita (daughter of Dr and Mrs Fitzgerald of Clonkee, North Circular Road), in St Stephen's Green Church at about the time the murders took place.

The shock was the same as once, long ago, when, as a small child she had stood behind the solid figures of her father and his friends in woods above Rathfarnham, marvelling at the sudden darkness of birds overhead, the great rush of their wings. Then the nightmare of guns, dogs, small thudding bodies and the congratulatory shouts of people whom, up to that moment, she had believed kind.

She didn't notice the doorbell until Ellen burst into the bedroom. 'It's the Tans, missus! They're outside!'

'Well, let them in! See them into the sitting-room, and tell their commanding officer I shall be down shortly!'

She needn't have bothered wondering what to wear. Into her bedroom without a by-your-leave they came, rough men smelling of riding macs and the badgery scent which Frank had on him sometimes when he arrived back from those trips of his. Such a noise they made, and the rudeness! Really, the English could be the most cultured and civilized people one might wish to meet, but there was no getting away from it, their urban masses, these uneducated lumpen creatures tearing about her house, were little short of animals. The dull pleasure in their eyes as they ripped and smashed about the bed made them more like the foot soldiers of Genghis Khan than servants of His Majesty. Indeed, you would not find such craven, ignorant destructiveness amongst the lowliest peasants of Europe, certainly not of Ireland. She would say so when she wrote to their superior officer. The letter was already composing itself in her head. She would add that she quite understood why these scrappily dressed troops had been nicknamed Black and Tans. They behaved like dogs in full cry, though more like hunt terriers than hounds.

Afterwards it was hard to recall exactly what she had said, to remember the details of a bad dream. It didn't matter anyway. Frank was not at home, that was the long and the short of it; as to where he had got to, their guess was as good as hers. She must have been in shock. Otherwise how could she have sat in bed with that nasty young man sneering from the armchair by the fireplace as tea stains spread over the scattered newspapers and sounds of a home being turned upside down were punctuated by the girl's screams and Mrs O'Reilly's roars. 'Ye filthy gits! Ye ignorant bowsies!'

Nobody asked her to confirm that Frank had prayed beside her at the mass.

When silence fell at last, the young man hawked a spit upon the floor. 'We'll get him, don't you worry!'

It was surprisingly difficult to get out of bed. Her legs couldn't seem to support her. With the slam of the front door she slid to her knees, burying her face in the sodden blankets, her hands thrusting beneath the mattress until her fingers touched the first hard little bundle.

'Thank God!'

She scooped them out, one by one: the silk camisole with a multiplicity of buttoned pockets which a Chinese man in New York had made for her (she had recently added panels to accommodate her increasing size); the cotton money-belt which she had fashioned out of elastic bandages; the heavy cotton underskirt, weighted like the others with precious tucks, seams, hems and layering. Honestly, if the nuns could see the handiwork, they might have changed their tune about her abilities with a needle.

She knelt like that for a long time, an unfamiliar image of piety reflected in the smashed mirror glass above her dressing-table. She *was* giving thanks, in a way, if she could only find the words of gratitude that the jewels had been spared, that she could hold them to her in the blessed calm after the storm. It was then she recalled a story Nina had told once, of a massacre in some city in Russia where Nina's father had been killed. That was it! Nina had called that day Bloody Sunday, and they had comforted one another for the innocent people who had died.

Later an indignant Mrs O'Reilly informed her she must have knelt like that for two hours. A long time, apparently, for the cook and the girl left locked with the brooms under the stairs. Mrs O'Reilly couldn't understand why Rita had been so slow in answering their thumps and shouts or responding to the concerned hammering of neighbours.

And now she was upstairs again, the bed freshly made up and sounds of the mess being cleared, the builders and a stream of busybodies from the road adding more hulla-baloo in the kitchen as facts of the drama were buffed and bent into fiction. Well, she would stay here in the darkness for as long as it took to grow strong. Frank had his mission to complete, but did he care that she had been struck down twice, first by his deception and then by such added public humiliation as he had brought upon them? In this violent new world few things were certain, could remain inviolate no matter what tyranny might touch them. Of course he was right, the jewels would be safer in the kitchen. But meanwhile, they were here, tucked up warm beneath her. And there was another thing to thank God for: those people had not found her husband.

V

Incarceration

* * *

When they telephoned her about Frank, Rita wasn't a bit
ready. It was a glittering December afternoon. She had
drawn the curtains against it and was standing in the soft
light of candles in front of the long swing mirror. Her
saffron silk nightgown with its low cutwork bodice was the
only dressy thing that would fit over her stomach the size
it was now. Teamed with Mama's embroidered Chinese
shawl, she rather liked the effect, even if the mirror was
still cracked and she looked somewhat larger than life. It
was a style which suited her favourites, the ruby and pearl
earrings, the matching ring, the pearl choker with its
diamond cherub clasp, plus any number of necklaces and
brooches which Rita could find places for.

The bed shimmered with more pieces waiting their
turn. Lovely to liberate the jewels in this way, to release
them one by one from the bonds of her underwear, greet-
ing each item like a long-forgotten friend.

Of all the combinations of clothes and jewels she had
tried in that dreamy Sunday after Mrs O'Reilly and the
girl had finally vacated the house, this was the finest. She
had taken her time putting it all together, selecting baubles
from where they lay twinkling up at her like babies
kicking in play. She had all the time in the world; the
servants were gone until suppertime.

It was the same ritual any Sunday that the house was
hers alone. First of all she would dress herself up in the
gaslight, laying on scarves and wraps and bits of lace.
Such stuff was a rich foil to her darlings, cold, hard, oh so
beautiful Russians which seemed to dominate her thoughts
more than ever with the isolation of each day. Only when

she had done all she could with dress and make-up would she light the candles grouped about the room, trying not to hurry, savouring this still, quiet moment. The excitement was exquisite. Turning down the lamps, she felt like a young girl at her first ball, her shallow breath panting high in her chest, walking with the dignity of a princess towards the mirror near the window.

That was always the best moment. The shock and recognition of this stranger, a woman dressed for fantasy, and (if you tipped the mirror slightly upwards) tall, imperious. All about her in the candlelight the bewitching, beckoning, whispering messages of her guests, beams of pure light sighing out their stories of occasions more fabulous than any one mortal could experience in a lifetime.

The sudden ringing made Rita almost faint. Had someone guessed what she was doing? Why did they not give up? She had never realized that the machine could continue to shrill like that, insisting she pull herself together, give up this play-acting, face life.

The jewellery clanked and clicked as she sank down on the linoleum. Nobody ever telephoned at this time on the sabbath; Mama had a charity whist drive that afternoon; Mary was down in the country for the weekend; neighbours were kept busy with visiting family and sporting events. As for Frank, everyone must know by now that he was a wanted man. They should also realize that for all his talk about the togetherness of 'The Irish Family', the last thing Frank ever managed was a Sunday afternoon in the bosom of his wife.

The jewels prodded her out of her panic. The way the bracelets cut into wrists made puffy with pregnancy and the lilac spray brooch tried to pierce her enlarged breasts suggested that they did not consider loss of nerve the correct response to such a challenge. Suppose they judged her a coward, not worthy of them? They pulled her, ashamed, off the floor and out on to the bright afternoon landing.

The telephone went on ringing, as lusty and certain of its demands as a baby in a tenement. Gliding downstairs, she glanced out the long window on the half-landing and saw Mrs Gorman and her big prayer-book walking up the road. Back from her umpteenth trip to the church that day, for all the good it would do. The veil over the face made it hard to tell, but for a second Rita thought she saw her neighbour's eyes fix on the blaze of stones, the flash like a thousand beacons in the sudden sunlight. Well, if Lizzie Gorman thought she had seen a vision, God knew she deserved one.

'Hello?'

'Ah, yes, good, Mrs O'Fiaich?' It was an Anglified voice, clipped, impersonal, slightly annoyed.

'Speaking.'

'Mrs Francis O'Fiaich?'

'Yes?'

'Right. Lieutenant-Colonel Myers here, Royal Blues. I am calling from the Bridewell . . .'

It was about Frank, of course. Hadn't she known it was only a matter of time. Manoeuvres how are you! How could he leave her pregnant and alone like this? She touched the wall barometer for support; the needle pointed to 'changeable'.

'. . . to inform you that your husband, Mr Francis Xavier O'Fiaich, was arrested at two o'clock this morning in the Sally Gap. He has been charged under the Restoration of Order in Ireland Act. Due to the wounding of an officer at the time of his arrest, there is also the question of a further, more serious charge . . .'

The collar of pearls had tightened around her throat.

'. . . a tribunal on Tuesday next . . .'

She felt for the huge diamond clasp at its centre. The two fat cherubs danced blithely on, just as they would have when the soldiers entered the basement room in which the family had been assembled. Nina had whispered once that the Grand Duchess Olga wore it that day. At least, Rita was almost sure she had said so, though at the time of telling her mind had been on other things.

'Hello? Mrs O'Fiaich, are you there? Hello?'

'Yes, yes.'

Were they trying to choke her or to pull her up straight? She must raise her chin above such impertinence. What was this voice suggesting? That Frank, her husband, had been charging about the Dublin mountains playing cowboys and Indians?

'To whom am I speaking?'

'My name is Myers, Mrs O'Fiaich, Lieutenant-Colonel Donald Myers, First Royal Blue Infant –'

'And what is your role in all this, Lieutenant-Colonel Myers?'

'I beg your pardon, but I am merely detailed to follow procedure –' He sounded rattled, as well he might. 'I have other families to contact in relation to this incident. I am merely passing on information to next of kin –'

'Next of kin, Colonel Myers? Is my husband ill?'

'On the contrary, Mrs O'Fiaich, as far as I know, he is in rude good health, but with guns involved you will appreciate that your husband's part in the matter must be regarded with the gravest seriousness.'

'Oh, don't be ridiculous! Isn't everyone carrying guns these days? I'm sure you have one.'

'I am a servant of His Majesty's forces, Mrs O'Fiaich.'

'And Mr O'Fiaich is a servant of the Irish people –'

'The prisoner will be represented by a person authorized by the court . . .'

Why had Frank never taken her into his confidence? Why was she sitting here humiliated by this uppity voice and her own ignorance? If only she had been with him on the mountainside; she could have shielded her husband's body with her own, prepared to die with her unborn child to save Frank for the great service he was destined to do for Ireland. She would gladly give up her life for Frank. But he had asked only that she guard the jewels. That was another question. If anything were to happen to her husband, would Mr de Valera take away the jewels, put them somewhere else? Could she refuse to surrender them?

Hanging up the earpiece, the horror struck. Frank had been arrested, might indeed be executed like many before him. She had a sudden image of his dear face, slanting blue eyes, long nose, flat cheekbones, the icon of a dead saint. And here she stood, as powerless as a child in fancy dress.

Bolts of late afternoon light shot through the coloured glass panels of the front door, playing tag across the wallpaper with the faces of emeralds, diamonds, amethysts, zircons, rubies . . . She had never seen the jewels so gay. Even in the most perfectly stage-managed candlelight her diamonds had never before released such brilliant colour, nor had the softness of gold glowed with such an implacable joy.

A solid bulk on the other side of the glass blocked the light. Maura Regan pressed the bell. The hall was suddenly shadowy with the stillness of those who hear the footsteps of their assassin.

'Yoo-hoo! Rita! It's me!'

The arm reached up to hammer on the knocker, down again to pip the bell. And yet Rita stood there, frozen to the mosaic tile floor, afraid that if she moved at all her pursuer would sense the change of light and colour only a few feet within.

'Rita, dear, Rita O'Fiaich! Listen! It's only me!'

As the letter flap was lifted to the brightness outside, an image flashed into Rita's mind of a black package sliding in to bounce on the green hemp matting with 'Fáilte' woven at its centre, an explosion of death by coloured glass and a roar of sound. The silence was intense. Only Maura Regan's wide-open eyes sliding in, flickering across the gloom to the foot of the stairs. To Rita.

'There you are, girl dear! I suppose you've heard the news? I'm that sorry, but Con says there's no need to be worried. We can get something done. Only open the door now . . .'

Rita was halfway up the stairs before she could release her voice. 'It's all right, Mrs Regan, there's really no need to bother . . .'

'What's that, dear? I can't hear. But I told Con I'll go straight round to her now and see what I can do . . .'

Breath coming in choking sobs, hands running with slippery jewels as Rita plucked them from her hair, her shawl, tearing clasps at neck and arms, fingers pricked and scratched as her pets registered their protests with sulky thuds upon the dressing-table. It was too much, this invasion. Poor, dear Frank. How dare he allow this to happen to her?

Downstairs Maura Regan's voice moved from wheedling to plaintive to piqued. The bell shrilled as Rita dragged her precious pile together and swept it into a drawer. What else? The bed. Strings of stone and metal and pearl hid themselves in the valleys of eiderdown, rejected earrings glinted, chameleon-like, against the silken sheen. An enamel brooch with a ruby at its centre slid softly down beside the bed. They had become naughty children giggling behind the shrubbery when Nanny called them in to tea.

Another voice. The front door was opening to admit her neighbour's thrilled mumble of explanation and Mrs O'Reilly's 'Oh God forgive us! Oh Jesus, Mary and Joseph, save us this day!'

No time to tidy up, only to push bundles of evening clothes behind the wardrobe doors, drag pins out of her elaborately rolled-up hair, kick off the white satin dress shoes.

'I saw her with my own eyes –'

'The shock, you see.'

'Was she off to some fancy do? There'll be no more gallivanting now.'

'The poor man! The poor, great man, to be cut down in his prime!'

'I'd better come up with you, so.'

Too late to dress. Anyway, her day clothes were somehow lost in the exodus to the wardrobe of shawls and the rest.

'Rita, dear?'

Maura Regan was tapping on the bedroom door, the voice like treacle. If this was the tone she took with her children it was no wonder her eldest had run off to Australia without a word of goodbye. Mary said there was talk of a young teacher compromised, but Frank was like a clam on the matter.

'It's me, dear, Maura, I know you've had a shock.'

'I'm here along with her, missus. Didn't I tell you only this morning them chicken's entrails were a shocking colour? And a bad day it turned into for the both of us, with that fella the sister married only stiff with the drink!'

Into bed, pull coverlet up to chin. Something clattering on to the linoleum; an earring; drag it back and under the pillow.

'We'll come in, so?'

This was how a vixen felt as the terriers scrabbled deep into her lair. Papa used to hunt, took her sometimes though she knew her pony slowed him down. She had never liked that smell of horse sweat, nor the blood the time they had wiped a pad on her cheek.

'Just to see you're all right.'

In already. Mrs O'Reilly still in her hat and tight-fitting coat, the ruddy glow of Maura Regan's cheeks no match for an unflattering puce wool dress.

'It was Dermot Quinn phoned, you see, told us the bad news. I thought I'd better pop in.'

'Will you look at the mess!' Mrs O'Reilly was staring about the room in angry amazement. 'Wait till I get my hands on that girl! What does she do with her time at all!' She had plonked her big handbag on to the bed and was unbuttoning her coat. Maura Regan was gazing about her in delight. She would have a good story to tell, the bedroom like a scene out of Bedlam, banks of burning candles jostling aside the usual knick-knacks, dressing-table spoiled with spilt powder, the big Reynolds print hanging askew with its burden of dressing-gown and scarves, other fragments of finery scattered about the room.

'Ah now, Mrs O'Reilly, you don't need to be tidying up for the likes of me. Aren't we good friends, Rita?' The woman Regan had sat herself down on the bed, pinning Rita's legs, leaving her powerless to do more than watch Mrs O'Reilly pick up odd shawls and underwear and head for the wardrobe.

Rita struggled upwards. Her big stomach didn't help. 'Leave that!'

'I'll do no such thing, Mrs O'Fiaich! I won't have youse living in a pigsty, even if that girl comes from one herself. Didn't I warn you before you engaged her, missus, it's a well-known fact that the Leitrim people do eat their young!'

'Stop fussing! I need to be alone!' Her voice tore out in a scream.

Mrs O'Reilly's hand froze on the wardrobe door. The stretched flesh around her eyes had darkened to a deep purple.

Maura Regan whispered, 'Better go on, so. She's upset!' at which the cook gave a sort of 'Huh!', picked up her things and marched from the room. Her shout, 'I'll be downstairs if you need me, missus!', was clearly directed more at the visitor than at her employer.

Rita wouldn't have minded if the cook had packed her bags then and there. All she wanted was to be left in peace in her own house. If that meant taking a gun and shooting both women stone dead she might just have done it. But, it seemed, Frank was the one with the gun and they had locked him up. The kicking within her suggested that the baby too wanted to get out and strike a blow for freedom.

'You're upset, dear, who wouldn't be.' Maura Regan had risen to shut the bedroom door. 'Mr Quinn said not to worry. The men are keeping a close eye on things and they'll let you know the minute –'

'Please, Mrs Regan, Maura, you're very kind, but I must rest.'

'Are you feeling sick, dear? Is it the baby?' The woman

had the audacity to stroke her big hand across the bulge of stomach. 'Shocks are the worst thing at a time like this. Now, let me see . . .' Unbelievable. The woman was on the prowl, crossing to the dressing-table to open drawers.

'What in God's name are you doing?'

That halted her in her tracks.

'Smelling salts – I, I just thought you might have some handy, you know, to give you a bit of go.' She was trying not to stare at Rita's *décolletage*, at the transparent silk of a nightdress which had lain defeated in a drawer since the honeymoon.

Rita sat back for decency's sake. 'Please, I merely feel tired. It's all been such a shock.'

'Indeed, you must be worried sick! It's a disgrace, so it is, arresting the husband of a lady in your condition. What torture will they think up next? Wouldn't you think even the English would have the wit to know when enough is enough?'

Too dangerous to close her eyes. The woman would seize the excuse to search her drawers again. Better to sit there on the bed, trying to look like a normal woman, not someone who spent her Sunday afternoons dressing up in a candlelit bedroom heaped with discarded underclothes. Better to smile politely and wait for her to go, for some semblance of peace to creep back with the dark.

Prison Visiting

* * *

Seeing Frank in the state he was in would have been enough to put any woman into labour. It was not a bit nice to realize that your husband looked happier in prison than you had seen him look at home in ages.

She had waited in the visitors' room for such a long time, watching damp sunlight come and go through the huge barred windows, listening to shouts, whistles and occasional howls filtering up to her from that bare, male place. It was important not to cry. Mrs O'Reilly had been very certain about that when she had seen her off – 'Remember, now, they don't like the women roaring!' – which made Rita wonder about her cook's own experiences of prison visiting. Mary had advised she carry a large lace handkerchief, 'for the photographs'. To hear her talk you'd think Rita was preparing for a tableau, 'Condemned to Death' perhaps, at a gala evening with the Gaelic League.

'Did they give you the parcels I left?'

'Will you go on home with yourself, woman!'

His voice was an exasperated hiss. Yet she should be the angry one. Often since that horrible Sunday she had rehearsed expressions of her deep hurt and pain, planning to frighten him with her sense of betrayal as she had done only once before when he tried to leave for America without her. This was not the time. His fury made her want to reach across the table, to feel his familiar warmth. But the guard had warned her that they could not touch, and the way Frank was glaring at her anyone might think she was a faithful dog being sent home by its master.

'I had to see you, I insisted! I've been so worried!'

'Listen to what I'm telling you, woman! Get off out of it!'

He was embarrassed, that was it, by a wife's presence, by this intrusion into a world pungent with limewash and carbolic.

And there was a bruise on his right cheek.

'Have they decided yet – the sentence?'

'Sorry, ma'am, no talk of the trial allowed!'

The old guard's voice was Cork, kinder sounding than her own husband's. She had to persevere, to be reassured, but sometimes it seemed too much to bear. Everyone said that, even the newspapers. Hadn't the Governor only let her in because of her delicate condition, and maybe because he knew Papa slightly? He probably thought Frank would be dead by the time the baby came.

'Well then, have they given you a decent bed? It's very important to get enough sleep.'

The visitors' room didn't promise much comfort for the place. The walls looked grey and damp even on this bright day, the scrubbed floor seeping a crumbling grittiness suggesting underground caves.

'Ah, will you whisht with your questions! Don't you know this isn't a spa?' When he looked at her at last, there was no warmth in his eyes. 'And while you're about it, would you stop the fussing? Don't you know most of the lads here are from the country; they don't have their people bringing such stuff.'

So, the food she had ordered with such care, the little extras of hot-water bottle, feather pillow, the new novel by Mr Wells slipped in to take his mind off the worry, had only annoyed him, made him ashamed at being different, being loved.

Sitting before him with tears running down her cheeks, she felt a sudden sting of anger. It was simply unfair, and a little ridiculous. 'I'm sorry, Frank, if you would only let me help.'

'Time's up!'

The guard's chair scratched like a knife on a plate. She

watched Frank stand to attention, only the briefest nod to herself, relieved to be led away.

She had not known it was coming: the moan which leapt out of her to bounce about the walls, escaping through the open crack of window into the yard outside. She was aware only of the warder at the door stopping suddenly as if in shock, and the guard who had handcuffed himself to Frank giving a guilty glance backwards. Her husband remained steadfast, head held high as if determined to be led straight to the gallows, to be removed from the life in this room and a foolish woman's scream.

He wanted to die. Until she had seen him here, witnessed his commitment to that awful, final destiny, she had expected him to fight back. Frank O'Fiaich was a winner, ordained for greatness. Mr de Valera had described him once as 'the most able man on my team'. She realized now that he might leave her like this, abandon her and the new life they had created together to join the roll-call of Irish martyrs.

Reprieved, 1921

* * *

Years afterwards it used to make Rita smile whenever the books claimed that Liam's birth saved Frank from the firing squad.

Well, if that was what they wished to believe, so be it. Such myths were part of the romance of history, the inspiration for many apparently hopeless acts through all the hundreds of years of British rule; part of a heroic tradition which had, after all, inspired her to leave the complacent certainties of Papa and Mama's lives.

One day, when everyone involved was dead, the official papers might be released. Then some sharp-eyed student would notice that her husband had, in fact, been spared from execution a full twenty-four hours before Rita went into labour. Facts like that would not be welcomed. Rita suspected that, like de Valera's birth certificate, the information would never be deemed fit for public consumption. It would take some tenacious historians to get at such truths. Perhaps they had not yet been born. In the meantime, she had no intention of doing their work for them.

She recognized Lieutenant-Colonel Myers's voice straight away.

'Felt frightful about our last conversation. Hadn't realized you were the daughter of Dr Fitzgerald. Done some excellent work for some of our chaps in the asylum. Anyway, thought I could bend a few rules in the circumstances, let you in on a little secret, Mrs O'Fiaich. Word has it he's going to be pardoned.'

One of Mr Noone's men walked past with a short piece of board trailing plaster and sawdust. The clatter of his boots down the kitchen steps and through the swing door was met by roars of anger from Mrs O'Reilly. Difficult to concentrate on the voice, this eager, whispering presence inside the earpiece.

'Mrs O'Fiaich? Hello!'

'I beg your pardon, Colonel Myers, but am I to understand that my husband is not going to be executed?' Her voice was pleasingly steady.

'Ah, for a minute there I thought I'd lost the line. Yes, but it's all under your hat at the minute.'

Spared! Dear, darling Frank, allowed to live.

'... a tricky decision here amongst the high-ups – keeping martyrdom down to a minimum and so on. A matter of counting heads. Plan seems they'll all get the death sentence tomorrow, but they'll pardon a few people like your husband at the last minute. Show a little humanity, and not many more prominent wallahs made heroes of.'

It was probably the shock. She felt nothing at all, as if her mind had soared up above her head, tumbling away from her in pursuit of one panicked thought. She ought to feel euphoric. But after the initial relief, she could think only of the jewels. Was it because she had never quite believed Frank would be taken from her? Dev had given his word that Frank would get the best legal representation even if he didn't recognize the court, and hadn't Mr O'Kelly been on the telephone only yesterday telling her the trial might be delayed indefinitely? Judging by all the letters and newspaper fuss, her husband seemed to have become some sort of folk hero. A sudden image of his face, the sharp-toothed smile, made her reel. The man she loved was being allowed to live. So why did she keep trying to remember his grim prison face? Was it to goad her fear that if he returned to her now, her plan to save the jewels, the one she had been working towards rather carefully, would come to nothing?

'I don't quite understand how you can do this.'

'Ah, as I said, Mrs O'Fiaich, this telephone call is highly irregular, but I realized from our last conversation that you were not, well, let us say, like many of the wives with whom I have had to communicate. As a military man, ma'am, even I have been shocked at the sort of language some of those ladies deem fit to employ . . .'

How much time did she have? Mr Noone had said he would finish fitting the safe today. The wood in the hall was probably part of the covering panel which Frank had ordered.

'Could I trouble you to ask exactly *when* my husband is likely to be released?'

'Ah, well, you'll understand I am not privy to that sort of information.'

Time was running out. Maybe it was tension, but in the last few minutes Rita had become aware of a new kind of pain, a flutter from the top of her left leg to her breast. The baby wasn't due for three or four weeks, but perhaps there was less time than she had thought.

'Thank you, Colonel Myers. I appreciate your contacting me like this.'

'Least I could do. Kindly convey my best wishes to your parents.'

She stood for a long time in the hall. The hammering in the kitchen was of nails into wood. The false panel. It would be fitted in place, flush with the chimney flue. She needed all her wits about her before Frank came back to spoil everything. The hall was almost dark. The workmen would soon be finished for the day and Mrs O'Reilly might begin to put together one of her grainy meals.

'Mr Noone! May I see you in the study?'

He looked like a guilty schoolboy, as well he might, the pig's mickey he was making of the job. 'If it's about that split skirting board, missus, I'll have it fixed in the morning as quick as blinking!'

'It is not about that, Mr Noone, though I have some grounds, I think, for feeling dissatisfied with much of what has gone on. No, it's about that safe. As you know, Mr O'Fiaich was most insistent that it be available for use as quickly as possible.' The man blessed himself as if Frank were already dead and beatified.

'And I am sure you would do all you could to meet those wishes.'

'Indeed and I would! Sure isn't Mr O'Fiaich the finest man this country has ever known —'

'And what I need to know from you, Mr Noone, is how I can open and close that safe. There are a number of important papers which my husband is anxious to have out of harm's way.'

Mr Noone looked confused and slightly foxy. He was not a party man for nothing. He had probably asked himself many times what there was, in this bare house, which needed such security.

'They're the divil to open, them combo things. Haven't the men been trying themselves, just out of interest, so to speak?'

Rita pushed on through his blushes. 'Precisely. There is a number, is there not?'

A vulnerable line of pale skin ran beneath the oily hairline where his bowler usually sat.

'It's funny you should ask that, missus. I was chatting to the Northerner fella who delivered that yoke and he said to me there isn't a living soul can get them numbers, saving the owner. Oh, God forgive me!'

'Come now, Mr Noone, Mr O'Fiaich isn't quite dead yet. But surely the company keeps records?'

'He said to me all their records is destroyed, you know, after the thing is delivered.'

'But the safe arrived when my husband was away on business, before he was arrested. Do you have the supplier's name?'

Negotiating a Treaty

* * *

The man in his shiny brown suit clearly wished to be anywhere but Rita's sitting-room. These were not the circumstances in which he was accustomed to do business. She could imagine his life up an uncarpeted stair in Molesworth Street, dealing with banks and insurance offices, talking to men like himself, a tight-mouthed Protestant from Belfast with a talent for concealment and decent living; a man to be trusted with the secrets of the business world. Yet here he was seated opposite a heavily pregnant woman in Terenure, in the home of a known papist Republican who, for all he knew, would be shot at dawn.

'While I completely understand your need for discretion, Mr Patterson, I am sure you will appreciate my own delicate position?'

She had chosen to wear the ruby earrings and the matching ring. She had been right. He seemed mesmerized by them in the soft light, his spectacles flashing each time her hand brushed a stray hair behind her ear and returned to its resting place on her stomach.

'After all, it was for my protection, or should I say for the protection of our property, that my husband engaged the services of your firm.'

Frank wouldn't have recognized her tone. It was Mama's, rather 'far back', what they called Castle Catholic, still the accent of authority to this commercial type.

'So, I must ask you to think again. Are you seriously telling me that since Mr O'Fiaich is unavailable to receive the number of the lock of our safe that you intend to withhold that information from me indefinitely, or at least until my husband is cold in his grave?'

Mr Patterson looked shocked, the small scrubbed hands nervously polishing the high shine over his thighs.

'Because that frightens me, Mr Patterson. We have had your safe lying about here for some months now, paid for, you say, yet quite unusable. I am a woman alone, an extremely vulnerable woman.' She leant forward and looked into the thick glass of his spectacles. Black pupils gazed back at her, huge with fear. 'Blood has been spilt for less. I seek your protection.' The shudder she gave as she sat back in her armchair was quite involuntary. A pattern was establishing itself in these hot pains which shot downwards from her centre. Time was indeed running out.

'Are you all right, Mrs O'Fiaich?'

At last, a little human concern cracking the ice.

'Simply frightened, Mr Patterson, very frightened.' She allowed a tiny sob to escape through her shining fingers. She could feel him stare, speculating. The ruby and diamond ring would be hard to ignore. It was fortunate he was a hard-nosed Northerner.

'I fear for myself, for my child, and I don't need to tell you there are some wild elements running loose in our country. If they were to get their hands on, well, certain pieces of property, they would destroy things which, I think, you and I would both wish to preserve, family things which we would both agree are only dear and decent —' Was she sounding Unionist enough for him?

'Please don't distress yourself, Mrs O'Fiaich. It can't be right to be worrying like that, the way you are.'

The glasses tried to avoid the swell of her stomach. Had it grown bigger in the day? It felt tighter, an ache pushing upwards now towards her swollen breasts, the weight more anchored, pressing on some nerve at the top of her legs. But she still had weeks to go.

'That's why I telephoned you, Mr Patterson. You are my only port in this storm, my last hope!'

Not the sort of man to whom women would turn. She could swear from the haircut and the small hole in his sock that he was unmarried. That could be to her advantage. He did not know women. He would believe her to be weak, might not guess the strength, the tigress quality which surprised even herself.

'I would like to help you, Mrs O'Fiaich, but this is very difficult. Like I said, the arrangement was to deliver the code to Mr O'Fiaich himself. I don't know how, in all honesty, I could renege on that arrangement . . .'

He was capitulating, she could tell. Though if he could have picked himself up and flown out the door, he would have. Seeking escape from his weakness, his eyes came to rest on Murillo's *Assumption* in its huge carved gilt frame. She still found it inappropriate for a sitting-room, as formal as a portrait of royalty in a government office. The Virgin smiled sweetly down at them from her cushion of cloud. Mr Patterson was bewitched, as if he had never seen anything quite like her in his life.

'I know you must observe the proprieties, Mr Patterson, but you can understand that these are exceptional circumstances. Perhaps I might suggest a compromise? That you place the code number in my safekeeping –?'

He dragged himself out of the Virgin's orbit, looking worried again.

'Inside a sealed envelope addressed to my husband? On the absolute understanding that I open it only if, well, circumstances, require me to do so.' Her voice broke rather prettily, she thought, as she held his eyes. He sat up straight and smoothed his tie further into the high-buttoned waistcoat. He was listening now, even though his eyes were dragged back again and again by the power of the Virgin's glorious ascension to the heavens, to her dimpled feet loosed from earth's bonds in a circle of fleshy putti.

'I would give you my word of honour not to open that envelope unless . . .'

The eyes, when they returned to hers, looked dazed, like a man awakening from hypnosis.

'. . . unless there was no other course left . . .'

'It's a hard one all right ...' His voice had lost its edginess, dropping to a whisper as he wiped his brow. 'But maybe it's the only thing we can do, in the circumstances.'

'Allow me to fetch you a nice white envelope.'

When she stood up, there was a new tightness at the tops of her legs. Every step was an effort, yet she managed to move smoothly enough to the writing desk and deliver the envelope without faltering. She watched him slip the wax-sealed note from his briefcase into her envelope, watched him lick the glue, write Frank's name on the outside, felt its sharp edge in her hand.

'Have you been in Dublin long, Mr Patterson?' Inside her ears a voice roared, 'You've got it! You've got it!'

'Six months, Mrs O'Fiaich. Transferred from the Belfast office.'

They were at the front door. He couldn't wait to be gone from this Catholic coven, but she played with him for a little, exhilarated by her success. Back in the sitting-room the envelope waited for her on a side table where she had so casually placed it.

'And how do you find it?'

'Och, it's nice enough. Maybe a bit worldly for my taste, a wee bit fancy for its own good.'

'In what way?'

Released at last into the smoky night air, he was meeting her again as another human, someone to do business with. The tough talking had been forgotten. He smiled, knowing she would understand.

'Let's say it's a lot more free than up there, you know, more free and easy. Down here ... you never know *who* you'll meet. I'll say goodnight.'

Confinement

* * *

It was only after she had memorized the number and practised opening and shutting the safe's heavy door that she finally admitted she was about to have a child. There was no getting away from it, those flutters of excitement, the stiffness, the lightning shots of fear and euphoria had to be recognized as pains which had deepened and lengthened with every hour.

Such fine timing. Indeed, her work today had been worthy of a politician, a master crook, a conjuror.

'Rasputin. Remember him?'

The jewels were bundled up in the underwear she had worn since America. No time to find something nicer for them, no chance of giving it a little wash. The larger tiara issued a flash of rage as she wound it into the elastic bandage. If it had a voice it would not whisper as she did, it would shout against the indignity of being stuffed into a hole in a kitchen chimney.

'Please don't be like that. It's for your own good.'

Spoiled children. Perhaps they hadn't liked the priest, but then, they wouldn't have cared about Alexis as he had. Did the poor child ever have to wear jewels?

'Trust me.' It was probably the same thing Rasputin used to whisper to the Tsarina, and look where it got her.

'What on earth are you at, missus?' The cook had appeared at the door to her room. 'Have yez any idea what time it is?'

Thanks be to God the safe was closed. Rita slid the concealing panel across it. 'I hope I didn't disturb you, Mrs O'Reilly. I couldn't sleep.'

'Yez won't get any rest checking up on the work of that

bowsie! If I was looking for something to do, ma'am, I'd be up all night writing letters for the lawyers, so I would, and I'd be getting meself another builder to do the finish!'

The very idea of such a thing, of someone else maybe ripping the safe from its hiding place and starting all over again, brought a new, more lancing stripe of pain.

'Are you all right, Mrs O'Fiaich? Here, sit down and rest.'

How must the chair on the tiled floor sound to them through a muffle of steel walls? It would be very dark in there.

'Don't I know only too well what ails you? I couldn't sleep myself this night of all nights. What kind of people would cut down a lovely man like that? A man only asking what's best for his country and his people.'

How shaming. In all the rush and worry of the last few hours she had almost forgotten Frank. Now there was nothing more to do she could think of him. If only she had been allowed to celebrate the good news. The telephone had been a frightful interruption all evening, first Mary offering comfort, then Mama trying to sound concerned, even some women inviting Rita to join an all-night vigil outside the jail. She had got Ellen to take the messages and tell them she was resting.

'What is your mammy thinking of at all, leaving you alone tonight? It's not right. And what that poor man must be thinking, his last night on God's earth. Did you see there was no moon earlier, though the sky was clear enough? I thought I'd take another look. Between the moon and the stars, don't they have our destinies all written out for us?'

'I've always favoured free will, Mrs O'Reilly. And faith.'

'Oh, there's Himself too. Aren't they in it together? Come on, so, maybe if we knelt down and said a prayer 'or the repose of the master's soul —'

Another lash of pain made Rita gasp.

'Jaysus, missus! Don't tell us you're at your time?'

'I don't know, Mrs O'Reilly. I've weeks to go yet, but something is happening.'

'Would the saints believe it! Wasn't I spinning the cards after dinner and I kept getting the Jack! Don't stir now until I telephone the doctor. God, but wouldn't it be just like a man to be getting himself killed at a time like this!'

Rita's body had become a violin, strung too tight. Now that she thought of it, she had glimpsed a nasty deposit earlier, something red and yellow as she flushed the lavatory. Perhaps that annoying bout of incontinence fitted with something the doctor had mentioned about waters breaking? Mrs O'Reilly was coming back. The new wood panelling looked raw. She had instructed Mr Noone to paint the whole recess in a rich navy blue, the same as the new kitchen cupboards he had yet to produce. God only knew what he might achieve in her absence.

'The doctor says to pack a little bag. You're to go into the hospital with him.'

Fine timing indeed, Rita Fitzgerald. Worthy of royalty. 'What are you talking about? I'm having the baby here.'

'Will ye whisht now, and wait for the doctor. Lay your head on the table there and rest yourself while I get your bits and pieces.' The woman stopped, gawping at Rita's ears. 'But, oh, Mrs O'Fiaich, I wouldn't go into any hospital wearing them things!'

The rubies. She had forgotten to put them in the safe.

'Aren't they only gorgeous!'

'Oh, these old things.' She tried to cover them, exposing the ring on her right hand. 'Paste, you know the sort of thing.'

'Paste my eye! Well, more power to you. There's fellas like that O Muirichiu could buy and sell Ireland, and all out of the politics!'

'My mother, Mrs Fitzgerald, lends me the odd thing for special occasions. But really, they're not at all as good as they look.' She must be very weak, making excuses to her cook!

'My last place, Mrs Cullen, she had some lovely stuff –

for all the good it did her with that face! Now rest quiet there till I pack your bits.'

Sitting in the cold, hushed kitchen, the scrubbed board of the table smooth and solid beneath her arms, the battered old clock ticking time away, Rita felt calm for the first time in ages. She touched the certainty of stone at her ears, each big ruby teardrop with its cool pearl tip, the clump of diamonds above clinging tight as a mollusc. Everything would be all right. They were safe with her, her good luck, her first-born children, the chosen ones who would share this adventure with her. They had helped her today, just as she was helping them.

Motherhood

* * *

Mama was right, she should have engaged James Power. He would never have allowed her here. But Frank had dismissed the man as a Castle quack. Thanks to his choice of Dr Dunne she now found herself in this vast Greek temple of a hospital, a place crawling with the fecund poor of Dublin and their insect life. She could only think that rubbing shoulders with such types was the reason why the staff addressed her with such familiarity.

'Will you look at her, lounging there like the Queen of England in all her finery. Come on now, girl, work to do!'

Horrid the way they harangued her to relax, to try harder, to concentrate. She kept her mind fixed on the jewels, touching the cool stones, pulling at them until she thought her ears would tear. Had any members of the imperial court worn them in their lying-in? How many had died of the pain of it all, as she was bound to do?

What then would Frank think when they returned her effects to him? Maybe he would have been better off not knowing, finished by the firing squad.

Her mind fluttered backwards like a book opened in a breeze, resting sometimes on scenes of childhood: a team of mild mongols pulling a roller over the lawn; Anne Marie swaddled in white lace, wailing as the priest poured water over her head; the teenage Mary chewing a blade of grass beside the tennis court.

'Right, me darling, we seem to be fully dilated, so let's have another little listen . . .'

That time Mary came on holiday with them to La Baule, unable to swim, looking surprisingly adult in her bathing dress. Papa smiling as she ran up the beach,

Mama oddly indifferent beneath her hat. Mama had never approved of her school friends. Used phrases like 'provincial types' and 'a trifle rough', meaning a distaste for pronounced accents or the way some young people did not think of London as the capital of Ireland.

Papa and Mama had gone to school in England and France. They only sent Rita to the new convent in County Meath because they were afraid the war would make travel dangerous. The nuns were from the order which had taught Mama in Surrey, but, as Mama liked to lament, 'Geography has a lot to answer for!'

'Lie back there, girl, and stop groaning. Aren't you having a baby, isn't that what the pains are for?'

The nerve of the man. Who did he think he was talking to? Concentrate on the picture show inside her head, another cool breath of chloroform, champagne bubbles distilled through snow.

'Look at her, Doctor, dolled up for a night with a prince!'

Hands everywhere. Her mind floating above it all, looking down on this Gulliver pinned to a bright bed. She was on another narrow bed far away, a place where the shouts mingled with horses' hooves, car horns, the distant groans of heavy machinery, and people, streets full of people in every shape and colour and nationality. There had been pain there too, or ecstasy? A thousand sharp stones dug into her flesh as she tried to roll away. Another pair of hands had strung them about Rita's body, pinned them in her hair, hidden them in places she dared not look at nor think about. Those dear hands would find them, they always did, probing gently as if they were tickling a salmon, easing it out of the water with that blissful, kissing caress, killing her in a pool of shivering joy until suddenly she was landed, beached, wrenched out of her element on to the cold, dry river bank, gasping for life, bucking, fighting to be allowed to plunge back into the dark and the wet.

'Nina! . . . *Dorogaia!* . . . *Milaia!* . . .'

'Listen to herself! Speaking in tongues we are, or is that the new Irish we're all supposed to learn?'

Oh, the brightness, the hard, flat light of this place to which they had dragged her, in pain and noise . . .

'That's it, one little push!'

A baby was squalling, crying for something it had left behind. There was no going back, it would learn that soon enough.

'A boy! Mrs O'Fiaich, aren't you the clever one, right first time! Will you look at it, a beautiful baby boy, fingers, toes, all sorts of unmentionables and a voice like an opera star!'

The pain had retreated to the lobes of her ears. She put out her hands to take her child. He was so soft, even beneath starched linen wrappings, soft and ripe. Two huge eyes. Friend or foe? 'Another Frank,' she said.

The nurse gasped and blessed herself. 'May the Lord have mercy on his soul!'

Exposure

* * *

'Will we say a little prayer now?'

Molly Nolan was taking out her rosary beads, a flashy mother-of-pearl set, not at all in keeping with the rest of her. The face was as innocent as a novice, animated for the first time since she had crept into the chair beside Rita's bed and whispered, 'Brendan said I should come.'

She wasn't the first of them. That morning's papers had published the list of men executed, with Frank's name absent. Later editions announced the birth of his son, and by the afternoon Rita's early delivery was being heralded as his salvation.

'Shall we offer up our intentions to the Blessed Virgin?'

Why else would every one of Frank's colleagues feel they had to get in on the act, or send their wives to plague Rita in her bed? All day she was told of the crowd of newspaper men outside, sending up requests for interviews, demanding statements from the likes of Molly Nolan. Didn't Rita herself wish she could comment on the leader in the *Irish Times* which had claimed the sparing of Frank's life as evidence of a new humanity in British rule. Frank hated that publication, called it 'Unionist rubbish'. If he ever got home now, you could be sure he'd try banning it altogether.

And after the streams of such visitors, all chattering around her bed as if they were at a mothers' meeting, why did it have to be Molly Nolan alone with her now, forcing her to pray? Why, if she had suffer such fools, couldn't she be left with Mrs O'Kelly or Mrs Mulcahy? They at least would have brought amusement and made more of an effort to look nice.

She examined the woman on her knees by the bed, the well-soaped cheeks and a weave in the tweed suit so rough you could drill potatoes in it. Was this the Irish womanhood of which Mr de Valera dreamed? Could anyone except Molly Nolan sustain such an impossible air of virginity after giving birth to six, or was it seven children?

'Blessed art thou amongst women and blessed is the fruit of thy womb, Jesus.'

Perhaps the constant repetition had put out a fire. Well, after the experiences of the last twenty-four hours, even the words of that prayer would never sound the same again.

Molly nodded at Rita to join the refrain, 'Holy Mary, mother of God, pray for us sinners, now and at the hour of our death.'

How would she die? Last night she had almost wished for death to deliver her from an agony which threatened to last for ever. Yet in all the uncertainty of the past months, she had wanted to survive, and triumph. Because of the child she carried, or the jewels? Frank might have died this morning.

'God Almighty! It's like the ambush at Kilmacross out there!'

A whirlwind, the blessed virgin Mary.

'Rita, you're the star of the show! You should see the mob. You absolutely must let them take your photograph!'

Molly Nolan got herself up off her knees. She had the nous anyway to know there'd be no more praying. Rita laughed. The world was not a veil of tears. You heard of Indian widows throwing themselves on the funeral pyre. Not here. The real world was Mary, perched on the bed in her cream costume, sharp perfume blessing the room like incense, suffocating the carbolic purity of the other.

Molly blessed herself, warding off devils as she backed towards the door. 'God bless, so.'

'I don't believe it. The man got some sense at last!'

The other visitor stopped mumbling.

'Decided to blow the lot in his final hour, did he? And to think I always said the fella was as mean as the Vatican!'

There was no concealing them.

'Well, I hope he can pay for them now the life insurance won't be coming through!'

Mary was roaring with laughter, drowning Molly Nolan's outraged gasp as that woman too leant forward for a closer look. It was too bad. The silly goose wouldn't have noticed a ring through Rita's nose if Mary hadn't made a fuss.

'Honestly, Mary, they're just some little things Mama lent me. Now, will you kindly let Molly get away out of here and stop your joking.'

Mary looked up at the other visitor as if she had just noticed a spill on the rug.

'Goodbye, Molly, dear. Give Brendan my love.'

Clearly, from the look she shot Mary Kelly, love was not what Molly would be carrying home with her. 'I'll say a prayer, so.'

As the door slammed, Mary doubled up with laughter. 'You poor thing! Are they all like that?'

'Thank Heaven you came! One more decade of the rosary and I'd have expired!'

'Did you see the cut of her rosary beads? Maybe there's a Parisian can-can dancer inside only desperate to get out!'

'Only her ghost.'

'So, go on, explain those things on the ends of your ears – and the ring.'

A ferret after a rabbit. What was it they did? Hypnotized their victim with a stare?

'Oh do shut up! Don't you want to know about the baby? They're bringing him in in a minute.'

She tried to gaze dreamily out the window, a serene young mother. Why did she always go hot when she lied?

'But hold on. Wasn't there a tiara, that night you had Dermot Quinn and myself to dinner?'

'I told you, Mama lends things to me, for receiving people and so on.'

'Sorry now, I must ask you to leave!' Rita's favourite nurse, the little dark one from Cavan, the baby at her bosom riding high before her like the cavalry gaining the top of the ridge. Too late to stop Mary's eyes finding Rita. 'So you have a secret,' they said. 'Share it, or I'll tell the whole school.'

'Can't you see Mrs O'Fiaich is worn out with the visiting . . .?'

From Rita's arms, Frank's eyes looked up, blue and guarded, waiting to see how the game would be played. Liam. Frank had decreed the name in one terse letter. In memory of a cell-mate who had gone to his death.

Mary was not to be shifted so easily. 'What about the newspapers? I promised a nice man in the hall I would ask for a snap.'

In America Frank had been agreeable to photographers, but Ireland was different. Here ideals and principles were supposed to win votes, not babies or gallows or women in hospital beds. On the other hand, there was Molly Nolan and her rosary beads to consider. If that was the face of new Irish politics, then Rita was on the side of American-style razzmatazz. 'Oh, send them all up.'

'You're a glutton for punishment, so you are, Mrs O'Fiaich! You'd think you'd had enough shocks lately without having them creatures swarming all over you!'

'Where's the hairbrush, Rita? It would be nice to show off your ears.'

Mary wasn't letting up. To see her fussing with comb and compact you'd think she was on her way to the races in the Park. She had hardly noticed Liam. Molly hadn't asked to see the baby either, though she had repeated that phrase again and again, 'blessed is the fruit of thy womb'.

Oh yes, Rita was blessed all right, as every woman who had ever held the warm peach of their child in their arms, stroked the soft down on the new skin, smelt the honeyed wax of cradle cap. She longed to show him to Frank, to show where the pulse trembled in the soft place on the little head, show him what she could do. He would surely be proud of her then, the bearer of his child, a citizen for the new Ireland.

It was that mood of happiness, a confused madness perhaps, which had allowed Liam and herself on to the front pages of the newspapers, had let the Tsarina's earrings gleam resentfully at an unknowing world.

VI

Romance

* * *

She telephoned on Rita's first day home.

'I can't talk now, Mary. The new nurse is here and we're just arranging a feed.'

'Spare me the details. I'm telling you my news!'

'Oh?'

'Dermot Quinn! We're getting hitched!'

The goose. Of all the men in Ireland, couldn't she see he was a most unsuitable husband? What Papa would call a bounder.

'Remember that day I visited, when Frank didn't get executed? Well, I met Dermot outside the hospital, Rita, and honestly, he was almost in tears. He was so moved by what he called your "strength and fortitude" that I didn't know where to look. There I was thinking, can he be talking about Rita? Kept saying how calm and wonderful you were, how you had told him not to fuss.'

'I threw him out, I'm afraid.'

'He told the reporters all about you.'

The man was a bore. All he had wanted to talk about were Frank's plans for the party, how they would manage with so many members in jail, exiled or dead – clearly wondering what was in it for himself.

'He waited until I'd seen you, then had me sitting in the Gresham saying how every great man needed a strong woman. And next thing, girl dear, he's asking me to marry him!'

Nobody had approved of Frank, not even Mary. 'You don't think he's a bit fast?'

'By Frank's standards, maybe, but he's a businessman. What do politicians know about getting on or making money?'

'Sorry, I'm really pleased. My mind's all over the place at the moment.'

'Though on the other hand, maybe some of them know more than they pretend ...' Here it came at last. 'Yes, sweetie, I'm looking forward to a few explanations. Dermot's taking me out to buy the ring this afternoon, but I'm coming to see you in a couple of days – lunch on Friday?'

'I have so much to do, I don't think I could manage luncheon –'

'Don't be ridiculous! Haven't you a cook sitting there on her backside with no man in the house? I'll tell you my romantic story, and you can tell me yours!'

Trust Mary to demand more than was good for her. Perhaps she and Dermot weren't so badly matched after all.

Confidences

* * *

So there they sat, Mrs O'Reilly's burnt pork and lumpy trifle congealed over talk of Dermot Quinn and the messages he wanted passed on to Frank's prison cell. By the coffee even Mary had grown tired of the subject, but for Rita, the alternative seemed treacherous.

'Now I absolutely *must* go and feed Liam.'

'Sit down, girleen! Didn't you tell me yourself the nurse would call when you were needed?'

She wanted to cry. How could anyone be friends with this brash, bullying girl with the eyes of a hungry giraffe? Why was she let through the door with her over-bright cheeks and unnaturally flat chest, talking you into a corner about the dreadful person she planned to marry? Sillier still, casting Frank and Rita as the matchmakers? And how could a best friend show no interest in your baby?

'You'll have to get used to the demands of babies, they usually come after wedding rings!'

'Oh yes, about that, you know we went shopping for the ring?'

Mary's face was crafty again, with that cunning look Mama disliked. Sometimes you couldn't help being reminded of Mary's origins, the parents' huckster shop in Mullingar which had spread into a rash of stores across the country.

'Dermot thought I was mad. Between Johnson's and West's and everywhere in between we must have seen a thousand rings and they all looked the same. In the end, do you know what I said I wanted?'

'Something Irish?'

'No, you eejit, I'm sick of all that Celtic twilight! Anyway, since you left the League has gone all political. No, I want one like yours!' She wasn't talking about Frank's modest claddagh ring. 'I kept telling them I'd seen just the ring I wanted. You know, that one you were wearing in hospital? It was dreadful. No one would listen. In the end I had to walk out.'

'Oh dear.'

'You should have heard the sort of things they were saying, the manager, the chief salesman, a lot of know-nothing snobs! They got the head designer down to me in the end and I drew your ring for him, clear as anything. Well, first of all this fella laughs in my face, and then he takes Dermot aside and whispers about it costing hundreds. The cheek! Dermot got all embarrassed and sort of ganged up on me. Tried to talk me into all manner of inferior gewgaws. To hear those men, Rita, you'd think I was a child. I said, "Right, so, the friend with the ring I'm talking about is no millionaire, in fact, I said, she's the wife of a prominent Irish nationalist." That shut them up, I can tell you, the jumped-up shoneens! I said, "Fair enough, I'll bring you the ring and you can copy it for me!"'

'You can't!' Rita's voice was a frozen whisper. Her breasts felt like they might burst.

'Of course I can, sweetie! If you're worried about it, you can come in with me!'

There was a pair of Adam and Eve candlesticks on the mantelpiece, solid brass figurines Rita had bid for at an auction in the days when she had tried to make this house beautiful. She often sat at the table and wondered who was the sinner and who the sinned against? The gleaming little woman offering the apple, Adam reaching forward to grasp it. Surely the story should have been the other way round? Surely, for so many women, you accepted what your husband offered. What wife would question if it was his to give?

'Rita! Will you stop listening for that brat of yours and pay attention. This is important!'

Nina, Sergei, Piotr, Frank, Eamon de Valera, Mary, Molly Nolan ... Now it seemed even the entire staff of West's knew of the precious apple she had been given to hold; the circle was widening, ripples fanning outwards long after the stone had dropped in the water, after the jewels were locked away.

She looked down at her hands, maddeningly square and plump as ever, fingers bare now of everything except for her wedding band and the gold claddagh which Frank had suggested would be more modest and Irish than a diamond engagement ring. Was it her fault that since the baby she found it hard to think straight?

'It's in for repairs, I'm afraid. And then I must return it to Mama.'

'Which jewellers did you use? I could borrow it for a few hours.'

'No, they've sent it to London. It needs some specialist work.'

She was only half believed. Mary was taking her time, waiting to see if she had any more cards to play.

'I'm sorry, darling, but I really must go upstairs. I don't know what has happened to that nurse!'

Mary followed her into the hall. She could feel the big eyes on her back as she reached the half-landing where Liam's hungry sobs filtered down to her, filling her mind, nudging every other thought out of her brain.

'What about the earrings, then? I'll bring them to the designer, to give him some idea of how the stones are arranged!'

A silver bullet between the shoulder-blades. She felt so tired, on her own in the house yet never alone, besieged by Mrs O'Reilly and the girl and the bossy nursemaid whom Mama had so kindly engaged for a few weeks, the ever ravenous child snatched away from her as soon as he was fed, builders turning up with some unfinished piece or other.

Now Mary, standing in Rita's own hall as sharp and unstoppable as a bounty-hunter. 'Of course, if you've sent them away too, I could always ask your mother for drawings. She must have some for the insurance.' Rita could hear the smile in her friend's voice as she drove home the knife.

'You'd better come up with me while I feed Liam.'

'Oh dear, couldn't you do that later?'

The nursemaid appeared like a crazed sheep on the upstairs landing, Liam sobbing in her arms. 'There you are, Mrs O'Fiaich, and about time! Haven't I had this one waiting for his dinner this past hour and myself in need of a bite!' The woman's hair was on end. She looked half asleep.

'I understood the arrangement was that you would call me, Mrs Crotty.'

'Never mind arrangements! Is it a mother or what is it you are? Wouldn't you come to a child when he needs you without a body calling? You're late and you'll have us all skewed now with the feeding. It'll be me has to put up with it!'

Rita couldn't trust herself to speak. Tears came so easily lately, but it wasn't just that. What was it about her which allowed servants and tradespeople to address her in this way? Only once had she found the authority: when the jewels were about to be taken from her. She was weak, hatefully ineffective.

'Isn't that what you're paid to do?'

Thank you, Mary, friend who stood by her at school, speaking out against bullies like Laura Ryan and that snake in the grass, Bernadette Ross. This was why she loved her, for the fierceness which Rita could never quite summon when it was needed, for anger and passion enough for them both.

Nurse Crotty was panting with suppressed fury. 'Mrs O'Fiaich knows what I'm saying.'

'Indeed, you are finding the care of this new-born baby cuts into your sleeping time. In which case, perhaps you should suggest someone who is up to the job?'

The soft warmth of Liam as he was thrust into Rita's

arms made the tears flow unstoppably. Nobody noticed. Mrs Crotty was pushing past them down the stairs and Mary pushing Rita ahead towards the bedroom.

Liam was beautiful. She thought of him as a kind of love-child.

In the blue of his eyes she could see the Empress Sophia's sapphires which Nina had wound slowly round and round her throat; in his earlobes the fat diamonds and opals which swelled the Tsarina's court bracelet; in every soft bump and bend of him the myriad small pieces for ear and finger which had pricked her skin as Nina pushed her down on lumpy hotel beds. Kissing Liam, his breath was sweet, like the tiny raspberry lozenges which were the taste of Nina's mouth; and when she held him, his softness was a drug, his hands and knees tiny grids of location on the fading map of her memory.

Mary obviously felt none of that. She sat in silent horror as Rita unbuttoned her blouse and put Liam's mouth to her breast. She stayed on, silent for once, as the baby suckled, afternoon noises of the road outside flitting like gasps through the darkening glass, listening to the postman's bicycle and the creak and clang of each gate, a coalman's dray, the cries of children returning from school.

'What does it feel like?' Mary sounded like she was in church, her voice at last breaking the gloom across the fireplace.

'Nice. You'll see.'

The suggestion seemed to irritate. 'So, are you going to help me with the ring, Rita Fitzgerald, or what will I do?'

Nothing mattered any more. Sitting there with firelight colouring the tulip-patterned tiles, Liam so close and content and Mary sharing something too powerful to speak of, the enormity of the secret seemed to drain away with each push and tug of Liam's bony gums. This was peace, the closeness of friend and child in the sort of moment rarely recognized as special until it had been reduced to a mere snapshot in the mind.

If Mary asked her a straight question now, she would be unable to lie. It would be pointless to try. Her friend would sniff out an untruth, she always did. She would scrabble at that fox-hole until the animal leapt out whole and alive from its dark hiding place, and then she would bite it in the throat.

Liam started to cry. Rita could feel Mary's exasperation as she walked him about the room, jigging him on her shoulder until he burped, murmuring into the sweet milkiness of his neck.

Outside, Mr Noone was directing three of his men in their struggle down the path and through the gate. She watched them drop a heavy black object on the pavement before heaving it in a series of grunts and clangs on to the waiting cart. The old horse staggered as the belly strap almost lifted him up between the shafts. Then the men were up and gone, rumbling down the street into the lights of the main road.

As they turned the corner, she saw the thing again beneath a street light, a hard, shining metal shape; she hugged her baby with relief.

'What is it?'

Mary had joined them at the window, looking out at the lighted windows across the street, at Mrs Gorman at her front door, blessing herself with holy water as she slipped out for another church visit. All was silent again, the cul-de-sac guarded only by the tightly pruned cherry tree in Number One, proclaiming the endurance of an Irish marriage.

'For a moment I thought they were taking away some equipment we've just had installed. But it was only a bit of the old range!'

Her helplessness was replaced by a rush of strength. the

pleasure of being a woman alone, struggling to hold hearth and home together for a hero barred from such softness, languishing in jail without family or friends ... No, he had friends there, too many, she sometimes thought. They were the reason he had refused her any more visits, even after de Valera had sent instructions that she turn up with Liam at the prison gates to meet the press.

She sat down again and moved the baby to the other breast. It was getting dark. The coals sucked and hissed, their lights turning Mary's strong face to alabaster.

She was so lucky. This warm room, this baby, and downstairs, safe in the kitchen, the precious jewels. No point in getting all hot and bothered about the range. Mr Noone was hardly stealing it. Wasn't the man a faithful old donkey, which was why he had been chosen? Frank must have told him he could have it. Judging by what was printed in the newspapers Frank seemed to be able to communicate with all sorts of people these days, except herself.

'I like these old lights.' Mary was lighting the gas. 'Though Dermot wants electricity, says it's the future.'

The red patches on her cheeks were glowing brighter, reminding Rita of the big schoolgirl puffing across the wet hockey fields, whacking the ball into oblivion with 'This is for Sister Annunciation and this one's for Sister Christopher!', reducing both teams to fits of helpless laughter. They had shared so much together. Why could they not share this secret?

'About your ring ...'

'*Your* ring, girleen!'

Mary's look was the same as she gave the men at Gaelic League ceilidhs. Rita had always wanted to advise her not to appear quite so fierce, causing dance partners to avoid her eyes as they reached for Rita's hand.

'It's a long story, but I simply cannot lend it to you.'

'But you have to! Surely you don't mind if I have the same?'

Her wail almost woke Liam. He must need a change. Where was that nurse woman?

'It's not that.'

'What, then?'

'Hush, please! I don't want the servants to hear! But the jeweller was right, you couldn't possibly afford a ring like that – no more could I.' Such a struggle to think straight, to sound convincing. But she had to get it right, for Frank, for Ireland.

'Right, so, it's your mother's, but she'll let me –'

'No.'

Mary's eyes flashed wide like harbour lights, her whole body leaning forward, determined to catch every nuance.

'You have to promise not to tell anyone, but the rubies aren't mine, not really. I got them with a few other things, from a friend in New York. I'm just looking after them for a bit.'

'A *friend*?' The eyes bulged with excitement. 'You, Rita Fitzgerald, were given jewels from a "friend"! I presume you're talking about an M.A.N., what the songs call a sugar-daddy?'

Try to laugh, pretend modesty. She *had* to leave it at that, allow this misunderstanding. A white lie, nothing more. Yet Mary's delight seemed so unfair to Frank.

'To think of little Rita Fitzgerald, always the pure innocent at those awful Irish dances. Why, I used to have to beg some of those fellas to drag you on to the floor!'

'You did not!' It was Mary who hadn't got the dances. Hadn't she seen the men's faces when she stood up, watching her unfold like a music stand? 'But listen to me, you have to swear on your honour not to tell anyone.'

'Even old Frank?'

'Of course not Frank, not anyone!'

He must never guess that anyone had seen a Russian jewel, that Rita had worn a single one. What had she been doing, letting herself get photographed in them? But, she had been so worried lately, all alone, and they were such a comfort. Anyway, you'd need to be a magpie

with a magnifying glass to spot even a glimmer in the newspaper.

From the main road the angelus bell began to toll, early
as usual.

'Wait a minute, what about that tiara?'

'It's one of the things I'm looking after.'

'But surely Frank saw that?'

Oh, it was so complicated, this lying, one untruth
leading into another. 'You know Frank. He thought it
came from Mama – if he thought about it at all.' That at
least was true.

'Aren't you the quiet one!'

Mary's voice was almost reverent. Rita dropped her
eyes to the bundle in her arms. Where was that nurse?
Mama was right: civilization as they knew it was breaking
down; the country was being delivered into the arms of
robbers and gangsters.

'I hate to rush you, but shouldn't you be getting back
before curfew?'

'This has been so thrilling I hadn't noticed!'

'Remember, what I told you is strictly between us?'

'Of course, silly girl! But some day you have to give me
the whole story!'

Rita laughed. She could never tell about Nina. Mary
would not believe it possible.

A Release, 1921

* * *

Frank walked in one morning in early March. It was a
blessing she was lying down, stretched in the bed with her
first cup of the day, Liam at her breast and the *Irish Times*
spread over the eiderdown.

Typical of the authorities. Wonderful he was back, but
if only she had known, had been given some warning.
Mama always said men liked a little glamour: a pretty
nightdress, a touch of rouge, not this frowsy slug-a-bed.
No wonder he hardly glanced at her or attempted to kiss
her.

He sat down on the bed, taking no heed of the newspaper crackling beneath the heavy winter overcoat. He
was staring at Liam who had stopped sucking and was
gazing up at him with that blank, baby gaze.

'I thought he'd be ugly.'

Horrible, the way he avoided her eyes, as if he were not
glad to see her, could not feel her love.

'I brought him to see you, but you wouldn't receive
us . . .'

The skin on his face had become white and waxy, like
asparagus forced up in the dark.

'Some of the lads I was with, they said they're awful
looking for the first while.'

'Not our baby. Anyway, he's hardly new born!'

She took Frank's hand, but he appeared not to notice.
Indeed, the way he sat there so still, passive almost, he might
never have left his prison cell. Yet he must surely have
looked forward to this moment when he would be returned
to his family. Like her he would have longed and prayed
for it through all the long uncertain months.

'Oh, darling, am I dreaming this? Are you actually here?'

He was looking at her at last, but not as a wife, more as if she were stock in a field. Maybe all he needed was a hot bath.

'You're fit, so.'

'Here.' No point in pressing herself to him, offering tenderness. He wasn't good at it. He preferred to do things in his own time. Still, something had to melt the hard glaze of indifference. She put Liam into his arms. 'He may bring up a little, but that coat needs a clean.'

The lines in his face relaxed as he looked at the child. He was still human. Prison hadn't entirely blunted the gentle man she loved. 'Cooch, cooch!' It was the sound used to lead calves to drink from a bucket. He was nuzzling a rather dirty knuckle into Liam's mouth, but this was the wrong moment to bring up matters of hygiene.

They looked so alike, father and son. Though Frank had filled out a bit, there was the same smooth flatness of cheekbone, the long nose, the wide forehead jutting over the eyebrows, the long, thin mouth over a dimpled jaw which, in Frank's case, was badly in need of a shave. Liam seemed to recognize the resemblance too. He was staring up at his father as if into a mirror.

'Jesus, Mary and Joseph, Mr O'Fiaich, but isn't he the spit of you!'

Would the woman never learn to knock?

'I heard the footsteps going up the stairs and I said to the girl, "That's himself or that's his ghost, God save us all!"'

Mrs O'Reilly blessed herself. Frank joined the mumbled prayer. Had he grown even more devout in his confinement?

'Have yez escaped?'

'No. No.' He spoke so slowly and quietly that Rita held her breath. 'They let me out.'

To hear the sadness there anyone might think he had been condemned to death all over again.

'But Frank, that's wonderful! You're free!'

Mrs O'Reilly looked black as thunder. 'What are they playing at at all? Released you, did they, on account of the child? I suppose they think they're the clever ones, snatching a man from the grave so that all Ireland will think they're the decent Christian boyos? Well, they needn't think they've got me fooled. Oh, no!'

Frank was nodding his agreement at such ravings.

'And, missus, I hope you're not planning to take this codology lying down?'

'Oh, Frank, let's just be glad you're here.' He was such a bumpkin he'd have entertained the cook all morning, listening to her burbling on about maggots in the meat safe being portents of new life. 'Perhaps, Mrs O'Reilly, you might be good enough to remove my tray and bring Mr O'Fiaich a fresh pot?'

'I want nothing, only sleep.'

The silence after the banged door was almost frightening. Frank sat staring at the handle, his face a pinched mask, reminding Rita of her Great-aunt Lily's monkey which had entertained her as a child.

Without a word of apology Frank stood up suddenly and opened the door. He must be very tired. Papa had written a paper in a medical journal once about people in prison not having enough to do and being prone to mental problems. There was quite a fuss about it at the time, letters to the newspapers. But you couldn't blame Frank for being nervy. One of the boys executed was twenty years old, her own age, many a few years younger. She must not expect him to behave as other men. However, his reactions to the baby's sudden screams and the unpleasant smell which accompanied it was quite normal. Rita reached for the bell.

The new girl from Bunclody was as bad as the cook. You'd think Frank had risen from the dead for all the nodding and bowing and the way she jumped like she was burned when Frank's hand touched hers as he handed over the child. 'Isn't he the spit of you, Mr O'Fiaich?'

What was it about Frank which made servants gabble so? 'Sure he's another patriot born for Ireland!'

Frank was smiling. 'Right enough.'

'And if there's still a fight when he grows up, isn't he made for the job!'

'I think we're all tired of that sort of talk, Bernadette. Mr O'Fiaich is home now and we must do what we can to forget the recent unpleasantness and get back to normal.'

'But blood must be let, missus; blood will out.'

They were both staring at her. If Liam hadn't smelt worse every minute, she feared the girl might have challenged her.

'*Dia daoibh.*'

At last she was backing out the door.

'*Dia is muire duit.*'

When Frank turned back to her, it was as if she, Rita, were the servant who had failed in her duties. 'Are you blind, or what?' He didn't wait for an answer, just went on in his slow voice-for-eejits. 'There is a war on here. Four of the lads in with me died for the crime of wanting to run our own affairs.'

'I know, darling, goodness knows I do.'

'Then maybe you know there's some dispute about who should administer power when we get it? People are being killed, Rita. Yet you, the wife of an Irishman who would gladly give his life for his country, *you* persist in pretending that everything is great altogether, that we can go on with the world as it's always been. Well, by the time this struggle is over nothing will be the same, no matter what lying rags like this one choose to tell you!'

'Really, Frank, there's no need to shout!'

He sat down on the bed again, then suddenly leapt up as if stung, ripping the *Irish Times* out from under him and flinging it across the room. So he had noticed it.

She hadn't seen him this angry since Washington, DC, when a group of Congressmen had tried to prevent Dev from pursuing his bonds scheme.

No use arguing. In two years of marriage he still didn't appreciate that she turned to the newspapers for the social and cultural events he hated, the excitements which Mary and Dermot might attend every day of the week. Who on earth could be bothered with the litany of lock-outs and ambushes and some skirmish on a God-forsaken bog published in the other journals? Of course she agreed with Frank about Ireland and so on, but honestly, she felt all the difficulty of achieving it had been going on for ever.

'Please, dearest, don't give out to me. Baby makes me forgetful, and I've been so worried!'

Her tears softened him. He sighed as he stretched out on the bed beside her and silently dried her face. She wished she could ask him to remove his boots.

He had stopped talking at last. If only she could argue like Anne Marie; but there was no way she could go to the National University like her, not as a married woman with a child. Still, she longed to talk to Frank about this thing which Papa said wasn't a war, just 'damned unsporting'. Surely her husband didn't want to be involved in grubby, back-street nastiness, ambushes on empty hillsides, attacks on village roads, shots fired at the King's soldiers from street corners? She put her arms around the dark bulk of his coat. Maybe it was its sour smell which made him somehow different, a bitterness which seemed to poison the air, a vapour rising from within his very skin.

She couldn't blame everything on the prison. Frank was changing, hardened by every setback, toughened by each atrocity, encouraged and even elated by the mounting death-toll of soldier, policeman, civilian and child which the *Freeman's Journal* printed daily within a black frame.

The hands sliding into the front of her nightdress were softer than they used to be. 'Be careful, I've milk.' She felt so unready. He wasn't listening. He was pushing against her, the thick overcoat bunching into her side almost as sharply as the knees which bruised her legs. His face was buried in her, rubbing into her chest as if he wished to drink her, absorb her into himself.

She tried to unbutton his coat, but he only pushed closer to her, moving against her, pulling on her left nipple, until a long, shuddering gasp and then he was still.

'Frank?'

Men were so peculiar. His whole body trembled with sobs which welled up louder and deeper with each breath. She could only pray Mrs O'Reilly wouldn't choose this moment to ignore instructions and walk in with tea.

'Frank, what is it? There's no need to upset yourself, you're home safe, it's all over . . .'

Her words appeared to make him worse. She held him then, the mother she had become, rocking him until he fell asleep. As she pulled herself away, she noticed some milk had spilled on to the lace of her nightie. Watching him lying there, he was no longer part of their floral-sprigged bedroom. His world was somewhere else, a secret place out beyond the humped ridge of mountains which began only a mile or so up the road.

The jewels? For a second she resented this unclean bundle on her bed. But that was silly. She loved her husband more than anything in the world, except Liam. His return would save her from herself, block an obsession which lately, in his absence, she had feared was becoming too powerful. It coloured her every thought with plots and plans for releasing her Russian guests from their own prison and holding them in her arms. Now she could concentrate on Frank's needs, and her country's. This was what was important, her struggle too. She would do everything in her power to see Ireland grow up confident and strong: beautiful, complete, purified by fire.

The only drawback was, she couldn't think what was best to do. She wished she could wake Frank and ask for guidance, but she could not be sure of his sympathy. The way he slept, clenched and folded in upon himself, holding sleep like a tramp with a full bottle of whiskey, did not offer a way in.

Domestic Life

* * *

Frank had slept only a few hours before he was off again, telling her not to wait up. It had started again, this married life without a husband; only now, as she sat alone that evening with Liam asleep upstairs, she couldn't help thinking about the black darkness out there, of men scurrying down back lanes, hugging walls, hiding and dodging. Were they poor Irishmen, or Tans out for revenge? She tried not to put faces on the people who stood against the Englishmen, young fellows like the six executed in the first week of March whom a local priest had claimed had gone to their deaths 'like schoolboys going on holiday'.

Was it the next night or the one after that when the Mayor of Cork's home was raided and his wife shot trying to shield her husband from the bullets? She wasn't the only brave woman: the wife of a city councillor and another, married to a member of the Gaelic League, had struggled with masked men in their sitting-rooms before witnessing their husbands being shot dead before their eyes.

Such events were too unpleasant to contemplate. Best not to think about the mess afterwards: blood stains on rugs would be difficult to remove. Bad enough to contemplate the damage done in her own home, the lamps, ornaments and crockery smashed by the soldiers that day they had come looking for Frank, the rips in curtains and upholstery she was still attempting to repair. Knowing Frank's dislike of expense, unsightly gaps would remain about the house for the rest of their days.

Only the thought that if they returned, His Majesty's forces might destroy Frank's mother's pink glass bowl and maybe even put a rip in *The Assumption* for good measure, gave some guilty comfort.

Frank was home for luncheon the day Mrs O'Reilly marched into the dining-room.

'Are youse going to the funerals?'

'Oh dear, who's dead now?'

'Listen to her ladyship! Who indeed!'

Frank looked up from his newspaper, eyebrows raised. He had got into bad habits in prison, reading at meals no matter what she said.

'In Cork, missus, those poor creatures!'

'Oh yes, that is sad, but we don't know their families, do we, Frank?'

'Don't know a man who has died for Ireland! Doesn't everyone know them? They're public funerals, missus. Sure anyone with their loyalties halfway straight will be there!'

That was another annoying thing. Meals should be enjoyed in peace, times for intelligent conversation. Frank didn't seem to mind that they appeared to live in a railway station. They had already entertained Mr Noone throughout the soup course, mumbling on about drainage runs for the new kitchen sink he had insisted on fitting despite the fact that there was a perfectly good one in the scullery. Now she would have to take Mrs O'Reilly aside and ask her not to bring up politics when Frank and she were at table.

'God willing, I'll get away first thing tomorrow. There's a party of us travelling.'

'Perhaps I'll come with you.'

'You will not!' His ferocity made her feel quite faint.

'But I'd like to. The girl could look after Liam, if I came straight back.'

Impossible to argue with the man. She so wanted to go. For a moment it had offered an opportunity to get back into the fray, to take some small part in the endless ritual of this war, to become Frank's full partner again. Also, those deaths seemed different to all that had gone before, people home with their families, just as she might sit sometimes with Frank and Liam. Violence had come to them, crashed through their front doors to strike at women like herself, wives and mothers kept at the edge of the

165

political fray, grateful only for spending an evening across a hearth from the men they loved.

Frank never offered information about his movements. She had learned long ago not to ask if she could expect him. She no longer inquired about grass marks on the knees of his trousers or the scattering of seeds and dry turf in the turn-ups.

That was why, when he returned from Cork, she was surprised when he asked, 'Are you all set for tomorrow?'

She was in the kitchen at the time, endeavouring to enlighten Mrs O'Reilly in the making of *œufs gelés* as a variation on her boiled offal consommé.

'Why, yes, I'm looking forward to it.' Mary had only telephoned that morning to tell her their good luck. 'But I didn't realize you would be interested! Mary says the tickets are like gold-dust!'

'Tickets? Don't tell me they're turning the thing into a side show? Though that pal of yours would make a great madam, knitting beside the guillotine!'

It was the first time in ages she had seen Frank laugh.

'Let me telephone the Gaiety and see what they can do.'

'The what?'

His shout made Mrs O'Reilly drop her spoon.

'You mean to say you were planning to go off to a show, in a theatre, on the night before some of our finest young men are put to death for Ireland?'

She knew what he meant now. Weren't the papers full of it? But weren't the papers always full of some execution or other?

Mrs O'Reilly had stopped stirring the gelatine. It would go lumpy, but what did it matter? There seemed to be more to this cooking business than Mrs Beeton would have you believe. Anyway, Frank hardly cared what he put in his mouth, and she only had to look at food to put on another pound.

'The march, missus! You'll be going, surely, for the all-night vigil and all? Aren't all the women in the country only dying for it? I'd go myself but for me veins.'

166

Frank was silent, examining Rita as if she were a tiny flaw in a piece of Waterford glass.

'I'm sorry, Frank, I honestly never thought.'

The cook snorted. 'The wife of Frank O'Fiaich, never thought about lining up behind our heroes!'

'I sometimes wonder what's happening to you, Rita.'

She saw the cook's smirk. Could the jewels hear her humiliation inside their dark cell and think the worse of her? An old childhood stammer stumbled into her mouth. 'N-naturally, I would be delighted to participate. You know how I have always asked to help in any way –'

'As Mrs O'Reilly says, my wife has an important role to play.'

'With the baby, I suppose, I haven't kept up.' She could feel a headache coming on.

His voice was cold and grating. 'You've thought enough to arrange jaunts and high jinks with that friend of yours and her shyster husband. Have you no idea at all, woman dear, what's going on, or what it would look like for a wife of mine to be at the theatre on the night six fine young men prepare for their deaths?'

She wished she could say that she hardly thought his colleagues would be at the theatre to see her. Apart from the Bartons and perhaps that young Mr O'Malley, none of them showed any interest in such events. She wouldn't dare suggest, playfully of course, that a high mass was the only art form most people in his party would appreciate.

'I suppose Mary could find someone to take my ticket. It's *La Pompée*, you see, with the full chorus.'

Frank stood like a lost dog for a few moments. Only the noise of Mrs O'Reilly scraping the contents of her saucepan into the sink roused him. 'You'll be there tomorrow, so, with the other ladies. I'm out tonight,' and he was gone. It would never occur to him to apologize for using the house like a hotel, and hardly using his wife at all.

She was woken later by the bombing of a military lorry in Dawson Street. Even three miles away, in the silence of the curfew the blast was unmistakable.

Marching for the Republic

* * *

She couldn't help thinking they made an uninspiring sight. Not that the women should have dressed up to the nines or anything. She was simply of the opinion, for the sake of all those rude men they passed, that a little colour or the odd bit of jewellery would not come amiss. At least it would relieve the black. She was feeling extra sensitive about that. How like Frank, with his mind on higher things, not to have told her that every woman there would be in mourning, head to toe.

When Molly Nolan saw Rita's best blue tweed she sniffed her pug's nose. 'We have you here anyway,' was all she said, as if she were a school prefect who had caught Rita on the street without a hat.

If only Mary had come, she would have enjoyed it. Though Rita could tell from the long pause down the telephone line there was no chance of that.

'It's a teeny bit political for me, sweetie . . .' She let her voice trail away. There was a new note of certainty in it, a distance from the Mullingar schoolgirl with the rosy cheeks. 'Now I'm married to Dermot it doesn't do to come across too strong – mixing business with pleasure, so to speak.' She laughed. 'Of course, it's different for you, we all know Frank is up to his neck in that stuff! But really, Rita, let's be honest, don't you think it's getting a mite dreary, now we've grown up, a touch of the old *déjà vu?*'

It had taken all Rita's self-control not to hang up the phone there and then. After all, it was Mary who had started Rita on this road. If it had not been for Mary getting all worked up about Home Rule and Cathleen ni Houlihan . . .

Marching along Sackville Street, looking at her companions' plain clothes and scrubbed faces, 'dreary' did seem remarkably apt. Rita had to remind herself that no lady can look her best hunched up against the elements while being taunted like a common streetwalker. Besides, what did fun or glamour or any of the other things people like Mary thought so important have to do with reshaping a nation?

All the same, she was glad she had extracted the Paisley-shaped sapphire earrings from the safe. They picked up the bright fleck in her suit and lent some dignity to the occasion.

They were passing the Gresham Hotel where a group of rather angry-looking people stood gaping at the women across the street. Traffic was piling up behind them. Motor cars hooted and stalled. There was a common – if outdated – misunderstanding amongst the populace that the women were something to do with the Suffragettes.

'To hell or Lesbos!'

'Find yerselves a man for Jaysus' sake!'

'Leave the votes to the men!'

'A disgrace is what youse are!'

The cabmen were finding their voices, gunning engines or whipping horses to a frenzy as the constabulary waved them past.

'Go on home to your children!'

She was glad she had not brought Liam. Mrs O'Reilly had suggested it – even wanted to send the girl along to push the pram – but the weather was quite unsuitable. A chill wind whipped rain upriver from the docks. Also, it was nice to get out alone. If her right shoe had not been beginning to pinch, a day out of the house might have been quite pleasant.

The girl beside her was a stenographer from Athlone. 'Have you come far?'

'Only Terenure.'

'Are you married?'

'Yes.'

'Well done, well done!' From the way the girl's frizzy little head turned to stare at any passing male there was clearly more than the future of Ireland on her mind.

The woman on her other side was a middle-aged creature from Dartry, a superior sort, though married to a grocer. 'I told my husband he'd just have to manage! Haven't the men made this madness and now they're leaving us to get sense!'

'You mean you're not a member of Cumann na mBan?'

'Indeed I am not! Haven't I enough to do keeping that man and his children going without leaving them every night to be praying and marching and learning that useless language!'

'But Irish is beautiful, we've got to get it back.'

'And give up the English? Sure we might as well learn that dead old Latin – it might do us more good knowing what the priests are talking about!'

Frank dismissed Dublin opinion as irrelevant. He said countrified nationalism was purer, bred in the bone. Maybe he was right. Rural life made people more accepting anyway. Whatever they really thought, they would no more argue basic political tenets like the revival of the language than they would disagree with the Pope.

By Parnell Square her brown crocodiles were not only tight, they were rubbing blisters on both heels. She tried not to think about the effects of horse manure and rainwater on their delicate constitution. The Bullocks standing outside the Black Church were a very welcome sight. A perfect excuse to rest.

'Mr and Mrs Bullock! How marvellous! Fancy!'

For a moment Rita feared that the dirt on her shoes was emitting an unpleasant smell. Dottie Bullock was a bridge partner of Mama's, yet the way the two of them stared anyone might think Rita was the devil himself. Mr Bullock nodded, took his wife's arm and hurried her away.

'Rita! There you are at last!' Elizabeth Hoyle, bearing down on her like a mother hen, the chest swelling triumphantly under black serge. 'I need you up at the front before we get to the jail. It's a pity about that suit, but no harm, you'll stand out in the photographs.'

She was pulling Rita along, past the lines of banners, up to the front to march with Countess Markievicz and her band. It was much nicer at the head of the march, walking beneath the street-wide banner which read BRITISH MURDERERS OUT, forgetting her feet as familiar streets transformed before them, the inhabitants scattering to corners and shop doors, hanging from windows for a better view. This must be what it was like to be royalty, driving in state through a city. The sapphires would feel at home anyway.

Everyone congratulated her on the baby. 'An excellent piece of publicity – beautifully timed!'

Countess Markievicz was smiling, bending down to Rita. A wide-brimmed hat accentuated her cheekbones. The voice was county. 'Where is the blighter? Didn't you bring him?'

'Don't worry – I'll get her one.'

Next thing Rita found a smelly bundle in her arms which shrieked pitifully as they approached Mountjoy.

'He needs a change.' Nobody took any notice except a woman who may have been its mother. 'Isn't it great to get your hands free for a minute?' She seemed in no hurry to take back her child.

The scene outside the gates was like Grafton Street on a Saturday morning. Rita was soon being greeted by all the wives of Frank's colleagues and a number of women who didn't have the good manners to introduce themselves. She was busy trying to say that this was not Liam when the journalists appeared.

'What would you say was your most exciting moment, Mrs O'Fiaich, having the baby or getting your husband reprieved?'

'Hold him up there now and we'll get a few pictures!'

'Give us a statement on these executions, Mrs O'Fiaich, as a wife and mother!'

Where to begin? Nobody had asked her what she thought for ages, not since America.

'Well, first of all I should say that this isn't my own baby. I don't know what kind of mother would bring a child out on a day like this —'

'Hush up and read this — loudly!' It was Molly Nolan, snuffling into the circle with her ragged sheaf of paper.

'Thank you, Molly, but I think I can manage —'

Molly Nolan's voice roared over her own. 'As you have been told, gentlemen, the women of Cumann na mBan are making no individual statements. Our commitment is a joint one: to rid this country of the stranglehold of British imperialism which tears our fine men from us just as they have stripped the great oaks from our forests to service their wars. The women of Ireland demand justice and liberty now — the right to run our own affairs, with the establishment of the one, true Irish nation. Ireland free!' She looked more like a British bulldog as she thrust her wet nose close to Rita and growled, 'Go on, read it!'

'But I'm not really a member —'

'Are you really an Irishwoman? Go on, and shout!'

It was photographs of that speech which were in the books. Nobody bothered any more to record exactly what she had said that day about spilt blood and the birth of a nation.

She saw the pictures reproduced sometimes: she didn't look too bad, though her face appeared a little flat. You could just about make out the earrings, which helped emphasize the strong line of her jaw and curve of her ears. In some of the photographs her large, milk-filled breasts were covered by the baby, taken before he had begun nuzzling so fiercely for a feed. Liam still liked to claim that was himself. She had given up trying to tell him it was not.

A Letter from Mama, 25 March 1921

* * *

Clonkee

North Circular Road

Dublin

Dearest Rita

Couldn't help overhearing what your papa said to you on the telephone about that march. It was Lord K.'s secretary, cancelling our weekend like that. The way the *Irish Times* keeps linking your name with ours anyone might think Papa and I had arranged your alliance! He complained to Major McCormack a number of times, but I get the feeling the Protestants have closed ranks. Did you see the Fowlers have sold their lovely place in Mount Merrion? Gone to Sussex, I think. Not a word of farewell and no change of address card. I hear it's going to be a seminary. That's something that's doing well anyway – the religious! Have you noticed how many orders are opening schools here? No doubt your husband would tell me it's good for education. Employment, more like, for unmarriageable daughters and sons who don't get the farm!

When do you think Frank and his friends will stop this nonsense? Too many more evenings sitting at home with your father may drive *me* into a convent. The curfew is killing the theatres, you know. Has Frank thought of that? I'll never understand what you see in those people. Few enough of them could appreciate more than the price of fat cattle.

Such a relief to escape to Liverpool, though I wish I had not witnessed the race. You know how I love horses. And mine was one of the fallers! I sat in the tea bar for the rest of the afternoon talking to a very nice woman from Tipperary. She was quite charming until the men turned up and your papa made some remark about the terrorists at home. The lady and her husband turned out to be dyed in the wool nationalists – I felt quite frozen out! Isn't it interesting how one can't read people any more? Where is it all going to end – bombings, shootings, executions? I saw that Mary Pickford has set sail for a visit to Europe. Don't suppose she'll be interested in seeing Dublin in its current mood. One feels so provincial.

Found the loveliest oyster satin in town last week, a fitting in an hour. Noreen and the Martins are coming this afternoon to make up a hand.

Do get that man of yours to see sense soon.

Your Mama

VII

A Meeting with the Chief

* * *

She recognized the voice, high and off-key.

'Don't say anything, Mrs O'Fiaich. Is he with you?'

Honestly, you couldn't be doing with it, this cloak and dagger stuff. They were like children, these men.

'Hello, Mr de Valera, how are you? If you mean Frank, he's away again, but you probably know where better than I!'

There was a sharp intake of breath and then the telephone went down. All that time in America had not improved the man's manners.

It was only later, remembering the clarity of the line, she wondered was Eamon de Valera back in the country. If so, Frank would be annoyed she had not got his telephone number. Well, it was his own fault. Wasn't it only a day or so after the dreadful march and executions that he had taken himself off again to God knew what carry-on. It was true what those war songs said about women left behind to worry and suffer. The blisters on her feet were still very painful.

Whenever the doorbell went, her heart was in her mouth, thinking was it bad news or a gunman. Mrs O'Reilly might complain all she liked about the climb up a few steps from the kitchen, but Rita had no intention of answering such a summons, not (as she told Mrs Winn who called about the church flower rota and was left ringing the bell for a good ten minutes) for all the tea in China. The newspapers were full of stories of decent people being shot on the threshold. Mama would never be seen dead on her own doorstep.

If only Frank would realize how awkward his disappearances were.

'On your own again, Mrs O'Fiaich?' Father Dineen's eyes were cool as Connemara marble. 'Where is the great man this time?'

She disliked the way he made her blush. 'Oh, you know how it is, Father, some meeting in town. He'll have to fit in a mass there, I'm afraid.'

Priests or nuns, how was it they could turn you into a liar and then smile like Beelzebub to see you do it? Straight after mass too, with bits of the communion wafer still stuck to the roof of her mouth.

He hadn't finished playing with her. 'Wasn't that a dreadful business in Rialto the other night? Do you know about it? A dispatch rider shot on the bridge and another soldier wounded. Where is it going to end at all?'

'I keep well out of such things, Father Dineen. So much unpleasantness! We can only keep our heads down and hope the madness will pass.'

The look he gave her, a fly which had escaped before he could tear off its wings! Mama would have been outraged at such blatant prying. She never could stand the familiarity of the religious – particularly the country ones – but Frank encouraged it; he didn't appear to mind their intrusion into his private life, what Papa called 'overstepping the mark'. Mama said her spiritual life was one thing, but if nobody stood up to the clergy they'd turn into a secret police force with the right to spy on everyone, and know far more than was good for them.

She should have guessed Mr de Valera would not waste another telephone call. His note, when it came through the letter-box long after the last post, was almost as brief as their conversation.

Your presence is expected at Buswell's Hotel, 2.00 p.m., Wednesday. Tell nobody. Destroy this.

He hadn't signed it, but who else would think a mother of a small child with a house to run would have nothing better to do than take herself off into the centre of the city? And for what? The fact that another ungrateful girl

178

had run off on the mail boat two nights ago didn't help the situation. Mrs O'Reilly had been most uncooperative about Liam. She had done nothing but groan and pray to herself since early morning when the cards dealt the Ace of Spades. Having the tram brought to a halt on the Rathgar Road was another blow. Wild-looking men they were, in scrappy uniforms: the one who stopped by her seat had traces of blood on his jawline.

'Where you going, lady?'

They were asking everyone the same, moving between the seats with guns waving, their stiff clothing and things strapped around them bumping and rustling like animals barging through woods.

'To Grafton Street.'

'What for?' His accent was thick cockney – 'Wah faw?' – difficult for some of the passengers to understand.

'Shopping, since you ask.'

He had moved on. What would he do to her if he knew the truth, if she blurted out the real reason for her journey? She felt pleased at how she had spoken up for herself, not like the ragged boy in front.

'T-t-to, Sssssss . . .'

'I beg your pardon, but I believe the young man is trying to say he is going to Sackville Street.'

It seemed polite to be helpful, and at fifteen minutes to two, time was marching on.

'Shut up, missus!' The voice was excited, the razor nicks in the face hinting at something darker, more threatening than what he really was, a scruffy youth in mismatching uniform. Then Liam began to wail. His screams only ignited the soldier, who suddenly jerked the boy from his seat and out on to the pavement, where he stood pale and not retching until one of them kneed him and another hit him with the butt of a gun.

Behind them the brasses on the front door of old Mrs Desmond's cottage-style house gleamed in the sunlight. How well Rita remembered visits there, climbing the high steps with Mama to pull the bell, a collection of rare birds' eggs, being sent out to play beneath the ceanothus with a wheezy Pekinese called Tang. She wondered who lived there now. Mrs Desmond had had the animal stuffed after he died, preserving the dog to greet her visitors from a glass case in the hall.

Rita heard the conductor whisper to someone that they would probably shoot him later. The tram seemed very quiet after that, its shrieks and groans suggesting human noises, a keening against the sobbing hysteria of a woman across the aisle and a small group saying the rosary together near the door. They got some queer looks from people boarding along the way, but nobody tried to explain. Hard to believe that anything had happened except that Liam continued to cry as if the sky had fallen in and for once no kindly soul offered to take him from her.

Rathmines looked just the same. Only a few hundred yards down the road and there was an RIC officer outside the station taking a jug of milk from Mr Kennedy while his fat piebald nibbled the hedge. Should she dismount and report the incident? One could never be sure whose side the law might be on. For an awful moment she wondered about Frank, about games of hide and seek played on dark boreens. Then Liam let out another roar and it was all she could do to sit tight until they got to Grafton Street.

'You're late.'

As she nearly said to the little pipsqueak on the hotel steps, the first priority for his political life was a few lessons in charm school. 'I am so sorry. There was an incident on the tram. The Black and Tans —'

'And he isn't expecting the babby.'

'Then he should have done me the courtesy of a consultation about the hour of our meeting!'

By the time the rude young man had driven them to Phibsboro by a most circuitous route Liam was screaming again and the strain of the day was beginning to tell on Rita's nerves. The gloomy hallway into which they were led smelt like a church, wax and wet mackintoshes. The parlour confirmed the residence of country people, the Holy Child over the fireplace, the dark, unused furniture and the squeaky grandfather clock marking time until deliverance.

'I'm afraid I'm going to have to feed him. You must allow me ten minutes or so.'

That took the wind out of his sails. 'The Chief isn't used to being kept waiting.'

'Nor is this fellow.'

He was just the same, unchanged since that long year ago in New York, his dark suit maybe a touch shinier and the olive skin stretched tighter over the face. Even in these circumstances the pressed uprightness of him seemed careless of the fact that he was a fugitive who shouldn't be in the country at all.

'So, Mrs O'Fiaich, how have you enjoyed being back amongst your own?'

When he sat down and crossed his legs, she was struck anew by their thinness. She would have liked to lean across the hearth and wrap them round and round until his polished black shoes became the dark point of a corkscrew.

'You're looking well, Mr de Valera.'

'Kept busy, I hear?'

'I've had a baby if that's what you mean, but he should give us a bit of peace now.'

'So you did, so you did.'

She had forgotten how bad he was at small talk. He had hardly glanced at the child tucked between cushions at the back of the couch. There was something on his mind and he was wondering how to put it.

'He was born when Frank was in jail. It feels like ages ago now!'

He fired her a beady look then, a crow which has suddenly spotted a soft-eyed lamb.

'I've been meditating how you view that time, Mrs O'Fiaich. Indeed, for all our travels together, it occurred to me that we never really got to know one another. So tell me, how do you see the current struggle; where exactly would you say your own heart lies?' Now they were coming to it. The reason for all this inconvenience. 'I ask because it has been brought to my attention that you have become a somewhat public figure of late, even quite famous.' He did not return her bright smile. 'For example, there was a photograph I saw of you, taken in your hospital bed?'

'Wasn't that amusing? The way people thought that having the baby had saved Frank's life!'

Watching him glare and retwist his legs in that irritated way, you'd think he was not pleased by Frank's pardon.

'Though it became rather a bore in the end, all those press people knocking on the door for pictures. And I only got to see Frank once. You should talk to him about that – I'm sure you'll agree that we women have an important contribution to make? But I was left rather on my own then, and as I said to the newspaper people, "I only wish you'd come back in a few months!" Having a baby, I'm afraid, for all you men or the Church may tell us, is not a woman's finest hour. Not in a photographic sense anyway!' Her laughter sounded too loud as it sank into the horsehair furniture. She was talking too much. Only the statue of the Holy Child continued to smile, offering her his heart.

Mr de Valera leant forward, his voice a hissing softness. 'And tell me, was it last week I saw you were on the ladies' march for those poor lads?'

His face in the gloom reminded her of a picture in an encyclopedia at home, a bishop in the Spanish Inquisition, nostrils flaring, the stiff figure arching almost voluptuously over a body stretched on a rack.

'And those other times you got yourself in the newspapers, out on some skite to the theatre and the like, at night.'

'Don't tell me you read the social and personal pages, Mr de Valera!' His look could stop a rabbit at fifty yards. 'But yes, I try to keep going, you know, fly the flag. It's important to put on a brave face for Frank's sake, and for what we all believe in.'

He pressed his fingers into a church spire and stared at the nicotined ceiling. 'I think you know, Mrs O'Fiaich, that Francis and I share the same objectives. Our vision for Ireland, for an Irish way of life, a truly Irish people and nation, is as one. But I have been away for a while, so perhaps you should remind me of *your* hopes for the country?'

'Well, obviously Frank and I are agreed too . . .' Why did this cold foreigner always have this effect on her, a nervous feeling that she did not quite measure up, a schoolgirl again, standing before the Reverend Mother to discuss her lack of team spirit on the hockey field? 'I, I mean we, I, want a free Ireland, a nation with its own government, laws and, oh yes, culture and so on . . .'

He leant forward again, not an easy task, she would have thought, for someone with legs crossed up to the crotch. 'Indeed, the Irish culture, and how would you define that?'

Be careful now. 'Well, I know you and Frank favour bringing back our own national language as a first language, and all the cultural things, but it's more than that, isn't it: a whole way of life, I suppose . . .'

Could the Chief detect her nagging doubts about what their dream might become, reduced, as she had suspected lately, to a hatred of great music, theatre, art, even food, which Frank dismissed as 'English' and therefore decadent? Why, only a matter of months ago Mr de Valera himself had been arguing to make Ireland a member of the League of Nations, part of the international community. Now it was as if the binoculars had been reversed, their field of vision narrowed to the boundaries of this tiny island. When had that changed? Or was it simply herself who was out of step?

'And tell me, Mrs O'Fiaich, do you regret any changes in Dublin life?'

That was another, more worrying element she dared

not question: his dream of an Irish Catholic culture, pure and simple, a rural family of innocents informed only by their Church. 'If you mean Castle society, I should think those days are long gone.'

'So they are, *deo gratias*. But fancy clothes and the like; would you agree with me that vanity is a terrible weakness in all of us, especially in the women? Eye-catching jewels, for example, mightn't they cause a certain unease, awaken appetites which are foreign to the Irish way of life?'

Dear God, had he recognized the jewels? 'Foreign, Mr de Valera? Surely if you look at the number of torcs and pins in the Museum, Irish women have been wearing jewellery for a lot longer than English times. We women must manage how we can to look presentable, not an easy task on my husband's remuneration!'

His eyes were chips of coal.

'But needs must! I try to dress up what I've got with the bits and pieces my mother lends me.'

The legs were slowly unwinding.

'Ah, now, yes. Those sparkling gewgaws I noticed in photographs, on your ears? And I've had reports of odd items worn about your person on other pleasure-loving occasions. Do you understand me? The sort of thing not befitting the wife of a man who is even now offering his life to rid his country of corruption and waste?' His voice was a wasp, whining, circling, preparing to sting. She must sit very still. 'I know you are a Dubliner, Mrs O'Fiaich, and, having grown up here, you may be blinded to the rottenness which has set the people of this city apart from the rest of the island for three centuries. As you say, the pillars which supported Dublin Castle are crumbling away. Therefore, if you have not understood the personal mission which each one of us must bear, then I must give you a very severe warning: as Frank O'Fiaich's wife, you cannot continue in your Castle ways. Irish men are offering up their lives to reshape this island. Any break in that endeavour, any weak link in our outward show or fall into the sin of vanity cannot and will not be tolerated!'

The nerve of it! The indignity! Bad enough to be addressed like a public meeting, but this threat, this ridiculous message, was no different in substance to the homilies which the nuns at school used to preach about modesty and purity!

'I must confess, Mr de Valera, I cannot quite understand what you imply. I wish you would speak plain English.'

'I would prefer our own language, Mrs O'Fiaich, but I believe you might have some difficulty in understanding me there too?' The way his mouth stretched slightly, almost smiled, he seemed to think he had scored a point.

'Actually, Mr de Valera, I have attempted to learn Irish, but find limited opportunity to practise it. As you must recognize by now, most of the people one meets, even outside the Pale, speak only English.'

Dev looked pleased with the debate. He was standing up. 'Sharp as ever, Rita O'Fiaich. But let me finish by reminding you that this is a nation in its infancy. It is a child which, with the right example, the right practices, can be led towards goodness. However, as you know, the leadership of our nation is in the balance, and any stumble backwards into old ways, any sniff of tomfoolery, could have our enemies making hay with us, swinging the thing in the wrong direction altogether.'

It was all right. He was finishing and he hadn't recognized the jewels. He had even used her Christian name. Funny the way he described Ireland as a child; Nina had used the same term about her country.

'You need have no worries on that score, Mr de Valera.'

'We understand one another, so. Give my regards to Francis.' His handshake was surprisingly warm. Did he like her? Strange how she always wanted him to.

The relief had carried her out into the dark hall and on to the front step before she remembered Liam still sound asleep inside. When she returned for him, Mr de Valera had disappeared.

The shock didn't hit until she had her key in her own front door.

'Jesus, Mary and Joseph, missus, will you look at the state of you! What happened at all?'

Only then did her legs give way beneath her and Mrs O'Reilly was pushing her up to bed.

'You just lie still and I'll bring you up a cup of tea. The child will be grand with me!'

'Oh, Mrs O'Reilly, it was awful!'

'Whisht now or your milk will sour!'

Her shoes were removed and the eiderdown pulled up to Rita's chin.

'Was it them Tans again?'

'Why, yes, on the tram!' An excuse for the fear and rage which churned in her stomach. 'They pulled off a young boy with a stammer. I think they were going to shoot him.'

God forgive her, she had forgotten all about him until that moment. It carried her through the evening, made a heroine of her, gave her the peace of the dark bedroom with the curtains drawn and a nice fire in the grate. Peace in which to think about the Chief's warnings and to resolve that, whatever he might say, whenever the opportunity arose, she owed it to the jewels to bring them out, to introduce a little brilliance to his new Ireland.

It annoyed Frank that she no longer read the newspapers, or not the news bits anyway. The only way she could explain it was that having a child had opened a wound. There was too much horror about. Every mother's son had become her baby, every mother's loss was her own.

On the occasional mornings they breakfasted together she tried to talk about such events. 'But how can it happen, "Fifteen-year-old shot dead at crossroads"? How did that boy's mother let him out of the house? Didn't she know he might get into trouble?'

He would become sulky, pushing the newspapers across the table at her before he stamped off, muttering something like 'Jesus, woman, would you ever think!'

Once, for no good reason, Frank had shouted at her so loudly she could have been at the bottom of the garden, 'What do you want, woman? What did you expect? That we'd get the country we want without a drop of blood?'

She was so startled her mind had gone blank. She could think only of Liam, the trusting smile, the solid weight of him, the sweet breath on her cheek: all as calming to her now as the cold certainty of the jewels. How much blood did good men like Frank and Mr de Valera, fathers of children both, expect to spill to achieve their dream?

No wonder Frank was edgy. Out all hours, probably sleeping in his clothes, judging by the state of them. It couldn't be good for him. That awful smoker's cough in the mornings was like waking beside an old sheep. Bad for his nerves too, the way he peered out windows, arranged himself to face the door, jumped when the new girl entered to clear the table or the doorbell rang. Rita didn't like to think what made him like that. She didn't like to think about any of it.

And he had become sharp with her lately, as if she were a prisoner brought in for interrogation. He hardly believed her when he came home a few nights later and she told him about her meeting with the Chief.

'Go over it again.'

'Just as I've said, he was looking for you and then he summoned me.'

'And you went to see Eamon de Valera with the child?'

'It was most inconvenient. I had to feed him in the house.'

'Say exactly what he said.'

'He looked at Liam, of course, said he was a soldier for Ireland. I said I sincerely hoped all this unpleasantness would be over by the time he grew up!'

'Great God, preserve us!'

It was the first time she noticed the mottling which surged over Frank's face, reminding her of the neck of her first pony, a strawberry roan.

'And before you ask me again, he gave me no message. We talked about me, really, about the role of a wife, the image, you know. We seem to be on his mind, the women of Ireland. He had seen me in the newspapers, at the march, I suppose, and other times, and he said it was important to look right. I must admit I thought his ideas rather drab. But you know the Chief: once a spoiled priest, always the spoiled priest!'

'But he said nothing about future plans – co-ordinating units – changing the chain of command?'

'No! No! No! Please, Frank, we've been over and over this and there's nothing more to tell.'

'Then why in the name of all that's holy did he waste his valuable time on *you*? The man's not even meant to be in the country. He could have been shot!'

'Indeed, and I hope he realizes he put your wife and your child's life at risk!'

'He must have had something on his mind.'

She knew full well that if the jewels had been mentioned at that moment, Frank would have asked, 'What jewels?' They were of as little interest to him nowadays as the pins in her hair.

Burning Your Own

* * *

Mama was right. You could no longer tell by the look of them what people thought.

There was Frank getting all hot under the collar about a meeting between the Chief and Mr Craig from Ulster when any fool could predict they hadn't a hope of understanding a word the other had to say. Yet he was dismissive of the most important event of all: a Catholic viceroy.

When Rita had joked about their chances of being put on the guest list to the Park, Frank had muttered something in Irish which sounded most impolite and walked out of the room.

She disliked the way he talked Irish in the house. It was like so much of his general demeanour these days, even in bed: correct, detached, nervous, as if there really were spies behind the prints of the Donegal mountains or hiding in the wardrobe. So different to how he was in America, after she got to know Nina.

Anyway, it was all very fine for him having grown up in the wilds of the country where a few people saw fit to speak the language, but she wished he would remember sometimes how hard she tried. When she complained she couldn't find a proper Irish–English dictionary, he insisted Irish was special, it shouldn't be taught through the contamination of English. He held to the view that it could be 'absorbed', like ink on blotting-paper. Only Mrs O'Reilly was allowed to joke about such things. 'Ah, get away outa that, Mr O'Fiaich! If youse want yer eggs done different, you'd better tell me so in the King's English!'

For all his ideas about equality, Frank made allowances for the servant classes. Why else would he have ridiculous conversations in Irish with the new little maid from Tipperary. As far as Rita could gather, they chattered on and on endlessly in idioms about the hardness of rural life. When he had questioned the girl closely about some problem with a creamery co-operative, they had slipped into English. It felt horrible, that exclusion; the same queasy sensation as when he held Liam sometimes and spoke soft Irish poems and prayers at him, as if he were stealing her baby, spiriting him away from her with all the artfulness of a fairy in one of Mr Yeats's poems.

The telephone rang.

'Did you see it, Rita?' Mary's voice crackled with fireworks and parties, an optimism which marriage had not diminished one whit.

'See what?'

'The fire! Oh, Rita, you goose! Don't tell me you haven't heard? The Customs House – it's on fire! The IRA are burning it down! I thought Frank would be crowing!'

'He's away at the moment.' Some fresh spider webs stretched from the barometer to the telephone on the wall. That little Nora was not doing her job. And by the time you had her trained she'd have her fare saved for the boat.

'There was an awful battle. More martyrs, I suppose. Couldn't you get into town for an hour? All the smoke and the noise and the size of it, I can't tell you how exciting it was!'

'How awful.'

'That's all our records gone up in smoke: births, marriages and deaths. Handy, when we have to lie about our ages!' Her voice dipped. 'Standing on the bridge, Rita, looking at it, I felt quite melty – you know, like with a man . . .'

It was too much, the crudity. And that sinking uncertainty again, never knowing what she might come out with next. Still, the girl had always had an overactive imagination. It was she who put out the rumour about

Sister Anthony being pregnant, the time she went into hospital with her nerves; and the story about the school becoming a nursing home for shell-shocked soldiers. But mixing up the destruction of that beautiful eighteenth-century building with what men and women did together in private!

'Talking of which, it may be rather a good thing for Dermot. *My* idea, of course. We passed the fire on the way home from the McVeaghs' last night and when I woke up this morning, it struck me. I said, "Ring Dev, he'll know if it's to be mended or knocked. And why shouldn't it be you who does it?" As I said, it's the least he can ask after all Dermot has done. Sure what are politics for only helping your friends?'

'I'm sorry, I don't quite —'

'The building contract! *Somebody* has to get it!'

'That really isn't how the world works, Mary.' As if Mr de Valera would have a say in the restoration of public buildings! But that was Mary Kelly, the horse-trader's view of how things got done.

'Open your eyes, girleen! Anyhow, let's have dinner soon. I was only saying to Dermot last night, we never seem to see you and Frank together now, and we *are* supposed to be best friends.'

But Frank disliked the people Dermot went around with, his racy social life, and that tendency he had of asking favours. Mary was right, they didn't see each other enough. Not that Mary needed Rita. Quite the reverse. Mary and Dermot seemed to be off gallivanting every night, while she sat home with Liam, waiting for Frank.

A Letter from Mama, 26 May 1921

* * *

Clonkee
North Circular Road
Dublin

Dearest Rita

Our congratulations to Frank on his extraordinary election success. However, I have to say that your papa and I are outraged by the dreadful fire. The building was a national monument, almost a work of art. Surely he and his henchmen should be celebrating Irish buildings, not burning them? I suppose I'd get short shrift if I said as much in your house. Still, if they want to be taken seriously in that new parliament, I do think the left hand should be telling the right hand what it is going to do. Silly too, since the net result is that he and his friends can't come out of hiding and form a government. Your papa has grown quite agitated, says this sort of thing only displays the inability of the British to understand any other point of view. They are certainly playing into the hands of the nationalists, and I have no doubt your friends will use it to their advantage.

So, Rita, what does this mean for you? Have you thought about clothes? It was all very well saying you had no need of fancy stuff when you were plain Mrs O'Fiaich of Terenure, but a politician's wife is quite another matter. Mrs Roche has got rather past it, I'm afraid, but I have heard of a good woman in Ranelagh whom you might be able to afford.

That is another thing. Papa was asking what sort of income goes with Frank's new seat? What I mean is, could it stretch to moving you nearer town? Terenure is all very well but hardly *comme il faut*. They're putting up some reasonable houses in

Donnybrook, I see, so much more convenient if Frank prefers to do his politics on this side of the water. More's the pity. Mrs Charles so enjoyed travelling back and forth to Westminster. You remember Papa and I visited them before all this unpleasantness? They had a charming apartment in Pimlico, ideal for theatres and the shops. Your papa, of course, still believes the worst, says the whole thing will collapse like a house of cards by Christmas. All those executions have made him quite tetchy. He has stopped calling everyone 'bloody savages' anyway.

We have our own revolution here. Anne Marie is learning to drive the motor! I do wish she had chosen a nice Swiss finishing school or Trinity instead of that awful National, but she says they give full degrees to women! Why?

If you get a chance, do try to talk Frank out of letting the Church into politics. Those people never know when to stop. Papa and Anne Marie were talking about it last night at dinner and left me with a splitting headache.

Your Mama

Inaugurating Dáil Éireann, 16 August 1921

* * *

'*Macushla, macushla!*'

He was chewing her ear, licking the tight skin over the eardrum, sending a shivering message into some chamber deep within her. She feared he might devour her. She hoped he would not swallow the earring, which she had not had time to remove. Poor man. He groaned with pleasure as she twined her legs around his. His calves felt thick and knotted beneath her feet and his back was sweating. He was putting on more weight. 'My girleen, *macushla*, my girleen!' Tonight, when they had come home, he had helped her undress. He was so eager, with that bright-eyed stare she had seen sometimes during the emergency.

Everyone had been so sweet. It was only a pity that the new assembly could not meet somewhere more fitting, more parliamentary looking, than the Mansion House. But it had been most pleasant. She had rarely seen so many familiar faces gathered together in a single building. As she remarked to Frank, if the British were to change their minds now and shoot the lot of them, it might be the end of the Troubles. Frank hadn't even smiled, but everyone else had been most sociable. The quality of the speeches showed it wasn't quite Westminster, but it was a start.

At the reception afterwards Mr Barton inquired about Papa and Mr de Valera himself was almost chatty. He bent down and listened when she voiced her fears about giving power to gunmen, though he looked surprised. Perhaps he did not expect her to have opinions. There was no reference to their secret meeting in Phibsboro. Did he even remember it?

'Not to worry, dear lady. I have the priests with us, and

there's nothing like fire and brimstone for silencing a bully boy!'

'So long as they don't try frightening the rest of us too!'

'We are not in Mexico, Mrs O'Fiaich. The Church will tame the wild lads for us when the time is right – given a bit of rope.'

'Don't ropes hang people, Mr de Valera?'

'In extreme cases, perhaps, but they can also restrain.'

The way Frank had rushed her, nuzzled her breathily on to the bed, as if she were a little pig in some children's story and he a wolf, hadn't given her time to take the jewels off. She was glad she had worn them. She had kept it simple, only the ruby earrings and ring, and all the wives were in their Sunday best. The Chief would have had his work cut out with homilies on plain dressing. Indeed, women like Mrs Childers could be surprisingly outspoken.

Surely one of the duties of a wife was to be properly turned out? Getting money out of Frank was like drawing blood from a stone. The asking and the sighs, then the slow withdrawal of a note or two from the wallet. It was so humiliating, so unfair. Mary had accounts in all the shops; she could walk into a bank and take out money any time she chose. Though, as Frank said, God only knew where Dermot got it from.

The only way to look halfway decent was to dress things up with some good jewellery. It was nice anyway to give her Russian guests a bit of an airing. Fitting, too, that they should attend the inauguration ceremony of the first Irish parliament in over a century. She hadn't been greedy. No one need be any the wiser, even if Mrs O'Kelly had given her a bit of a close look.

Her head was pressed sideways now and she could feel a gold post skewering into her head, pushing in, hard. Oh, darling one, sweet, sweet Nina. Where are you? Why do you never answer the letters which Frank ordered me not to write? Just a word would mean so much, would give me strength. For what? Pushing, probing, driving on and in. Oh, Frank.

VIII

A Dinner Party in Harcourt Street, 1922

* * *

Mary had changed. At her own dinner table in the peculiar little flat she laughed at Rita – ridiculing some comment Rita had made to Mrs McNally about the people in the North being as Irish as the rest of them.

'Listen to her! Never been there in her life, but still the little romantic after all these years!'

All these years! How long was it anyway since the two of them had been girls together, imagining a Celtic revival, talking about the binding twine of Irish culture?

Looking at her made you wonder if everyone was supposed to change. She glanced down at her own childlike hands, only too aware of the plump softness which still clung to her body long after it could be excused as puppy-fat. Mary had become a willow wand, rustling quietly in green taffeta at the head of the table. When she gave one of her long, tinkly laughs, the men paused in their talk and regarded her thoughtfully, pleased somehow, smiling. And when she spoke, leaning forward with her great eyes wider than ever, Mr McNally and even Frank would put down their forks, amused by the most mundane comments which dropped from her too large mouth.

That was another thing: Mary's accent. The ignorant hawk of Mullingar had been polished to the warbling notes of a thrush. Her face too was longer, more refined. All the weight she had lost since meeting Dermot drew attention to the artistic lines of arms and back, the leanness of collarbones and joints.

Dermot wasn't such a bad husband for her. He might even be amusing. Everyone except Frank enjoyed his story about being caught in his new motor car after

199

curfew – how he had given the army officer who stopped him a test run and they were both nearly shot at the next roadblock.

Frank didn't laugh. Perhaps he was over-serious sometimes, but then it wasn't nice being a wanted man, skulking about like a mouse in the home of an invisible cat, never knowing when he might be locked up all over again. It put a strain on the household too. Only last Monday she had had yet another visit from some extremely rude soldiers who tramped all over the house and garden, poking into areas where they had no right. No sooner had they gone than Father Sugrue called, mumbling messages for Frank about eternal damnation and excommunication. Then this morning a young priest had appeared at the door and offered her a telephone number, saying something about hearing Frank's confession and 'sympathy for the cause'.

It was difficult enough getting Frank out with her tonight but, as she told him, it might be safer at Mary's than sitting at home. The way people welcomed him like a returning warrior Rita wondered if his notoriety might go to his head. Only Dermot seemed unimpressed. Was it because Frank was always so solemn now, making no effort to please. His face was granite as Dermot related how he brought the English soldier home for a drink and they sat up all night like the best of friends.

Mary's little wink didn't help. She seemed perfectly happy with her attic, the cheap furniture made just about bearable by artistic arrangements of shawls and rich fabric-ends, the lack of a proper dinner ignored in favour of charcuterie served with an endless supply of wines and liqueurs. It was how Mary and Dermot carried on, all show: the motor, the clothes, the going about. Dermot claimed it was necessary for business.

Was she being overly critical? Liam had been teething and he wasn't giving any of them much sleep. When she mentioned that, Mary threw up her arms and hooted, 'You poor dear! Don't say you're still at that messy old breast feeding?'

Rita was sorely tempted to remind her of the women's groups at the League, the talks about rearing healthy Irish children. How patronizing she had become! The swank she put on! Two or three maids in fancy uniforms hired for the night and flowers everywhere. Where had Mary learned all this? Rita could still remember the first time she had taken her home for the holidays and seen her quite overwhelmed. Yet here Mary Quinn now reigned, the *grande dame*, opposite a husband who would proudly tell anyone he was the son of a docker.

Such unkind thoughts. She reached out to touch the lily of the valley at the centre of the old gateleg table. 'These are lovely, Mary. Mine came up blind this year.'

'Shame on you, Rita, and that great man of yours preaching to us all the time about the pleasures of living off the land!' Irritating how such a remark from Mary could make the whole table smile.

'The church flower committee does very well out of my garden, I can assure you!'

Just lately Rita had felt quite exploited. What with special masses and all the baptisms, marriages and funerals, she was going to have to extend the herbaceous border or there wouldn't be a thing left. Compliments for her arrangements were nice, though. More than one parishioner had suggested she go into business.

Then Dermot chimed in. 'I suppose, Frank, you'll be telling us everything you eat in your place is home grown?'

'Indeed and I wouldn't mind putting in a few Kerr's Pinks if I had the time.'

For some reason that made everyone shriek with laughter.

'Why not go the whole hog, Frank, and put an old sow in that big garden of yours? Haven't you a lovely bit of lawn only wasted out there!'

Dermot could be quite rude. He clearly enjoyed baiting Frank as if there were something funny about his ideals, as if he couldn't admire all Frank was doing for Ireland, the dangers he was running. Yet it hadn't always been like that. When had it begun, Dermot's loss of respect? Was it at the end of last year when Frank had been kept back from the negotiating team for the Treaty? Surely everyone knew that Eamon de Valera needed Frank in Dublin, that he considered Frank O'Fiaich his right-hand man? And a good thing too, considering the condition of the men who did go to London.

Dermot raised his glass for a toast. 'Well, here's to the Chief! I hope he's not expecting us all to be running around with guns over that Treaty of his!'

Mary was the only one to laugh. The rest of them were looking at Frank.

'What, in God's name, makes you call it Mr de Valera's Treaty, or suggest he wants civil war?'

If Frank had been a dog, his hair would have stood on end.

Dermot was too well on to notice. 'Sure hasn't he got all his old cronies out against it – even Rita's band of marching banshees! Though from what I hear he had to do a bit of arm twisting to get certain parties round to his way of thinking.'

From the look Frank shot at her, it was clear he thought Rita had been telling Mary his problems. He pushed the pudding from him. 'Mr de Valera wants peace. But what true Irishman would think Ireland could be free without full Republican status?'

Dermot refilled Frank's glass. 'Come on, Frank me lad, aren't you amongst friends? Tell us what Dev is up to at all. Didn't he send Collins to London with instructions to get the best deal he could? If he wanted all or nothing, he should have said so or gone himself.'

'Collins was duped.'

'We'll be making more eejits of ourselves if the English see us scrapping over the oul' North.'

'I hadn't known you were a Collins man, Dermot.'

Dermot paused, looking slightly shaken. 'Don't you know I'm behind you all the way, Frank, only I'm worried about the Chief, what he's doing. Is he afraid maybe his crown is slipping, that Collins is taking the lead?'

'Michael Collins will never run this country.'

Pattie MacNally tried to smooth things. 'He's a fine-looking man, all the same, and always out and about. We need somebody with a bit of style.'

Frank smiled as if the worst were confirmed. 'He has a bit too much of the boyo's swagger for my taste.'

'Well, like I say, you're amongst friends here.' Dermot was suddenly desperate to please. 'Wasn't it myself who was sent to visit Connolly in the Bridewell, and wasn't it Griffith himself who said you and me were the two ornaments of the organization?'

Rita could almost see Frank's top lip curl. Mary broke the silence. 'God, Rita, do you remember the lock-out? The time Larkin's strikers stopped us getting back to school?'

'Larkin? Isn't he in America now, Dermot?'

'Russia, more like, and I'd take a bet that fella's in clink. A right communist, what, Frank? Sure if his type had their way, there'd be no chances for a man like me to put his shirt on a good idea!'

To see how Dermot lit up his cigar one might think there had never been a *froideur*. 'And they have plenty of friends behind! Did you see all the ruction in the Socialist Party last autumn – that writer fella O'Flaherty and his pals threw out the two big shots because they weren't communist enough! Dev would need to silence that shower, Frank. They're bad enough in Russia!'

Frank remained tight-lipped, behaving like he wanted to slip away and warn Mr de Valera of his enemies.

Pattie MacNally nodded. 'The coal industry has it awful. Strikes every time you turn around and turf hard to get.'

Mary snorted. 'Turf? You might as well burn bricks for all the heat it gives!'

'Ah now, Mrs Quinn, I wouldn't condemn our home grown.' Owen MacNally was as emollient as ever. 'But true, there are a lot of wet sods about with the strike.'

203

Frank was breathing fast when he stood up, as if he couldn't stick in his chair a minute longer. 'It might serve you to remember, Mary, that the turf you condemn is our own, not another frivolous luxury keeping the country in debt!'

Dermot looked interested. 'Do you think there's a market for the bogs, then?'

Mary stood up. 'Dull, dull, dull! Time to retire, girls.'

She was right. And Frank had behaved crassly. Not pleasant to see him lose his temper like that. Heaven knew, Papa had a temper, but he never let it get out of hand in company. It wasn't hard to imagine his reaction to tonight, his amusement as the ladies crossed the room to the easy chairs around the fire.

'Frank is tired, I'm afraid. He's got so much on his mind, you know. And the authorities have been looking to question him ...' She had to stop herself or she would have rattled on about the worry of it, the loneliness at night, the state Frank came home in sometimes. 'Though I do wish they could all shake hands, and get on with running the country now they've got it!'

Pattie MacNally looked puzzled. 'What ails you, girl? There's no chance of that! Aren't Dev and Collins squaring up? All you can do is see your husband is well fed and ready for the fight.'

Rita smiled politely. She never knew quite how to respond to such sentiments, which nowadays were expressed by the most unlikely people. It was the sort of thing Mary and she used to laugh about at school, when the nuns droned on about 'preparing for a good Catholic marriage'. Mary would hiss into her ear, 'Poor things – they haven't a clue!' Lately Rita couldn't help wondering if such rhetoric had got into the water supply, causing everyone to speak in tongues. Or were they quoting lines from a play for which she had not even been offered a ticket?

That was another thing: the rules were changing. Who had decided that good manners had no part in Irish life?

If Mama had been at Mary's tonight and the men had failed to rise as the ladies left them to their cigars, she would have taken herself off to bed very early indeed. You wouldn't see her again before midday.

'God but your husband's great, Rita, he's the man to watch!' Dermot had returned with the men, his charming self.

'He is indeed,' Owen MacNally mumbled. Rita thought he added, 'A future leader, maybe.'

'There's a lot to be done.' Frank was staring into the fire. His mood had improved.

'He's a bit of a dreamer, Rita, am I right? And isn't that what this country needs?'

She couldn't help herself. 'Well, dreams are cheap!'

Only Dermot laughed. 'All the same, I don't think any of us will get rich on sods of turf! I'll put my money on coal: there are some great bargains to be had at the moment with all the bankruptcies!'

Frank looked up from the grate. 'Who ever said anything about getting rich, Dermot?'

'Ah now, Frank, we can't all be saints like you!'

It was that night, when they got home, that Frank announced he wanted nothing more to do with Dermot ('that foxeen') Quinn. Rita didn't ask if he meant Mary as well. It was not a time to argue. The drink, or the silence from Liam, had made him amorous.

The Home Front

* * *

So now they had their own little Eamonn. Frank had named him. It was a good thing the baby was so small, it gave her time to get used to saying it. She tried 'Aye' and 'Monney' in an attempt to stop the sounds from sticking in her throat, the feeling that every time she said 'Eamonn' the long shadow of the Chief darkened the cradle.

If only Mama hadn't said, 'How American! Like the slaves, I suppose, given the name of their master!'

There was something not quite proper about using Dev's name, even with an extra 'n' on the end, even if she had liked it. If only Frank had agreed to calling him Michael, which she preferred. There was no chance of that: he had mistrusted Michael Collins for long before the Treaty, and now he had every reason to hate him. Sometimes, overhearing Frank talk about their fight, she was shocked by the sour malignancy which could pour from within like some ancient dragon fire. Perhaps she was imagining the darkness within him. The mind played tricks after childbirth, exaggerated every little worry into some living nightmare, keeping her awake in the brief moments of peace from the demands of her children.

Yet things did feel worse after the Truce. Frank was gone so much of the time, returning with a hooded look in his eyes, his skin sour from the places where, this time round, Irishmen lay in wait for their own. Rita didn't know what bit of news upset her more: the destruction of the beautiful Four Courts or that horrible siege of the anti-Treaty headquarters in which Cathal Brugha was fatally wounded. Rita had represented Frank at the funeral. Looking at the coffin, it was odd to think of Mr

Brugha silent. For a man of so few words, he had always seemed noisy to her, to fizz with some dangerous, inner electricity.

Eamonn was a good enough baby, much easier than Liam. Mama had offered to send Nurse Crotty again, but Rita preferred things as they were. The current girl, Eily, came from a big family in Cahirciveen. She had been with them a few months now and it seemed no trouble to her to take the children under her wing. Besides, with Frank out of the house so much Mrs O'Reilly and herself had little enough to do.

Mary's reaction to a second child had been strange. 'Another one! How can you stand it?'

A new baby was a blessing, everyone knew that. It was just like Mary to be contrary. She and Dermot appeared in no hurry to produce one of their own.

How do you ask your best friend about such things? If their roles were reversed, Rita knew only too well that Mary would speak her questions out straight, and be delighted by any embarrassment she might cause.

'Do you and Dermot have, you know, relations, in bed?' She could imagine Mary's little jokes about sleeping with her relations. But what else could you say about the intimate things two people did together in the dark? Could Mary name the places which she could not see, which Rita remembered only as raw and untidy those few times Nina had insisted she look?

Nina had known such names. In Russian, French, English and languages which Rita had never heard before or since. She revelled in them, rolled them around on her tongue, licked and spat them out like cherry stones, making them all right, almost ordinary and everyday. She had made Rita learn some of those words, especially the Russian ones, and say them to her in the darkness. Well, they were of no use here, in the Irish Free State.

Papa always said, 'If you want to know something, just ask! And if you don't know the question, look it up in a book!' She had asked Frank once, only once. She would never forget the amazement in his face, the way he had drawn back, iced over. Maybe he didn't know them either, even in Irish. There was certainly no book she could check.

She wondered if it was her fault that Frank had been talking about 'dangerous influences'. He and Dev were promising some sort of censorship, telling everyone they would save Ireland from the corrupting influences in the art and literature of its godless neighbour.

She was sitting by the cot when the idea had popped into her head. Awful really, how once a fancy lodged there, it would not go away. Glancing down at Eamonn tucked up warm and snug in his lace and embroidery, she was surprised how worried he looked, more like a little old man or a priest than a baby. In fact, it was hard to cuddle him the way she had Liam. He reminded her of what Mama called 'the worst sort of country priesteen', wringing together his podgy little hands, mouthing quiet prayers to himself.

She made a joke about their 'priesteen' to Frank and he frowned. 'If it's God's will, I'll be a happy man.'

'You make God sound like Lord Kitchener! Do you really think he's up there pointing a finger at our little bundle?'

From the way Frank's mouth tightened, she realized that her teasing words came as a shock. An easy humour had gone from him, the springy, bendable quality. In just three years of marriage he was growing stiff and brittle, thickening into a stump like a tree on the edge of a bog.

When had it happened? Perhaps this calcifying disease had been within him since they met. He had always been serious, but since the mess of the Treaty, and now this new fight with Mr Collins, Frank had aged, grown slower, more indulgent to his own impulses to anger or desire.

After a little silence he mumbled, 'As you know, Rita, I don't think the Lord Jesus Christ or his Church are subjects for mirth.'

She hadn't felt that bitter mixture of shame, anger and

bafflement since the nuns had made her stand up in front of the whole school at assembly. That was the spring term when Rita was thirteen. Something about her body had worried them, fussed them every time she ran about the playing field or walked down a corridor. 'Margarita Fitzgerald! Have you no shame?'

Standing by the cradle like a chastised child, Rita realized how inhibited she had become, how careful she was with Frank in every word and deed. As the nuns would have wished, she was learning her lessons well, keeping her thoughts to herself, walking in his shade.

The Death of Michael Collins

* * *

Frank was in a bad mood these days. Of course, a civil war would upset anyone, but it didn't help that Dev and his cronies had taken to dropping in at the most inconvenient times. Frank was always especially tetchy after one of those sessions. She would have liked to tell him, if she ever got the chance, that all the waifs and strays he was now in the habit of bringing home from his travels upset her too.

On the other hand, Mrs O'Reilly revelled in the uncertainty, happy to dance to whatever tune Frank's rough young acolytes might play. Those mornings, when she inquired about breakfast or bath water, it was 'You'll have to wait, missus. Can't you see I'm run off me feet?'

Just once Rita had taken it upon herself to suggest that, as mistress of the house, her own needs were surely a priority. She had tried to make a little joke of it, to argue that after all armies may march on their stomachs, but as general of this barracks there could be no battles fought unless she got her tea and toast, first thing! Mrs O'Reilly had looked agonized. She glanced over her shoulder before whispering, 'I wouldn't make sport of armies nor battles, missus, not these times with Collins prepared to shoot any decent man who'd stand against him.' She had crossed herself three times then, and offered no breakfast that day.

The best Rita could get from Frank was 'Are you aware we are trying to fight a war?'

Well, it was a funny sort of a war. Frank, like everyone else, claimed it was over the Treaty and the Oath of Allegiance. He had even told her with a straight face that an Ireland without all the counties in the North was maimed, becoming impatient with her when she asked what he wanted with those impossible Unionists. She had said as much to the woman on the telephone from Cumann na mBan who invited her on some anti-Treaty march. Well, after the last one they could ask away.

Besides, even if this was a civil war, it was no excuse for behaving discourteously. Frank never introduced her to the strangers he brought home, nor even told her they were in the house. By the time she was up and dressed they were asleep in the spare room or gone. Once, when she complained about the household budget, he opened his wallet and handed her a banknote.

And now that girl, Eily, was creating her own fuss. Apparently her people were sympathetic to Mr Collins and here she was, as she kept repeating, 'In the bosom of the enemy!'

'Just be grateful, young woman, that you have a job and a roof over your head!'

It was plain disruptive. The silly child wanted to go down to Cahirciveen to see what kind of state the family was in. Standing blubbering in the kitchen, face all swollen, a letter full of the most unhelpful sort of news a mother could send to a homesick daughter. The parent had written in Irish, another inconvenience.

It was Mrs O'Reilly who insisted on the translation, pushing the girl into a chair at the kitchen table. 'Now, will you for Jaysus' sake tell us what all that gobbledygook says, and let me get on with the dinner!'

And then the child had to be stopped from bumbling on in her native tongue, pulled back to translate stories of dead children, disappeared sons, burned-out houses. All done, according to the letter, in the names of Mr Collins or Mr de Valera.

Strangely enough, it was the paragraph about the maiming of one of the family's cows that reached Mrs O'Reilly. 'Jesus and Mary, spare us tonight! What kind of wild animals are they at all, cutting the tendons of an innocent beast? Well, there's no chance you're going back to that sort of carry-on!'

In less trying circumstances Rita would have enjoyed teasing her cook about the joints of meat she roasted with such relish. It was the sort of amusement which might dance in the mind at such times, a fault which had got her into difficulties at school assembly. Rita forced herself to concentrate on this crisis, to think through the implications for Mr de Valera, and therefore Frank, which the letter suggested. Of course, the papers were full of such tales if anyone could bear to read them. But with two children to care for and a house to run there was little enough time for reading.

'Tell her she can't go, missus! Not now. Coming from this house, she might find Collins's men down on top of her.'

'But they're all split, missus, the whole family and the neighbours: for the Treaty, against the Treaty – and prepared to kill for it!' Off the silly girl went again, with a banshee wail loud enough to wake the baby.

'Control yourself, Eily. Look, I shall have a word with Mr O'Fiaich when I see him next. He knows people down there, you know, good men who I'm sure would be able to help.'

The way the two of them gasped and gaped anyone might think she was calling God a communist.

'I wouldn't want that, missus, if it's all the same to you. You'd be better off saying nothing to no one.'

'That's right, ma'am, leave it be. Sure won't they learn soon enough, those eejits?'

Really, these people were quite impossible. They didn't deserve help. 'It's up to you, Eily, but I'm sure a word from my husband and it would all be dealt with in a trice. That's how things are done nowadays, you know, now we're running our own affairs.'

'Oh, indeed and I know, ma'am, indeed I do!'

Things seemed settled for a while after that, and just as well. It was no time to be left with a cook grown too uppity for her own good. Sometimes, living with staff in a house this size, she wondered if she would ever have a moment's privacy. They were out this afternoon, thank goodness, Mrs O'Reilly to see family in the Liberties and the girl sent to Palmerston Park with the children under strict instructions not to return until five o'clock, hail, rain or summer snow.

She had sat in the sitting-room since luncheon, listening to the clatter of plates downstairs, the murmurs of the two women as they put on their coats at last, the quick steps of the girl about the house gathering children and equipment. Rita forced herself to remain still, tracing the cabbage-roses on the chair arm, avoiding the shocked gaze of the Virgin. Easy for her to feel superior, picked out to be the mother of God, then raised above the mess to become Queen of Heaven. What ordinary women didn't need escape too, just a few hours of innocent pleasure?

The side gate had hardly clicked when she flew to the kitchen, her fingers flicking through the combination. It was always a thrill when the heavy little door swung open, allowing her to reach into the darkness. They jumped into her hand, favourites first: the satin drawstring bag with pearl choker and bracelet, the children's shoebox containing bigger pieces with necklaces and brooches, the velvet-lined casket in which she kept earrings and rings.

Anyone would think she was committing a robbery with her heart banging like this, every detail of the moment so precise and clear, right down to some greasy marks on the tiled wall which Eily had missed.

Now to be calm, securing the bolt on the bedroom door installed after Bloody Sunday. Ahead stretched a whole afternoon to indulge herself. Today she would dress for a grand ball. She would meet someone there, someone who could look into her heart, touch her as Nina had.

Mama's old ballgown, the blue Kippure lace with the orange silk lining, was just going over her head when the side door slammed. Frank? Oh dear God! If he found her with the jewels . . . But surely he would use the front door? She tore off the dress and reached for the treasures heaped upon the bedspread, pushing them into box, bags, wrapping them in scarves, anything to give them cover, to hide her shame. If he were to walk in now.

Quick footsteps tapped up from the kitchen and into the hall, followed by the wail of a baby from down below. Eamonn. Then Liam's infant voice, complaining as it followed Eily's rush up the stairs, undaunted by the girl's 'Will ye whisht, child, will ye whisht for God's sake!'

Thank goodness for the lock, a barrier against Eily's frantic rattling bleat. 'Ma'am! Ma'am! There's something desperate I'm after hearing. Are you there, ma'am?'

'Just one moment!' Oh, the unfairness of it! The girl could cool her heels on the landing all afternoon for all Rita cared. Liam had got there too, beating on the door with his fat fists, his 'Mama! Mama!' adding to the general bedlam rising through the house as the baby screamed blue murder from the pram in the kitchen.

No time to put on anything now but a wrap. Better to be thought indolent by one's servants than have them suspect . . . 'What in heaven's name brought you back so early?'

'The most terrible thing, madam, I only heard it on my way down the Terenure Road. It was Mrs Winn stopped to admire the baby and she let it slip. I had to come back and tell you, ma'am. I can't stay!'

'What thing? What are you talking about?'

'He's dead!'

No. Please. Surely not. Not Frank. Sinking to her knees, she grasped for her first born, Frank's child, pressing the warm, stiffening softness of him against the chill of her breast, hugging him blindly until his keening wail bounced and echoed about the height of the landing ceiling.

The little maid was shaking her, weeping also. 'No, ma'am, you've got it wrong, it's not himself at all, it's Mr Collins! He's dead! He's after being shot by yer crowd, in an ambush in Cork! Oh, ma'am, there'll be terrible blood spilt now, I don't care to think . . .'

Thank God. Frank was alive. He would come back to her. Mr Collins it was who had died. He was young, and not married, which was a blessing. There would be no wife reduced like this, trying to gather her Chinese wrapper across her chest, to soothe the hysterical sobs of a child.

But who would shoot such a fine-looking man? People spoke of him as a ladies' man, and when she had sat beside him at dinner once, he had been quite charming. She remembered they had talked about music and poetry. That's right, he recommended an Irish novel, and sent it round the next morning as good as his word. Dead.

'They'll be going mad at home, ma'am –'

'Well, let's hope it's a rumour, Eily. You know how stories get distorted these days, and I have heard nothing. Meanwhile, I really don't see why the children should be denied their nice walk on this lovely day.'

The shriek which the girl let out of herself was as fierce and heavy as an anvil blow. Liam clawed the air, clinging to his mother for rescue from this mad creature.

And then there was the calming down, the cup of tea which she, the mistress of the house, had to make for the girl slumped at the kitchen table, the long, sobbing, oft-repeated litany of names of young men of Eily's acquaintance who had apparently died for Mr Collins, the wondering whys and wherefores of what was to follow.

She felt sorry for the girl, of course. But the way she was carrying on anyone would think him a member of her family. That had been the man's quality, a sort of humanity which shone through his photographs and his speeches, despite the awful things Frank said. Still, it was unfair to blame her husband for the killing. Indeed, Rita did her best, more than any employer could be expected to say or do. Which was all the more galling when an hour after the girl had returned with the news she was standing in the hall with her bundles whispering about money owed.

Mama of course would never have paid a servant who went off like that in the middle of an afternoon without a minute's notice. She would have searched the bundles too. But Mama always believed the worst of such people. She never realized how much the Great War and the Rising had changed everything. Also, Mama would never have had the Russian crown jewels bundled beneath her bed, crying out to be put back in safety before her cook returned. Nor would she have allowed special hugs for Liam and baby Eamonn, and certainly not a kiss on the cheek delivered as Eily went out the front door. 'I'm sorry, ma'am, you do see, I can't stay? You do see?'

Funny, the girl appeared to have become quite fond of them. Yet she was gone, with the day to which Rita had looked forward and planned for so long left in ruins. And she still had to tell Mrs O'Reilly that once again there was no help in the house. Maybe Mrs Finnegan next door could help. She had an endless supply of such girls. From Mayo, wasn't it? Now that Rita came to think of it, she had an idea that the west coast was generally anti-Treaty. One of these days she must get Frank to sit down with a map and explain the whole business. In the circumstances, it was obviously the sort of thing any good employer needed to know.

Dinner at Jammet's, 1925

* * *

It was her song from the time Eamonn was born. She had whispered Moore's melody, 'Just a Song at Twilight', to herself when waiting for the midwife to arrive, timing her contractions by seeing how far she could get before pain tore the words apart.

> When the lamps are low,
> And the evening shadows
> Softly come and go . . .

She rarely got to

> Tho' the night is weary
> Sad the day and long . . .

but then, she was always hazy about the words of songs and it was the first verse which was important. It had become a sacred chant, her secret comforter for three years now, the golden cloud on which she could rise above Frank's mulish refusal to change his linen more than once a week, Liam's tantrums when she tried to teach him his prayers, or the blocked kitchen sink for which Mrs O'Reilly blamed the long-departed Mr Noone but which was really the result of the woman's wilful insistence on pouring meat juices down it.

Only hum 'Softly come and go' and the daydream would slip into her mind. An image of palatial rooms, a low afternoon sun slanting through long windows, ornate samovars, pale figures drifting like shadows, the gleam of pearls on a long throat, a glitter of diamond on cushiony lobes.

The dream was her escape. It soothed the nagging

217

worries about her guests, abandoned for such long periods now in the darkness of their foreign cell; lightening also a fear that now things had calmed down at home Frank might suddenly take it into his head to move them elsewhere. Then there was Mr Lenin, dead for over a year; changes in Russia might cause the jewels to be repatriated. She often felt tempted to inquire about events there, but with so much to arrange at home Frank would probably know as little as she did. Best to let sleeping dogs lie.

The horrid fighting was over anyway. That was a blessing. But with Frank about the house so much, there was always the danger that Mrs O'Reilly might report Rita's special interest in the safe. The cook and he seemed to have a great deal to say to one another. He would seek her out in the kitchen and hold a conference over the washing-up, discussing some dreary problem like the Ulster Boundary Commission. Rita had overheard him quote his cook when talking about such matters on the telephone. It made Rita so angry she had ripped the entire sleeve of an Aran sweater with which she had been struggling for months. Ridiculous really, but she sometimes felt almost jealous of Mrs O'Reilly. Not that she feared the woman would steal Frank's affections. The very thought of Frank in the arms of that shapeless apron made Rita smile. But listening to the intense hum of their chat rising up the kitchen steps brought on a peculiar sense of emptiness.

She didn't complain. He had grown aggressive lately, rude and angry when she had to refuse his advances, behaving as if he didn't believe Mr Dunne's insistence on some rest before the next baby. But then, he had become suspicious of everyone, returning her politest inquiry about items of news with 'Why do you ask?'

Well, simply because she wanted to know. He never shared his problems now, and there was less than ever she could do to help. Her mild suggestion that politicians should keep away from the fuss surrounding the death of the celebrated eccentric Matt Talbot was the closest they had come in years to an exchange of views.

'Don't you know the man may be canonized – independent Ireland's first saint?'

'I'm sure that would be very nice. But it's Church business, isn't it? And a lot of people are saying the way he lived, with the ropes under his clothes and flagellation and so on, the man must have been mad. I mean, it's not a healthy image for Ireland, is it, hardly the sort of thing we'd want our young people to take up?'

'Who's saying that? What kind of people would destroy the name of that poor man, God rest his soul?'

His sanctimoniousness annoyed her. He seemed more religious than ever these days, blessing himself as he passed churches, saying a little prayer to himself before going out the front door. She didn't like the sense of superiority it gave him, an implication that she was the sinner, he the saint. Her refusal to attend Matt Talbot's funeral was silly, a tiny show of rebellion, and she was surprised to discover how much she enjoyed Frank's discomfort.

In the years of conflict, when she had asked to be taken out, he had put her off with 'When there's time, when all this business is over.'

Well now it was long over. No more fighting, no more cloak and dagger stuff. Frank was an elected member of the opposition, even if he refused to take the Oath and sit in the Dáil; into town on the tram every morning, back every evening, away only for the odd night or two organizing Dev's new party around the country. Yet he still would not behave like a normal Dublin husband. Now, when she suggested a concert or a meal together, he became agitated, even snapping at her. Yes, 'snap' was the only word for it.

'Are you mad, woman?' Or worse, 'If it's a night out you want, aren't there plenty of Irish events you should be supporting? Would you find something you fancy in the newspaper and leave me to get on?'

He meant the events advertised in the *Freeman's Journal*. There was more and more of it: Irish dramas, music, dance, poetry, some of which she had gone to for his sake but found incomprehensibly dull.

That was why she was out with Mary and Dermot that awful night. She knew Frank would disapprove, but he offered no alternative. He could not expect her to sit home alone all the time; she was not a broody hen. At least Mary needed her, had begged her to come and talk to a difficult Englishman with whom Dermot was trying to do business.

'You could charm him, Rita. You always have so much to say when you put your mind to it. Wear some of your sugar-daddy sparklers, sweetie, and the pink chiffon!'

'It's a bit tight, since Eamonn.'

'All the better, my dear! The fella's a big developer, Dermot really needs him!'

It was preferable to watching coal burn in the grate. So there she was in Jammet's with Mary sleeked and bobbed in bias-cut coral silk, Dermot glossy in black tie and their Mr Johnson, quite a sweet man who turned out to have holidayed in Dinard as a child and knew the house Papa took for the family. All was going well until Mr Basset joined them for coffee, suddenly holding Rita's fingers far too tightly and inquiring about her rings.

'But of course, I know your mother well. We have done battle at auctions. I had no idea she possessed jewellery of this quality.'

'They may have come from Papa's side – I really can't remember . . .'

Why had she been so greedy tonight? Why hadn't she settled for just one ring? Why had she decided her chiffon needed improvement, needed emeralds and rubies *and* sapphires. Her pudgy little hands glittering in Mr Basset's looked ridiculously overdressed.

She could not meet the man's eyes. Even her voice was shaking. It was so embarrassing. The man was an expert, the best truffle hound in Ireland, Mama always said. He would be doing well for himself these days, with all the big houses selling up. At Sunday lunch recently Papa had joked that Mr Basset probably did more for the Free State's balance of payments than the farmers. It was the sort of humour Frank did not find amusing.

Mary was laughing, the slight edge in her voice betraying annoyance at the interest Rita was attracting. 'Don't waste your time asking Rita about those baubles, Louis. She's as tight as charity with them, and I'm her best friend!'

'But they are quite exceptional.'

Mr Johnson was leaning forward now, scrutinizing fingers which felt red and swollen.

'Indeed, Mrs O'Fiaich, you are right to be careful with such pieces. They are extremely valuable. The quality of the stones, the artistry of the goldwork, quite fabulous. Continental, of course.'

'Valuable, are they?' Mary was gleeful. 'Rita's husband won't be too happy to hear that, Mr Basset, you know what a fuss our home-grown politicos make about show!'

Dermot roared with laughter. 'Will you listen to the woman! Don't you know politicians cut the same cloth as the bishops? It's all "Don't do as I do, do as I say." And sure why not, doesn't it keep the populace under control?'

Mr Basset remained deadly serious. 'Crime going the way it is these days, Mrs O'Fiaich, your husband should be more worried about theft. I hope you've got a good safe in the house? As a matter of fact, some of my customers have been asking me to dispose of their jewellery, at the best price, of course, which I'm happy to do . . .'

As the man rattled on, gripping her hand, Dermot seemed to be concentrating on his brandy, swirling it around the glass, breathing in its bouquet. When their eyes met, locked for a second, Rita realized how dangerous the situation had become. She recognized that look. She had seen him fix it upon others, the sudden relaxation of the big prop-forward's shoulders, the lowering of the handsome head like a supplicant before the altar. He was gazing at his cigar stub, but she could tell that suddenly she was no longer Frank O'Fiaich's little wife nor Mary's friend. He had spotted something which might be useful to him, if he could only discover how.

She had to get away. Next thing this dealer would be

pulling the rings off her fingers, taking out one of those jeweller's eyeglasses. Mama had always said Mr Basset was shameless when after treasure.

Despite all their protests she was up and out of there, goodbyes made, coat fetched, into Nassau Street with Dermot grumpily insisting on calling a cab before any more could be said. For that night, anyhow.

On the way home she hummed her tune. The words calmed her. They revived the magic which the night should have brought, the pleasures of a society to which her jewels had been born. Not for them the suburban house in Terenure growing shabby with years and children and Frank's economies.

The lamps were low over Portobello, casting a yellow halo on a barefooted urchin and his mongrel. Rita pushed the sharp stones of her rings into her lips. She liked the feel of them, so cold and perfect. They had witnessed great beauty, cruelty, pain, neglect and history. In their company she too had experienced moments of greatness. According to the papers, Russia had become run down lately, quite horrible in fact. The newspapers told of another shake-up in the government, more arrests and disappearances. Only last Sunday Father Quorn had preached against the Soviet Union, referring to revolutionaries like Nina as 'servants of the devil'. Rita had wanted to stand up and shout. She prayed for patience instead. These days she found she needed it more and more.

The world was growing darker. Outside, the dog flung itself at the wheels, snapping and growling as it chased after her over the bridge and down the Rathmines Road.

Friends in Need

* * *

'I may have to kill myself.' She spoke quite seriously, tipping her tiny cup of coffee down a throat still glowing from a holiday in the south of France.

'Oh, come on, Mary, things can't be that bad!'

'They're the worst.'

She waved a limp hand at the waiter as if ordering strychnine. Rita couldn't help thinking her friend would make a beautiful corpse, a slain warrior by Burne-Jones.

'Honestly, darling, I think if I didn't have you to turn to, my one true friend, I'd have done it already!' It was a surprise to see real tears wetting Mary's mascara. 'Dermot is finished – and me along with him!'

A waft of perfume from the handkerchief soared into Rita's nostrils like some powerful drug.

'One day you'll know what I'm talking about. One's friends are what count – not Dermot's rotten colleagues, not family.' Her voice dropped to a snarl, the accent suddenly less polished. 'That shower! That mean, penny-pinching bunch of hucksters and gob-shites – fellas Dermot has given his life blood for –' She was staring hard at Rita, oblivious of the waiter refilling their cups and, for once, of who else might be lunching at the Dolphin that day.

'Is there anything I can do?'

The long nails digging into Rita's forearm withdrew slightly. Mary's smile reminded her of the night when a tiny bat had flown about the dormitory. Mary had caught it in her bare hands, and the next day a bat had flown out of Sister Anthony's desk as she lifted the lid, bringing on her annual bout of nervous troubles a little earlier than usual.

'No, no, please forget it.'

She was rootling in her handbag, a brown pigskin for which Rita knew this broken woman had paid twelve guineas in Weir's only last week. Rita had helped her choose it, or, more precisely, tried to talk her out of such extravagance.

'Please, tell me how I can help.'

The silver cigarette case looked new too.

'I'm desperate. If Dublin gets a sniff of this, Dermot is as good as finished. We'd have to go away.'

'Of course I won't tell anyone.'

Dublin without Mary. Over the years gallery openings and theatre tickets, restaurants, concerts and coffee mornings had become as essential for happiness as Cadbury's chocolate or the latest Edgar Wallace. Of course, Rita had her work for the Legion to keep her busy, and her flower arrangements, not to mention her most important role as mother of two demanding and rather wild little boys. But it was Mary who made her feel part of a wider world, like the time she had smuggled a copy of *Ulysses* from Paris. Never mind if Rita had found it difficult and kept it hidden from Frank in the safe.

'I told Dermot nobody would want that awful heavy furniture he's been importing. Now we're on our uppers.'

Frank always said Dermot sailed too close to the wind, whatever that meant. The Quinns were certainly *flaithiúleach*, living like millionaires. When they took Rita to the first night of *The Plough and the Stars*, they had the front row of the stalls (attracting some uncalled-for comment in the newspapers about Frank O'Fiaich's wife attending such a scandalous play). Then there was their big car, and that gin-palace of a house in Foxrock.

Mary looked broken. Perhaps, after so much pleasure, the loss of everything would be harder for her.

'What are you going to do?'

'We have one last shot. Have you noticed all the bogmen moving into Dublin? Whole families of them? The north side is bursting.' To listen to her no one would guess that

Mary's own family had only moved to Dublin when she had almost finished school. 'They'll need to be housed, and Dermot has heard from a little bird in the government –' Her wink reminded Rita of the phrase 'a cute hoor' which Mrs O'Reilly used about the bread man with dirty fingernails and a blue-eyed horse. 'Whole farms are to go for building. So, if a person were to know exactly which ones and where . . .'

She was asking too much. 'I'm sorry, but Frank would never divulge information like that. You know how he hates that kind of thing –'

'For the Lord's sake, Rita, if we were all reliant on that clam of a husband of yours we'd be in the poorhouse!'

Rita had a good mind to remind Mary that it was the Quinns who were heading for that particular establishment.

'Dermot's got all the information he needs, it's raising the money to buy the land that's the problem. It's really cheap, you see. Who'd be a farmer these days? Sure isn't that why the whole population is moving in on us, no matter what Dev has to say about the joys of country life!'

'Won't the bank lend it?'

Mary's neighing shriek made the waiter shy like a horse as he slid the bill on to the table. It had grown late; the restaurant was empty. 'Oh, sweetie, you are such an innocent! This is much too big for some petty-minded little bank person to deal with. No –' She leant forward to whisper, 'Tomas O Muirichiu is our man!'

Frank disliked him too. He called O Muirichiu a jumped-up jackeen. Certainly the man had come from Beggar's Bush, where the father, called Murphy, was a common street hawker, but the son appeared to have done well for himself, judging by what one read in the newspapers. Extraordinary how people like him were making a king's ransom as bit-players in the government, yet Frank and she seemed poorer than when they had begun.

It was probably the man's bad Irish Frank couldn't forgive. Frank had this bee in his bonnet about anyone holding a government post having to be fluent in the language. O Muirichiu had learned it all right. He spoke it sometimes in debates when he wanted to fox the other deputies. But the accent remained strong Dublin, not quite pukka, according to Frank's rigid standards.

'I'm sorry, Mary, I don't really know the man. Frank isn't awfully keen –'

'Don't worry, Dermot knows him well enough. No, I'll tell you where you come in, if you *really* want to help . . .?' She paused, waiting for Rita's slow nod. 'Tommy O Muirichiu has the cash all right, but Dermot has to let him know he's a sound man, that we're doing all right and so on. And what makes a fella like O Muirichiu think that?' She raised her pencilled eyebrows like a schoolmarm.

'Champagne?'

'Silly! Businessmen know a man's doing well when his wife is wearing furs and, listen to me now, jewels!'

Had she any conception of what she was asking? Rita still had nightmares about Mary's seventeenth birthday, the night she had been made to steal the communion wine. 'You know I can't!' It was maddening to hear her own voice like that, a bleat of defeat.

'We're talking life or death, sweetie! But this may swing it, men only have to see a few diamonds to think you're Lady Lavery.' She ignored Rita's shaking head. 'Now, I need your advice. I'm going to wear my new Chanel evening gown, the clingy green velvet with the low back and those tiers from the hip – Dermot adores it and you know what men mean when they say that! So, I'll need some emeralds, or do you think that big jewelled cross you had on for a poetry reading last year would be better . . .?'

'You know those jewels are in my custody! I can't possibly take any chances with them, they're a secret!'

'Exactly, Rita dear. I often wonder what that man of yours would say if he knew how you got them. Does he go round with his eyes tight shut or what!' She was staring at Rita, hypnotic, hard eyed, the way you might look at a dog when teaching it to sit. 'But don't worry. I won't tell on you if you don't tell on me!' She had dropped her eyes to the bill. 'I'll just take them away one day, bring them straight back the next, and you will have done Dermot and me the most enormous favour – probably saved us.'

Her big loopy handwriting streeled across the bill. The way she turned to find a waiter it was clear the subject was closed. She was more right than she knew. If anything happened, if anyone ever found out, Rita would have destroyed Frank's reputation, wrecked his trust, ruined everything.

'I need to think . . .' Rita reached for her gloves, desperate to get home, to warn her darlings.

'Don't be a goose! I'll be round on Saturday to pick them up! Oh, and didn't I see a pearl choker with some kind of cheruby thing on the clasp? Better put that in too, just in case.'

She smiled warmly at the waiter. It probably wasn't the first time Dermot's credit would be found wanting.

IX

The Irish Times, *25 January 1927*

* * *

Fitzgerald, James Albert, MD, FRCS, of Clonkee, North Circular Road, suddenly at home on 23 January. Deeply regretted by wife, May, and daughters Margarita and Anne Marie. Funeral at St Cecilia's, Clonsilla Avenue, at 11.00 a.m. tomorrow. Family and friends afterwards at the house. May he rest in peace.

A Kerry Cottage

* * *

The cow in the garden was unfortunate. Rita had been so looking forward to showing Mary the cottage. She had asked Mrs Cuddy to give everything an extra polish. Even the Elsan didn't smell too bad now, and the wild flowers bunched in the old enamel jug looked surprisingly pretty against whitewash.

But she had been relying on the garden for first impressions and now the cow was doing its best to spoil things. In just a few months the montbretia and rhodos had come on marvellously, and the O'Sullivan woman from the farm was always remarking she hadn't seen a fuchsia hedge like that one, not even in a kingdom going wild with the stuff.

'Don't say you've taken up farming!'

Wouldn't you know it. Mary was out of her little car just as Rita had given the beast a whack on the hip, sending it careering across the lawn with great muddy scoops, leaving a steaming puddle of brownness on the concrete path. Frank should be here to help, not back in Dublin still arguing about an Oath to the King. Watching the beast snatch mouthfuls of cotoneaster off the wall by the turf shed, Rita offered a silent prayer that it would poison itself.

'No need to swallow everything Dev tells us! What is it he wants for us – an acre of land and a cow?'

Her fox stole was pulled up high over her nose, as if trying to block out the very air on which she had been reared, the fitted suit and co-respondent shoes too precise in the huge landscape of ocean and mountain.

'Charming!'

Her eyes were arc lamps on the damp patch in the hall. The foolish decorator had sworn it would disappear under new paper.

'Dermot didn't believe me when I said you were buying in Rosbeigh.'

'Frank prefers it.'

'Frank!' She gave that annoying little laugh of hers as she tapped out a cigarette. 'What he'll never realize, that fat-headed husband of yours, is the connections he could make on the golf course. I think Dermot does more business in Dooks than in the rest of the year.'

Rosbeigh was fine for them. 'Ordinary people,' Frank had said. Of course, he didn't mean the visitors like themselves. He had no time for the builders, teachers or civil servants who spent a few quiet weeks here, nor for the artists with their Anglified accents who lived the year round in cottages further up the mountain. It was farming people Frank liked, though Rita often wondered about his use of the word 'ordinary' for a man like Mr O'Sullivan, who beat his dog so savagely on the road most mornings she had had to tell him to stop, or old Mattie Sheehan, who managed to fill a day going to the new creamery and back with one churn on the donkey cart. As she had said to Frank in an unguarded moment, if these people were ordinary, then the rest of the world must be quite demented.

Yet Frank was more mellow on the days he exchanged a few words with them. He grew kinder, as if he had touched on something far greater than fat ewe prices or the details of someone's will. The way he carried on anyone might think he had discovered this place. But left to himself, there would have been no cottage in Kerry or anywhere else.

He had been annoyed by the kindness of Papa's last will and testament.

'How much did you say?'

'One thousand pounds each to Anne Marie and to me.'

'I'd better have a word with McGrath in the bank, so, see is there any way of making it disappear.'

'Disappear?' She was a bit slow on money matters, but all the same . . .

He was speaking to her in his tense, careful voice. 'It does not look good, woman dear.'

That was another thing, when had he started calling her 'woman dear' and omitting her own name altogether? Was it since the children came?

'A man in my position, it doesn't look right to have hundreds of pounds of my own mounting up in the bank.'

'But —' Always ahead of her these days, off somewhere else entirely, turning round in surprise sometimes and noticing her struggling up behind. She felt like roaring angrily at him, the way Eamonn had as a baby when Frank tried speaking to him in Irish. 'There's no need to bother the bank. Apart from the stocks, which Mr Montgomery advises I leave alone, there's only a few hundred in cash. I have decided to buy a cottage with it. County Kerry, I think.'

That put a stop to his dance.

'The children need some Atlantic air. We used to summer in some lovely places abroad, you know, when I was growing up, but I think we'll wait for France and Italy until they're older, when they're ready to learn another language.'

'Isn't their own country and language good enough for them?'

Somehow she had steered him into the idea of this place, a low whitewashed cottage on the Rosbeigh road, two bay windows and high fuchsia hedges in front, and behind them a view over the back strand to the Dingle peninsula. That was where Frank had wanted to buy, of course, in Dingle, an area where the language had never been lost or, at least, where Dev planned to pay a subsidy to keep it alive.

It was nice having her own money. The cash left over from the cottage and the occasional dividend meant she no longer had to ask her husband for every penny. She had bought a bicycle and on fine days would pedal to Dooks for golf with Mary.

234

The children were happy there too. Liam's raw energy found the space it needed, so that he slept soundly through the night for the first time since he was born. Eamonn was more of a home body. But in the simple seaside life she found herself less irritated by the way he followed her about, trying to share in her poor attempts at decoration and knitting, wanting to get close whenever she sat down.

'It's so quiet here, I can't believe it!'

Mary's long stockinged toes stretched to the fire. What was it like to have legs like that? Rita had Papa's legs. Safe inside his trousers, he used to describe them as 'beef to the heel like a Mullingar heifer'.

'It's like Kingsbridge station at our place. Only yesterday that widower Flanagan called to ask me for a game and the awful Hannay woman from The Shack walked in and behaved as if she'd caught us *in flagrante*!'

'Oh, Mary, honestly, as if you would!'

Did they know each other at all? Mary had changed, or was it herself? Rita looked down at her hands, so childish compared with Mary's polished claws. A sudden yearning for Nina, a stabbing pain like childbirth, caused her to flop back suddenly into the chintz armchair.

'What is it, sweetie, curse coming on?'

The jewels. Remembering them suddenly like that, left behind over two hundred miles away in the dark safe, was like remembering forgotten children waiting to be collected. All those years since the United States and not a word. Nina could be dead for all Rita knew, you heard some awful stories. The country had sealed itself off from the rest of the world. Perhaps that was how Nina wanted it. To the Russian, she had probably seemed an amusing interlude, but it was hard to stop the memories shining out sometimes from the darkness of her mind, bright-coloured bruises which hurt when touched.

And what of the jewels? She had abandoned them, cast them from her as she went off for this first long summer holiday. What did they feel? They did feel, she knew that. Whenever Mary had borrowed a piece or two, she worried for them, waiting up for their return like a mother, making them welcome again. It was foolish, really, but when she polished them before slipping them back into the safe, she fancied she could detect a sulkiness, a resentment she saw in Liam when she had sent him to play with children he did not know or care for. Like the jewels, Liam had no time for her explanations about making friends with children from good families.

'Whose is the car?'

A relief when the children appeared, sandy and wind whipped from their morning on the beach. She was proud of Liam, the way he had grown so clever and quick, with the sharp blue eyes which could see into her mind. Eamonn was like his little shadow, shy even with herself. Her pleasure in them muffled the hurt of Mary's silent appraisal of the décor, the raised eyebrow at the sunny yellows and pinks, the local *sugán* chairs which Rita had painted herself in primary colours and the shell mirror which had taken months to complete, even with Eamonn's help. She enjoyed her friend's discomfort as Liam sang his party piece, 'God Save Ireland', and Eamonn tried to distract her with his collection of sea snails.

When the gong sounded, Rita thought all would be well. Mary couldn't help but be impressed by the good leg of boiled mutton or Rita's own carrigeen pudding.

'Well, well, darling, best china and a gong in the hall? You'd think it was a great house we were in and not this little hovel!'

The way Mary made the children laugh with her was unforgivable. It nearly put Rita off her luncheon, though Mary didn't notice that at all.

Making Sacrifices, September 1928

* * *

'Well, *a bhuachaillí*, I've found the very school for you both. They'll have you speaking our own language like Finn McCool.'

'A new school, Frank, where?'

He had listened to her fears after all, her reservations about the dull teaching, brutish boys and rough and ready masters of the local school.

'The Chief himself is excited by this place, so he is. Brand new, Rita, and near the sea, which should suit your fancy ideas about fresh air.'

Liam looked thrilled. He was such an enthusiastic boy. Rita knew he was frowned upon by the masters, who thought his sense of fun dangerous and needing to be squashed. 'When can I go, Daddy? Can I start tomorrow?'

Only that afternoon he had come home in tears after being beaten once for his untidy handwriting then beaten again when swollen fingers made it difficult to hold the pencil. Standing there flushed with the chance of something better, he reminded Rita of his father: the young warrior concealed by layers of disappointment and compromise beneath his thickening flesh.

'Hold on, now! Next term will be soon enough. I was talking to the head brother on the phone, sure they haven't finished the dormitories yet.'

'Dormitories, Frank? You're not thinking of boarding school already, are you?'

'Total immersion, that's what the brother told me, the only way to learn the language. In a couple of years, he says, he'll have the lads dreaming in it or he'll want to know why!'

'But how can we, Frank? And Eamonn's only six, it's cruel!'

'Get them young, Dev says. Wasn't he a teacher, he should know.'

Only Eamonn had been upset by her reaction. He was growing up so sensitive, anything would set him off. An Irish-language boarding school run by Christian Brothers? It wasn't good enough for her lovely, clever boys.

'Small children, sent away to strangers, to a place we know nothing about?'

Liam pushed her off to stand by his father. Only Eamonn sidled up to brush the tears from her face.

Frank put a comradely arm around his eldest son. He rarely touched them, had little enough to do with either of them, but tonight he patted and stroked them like prize animals, or trophies he had walked into her sitting-room to bag for himself.

'Listen to your mother, Liam, still trying to tie you to the oul' apron strings. This is a great chance for them, woman dear, the first chance we've had to experiment with a truly Irish Catholic education. And the lads here will have first crack!'

'But what's wrong with Clongowes Wood when they're older, or Blackrock? They're good boarding schools, and they're Catholic.'

Frank sighed, smiling in mock sadness at the two boys. 'Will she never learn, what? Married to this woman for nine years, and she understands the situation less than ever!'

'That's because you never tell me anything, Frank. You never consult me!'

'Well, listen to me now. An *Irish* education, Rita, language, culture, the whole shooting match. Think of that. We're building an Irish-speaking society, root and branch. Believe me, when our side are in power, you'll need to be fluent in the language or you can forget getting a job. Imagine the advantages that will give the lads!'

'In that case most of your shadow cabinet will find themselves out of work!'

'What are you saying now? They've all learned the Irish.'

'Indeed! I had a word with Tom Derrig at that reception last week and as far as I could tell he knew little enough about education *or* Irish!'

She had gone too far. Frank's angry silence lasted until the children had gone to bed. She tried to reason with him then, wept, pleaded, promised extra home tuition paid with her savings, offered to return to a study of the language herself so that they might all speak Irish in the home. It was no use. He was adamant, too pleased with the arrangements to consider change. Her stupid outburst had lost her the argument. It had also lost her the children. Only a cup of tea in the dark kitchen and a quick rummage in the safe could calm her.

When Mrs O'Reilly appeared out of her bedroom to say it was a terrible thing to do, tearing young children from their homes, Rita thought she had an ally. Then the woman said, 'But there's no point arguing, missus, youse have to give example.'

So, she had become Abraham, delivering her own flesh and blood for the cause, for the good of the nation, still sending them to hell or Connacht. She could only hope that the new school in Ballyquin wouldn't sacrifice Liam and Eamonn to some unseen Irish god.

Investments, 1929

* * *

There was no stopping her. Once Mary got an idea into her head, she would hammer away at it for hours.

'Nobody need know. I'll take them to London myself. It'll all be done by a little man in Hatton Garden Lucy Cronin told me about. She says he's absolutely discreet.'

Rita could imagine her on the other end of the telephone in Foxrock, the hair smooth as a hat, body taut and imperious. She had worn them too often, that was the problem, grown to rely on borrowing one piece or another over the last few years, so that she had come to think of them as her own. Indeed, if there was any justice in the world, Mary should have had charge of the jewels.

Seeing them on her friend, Rita couldn't help thinking how unfair it was for them. Alongside the regal Mary, she was a gargoyle, a goblin jailer from one of the children's fairy tales. Still, she had read somewhere that the Romanovs were not tall, especially the women.

Short, Dr Dunne said she was when she went to see him last week, insisting on a measurement of five foot one inch when she had known all her adult life she was five foot three. Then he implied she was seriously overweight, which was a lie. 'Better cut out the sugar in your tea, Mrs O'Fiaich.'

As if she ever ate a sweet thing in her life. What fools men were, talking to women like that. It was bad enough the way one got measured and weighed in pregnancy. But to be condescended to by that ignorant man with his mouthful of bad teeth and dingy rooms in Leeson Street was simply too much. The man might as well be a vet. Third baby round she should have grown accustomed to him, but he still made her feel like a farm animal, a pig. She had gone straight home and spent a little time with the jewels. That day she had become Olga, though compared with herself and her increasing girth, the Grand Duchess looked slight in photographs.

Maybe it was as well those girls had not lived to bear children. They had been spared humiliating sessions with the likes of Dr Dunne and worse, the sinking sense of loss when Liam and Eamonn returned for the Easter holiday. It made her ashamed to remember how little Eamonn had skipped on to the train like a lamb to the slaughter. Frank didn't seem to notice that Eamonn came back to Dublin like a dipped sheep; he would not acknowledge Liam's closed fist of a face, his refusal to be hugged or held close, the paleness of his cheeks. Even Mrs O'Reilly had failed to rouse him when she hooted at the boys over breakfast, 'You've got awful dull, so you have. Have you died for Ireland or what?'

There had been an item in the paper recently about the Grand Duchess Anastasia turning up from the dead. What must it feel like, to have lost so much? Sometimes Rita wished she could write to her, reassure her that all was not lost, that she had her jewels. But, of course, the woman was probably an impostor. Perhaps it would be better to be dead than to return like that with nothing.

'Couldn't you draw them, Mary? You were always so artistic.' She hadn't meant to say that. It was a first crack in the ice which would take only a few whacks of Mary's sledgehammer to break through.

'Don't be stupid, sweetie, it's the *detail* jewellers need to see. Come on, this is for you too, you know! And I'm the one who's paying, don't forget, for copies which I'll let you borrow any time.'

'I'm sorry, but when we talked you said they would be copied in Dublin, and we could bring them in together, just for an hour or so –'

'Well, I know better now. London is the place. If you want to come with us, you're welcome, but I really don't want to argue the whole thing through again. You agreed with the principle, but if you've changed your mind maybe I should ask Frank what he thinks. He's a thrifty man, he might be interested in the saving I'm suggesting.'

'For the millionth time, Mary, this is nothing to do with Frank!' Oh the mean, sneaking, bullying ... 'I resent this, this invasion! I thought we were friends.'

'Such a fuss over a few bits and pieces? Honestly, to hear you go on you'd think they were the crown jewels!'

When it came to it, to getting the right ones out of the safe in a hurry, Rita had panicked. She blamed her pregnancy. She hadn't managed a clear thought for weeks. And it didn't help having the chit of a girl from Leitrim in and out of the kitchen, about as much help as the devil at mass. Mary had made things worse with her last telephone call, saying they were off a week early and she'd be round in an hour to collect the jewels. Without the time to stop and think, it had been hard to recall exactly which items of the collection Mary had seen. Had she attended the dinner for Douglas Hyde a few years ago when Rita had worn the sapphire pendant? Had she ever borrowed the huge emerald brooch set with a spray of tiny stones like a mossy clod splattering into a rock pool? And what about the diamond bird's claw on a sapphire branch? It would look pretty on a blouse, even as a copy.

Trying to sort the jewels into some sort of order, it occurred to Rita that over the years she must have worn almost everything that was laid upon the bed. It had seemed only fair to give them each a little outing, to bring them into the light. It was easy enough to do. Mary took her to places where people were expected to make a little effort. As for Frank, on the rare occasion when he took her to an official function, he hardly noticed her. Too busy as usual talking, explaining, arguing about the events of the day.

Impossible to decide what to include, which to leave out. In the end, she thought she might let Mary choose from a small selection. That was another mistake. Mary

242

had fallen on the little heap with hoots of joy, purring like a cat as she pressed the pearls to her cheek, dangled the ruby drops to the light. 'Darling! I had no idea there was all this! How absolutely fabulous! What fun!'

'I wasn't sure which ones you wanted, so I put out a few extra.'

'All, sweetie, all! How could anyone possibly choose? And, looking at this lot, I can't help asking myself if your husband is as innocent as you say!'

No time to think of a suitable reply. Mary swept everything into her bright silk scarf as if she were removing bits of a broken vase, then off she went, suddenly in a dreadful tear to be gone.

'Hang on, Mary, you can't possibly take them all. It would cost a fortune to get them copied!'

'Let's just see what can be done, all right? Trust me! Now, I really must dash or Dermot will be furious. He's awfully in with a brilliant man in London, they're buying shares like mad. Quite honestly, sweetie, with the schedule he's planning I'm going to be pushed to fit in this Hatton Garden trip at all! But I'll do my best!'

After she had gone, Rita sat down and tried to make a list of exactly what had been taken. The big pieces were still in the safe, the two tiaras, the huge enamelled and jewelled cross, other items with complicated niello or filigree. Still, it was a worry. It made Rita feel very tired. By the time Mrs O'Reilly called her for dinner she was asleep in the chair.

A Letter to Mary, November 1929

* * *

21 Kerrymount Road
Terenure
Dublin

Dear Mary

I am so worried about you. Are you ill? Or are the rumours true? Has something happened to Dermot's business? I do hope not, but whatever it is that's troubling you, I feel hurt that you cannot tell me. This long silence and refusal to come to the telephone or answer letters is very upsetting. It's ages since you got back from London, and I need to know what happened there.

Also, the manner in which you finally returned the items I had loaned you in good faith was most disturbing. What on earth possessed you to deliver things of some value into the hands of my cook? Imagine my return home to find such a package lying casually in the hall. And then discovering some small but not insignificant items were not amongst its contents!

It is all very distressing to me, and for reasons which I am not at liberty to explain, the loss of certain pieces could be disastrous for my marriage and Frank's career. Goodness knows he's under enough pressure since he supported the Censorship Bill.

I am sorry if you thought my inquiries imply suspicion of you in any way. On the contrary, I know there must be a very simple explanation, but bland messages conveyed via your maid every time I call are not answer enough. So please, get off your high horse and talk to me about it. As you very well know, I am in a delicate condition and all this worry is making me ill.

Please, dear, let's forget all the harsh words and start again.

Surely you don't intend to go on avoiding me, your oldest friend, for ever?

With fond regards

Rita

A Letter to Rita, November 1929

*　*　*

Woodview
Brighton Road
Foxrock
Co. Dublin

Rita Fitzgerald

How dare you write to me like that! Mother of God, if Dermot
were to read it, I don't know what he would do. You claim
your precious Frank is under strain. Well, how do you think
Dermot feels being cut out of the electric scheme by his friends
when the whole country knew the bogs were one of his interests?
And now here's you, wife of the great O'Fiaich, putting her oar
in.

It's perfectly slanderous what you wrote. I always knew you
were a sneak, Rita Fitzgerald. Butter wouldn't melt, would it?
But I haven't forgotten the time I got caught for tying all the
gym shoes. It was you told Sister Anne, wasn't it? But oh no,
Little Miss Innocence as usual.

Now I discover, after all the ups and downs Dermot and I
have had to struggle through, you have had those 'items', as
you call them, stashed away for years. Worth thousands, the
man said, thousands and *thousands* of pounds! It was embarrassing the way he talked to me, in a most high-handed manner, as
if I had stolen them, simply because I had no idea of the value.
But he was glad to take them all right and do the work, and a
pretty penny he charged me too, for which, remember, I did
not ask a farthing off you.

You demand an explanation. Well, all I would like to know,
Miss Holier-than-thou Fitzgerald, is how you dared keep the
truth from me for so long? Sugar-daddy in New York, my eye!

No woman since the Queen of Sheba got that sort of payment for lying on her back! So where did they come from? If I'm such a great friend, surely I'm the one who deserves an explanation, and an apology? As for the other little bits and pieces (one measly pair of earrings and a ring, for God's sake!) don't you *ever* imply I am a common thief or I'll have the lawyers on you quick as winking. You may well ask for them back, but now it's my turn for a bit of trust and confidence from someone who has *pretended* to be a friend.

Yours in all sincerity

Mary

Possessions, 1930

* * *

It was like a nightmare. Her limbs felt heavy, her head like a sack on the pillow, pain suspended somewhere, tipping deep into her brain if she tried to move. Mary was standing at the end of the bed – a hospital bed. This was a hospital room. They had given her a funny gas and then something stronger. Complications, they said. But she had had a baby –

'Where is it?'

Noise flooded her ears as if a needle had dropped suddenly upon a record. The clip and rumble of traffic, birdsong, a man crooning drunkenly down the corridor, sharp scent and Mary's voice, harsh and throaty, splintering the fug.

'Have you any idea of the mess we're in? Of course not! Too busy with your own cosy world, "Fancy! Three fine children now, Mrs O'Fiaich, I don't know how you do it", and Frank so stuffed full of his own importance he wouldn't react if a ferret bit him on the backside –'

What was she talking about? Frank attacked? Three children . . . 'Mary?'

Mary plonked herself on the bed, pulling blankets painfully tight, almost hissing into her face. 'Come out from under the sheet, have we? Well, maybe now we can have that conversation you claimed you were so desperate for, about how you tricked me, Rita Fitzgerald, saying those jewels were someone else's. As if anyone in their right minds would give stuff of that value to the likes of you! Oh yes, over and over you lied, didn't you, pretended to be so poor and humble with that priesteen of a husband of yours, when many's the time Dermot and I were struggling, begging, down on our knees for a crust –?'

Mary's ears. The diamond star earrings. Hadn't she returned them?

'Then you have the audacity, the brazen nerve, to write the meanest things to me, leave all classes of telephone messages. I don't know what the maid thought they were about – not that it matters, she's gone anyway like everything else. Then just as our lives are tumbling about our ears, you, Miss Self-righteous Stuck-up Jackeen, take it upon yourself and that poker-arsed man of yours to pull out the rug altogether!'

A door banging open and silence, someone else leaning over the bed, smiling, pulling up the covers.

'Woken this minute, Nurse, and doesn't she look great?'

You'd hardly recognize Mary's voice, thickening swiftly from acid into treacle.

'That's the spirit, Mrs O'Fiaich. Would you like a nice cup of tea?'

'Where's my baby?'

'What's that, dear?'

'Great idea! If she doesn't want it, I'll drink it for her!'

The two of them were laughing like conspirators. She would have to shout to be heard.

'I. Want. My. Baby!'

'Ah no, girl dear, sure isn't she tucked up warm in the nursery. I'll bring her to you at feeding time.'

A daughter . . .

'I want her, I want her here!'

She could feel tears on her cheeks. A daughter to dress, to be an ally, to prepare for this strange male world, to shield from Frank's ridiculous ideas about education. Her own little girl. A miracle.

'Now, now, Mrs O'Fiaich, you're tired and why wouldn't you be? Your husband looked in earlier, but he had a meeting to get to. I said maybe he'd like to take a peek at the child, but sure isn't he very important altogether, a man like that, hasn't he a lot on his mind?'

'My baby!' The voice came out like a wail.

'Rita, will you whisht, you'll have us all scared!'

One of the fingers digging into her wrist wore the twisted diamond rope ring. A copy, though one would never guess.

'Well, I don't know. You break the routine and you've got trouble with the little mites ever after.'

'I'll stay with her.' The harsh, more dangerous note was creeping back into Mary's voice.

'No excitement, now. I only let you in because you said you were travelling.'

'We're old, old friends, aren't we, Rita? I couldn't leave without saying goodbye.' Even as the door closed she was speaking again, her voice husky, stretched, unstoppable, the earrings flashing. Yes, she had returned the originals. 'We haven't much time. I just came to tell you that Dermot and I are off, to London. We're broke, Rita. It turns out we never actually owned the house or the cars or anything.'

Interesting to watch the face, red cupid lips, blonde hair swept up inside a brown velvet beret. A face from *Tatler* or the *Illustrated London News*. Poor Mary, how dreadful . . . But a daughter, here any minute, to have and to hold.

'As for those little things I kept back, can't you get it into your head I have *borrowed* them, that's all!'

Please God, don't let her have sold the ruby ring or the earrings. Holy Mary, mother of God, pray for us sinners. Not the rubies. Blessed is the fruit of thy – Claire, that was a nice name, or Celia? But Frank had insisted on an Irish name, he had told her the one he wanted if it was a girl: Eithne? Mairaid? Siobhan? Nuala, no, pretty but not right. Nora? Or Niamh? Yes, Niamh O'Fiaich, that was it.

'So don't fuss, all right? They're not gone, just used for a little collateral, as Dermot would say, to see us out of the mud. I'm glad you're not angry!'

'There we are! A fine baby girl, the poor creature!'

The bundle was in Rita's arms, tiny, bound up tight.

'Is that the time? I must fly!' Mary was kissing her

cheek. 'It wasn't easy getting out to see you today, what with the packing and those dreadful bailiff people hammering at the door. But I thought I'd better explain. You do understand, don't you, Rita?'

'That's it. We'll give Mammy and baby some peace. Don't try feeding her now, Mrs O'Fiaich, or you'll be dogged for life. I'll get her a nice warm bottle.'

The silence when they had gone was wonderful. Liam had looked like Frank when he was born, nice, with that guarded wish-to-please expression Frank had had when they first met. Baby Eamonn had looked perplexed, worried about the world, as well he might be. This one was a little pixie of a thing, black hair, big brow, a set little mouth, almost sulky that bottom lip, the minute cleft chin. She knew what she was about.

'We're going to be friends, you and I, we're going to have fun.' Why had she whispered that? It surprised her. Wasn't she friends with the boys? Not really, not any more. Frank said the school was making men of them, but it wasn't true. It was turning them into strangers, as if by making them speak and think in another language they could no longer communicate with her. One night in the last holidays Eamonn had whispered, 'I miss you, Mammy. Why do you never write?'

That was when she discovered the priests had held back her letters, judging their use of English and their content too unsettling. Now Frank translated her letters for her, removing any bits of news he thought unsuitable, so that Rita felt like a prisoner in a foreign jail, writing into a void. Had Mary said she was moving to London? That the rubies were all right?

A look of disapproval on the tiny face. She was hungry. 'Sorry, darling, I seem to annoy everyone these days!'

Hadn't she owned a teddy bear once, an old, motheaten one she had taken to school, that time she first met Mary? It had disappeared too.

X

Mama said Mr de Valera was a dictator, but then, she had never understood what he was trying to achieve.

Sunday lunch hadn't changed, even in the little Regency house in Monkstown to which Mama had moved with Christine and the maid. Anne Marie's husband, Declan Hurlihy, sometimes stirred things up, especially when egged on by his maddening little wife.

'Has anyone seen the new play at the Gate?'

Rita could feel Frank stiffen, his mouth small and tight over his soup-spoon.

'Great stuff altogether, great stuff.'

The man wouldn't recognize Shakespeare from Puccini, yet he and Anne Marie seemed to get to every first night. And all he ever had to say about the play, ballet, opera or concert was 'Great stuff!'

'That fella's giving our people a bad image.' Frank was glaring at Declan. 'What class of greatness is it, to portray your own people like that, to blacken the name of Ireland?'

'I suppose he does get a bit of sport with the chancers and jokers, but sure isn't it true enough? And it's great entertainment, a lovely night out.'

Anne Marie laughed. 'I thought you wanted to call this place Eire, Frank?'

'That is one of our objectives, yes. Mr de Valera is planning a lot of changes, but it takes time.'

'He hasn't managed to close a theatre yet!'

Why did Anne Marie always try to bait poor Frank? It was so mean, and she surely knew by now he wouldn't have his mind changed.

'No, the Irish people will do that themselves.'

'Oh, and who are these "Irish people"? Aren't *we* Irish, the people who support the theatre?'

'In a democratic society the will of the majority —'

'Hah!'

Anne Marie was laughing into Frank's face. So rude to him, as always, and in front of the children. Like his father, Eamonn looked as if he wished himself anywhere but here, but Liam was interested.

'What's "democratic", Daddy?'

'Will you listen to the boy, Frank! Your own son, raised in the furnace of revolution, and he doesn't know the meaning of the word! Home truths, Liam, that's what democracy is, letting each man have his opinion and be respected for it, something this country likes to confuse with mob rule!'

It was always like this, the war between Anne Marie and Frank. Her degree in philosophy had only made her more impossible.

'Ah now, Anne Marie, I wouldn't go that far.'

Having started the trouble, Declan always played the peacemaker. So much hot air, yet Rita could never quite see what their arguments were about. Didn't they all have a good enough life? Declan, with the round child's face, as smug as any surgeon making a reputation for himself; Anne Marie, quite the bohemian in printed velvets and feathered hats, with her two perfect children and precious little literary society; Mama shrunken but still as sharp as ever, living comfortably with a view of the sea. They were all so lucky. You heard such horrid stories about Depression in America, and there were poor people all over the city, beggars at the door and able-bodied men playing tin whistles for pennies. She wondered sometimes if she might end up in the poorhouse, now that Mr de Valera had seen fit to cut all ministers' salaries by five hundred pounds.

'I'd love to go to the theatre, Anne Marie. It's difficult for Frank, since he got into government.'

'Is that what he calls it? Well, if your party can agree

anything between the lot of you, industry is what we need, Frank, manufacture, construction, not to mention the sort of world-class culture which goes beyond banshee wailing and hopping.'

The situation was not helped by little Niamh, who behaved as if everything Anne Marie had to say was hysterically funny, rocking and hooting on her high chair; nor by Mama, nodding from the end of the table. Frank looked like he might explode.

'If you want a little England, Anne Marie, why don't you move over there? I for one have no intention of allowing Ireland to turn into an industrial wasteland populated by amoral atheists!'

'Is that what England is? Well, then, have you ever thought what will happen if you turn us into a nation of pig farmers? Your biggest export to that shockingly sinful country will be your own people!'

Declan was delighted by his wife's sharp wit. 'Yes, and you can't pack them off to Catholic countries, can you, because you haven't given them the languages. Spent too much time and money beating in the precious Irish, for all the good it'll do them!'

Frank stared at the table, his big hands gripping hard at his knees, his face still flushed. Why couldn't he argue better? Rita had hoped that all those years with Mr de Valera would have improved his debating skills. Sometimes he reminded her more of a priest than a politician, single-minded, authoritarian, openly hurt and surprised by opposition. A relief when Christine broke the awkwardness.

'Ah, the roast! I thought you had forgotten us, Christine!'

'Indeed, ma'am, I didn't like to interrupt!'

'Frank, will you carve for us? You were always good with a knife.'

Mama still knew how to improve things. In another life Rita could imagine her a Romanov or a Galitzin. Why not? Watching her smile and chat with Frank as if she liked or approved of him, Rita wondered, just for a moment, what they had all done with themselves. Would it be better to live at full stretch, taking your fill of excitement, even if at the end you find yourself locked in a small room facing your assassins? Horrid, horrid thought. And not a word or a sign from Nina in all those years. Well, one must go on. She stared out the window.

'Aren't your camellias marvellous, Mama? Which reminds me, do any of you know if we'll get a production of *La Traviata* this year? Now that's something we could all agree about!'

They were all staring at her. Niamh was giggling again. Frank had twisted round from the sideboard in mid-slice, still upset after Declan's mean gibes. The groan he let out when the carving knife cut deep into his finger, anyone might think him a sacrificial bull at a feast. He was openly rude, too, when Rita tried to help, pushing her off before he slammed out to the bathroom. She had to explain that Frank was always upset by the sight of blood.

A Minister's Wife and Her Family, 1937

* * *

People were continually saying, 'I don't know where the time goes!' and 'Hasn't the year flown?'

Before the spring of 1937 Rita had considered such remarks sad, the stuff of lives rushing out of control. For her, time had felt slow and detailed in childhood, speeding up at boarding school, a mad whirl in the brief time at home before her marriage, then, during the Troubles, vibrant with fear or relief.

Frank's years in opposition, when the boys were small, had a static quality, a waiting for time to begin again, as if she were standing in a queue noticing every stain on the pavement, noting the trimming on a hat, reading and rereading posters on a wall. But in all those years Rita had felt in control of time. The jewels made that possible. They were old, they had seen it all before. With them in the safe she could see a continuum, and wait.

Holding the children, hugging them when they would let her, brought the same certainties. They were good-looking, and healthy enough except for Eamonn's asthma. Yet in family life she had begun to lose the pattern. Her own childhood had been full of people. In Terenure the cook and a raw girl from the country were hardly suitable influences for growing children. Frank did little enough with them, and she found it difficult to amuse them. The boys resented her suggestions of board-games or walks. A relief, really. The sounds of Liam's sheer physical aggression were unsettling, even if it were only a football being kicked against the house, and at fifteen, Eamonn's shyness could be awkward. He was content to stay with her for hours, watching her closely as she darned socks or dead-headed the roses, blushing when she attempted conversation. Recently he had borrowed her embroidery threads and completed a floral border on a pillowcase: surprisingly well done, but hardly a suitable pastime for a boy. Turned out to play, he did not seek other children. When she had looked into the garden yesterday, he was on his knees burying a dead bird and appeared to be praying. After Papa, Frank and those two, she would never understand the male of the species.

But her daughter's peculiarities caused the real pain. She had expected so much of her, looked forward to their friendship, so that at seven years old Niamh's refusal to do anything at all ladylike was most disappointing. A waste of time making new clothes. She would only scream if Rita insisted she wear them, or tear and muddy them in rough games with her friends. Such disappointments made Rita tired. Perhaps that was why she found herself repeating, 'I don't know where the day has gone!'

It was a feeling that somewhere along the line she had lost her grip. And now she had to look up into the faces of her growing boys, Frank had held two ministries, her country had changed and she was no longer part of it.

Mary left such a gap. Like the rubies she had taken, her disappearance from Dublin felt like an open window, a cold draught blowing in and out of Rita's mind. Without her life was dull. Nights out meant official functions and other party wives; the chat about domestic matters and family hardly varied at all. The ladies at those dinners and receptions were not expected to express opinions on the affairs of the day. Indeed, when she read the arguments in the paper about the Spanish Civil War or ideas for the new constitution, it was hard to decide what to think. Frank was not interested in her opinions. Sometimes, just to show a little independence, she refused to accompany him to a do. He only shrugged his shoulders and went alone.

Once, when consulting her doctor about headaches, she confessed that she felt unreal, as if she were living in a sort of limbo.

'Maybe it's a priest you need, Mrs O'Fiaich. Though I know many a woman proud to be in your shoes. They say that husband of yours is the coming man!'

It was an unnerving feeling, all the same, a sense that she wasn't quite there, she didn't matter. Frank spent more time talking to the cook. He seemed impatient with her, affectionate only after he had had a few drinks, and angry when reminded that she was not strong enough for more children.

Her own fault, she supposed, this breakdown in communications. After Niamh was born, she couldn't face going through all that again. There were things you could do to prevent conception, she knew, but she never dared suggest them. He had been bad enough about her failing in her Catholic duty, which, she gathered from his embarrassed mumblings, was to offer yourself up to your husband and welcome whatever God sent. Repeating Papa's theory about the dangers of having one child after another never helped. Frank reacted as though such talk might be overheard by the spies behind the fading wallpaper.

They had never talked about such matters, not fully. As far as Rita knew, nobody did. A priest in the confessional had asked about her family. 'Only three, is it? And do you and your husband still share a full married life?'

'As a matter of fact, we don't go out much, Father. Do you think it helps a marriage if you go out and enjoy yourselves together, from time to time?'

The way he was shifting about in the box it was clear the answer was not what was wanted. After a space he said, 'Drink can have terrible effects on family life.'

Only later, bathing Niamh, did it strike her what he had wanted to know. She let out such a hoot of laughter the child nearly jumped out of her skin.

She never told Frank. He disagreed with her view that they lived too close with the Church; he didn't appear to mind its increasing influence on Irish politics either. Another minister's wife had told her about the Chief's plan to give the Catholic Church a special position in the Irish constitution. He had stuck to his point and the bishops had gone to Rome for advice. When she asked Frank about it, he said such matters were none of her business. After that, when a rather hysterical young woman telephoned to demand she put in a word against clauses on women and their primary place in the home, Rita firmly told her that she preferred to leave such decisions to her husband. Amusing to look back and remember the ideas she had had about their partnership. She knew better now. Politics were for men. You only had to look around the world, listen to the talk of war.

Over the years she had observed her priest from the confessional. Watching him make a sort of royal progress along the pavement, she thought what a tyranny they had, knowing things about everyone, especially the women, the most intimate details of their lives. She understood now why Mama would never go locally to confession.

Yet Frank could see none of this. He carried the Church in his head, as if God, like some vengeful mother, were watching his every move, ready to swipe him with a wooden spoon if he put a foot wrong.

Judging by the way he talked to her these days, she wondered if he did, in fact, see her as a mother, a sort of plaster saint, without wishes or expectations or tastes of her own. Recently, after failing to buy the latest Sean O'Faolain short stories which had been so well reviewed, she tried to ask him about the Censorship Act, gently suggesting that his government might be treating its citizens like children. 'I mean, after all that's happened, don't you think the Irish can tell the difference for themselves between right and wrong?'

'What does it matter to you? Where in God's name would you find the time for reading books or going out to gaudy picture shows?'

She couldn't help thinking of his late mother, her drab life in Clare, ground into the mud by an endless round of poor farming and a husband who came and went to England for the work and the drink.

Niamh was a bad sleeper. The broken nights made Rita feel tired and disappointed. This was not the daughter she had imagined, so big and square for her age, awkward and strangely uncoordinated. She took her colour from the boys, always the first one up a tree or highest on the swing. Rita despaired of her ballet. Miss Griffin had a way of announcing, in her pretend French accent, to the tittering mothers, 'Even *I* cannot make a silk purse out of Niamh O'Fiaich!' The silly woman never could comprehend the trouble she was storing up for herself at next week's lesson.

The boys had been in the Irish college too long. Frank had refused to move them until the incident with the rat. They should have made some protest about that; it was a disgrace to have children sleeping in a room where a rat could climb on to a bed and bite your child's ear. Frank had ordered her to keep silent, claiming the Irish-speaking boarding schools were Dev's pet project and this trouble was only part of breaking them in. The move to the day school of Frank's choice was not much better. The priests who ran it seemed more interested in sport than learning. Mama said such places produced savages. She was upset, of course, by what the good fathers had done to the big house and grounds in Templeogue. A pity to see the lake drained and gardens gone to grass, Lord and Lady Dodd's gracious rooms partitioned into classrooms. Frank said it was progress, a symbol of the Irish retrieving what was theirs. Mrs O'Reilly went further, claiming if she had her way, she would raze every great house in Ireland to the ground. 'Aren't they only a reminder of the way the English had us all slaves?'

Watching her husband nod delightedly at such sentiments made Rita feel more out of touch than ever. Only the jewels remained hard and certain. She found her mind dwelling on them more and more. With Mr de Valera setting the style she did not flaunt them in public. Sometimes, though, she concealed an extra necklace beneath a high neck or bracelets underneath long sleeves. The din-

263

ners and receptions must have appeared dowdy in comparison with life in St Petersburg, but she felt sure they appreciated a night out. Judging by what the papers wrote of the Russian economy, Mr Stalin was in no position to ask for them back.

She still felt guilty. She had let down the jewels appallingly: betrayed them by showing them to Mary, lost some, and now left them locked up too long in that dark safe with only the crude smells of Mrs O'Reilly's cooking to keep them in touch with life.

Once, when Rita screwed up her courage to ask Frank when he might see the Russians again, he had looked blank for a moment.

'That shower! If we didn't have our hands tied with O'Duffy trying to help General Franco, I'd be tempted to go to Moscow myself to sort them out!'

The way he hid behind his newspaper again it was clear he did not like reminders of his deal with the anti-Christ. Yet it was impossible to imagine Nina, Sergei or Piotr in that evil light, no matter what was said of the persecution of their Church. She struggled with Russian novels from the library, trying to imagine life there, life for Nina. The stories did not illustrate the place Nina had described. Their country sounded carefree and rather beautiful, like Dublin in Mama's time, filled with pleasure.

A Letter from Mary, 10 March 1937

* * *

47 Montague Mansions
London W1

Dearest Rita

Long time no see! Sorry I never replied to all those letters and Christmas cards (which did find us via the Irish Club, clever girl!), but things have been a bit sticky in the last few years, and at times downright awful.

You are the only person in the world I could confess this to, my sweet, but there have been times when I thought I'd be better off out of it. Now, you're shocked, still with the keeper of Sacred Ireland, but I no longer believe life is such a great gift nor marriage a holy and unbreakable sacrament. Only priests (or spoiled ones) could say that.

Well, as you can gather, yours truly has turned rather outspoken living here. I've also become quite independent, with a little job in an accountancy firm in Holborn. I thank God that the nuns gave us a bit of an education in between the prayers – enough, anyway, to keep body and soul alive. It's quite a nice office. I have a desk and a telephone and I greet clients, make tea, file, that sort of thing. I'm not exactly Joan Crawford, but Mr Peters, my boss, says there's more to the daily grind than filing cards. He has been very kind to me, taking me about and introducing me to all sorts of interesting people, which is just as well as I could go mad in our little flat the way Dermot is away so much. He's doing all right with the import–export now, though he's so full of talk sometimes I don't know if it's the truth or a big front. Any bit of spare time he's off after that fella, Mosley, thinks they're still the coming lot. I ask him how he can trust anyone who's been in the Labour Party. Aren't

265

they the next worst things to the communists, and we all know how those Russians treat Catholics? Dermot just laughs. He has become rather hard.

How are you and yours? As you've probably guessed, we have not been blessed in that department. I had one scare, but it wasn't the right time anyway, and the doctor said there wasn't much chance of another. Just as well, in the circs. Your girl must be around six or seven by now? Such a tiny scrap of a thing that day in hospital. I suppose the boys are great sportsmen? I hear the Gaelic games are all the rage over there, but then if Frank and his pals had their way, they'd have rugby balls shot against walls. Where does Frank stand on hockey and lacrosse – or is it only English games he disapproves of? Tell him from me he can ban those two and save a lot of poor schoolgirls hours of agony. Will you ever forget those Wednesday afternoons, Rita? Do you think Miss McKetterick was the full shilling? There are women like her here who dress in men's clothes and get up to all sorts of funny tricks. I'd better not say what they are in case Dev has the customs men opening our letters. And you were always easily shocked.

As for the other thing you harp on about, as I said in the hospital, trust me. It is under control. With business the way it is at the moment you can hardly expect me to have the cash to recover them right now. But they're perfectly safe and they have been very helpful. Dermot is eternally grateful, though he, like me, can't understand how you could have such things and live like you do. And don't tell me that one again about 'a friend' in New York or I'll split myself!

Still, it can only get better. And, as my Mr Peters says, you have to laugh. At the end of the day, what would life be like without a few laughs and a secret or two? Though I am still a teeny bit angry with you, Rita Fitzgerald, you have a lot of explaining to do.

Do please write again with all the news. I miss yourself and the old sod. We only get the *Press* or the *Irish Times* occasionally and see Frank is doing all right for himself. He appears to have kept in Dev's good books anyway, which isn't the case with everyone, as Dermot knows to his cost. Times are difficult for us all, but it must be nice having a few diamonds in the bank. When I think of all the stuff the nuns told us about honesty and diligence . . . Nothing personal!

All love

Mary

Redecorating, 1938

* * *

St Patrick's Day felt like the coldest day of the year. Frank was away in America, so it was a great relief to be spared attendance at the dreary parade up Sackville Street (she could never bring herself to call it O'Connell Street), relieved from duty outside the GPO, legs frozen from under you and Niamh complaining she couldn't see.

The children didn't miss it, disappearing after breakfast to celebrate the day off school with their friends. Rita wondered sometimes how she had failed them. Perhaps she should have chosen their companions for them, been more careful about their playmates amongst the neighbouring offspring of bank clerks, teachers and small businessmen. To think of the hopes she had once had for a truly Irish society. Frank himself used to hark back to the Island of Saints and Scholars, but nowadays he seemed keener on the priests than the intellectuals. Where were the creative Irish, the musicians, writers and artists whom she had imagined as neighbours and friends? Compared with Mama and Papa's time there were fewer such people about, not more. If she had selected suitable playmates for Niamh, where would she have found them? Terenure might as well be a million miles from Rathgar, let alone Donnybrook or the Georgian squares in town. And, she found herself guiltily thinking, who were the good families now? The people Mama knew had become ghosts, their houses burnt, abandoned or turned into institutions, reduced to half-remembered names which flitted across the letters pages of the *Irish Times* from addresses in Greystones or West Cork.

Rather a pity how, in imposing the new order, so much

of the old had been swept away. She had said as much to Frank once and got a long lecture about 'Progress'.

'But I'm talking about people, Frank, a whole way of life. Why couldn't we have a new Ireland with them there too?'

'They didn't fit, woman, can't you see that? Listen, if a shoe pinched, wouldn't you throw it away?'

She had laughed, which she realized afterwards was a mistake. For the first time in ages he had been trying to convince her of something, to win her round. 'No, I would not, I'd have them stretched. And I'm surprised at you advising such wastefulness!'

He had not returned her smile. His face was strangely sad when he finally muttered, 'Ah, forget it,' and retreated behind his newspaper. For all his talk he was not very progressive. The house was still lit by gas, though most of the road had installed electricity. He said he saw no need for it.

On St Patrick's Day afternoon Mama called with some cuttings. She was in one of her picky moods, critical of Rita's gardening tools, the colour of the back door, even Rita's second-best skirt, which she informed her looked ready for the rag and bone man. Over tea in the sitting-room she had looked up at *The Assumption*.

'Isn't it time you got rid of that?'

'I hardly notice it. Mr de Valera always comments favourably on it, the odd time he visits.'

'That's what's wrong with Frank's party. Such piety makes the priests too sure of them!'

Rita pretended to disagree, but Mama was right. Once she had called her attention to the picture, it could no longer be ignored. As Frank had said, progress was about letting go, a clean sweep. She had seen the improvements in Number Twelve recently and there, hanging over a fireplace in Terenure, was a real oil painting. Rather a mess, she thought, too modern by half, but real oil on canvas, and done by the brother of Mr Yeats.

Anyway, after Mama had gone home, Frank's picture

began to depress her. Instead of enjoying the peace, she thought how shabby it had all got: not just the picture, but the room, the whole house, displaying eighteen years of neglect. His mother had been dead some years, yet even her pink glass bowl, which the Black and Tans had done their best to destroy, remained stolidly on the mantelpiece, undaunted by the cracks of that horrible day.

What if she were showing similar signs of wear? In the mirror her face looked young enough, though the hair needed colour in the grey and the clothes could have done with a major overhaul. She would cut out bread and potatoes again, no matter what Mrs O'Reilly had to say.

As for the rest, there was really no point in asking Frank for money to spend on the house or herself. It was hard enough to get shoes for the children. He seemed to think Ireland's dismal economy should be reflected in his own lifestyle, even though, as far as Rita knew, he earned a reasonable income. She suspected he spent the excess on savings bonds or something, some sort of patriotic gesture.

By the next Sunday her mind was made up. It was quite a struggle, even with the help of her cook, much heavier than they expected, and then the bolt in the wall fell out, killing two birds with one stone by smashing the pink bowl to smithereens.

What with the fallen plaster, the picture couldn't be put back even if she had wanted it there. It left a dark patch on the wallpaper too, which meant redecoration and goodness knew what that would cost. Like so much else, it would probably have to be subsidized by her own little nest-egg. Perhaps that was why Rita felt upset that day, in need of cheering up. She went to the kitchen while Mrs O'Reilly was out and removed some items from the safe.

On the bed upstairs she tried to remember what Nina had done; where she had put her hands and her mouth. It was surprisingly pleasant, thinking about Nina, feeling the jewels on her skin, touching herself. She had a sudden image of Sister Joseph's shocked face and laughed out loud. Had the nuns been mistaken in their belief that it was a sin to even think of one's body? There had been no reference to such practices in the Catechism that Rita could recollect, but then, she might not have seen them. Religious knowledge was like Irish, full of words she could not translate and answers she had never understood. Once Rita asked Sister Pauline to explain the word 'covet' in the Commandments and she had been sent to the chapel to pray.

It had grown dark outside. She could hear Niamh crashing in the side gate, arguing with Eamonn in the kitchen. They would find the desecration in the sitting-room soon and be upstairs, demanding to know what had happened. Funny to think how they would react: Liam probably offering to climb up there and knock out the rest of the plaster; Eamonn shaken by her rejection of the sacred image; Niamh delighted by the mess. Rita gathered the jewels into a rough pile and pressed them to her breasts. She was surprised when she saw tears drip on to her hands.

'I'm sorry, darlings. I know I can't possibly feel lonely. I love my children, and haven't I got you?'

Restitution, 1939

* * *

'Nine years! Can you believe it's been so long! Oh, sweetie, I have so much to tell you, and you'll not believe the half of it!'

Mary never did tell the full story of her time in London. Sometimes Rita felt her on the edge of it, but then she would look hard at her friend, like a parent wondering if a child is old enough to be told the facts of life. She always seemed to decide to leave the subject for later.

Her laughter had grown huskier, more modulated. Her accent had altered subtly again, as if she were speaking English with just a tiny difficulty, so that each word came out polished, poised, plopped into its proper place. Everything about her was finer, brighter, the effect as groomed and glossy as a racehorse in the paddock when the rug comes off.

'I suppose you have a few stories to tell me too?' Her wink over the teacup was demonic.

Rita felt very dull, especially beside Mary's crisp navy coat dress with the huge white piqué collar.

'How's Dermot?'

'Don't talk to me about that man!'

'But I thought everything was all right now – he was doing well?'

When could she bring up the question of the missing jewels? No sign of them on Mary. Her huge diamanté panther brooch was not at all the sort of thing one would expect to see in a royal collection.

'No worries on that score! But he has a great scheme for Ireland, says it'll have us all on the pig's back!'

'You're well out of London, with the war.'

'You're joking, sweetie! Even if Hitler bombed us, there'd be plenty of compensations!'

There was that familiar sinking feeling again, forgotten for so many years. Everything her friend said carried some hidden meaning which, for the life of her, Rita could not grasp. She was glad when Liam walked in.

'I don't believe it! Why didn't you tell me, Rita, he's gorgeous!'

'Hello, Mrs Quinn.' Liam was surprisingly polite, allowing Mary to wrap her arms around him like that and squeeze him quite excessively.

'He's so young, so fresh! I had no idea he was grown up!'

'I'm nearly nineteen, Mrs Quinn.'

'Never! So, what are you doing with yourself? The army?'

'No, I'm at National, for the law.'

'What, no fighting at all?'

'No, Daddy's against it. I wouldn't fight for the English anyway.'

'You wouldn't want to help Mr Hitler, though?'

Mary had meant it as a joke, but Liam was considering the question rather seriously. 'I don't know.'

Niamh had shouldered into the sitting-room. 'Mrs O'Reilly wants to know if your friend is staying for dinner.' Her tartan skirt was ripped and her white socks bunched around her ankles. Rita itched to spit on a hanky as Mama used to, to rub away the grime from her daughter's rosy cheeks.

Mary laughed. She appeared to find the sight of this daughter even more amusing than the son. 'Goodness, Rita, who'd ever have thought! Where's Eamonn, now, and we'll complete the happy families?'

'He's going to be a priest, the silly eejit!'

Sometimes Rita wondered about Niamh. When she thought of the efforts she had made over the years to suppress her own growing anti-clericalism, it was enough to make you despair of motherhood.

273

'Oh yes, you did mention something in a letter. But a priest! Poor you, sweetie, a spy in court! Don't let him ask too many nosy questions in this family, Liam, or your mother will get nervous. She'll be needing you to defend her!'

Impossible as ever. To think how she had longed for Mary to return and here she was, hardly in the door, hinting at all sorts of secrets to the son of the house. What would Mary know of losing a child to the seminary? Why couldn't she simply congratulate Rita, pretend like everyone else that it was a wonderful thing to give up your son to God?

'Will you look at your mother, children! My oldest friend and still can't tell when I'm joking!'

Niamh glared at Mary, thrusting out her lower lip, squaring up to her like a miniature boxer. 'My mammy doesn't need a friend like you!'

Mary laughed, waving aside Rita's apologies for such bad manners. 'With that kind of charm there's no need to ask who your father is!'

When Frank walked in, slamming the door as usual, Mary rushed to greet him. 'Ah, the great man!' She managed to kiss his cheek before he spun away. 'Living off the fat of the land, by the look of you! What are you giving the males in your family, Rita, monkey glands?'

'Well now, is Dermot with you?'

'He's around, Frank. We're back, settled our affairs in London, and now it's Dublin here we come!'

'Rita will be pleased anyway.'

'Is that all? Dermot's dying to see you, asked me to test the ground.'

'Why? What's he doing now?'

'Don't ask! Doesn't he always have a plan?'

'Would I be right in thinking he had a run in with Mosley's lot?'

'Don't mention those gurriers to Dermot! He's still owed for stuff.'

Frank gave Mary a long look, which obviously pleased

her. She threw herself back into an armchair, beige legs stretching into high, clumpy shoes.

'Anyhow, it's heaven to be back. You're both looking great, and this room, Rita, I love the plain colour. So fashionable!'

Mary was standing up. The shoes must have cost a fortune, and a dress like that wouldn't come cheap. Liam and Frank watched her with bemused fascination. She had become extraordinary, a free spirit rarely seen in this country off a cinema screen. Even there, she would probably have been severely cut.

'Must fly! Mind if I come and watch you perform, Frank?'

'What?'

'In the Dáil. I'd like to hear you debate. You do open your mouth there sometimes, don't you? Oh, and we've got a spare ticket for Saturday night, Rita. I'll pick you up at seven.'

It wasn't until Rita was alone with her on the front step that there was a chance to whisper, 'Listen, Mary, I have to ask you, what about those jewels?'

There was something triumphant in Mary's eyes, something of the schoolgirl tease. 'Don't tell me you were worried?' She pressed a little velvet bag into Rita's hand and was gone, clicking out the gate and into her car. Rita didn't wave. She was up the stairs and into the bedroom with the door locked, spilling out the ruby earrings and yes, the ruby ring. Thanks be to God. There they were: the huge uncut ring stone framed with diamonds and topped by a pearl; two teardrop rubies with their pearly points each suspended from a diamond earpiece. A great weight had been lifted, the same joy she had felt when Mary first picked her for a friend, when Rita won the Sixth Form tennis tournament, when she walked down the aisle with Frank or gave birth to her beautiful babies. But this love, this elation, could not be spoiled. She had not failed them after all.

A Diplomatic Reception, 1942

* * *

'You look terrible! Are you all right?'

All very well for Mary to act the Lady Muck. Her long silver sheath probably cost ten men's wages, and you could be sure that herself and Dermot had not got here by tram. Sometimes Frank took the government's austerity measures too far.

Niamh was just as extreme. Where a twelve-year-old girl got her ideas was a mystery, but it was not nice having your child scream 'Fascist!' at you as you tried to get out the door to a party. Things weren't helped by Frank's parting shot. 'I have a sight more understanding of the situation than you, you little spalpeen!'

They had curtains twitching up and down the road.

'Hypocrite! Liar!'

Niamh's rather square body had positively shaken with passion. The shorter hemline did not flatter the girl's legs, which Rita knew came from her own side of the family. Still, it was several years since her daughter had accepted any guidance on making the best of herself.

Then, after all the trouble Rita had gone to for this party at the German Embassy, here was Mary implying that she simply wasn't up to the mark.

'Time for an overhaul, sweetie! Come over tomorrow and I'll show you the sort of thing I mean.'

It had been an inauspicious evening. At dinner Dermot and Herr Hempel had been talking across her about the Russian front. It had taken some time to grasp what was being said. The Ambassador appeared apologetic. 'To be truthful, Mr Quinn, I think my government plans to starve the whole nation to death.'

'We can expect some vodka shortages, so!'

The German did not laugh. Rita asked, 'Surely cities like Moscow or Leningrad have food?'

'No longer, Mrs O'Fiaich. Many, many are dying.'

Nina. Was she hungry? That soft, springy body like a warm cottage loaf, strawberry nipples, legs knotted and white as winter celery. She had laughed at Rita's modesty. 'Is good, is good!'

How sure she had been, sucking out Rita's cringing inhibitions, drawing her further and further with one more taste from the bizarre bags of food and drink which she carried to the hotel rooms of their furtive meetings, closing Rita's eyes and mind with a kaleidoscope of sensations, textures and the jewels. How awful that Nina, of all people, should suffer. Hunger could destroy the spirit. Rita had seen for herself what it did to the chickens on the farm up the road in Rosbeigh, when Mrs O'Sullivan locked them in a box to starve for a day before the kill. Rita had arrived early once to collect the glossy broiler she had picked out the day before. Their eyes met again when the deflated creature was plucked from the box, its neck wrung in the damp sunlight of the yard. She had been tempted to write to Mr Bernard Shaw for some vegetarian recipes, but thoughts of Mrs O'Reilly made her lose heart.

Niamh was right. They should not be breaking bread with these people. Mrs O'Reilly had hinted as much this morning, stopping Frank in the hall to inquire, 'Has Dev had a conversion or what?'

'No chance of that, Mrs O'Reilly, I can assure you!'

'Can youse assure me about cavorting with them Jerries, so? They're no better than the Blue Shirts – some say worse!'

Frank had mumbled about friends of small nations and keeping the English guessing, but Mrs O'Reilly stuck to her guns. When she told Frank she was disappointed in him, he stamped out of the house, slamming the door, after which the cook went downstairs to her store of cracked delft and smashed it, piece by piece, against the high wall outside the kitchen window.

On the way home Rita asked Frank what Herr Hempel had meant.

'Don't you read the newspaper, woman?'

'Someone said they thought the Pope would intervene. About what?'

He looked gloomy. For a moment she felt sorry for him, for the rounded, balding man he had become almost without her noticing.

'It wasn't only the Russians Niamh was shouting about, was it?'

Frank sighed. 'It appears that Herr Hitler has been getting rid of Jews and some others: gypsies, communists and the like. Rounding them up. There's word he plans to kill them.'

She thought of the Jewish family called Crow who ran the delicatessen in Terenure, the only place you could get a decent bit of French cheese for miles. Their corned beef was good too, and their eldest girl was only the same age as Niamh. 'The men, you mean, they're sending away the men?'

'Whole families. Naturally, Herr Hempel is upset by it all. The fella's no Nazi, just got stuck here by the war.'

'Then maybe they're right, Niamh and Mrs O'Reilly? Maybe we shouldn't be accepting his hospitality no matter how different he is? Goodness knows, there are enough young Irishmen fighting on the British side.'

'We're doing our best. Didn't Dev tell the Minister in February to close down their radio transmitter?'

'And did he obey?'

Frank tore at his bow-tie as if it were an enemy of the people. 'Do you know what's not right, woman dear? The way people round here − the women even − think they can open their mouths and tell elected representatives how to behave!'

'I'm sorry, it just seems wrong. I'm surprised the priests don't say as much to Dev.'

'Arrah, what the layman never understands is that politics aren't all about right and wrong. They're about long-term strategies, Rita, and as I'm sick of reminding everyone these days, we've been at war with England for over three hundred years. We'll be fighting them long after this German war is dead and buried!'

'All the same, I'm not going there again.'

'That's up to yourself.'

Later she dreamed of Nina. A vision of her being pulled out of Crow's little shop by soldiers and beaten into a truck kept her awake for the remainder of the night.

Making a Contribution

* * *

She wondered was she still dreaming when she called on Mary the next afternoon. The whole elegant downstairs appeared to be covered in butter and biscuit tins.

'Goodness! It's like the Monument Creamery after an earthquake!'

'Oh God, Rita, I forgot all about you!'

'What on earth are you doing?'

'It's too disgusting. Dermot has this rush order for London and it has to be got on the boat tonight.'

As she whacked the butter into the tins, Mary didn't seem to notice it splatter on to the rosewood dining-table, nor the smears on the silver or stains on the huge Chinese carpet. Her maid was distraught, a black and white rabbit circling about them with cloths and dusters.

'If you've finished yours, Dorothy, would you ever make us a cup of tea?'

'Don't stop on my account!'

'You needn't think I help Dermot like this every day! It was an emergency. I've been out half the morning buying Mariettas and butter. The grocers round here must think I'm half cracked!' She slipped a square of greaseproof paper over the packed butter, fitted the lid and sealed it with tape. 'Thank God that's the last one done! Honestly, Rita, the sooner this war is over the gladder I'll be.'

'But why does he have to send butter in biscuit tins?'

'Under-the-table stuff, you eejit! I suppose that famous husband of yours would try and have it stopped like everything else? Well, Dermot says it makes a lot of people happy – including us – and what's wrong with that?'

'But isn't it illegal?'

'Isn't everything? Sure if this government had its way, there'd be a law against farting!'

'What else does he send to London?'

'Not the white slave trade, if that's what you're thinking – no call in wartime, apparently. Simply supplying what people can't get over there: food and drink mostly.'

Frank would go mad if he ever found out. It would be enough ammunition to try to stop her seeing Mary, and then what kind of life would she have? But he did things of which she could not approve. How often she had wished she could dictate for him the friends he saw. And, to be fair, her behaviour with the jewels might not be viewed as completely straight. If only Nina were here, laughing as she used to at Frank and Mr de Valera's agonized arguments, 'Ach, please, you stop this "I think", "I believe", stupid mans, and *feel!*'

'Oh dear, Mary, we make a right pair!'

'Partners in crime, Rita!'

Mary's arm was a nice, comradely feeling, worth risking a butter stain on the shoulder of the grey crêpe jacket.

A Letter from Mama, 1944

* * *

14 Fitzherbert Road
Monkstown
Co. Dublin

Dear Rita

Aren't these shortages dull? I said to Christine this morning I would give my eye-teeth for a freshly squeezed orange and she pointed out that nobody would pay good fruit for a set of second-hand dentures! I suppose you'd hardly notice any difference, the plain way you two live! Don't you dare reply with Frank's promises of jam tomorrow. As far as I can see, our city has become drab and dirty over the years, and not because of the war.

When will it ever end? I have told your husband often enough, Mr de Valera's high line on neutrality is another stupid mistake. An Irish fighting force would have pushed those Germans back in no time, brought employment too. Though Heaven knows, I'm thankful to be spared the bombs. The one they dropped on the docks was quite unpleasant. Did you see Mrs Traynor's boy, Peter, was killed in action? That's another letter of sympathy I must write – I've become rather good at them.

However, I'm getting wiser in my old age and know to steer well clear of certain subjects. I had a visit from young Dr Kennedy yesterday, mouthing the sort of sentiments Frank might approve (does Mr de Valera issue nationalist scripts?). Anyway, I said I got the impression that Anglophobia was now endemic in Ireland and, do you know, I don't think the fellow had the slightest idea what I was talking about! The baffled look on his face, Rita! I felt quite well after he had gone.

Such a sad note in the post from Philippa Gore. She gave up the garden shows after the two boys were killed, and we had rather lost touch. Apparently they're selling up and moving to Rhodesia of all places as soon as travel becomes possible. Such a loss. She won't find it quite so easy to create herbaceous borders in Africa, though at least labour is cheap. Their lovely house is going to be a nursing home. The nuns again, so we can wave goodbye to the gardens. Asked me over next week to take cuttings.

Lovely visit from Neive (will I ever spell this right? And is that the only skirt and cardigan the child possesses?) She told me her father is warming up for another election. I suppose he's never home, but you're used to that. I'm sure he has nothing to worry about; that ridiculous children's allowance has made Dev very popular, especially with the breeding classes. Did you see that Declan got a promotion? He seems highly thought of with a knife, but, *entre nous*, he's no great shakes on other medical matters. He will express no opinion on my aches, and when I asked him for a little diet for Neave(?), he came back to me with a list of nothing but fresh fruit and prime steak. In wartime!

Your Mama

Political Ideals, 1945

* * *

Frank was in an odd mood. He should have been pleased that Mr O'Kelly had finally won the presidential election, he worked hard enough for it. But she could tell by the decisive slam of the front door and the way he stamped straight into the sitting-room that there was trouble brewing.

'Success at last, Frank? I hope they got the count right this time!'

Best to pour balm on his moods, though she sometimes suspected that she only made things worse. And he'd never think to ask now how her day had been, or about her increasing success with flower arrangements in local horticultural shows. Amazing how long he could sulk over things which happened quite outside her realm, his silences implying that her last tattered wish for a happy home was letting the side down. Mrs O'Reilly was the same. The last few days, while the presidency hung in the balance, the woman might as well have worn sackcloth and ashes; worse, she appeared to expect her mistress to whip herself about the house like poor Matt Talbot. The stuffed lambs' hearts last night had been as tough as saddle leather.

'What do you know about Dermot Quinn?'

'I suppose he's a bit of a rogue, but he's always been very good to Mary – and kind to me.'

'Would you agree the man's a crook?' She was still thinking of a reply when he blurted, 'He's got the lads to put him up for Roscommon South. Do you remember Brady died? It's a safe seat.'

'Dermot? Going for the Dáil? I thought he was a businessman.'

'There's business in politics these days. He's not the only one who thinks so.'

'Fancy Mary standing outside church on Sundays kissing babies!'

'I tried to talk Dev out of it but it's the old story, his mind is made up. What with the Sweepstake and other schemes he had a hand in, Quinn's been putting quite a fair bit of money our way.'

'They're well off, all right. But what harm can he do?' When she thought of some of Frank's colleagues, awkward country types with few words, their horizons extending no further than the boundaries of their own tiny parishes, Dermot Quinn sounded like quite a good thing. At least he was articulate, almost cultured by today's standards, unless he took a drink too many.

'He'll not leave it at that. You watch, in no time he'll be strutting around with a portfolio under his oxter, making fools of us! An ex-pal of O'Duffy and Mosley!'

'Oh, I think he realizes that was a mistake.'

'The Chief says the voters have short memories. Well, I don't. So if you know anything about how that bastard made his money, I would be delighted to hear it!'

'And try to spoil his chances? Why?'

'I didn't fight for all these years to line the nests of fellas like Dermot Quinn! Where was he when there was a price on my head? I'll tell you where: sitting on his fat arse dreaming up schemes for fleecing the country. The Chief doesn't understand that, Rita, what those years on the run meant to me. And I might as well say it now: Dev wasn't so smart at that sort of thing himself, better behind a desk. But I was out there cleaning up, risking my neck, and for what? So that the country could be taken over by that class of jackeen?'

'Oh dear, let's not remind ourselves of those days!'

'Isn't it the God's truth? Don't you know what had to be done?'

He was trying to upset her. He did that sometimes, turning on her, claiming he was trying to tell her what he called 'home truths'.

'Well, it was a long time ago, over twenty years.'

'And you think I should give up the struggle, hand over to the likes of Mr D. Quinn?'

'Of course not. There's room for you both.'

'The Chief said I was tired, needed a rest. He won't make me Tanaiste, he told me that.'

'I had no idea you were in the running!' Hard to keep the surprise out of her voice. She would never dare say it to Frank, of course, but she had often thought he had not had his due for all the hard work and loyalty.

'That goes to young know-it-all, Lemass.'

And yet he was smiling suddenly, with that eager look she hadn't seen on him for years, not since blood, back-stabbings and boredom had beaten it back inside himself.

'I suppose he *is* Dev's sidekick.'

'I had a great long chat with the Chief, like in the old days. He said I was the same as himself, one of the old school, a bit out of touch maybe, with what he calls "the new reality". He said I should get out of politics in a few years.'

'Retire? But that would be awful! It's all you know.'

'Will you whisht, woman, and listen to this! He said he had me in mind for Seán T.'s job, when he retires, or, God forgive me, dies in the post. So, woman, how would you like to be the wife of the President of Ireland, living in that fine house in the Phoenix Park?'

An end to this threadbare existence. Frank and she could move on and up after all. It was better than she had ever dared imagine. She had always admired that house, the great Georgian mansion with views of deer park and woodland. Back in the old days when it was the viceregal lodge, Mama and Papa were often there, and she had vague memories of a huge ballroom and wonderful stucco ceiling, of herself at some children's party in her princess dress with the seed-pearls on the bodice. What a pity Papa had not survived to see her there again, understood at last how right she had been in her choice of husband.

'Oh, Frank! That would be divine!'

Wife of the President of Ireland. She would show Mary and her loud friends how things should be done. To fill those fine rooms with creative people, world scientists, statesmen and yes, why not, even royalty? She would make that great house sparkle as it had done in the old days, banish memories of the cottage parlour entertainments of recent incumbents. Best of all, she could bring the jewels there, to a setting they truly deserved. They, like herself, had been waiting a very long time.

XI

The Irish Times, *17 October 1949*

*   *   *

Fitzgerald, May Alexandra, *née* de Burgh, peacefully in Our Lady's Hospice, Mount Merrion, on 16 October 1949. Sadly missed by daughters Margarita and Anne Marie and their families. High mass at St Dominic's Church, Stillorgan, on 19 October at noon. No flowers please, donations to the Royal Horticultural Society.

A Will and Testament

* * *

How like Mama to have missed the point completely. She had never understood her elder daughter. What about that awful year someone told Mama she could make Rita's hair thicker by shaving it off? Rita was six by the time it grew back as thin as ever, when the same adviser told Mama it had been cut in the wrong direction. Papa intervened then, but Mama always blamed Rita's obstinacy for the condition of her hair. She had never apologized.

Old Harold Montgomery read the will. He had come out of retirement to do so, 'out of respect', he said. Rita thought he had other reasons. She suspected he enjoyed his profession as a sort of spectator sport. At dinner parties in the old days that was how he had spoken of it.

After a small bequest to the ancient Christine there wasn't much left to share between Rita and Anne Marie; the war seemed to have done a lot of damage to Papa's portfolio, and the pound almost cut in half recently had reduced it to even less. The little house would be worth something, though, if anyone wanted a damp Regency cottage these days.

'To my eldest daughter, Margarita, I bequeath my collection of ballgowns, fans, shawls and evening bags. There may be no opportunity left in this country to employ such items, but I am unable to resist blaming Margarita and her husband, Frank, for this being so. However, I recall it was she who appreciated these things, and perhaps they will remind her of the world she helped destroy.'

Anne Marie hooted. 'Trust Mama! Still wanting the last word, even in death!'

Mr Montgomery frowned, although it was clear he was enjoying himself. Thank goodness Frank was absent.

'To my daughter, Anne Marie, I bequeath all my jewellery . . .'

Anne Marie? All? The Victorian cross, the gold locket, the dress tiara, the diamond engagement rings, Great-grandmama's bangles and ormolu egg, the de Burgh gold seal . . .? It was so unfair!

The solicitor paused. 'I'm afraid there is another little aside here, which your late mother insisted be included. I did suggest an accompanying letter to the party involved, but . . .' He coughed and allowed a small silence to fall before continuing. 'When making this division, I am aware that my eldest daughter, Margarita, might feel disappointed by the absence of any family jewellery. However, I have made this decision to ensure that these pieces, most precious for their sentimental value, should remain within the family and be passed on to future generations. And Rita knows I disapprove of her chosen path. Over many years she has lectured her Papa and me about what she calls "the Irish way of life" and has made it quite clear to me that precious jewellery plays no part in such a life. Indeed, having seen the depressed state of the country and its citizens, I fear only burglary or barter would result if my family treasures were to fall into her possession.'

Anne Marie was the cat with the cream. Probably already planning what to wear at her 'First Fridays', the little literary soirées in the house in Baggot Street where she floated about the place dropping clever remarks as if she were Mrs Patrick Campbell incarnate. The pretensions those two had! Anne Marie's writers' group was nothing but a thorn in Frank's side, always sending letters to the newspapers about some government business or other. Frank said that sort of carry-on wouldn't help Declan when he came up for mastership of the hospital.

'The remainder of my property, house, furniture, pictures, rugs and all other effects, both general and personal, are to be divided equally between my two daughters,

Margarita and Anne Marie, to be disposed of how they will.'

The furniture might fill a few gaps in Terenure or Rosbeigh. As for the rest, Rita's legacy of old clothes, fans, handbags, they were nothing but a disruption. Her outfits were already worked out, the ones she dressed in the odd time she dared to open the safe. She had taken some jewels to Kerry once, been alone with them for one whole glorious week, but the risk was too great to repeat. Still, good things didn't date as much as Mary claimed. On a positive note, embroidered shawls and painted fans and dressy handbags might come in useful at Áras an Uachtaráin.

'Dear Mama, she was always a mischief!' Anne Marie's neatly gloved hand touched Rita's arm. 'Though she asked me ages ago about the jewellery, and we agreed it was hardly your style.' She would drop that condescending smile when Rita was first lady.

'Poor Mama, I never had the heart to tell her all that glistens isn't necessarily gold!'

Anne Marie's perfect doll's face was suddenly tight and rat-like. 'What do you mean?'

'Did I ever tell you I once bit her pearls? They peeled.'

'Since when were you an expert in fine jewels?'

Delightful to see how upset the demure little madam could become, the way her silly voice hissed with fury. 'Or could it be that living with Frank O'Fiaich has made you bitter? Oh yes, Mama never forgot those times you tried to spoil things for me, letting me down in front of my friends with your stupid revolutionary talk! As if you'd know the first thing about jewellery! Mama loved her things and she knew if she left any to you, you would sell them down the river like everything else that's precious in this country!'

'Exactly! She was afraid when I tried to sell them I might learn their true value. By the way, is that her musquash coat you're wearing?'

Christine was getting ready to leave. It would be only

decent to say a few words to the old woman. She was without a roof over her head now, and the money Mama had left wouldn't last long. Mama had never understood the value of the stuff. But then, Rita hadn't forgotten an occasion recently when she had tried to cheer Mama up with hints of her elevation to Phoenix Park. Mama had perked up all right. She had called Christine into the bedroom to share the joke.

'You'll enjoy this, Christine! Miss Rita says that husband of hers will be our next President of Ireland, living in the Lord Lieutenant's house! As if things weren't bad enough!'

The old housekeeper had sat down on the bed to laugh. 'They'll be making ambassadors out of our donkeys next!'

Anne Marie looked fit to be tied. She was clutching the fur coat to her as if Rita might pull it off there and then. 'Mama gave it to me, Rita, years ago! Oh, why are you always *so* mean!'

No, she could not bear to say another word to Christine. Better to smile graciously at this stupid sister, wave at the faithful housekeeper and Mr Montgomery and set off for the bus. They would realize it soon enough: living well was the best revenge.

Invitation to a Shopping Trip, 1955

* * *

She was potting out geraniums when Frank came into the garden. The sight of him out there was surprise enough. Had he come with good news, to tell her Seán T. O'Kelly had resigned, that Frank was on the way at last, to be elected President of Ireland? No, from the set of him, there was no hope of that. He walked tentatively across the lawn, as if clay and manure had become foreign to him, and rather threatening.

'Would you be on for a trip to London?'

'Oh dear, I wasn't expecting you home yet! Hadn't you some meeting with Mr Costello?'

'I'm asking you a question, woman. Are you on for London on Friday?'

'Well, yes, that would be lovely, but I don't quite understand why?'

Going anywhere these days with Frank was unusual. In recent years of coalition government she had rarely been invited to official functions. In fact, the last time she and Frank had been out together was to an unfortunate dinner in Iveagh House when she sat beside the Archbishop and asked for enlightenment on the Health Bill for expectant mothers. Frank was angry afterwards, though he too couldn't explain what all the fuss was about, only kept repeating that the moral question was clear. She looked around at her creation: the curving herbaceous border, smooth lawns, the rose-beds in formal ranks of floribunda and hybrid teas, rustic tripods draped with varieties of rambler and shrub. With the children grown, she seemed to spend most of her time in the garden, spraying, mulching, overseeing some rough labourer dig more rose-beds a

296

standard four feet deep. For all the talk of unemployment, gardeners were a thing of the past. She didn't mind the work. She had made a name for herself at the shows, and Sam McGredy had made a special point of meeting her and showing her round on a recent Rose Society trip to his nursery over the border.

'You're expected, anyhow. That woman wants to see you. As good as ordered that you should attend.'

'What woman?'

'I'm not surprised you'd forget her – that rude heifer with the bristles on her face?'

Nina? A lightning bolt, rooting her to the ground.

'By the tone of the message Dev got, her manners haven't improved either. They're stepping over the mark, so they are, dictating who should be appearing for our side. But as I said to the Chief, what harm, don't we need the money? And God knows I'd be glad to get them things out of the house.'

Nina. She was going to see her again. But the jewels would go. Frank looked edgy, glaring around the garden as if he expected spies to leap out from behind Papa's old sundial. His voice was almost a whisper. 'You understand the position? No questions, do you see, no letting slip we're talking to Reds. So have a story ready. Tell anyone who wants to know it's a shopping trip, clothes, stuff for the house, whatever you like.'

'Shopping? Coming from you, Frank, I'm afraid that might arouse more suspicion!'

But certainly she understood. She put down the trowel and walked as calmly as she could to the garden bench. She was to see Nina again. To look into her eyes, feel the tips of her long flat fingers . . .

'Don't joke now, woman. Dev told me himself, this is strictly between ourselves.'

At last they would meet again. Afterwards Nina would go, taking the jewels with her.

A magpie screamed from the top of a holly bush, raiding another nest. From the Terenure Road the rumble and screech of buses was like the noise held deep down in her own throat. So this was what it felt like. Stories of sundered Jewish families were appearing in the newspapers with haunting regularity, children torn from their mothers' breasts, killing, torture and deprivations which Rita feared she could never have endured. But this agony she must bear. She was not ready to surrender the jewels, but then she never would be. For years she had promised them the life they deserved. Instead, she would deliver them back into the hands of their enemies, to a grey world where they would be despised, ignored, or worse.

'We'll take the boat Friday evening, so. Better the same arrangements as before, under your clothes and so on.'

Seán T. would surely retire soon. Everyone agreed he was too old to carry on, that the Chief should never have let him run for a second term. Frank was next in line, hadn't Dev said so? Now she would go to the big white house in the Park, naked and alone.

'How long has it been?'

He didn't seem to notice the faint wail in her voice. 'What? Them things in the safe? Too bloody long! Jesus, it's over thirty years! Long enough for that shower to have changed from our pals to public enemy number one. Christ! If anyone were to get a sniff of this . . .'

The Atlantic cedar had grown as tall as the house. It had been such a little thing when she had bought it with Mary on a drive in the Wicklow mountains. And the climbing Cécile Brunner, a slip from Mama's garden in Clonkee when Eamonn was a baby, now nearly dwarfing the old greenhouse.

Thirty-five years it was since Frank and she had come here from America. She remembered the lawn under the apple trees, white with daisies. When the children came, she cleared some and put in a swing. Now the apples had gone, Liam was in London with the *Irish Press*, Eamonn had his own parish outside Limerick and Niamh had finished her physiotherapy course. One day someone might marry her.

Rita sat there for a long time after Frank had gone. Everything was sharp and clear in the evening light. She tried to think about each tree and plant, to concentrate on how they had come there, her plans for improvement. Anything to keep her mind from the void.

In the time it had taken to develop this garden so much else had happened, so much had come good: revolution, the Troubles, civil war, the Depression, Hitler, Stalin, popes, generals, politicians; risen and fallen like tides beneath the moon. How could it be that the jewels, solid, unassailable chunks of history, could now be slipped casually, silently back into a loveless darkness, rendering her period of care no more significant than the ticking of the clock?

'Mammy! Didn't you hear the gong? The food is on the table.'

Niamh was standing at the scullery door. How she had grown, and never the little girl Rita had dreamed of. They had all slipped through her fingers somehow, become citizens of this strange new world: Liam with the easy Dublin gloss which covered a deep, almost icy reserve; Eamonn slow and secretive like Frank, easily embarrassed even by his own mother; and Niamh, clumping about the place in ugly brown lace-ups. Only the jewels remained constant, kept their brightness in the increasing gloom, cushioning all disappointment. Without their hard certainties, would anything have been different?

'You're not wearing that uniform to table, are you, darling?'

'For God's sake, Mammy, the Brown Owl is retiring tonight and I'm presenting the gift!'

Without the jewels, would she have brought them up differently, insisted on opening the house to new people and ideas, forced Frank to take them abroad?

'Sorry. I feel like I've been living in a dream for thirty-five years, Niamh.'

'Well, wake up now. It's cold out here and Daddy's in a mood.'

Mutton chops and cauliflower cheese followed by stewed apple and Bird's custard. How could Mrs O'Reilly burn Bird's custard? When they got back from London, she would take the bull by the horns, insist the old cook retire to her sister's new house in Crumlin. And she might ask Mary to have a word with Niamh about her turn-out. The girl had to take a pull on herself or she'd never get a man.

'It was going cold.'

Frank hadn't waited. After all those years he still had the manners of a bullock. Watching him saw irritably at the meat, she remembered her vow to have and to hold. No sign of that now. Only separate bedrooms and the creak of the bed in the night after a prayer, the squeak of his door every morning as he slipped out to first mass. Was this where the dream had led, to this gloomy tableau? At last there was someone she could confide in: Nina would know the answers, she had always known where she was going.

Reunion

* * *

No sleep for a week. So much to think about, so much to arrange. First of all there was the unearthing of the silk underwear, laundering it out of range of Mrs O'Reilly's rheumy eye, stitching up moth holes. All of it painful, not just the pricking of her fingers, but the realization of what she was doing, her own complicity.

Upsetting, too, to find how her shape had changed. The lack of a corset could not properly excuse the way the camisole would hardly pull over her breasts, and the petticoat, which she had had to adapt to two layers, needed elastic to fit around her middle. She tried not to think about her body, how Nina would see her. But after all the years of dieting and self-control it seemed unfair that the curves and bumps which she had battled to keep under control had somehow fused into a smooth cylinder. That evening, when Rita entered the kitchen with the old underwear beneath her clothes, Mrs O'Reilly remarked from her armchair in the kitchen, 'You've got stout, missus! A fine figure of a woman!' From her tone anyone might think she was paying a compliment.

Afterwards Rita spent a long time in front of the mirror, trying to see herself as others might, as Nina would judge her when they met. Her face wasn't too bad for a woman of fifty-five though some bristles needed plucking and a sagginess along the jawline reminded her of a greedy hamster. The rest of her was at least alive. Milky skin stretching over rather bony shoulders and long red-tipped breasts to the rounded belly and thinning dark hair between still plump thighs. She touched herself there and saw the blush flood upwards, felt her whole body boil to waves of a memory which had not faded. She covered herself quickly, resigned to these hot flushes which still leapt upon her occasionally like some escaped animal from the Zoo.

Ludicrous, the trouble she went to for their meeting. She had given up asking Frank for new clothes years ago, and there was no point in expecting him to fork out for the petal hat with a veil, swirling poppy-print dress, red duster coat and rather tight stilettos. The handbag was an economy, a big one borrowed for the purpose from Mary. Of course, the hairdo in the Piccadilly hotel was more expensive than her little man in Terenure, but she only had to remind herself about ships sunk because of a ha'p'orth of tar.

When Nina sailed into the hotel room, she was barely recognizable. The woman looked more like somebody's servant than a member of a state delegation. There were no two ways about it: she had become fat, enormously so. The body buttoned tightly into a shiny brown suit rolled and swelled like some trapped sea monster, undulating magnificently with each stride. She appeared to be wearing no stays, let alone one of the two-way stretch which Rita had discovered on her shopping trip. It would have been nice to introduce her to such inventions.

'Rita?'

The arms were around her then, warm lips on each cheek, a familiar scent of raspberries. Grey hair scraped back from a wide expanse of face, moustache whitened and thinned with age, the dear mole on her cheek splashed large and untidy.

'But, what have they done to you?'

She was holding Rita at arm's length, buttony eyes scanning the outfit which the assistant in Switzer's had assured her was the nearest thing to a Dior copy.

'Where is Rita, huh? Where is wild Irish rose?'

Was that disappointment in the voice? Oh please, make it all right, like it once was. Please God, dear sweet Jesus whom I ignore, to whom I do not pray enough, show me that she cares; after the long years of silence, that I matter . . .

'So, is Ritushka, I think, I am not seeing.'

Her hands felt hot and strong on Rita's arms. Oh to yield to the soft bulk of her, without this stupid inquisition, this game.

'Western womans only I am seeing! Oh yes, even in motherland, we fight such womans. I say them, I say for what we fight? Is question for you, *chérie*. Tell me for what is these things we do, 1914, 1916, 1917 – is for this dresses, this shoes?'

The familiar snort. Rita felt nineteen again, vulnerable, cringing. Could Nina no longer see beyond the stupid, polite smile to the turmoil inside?

'Well, thanks be to goodness we're not fighting any more. We're a republic now, you know, all peaceful thanks to Mr de Valera and Frank!'

Neither of the men looked up. They stood by the big table near the window, as lost in thought as the two Russian men opposite.

'There's still the Six Counties to be sorted out, of course . . . people up there need freedom and justice –'

'Freedom! Justice!'

When Nina laughed, some spittle landed on Rita's nose. The weatherbeaten face had become polished with the years, like the hobs on Mary's Aga in her new house in the Dublin mountains. A number of lower teeth might have been made of metal. A Russian fashion, perhaps?

'Well, yes. As you know, Frank has given nearly fifty years of his life for such things –'

'You know for what mens fight?' She had forgotten this side of Nina, this angry passion. 'I tell you: Ava Gardner, Shelley Winters and what is this shiny lips? Doris Day! Oh yes, I see womans in London, many, many tight dress, yes? In, out, like you going, and stupid shoes – the Minnie Mouses!'

Or had she simply forgotten that youthful anger in herself? How silent the room was. The men were waiting to sit themselves on either side of the mahogany table, two navy-blue Irishmen, two brown-suited Russians. Outside in the corridor the childish voice of a bellhop repeated a name like responses to the rosary.

'Oh, Nina, please stop talking riddles! Look, when this is over, let's have luncheon, just the two of us. I've so much to ask!'

'Certainly.' Her smile was the same, direct and warm. 'I also, many questions.'

Frank beckoned impatiently, then cleared his throat. 'Perhaps we could begin by introducing my wife, Mrs O'Fiaich.'

'Darling, have you forgotten? I know them well, from the States, or at least I know Nina and Piotr!' It was ridiculous, a charade.

He ignored her, addressing his remarks to the men. 'We understood that although she is not, and never has been, any part of an Irish delegation, you wish to have her attend this meeting?' Hurtful, too, to be dismissed like this.

Nina interrupted with a snarl. 'You forget, Mr O'Fiaich, is your wife make arrangement for jewels and money. Me and Rita. Our idea!'

Dear Nina, never the diplomat. Rita did her best to smile, to soothe things, though she could feel the panic pressing into her lap as she took her seat at the table, fear emanating like an electric current from her heavy handbag.

'But Nina, where's Sergei. Is he unwell?'

She might have waved a dead rat under their noses. Eamon de Valera was staring at the hotel carpet. Piotr looked nervously at the third member of his group before shaking himself to murmur, 'Delighted to meet, Mrs O'-Fiaich. Now I introduce Mr Yaramov from Board of Cultural Folkloric.'

Noël Coward might have written this play, the bowing and shaking hands and formal smiles. The new Russian was like the undertaker who had dealt with Mama's funeral. His hands also felt too soft for a man.

'When you get home, Mr Yaramov, you must get Sergei Grigoryev to teach you some of our Irish folksongs. He had us all racking our brains when we were in the States, and how well he used to sing them! Do you remember, Frank, those evenings after dinner?'

'Comrade Grigoryev is not in Moscow, Mrs O'Fiaich.' Piotr was gripping the sides of his chair as he cast edgy glances from Mr Yaramov's stony mask to Rita.

'Oh, really, where has he got to?'

The way Nina rattled her tin box of lozenges suggested that Rita had asked something improper. But surely, even in their barbaric Soviet Union, it was only polite to inquire about absent friends?

Nina stared ahead, noisily sucking her sweet, Piotr smiled, nobody attempting to answer. Odd to see how Nina and Piotr had grown so much older, yet appeared less assured than when she had seen them last. Piotr was more like Don Quixote than ever, though more deflated than someone who had enjoyed a life tilting at windmills.

'Perhaps we could get down to the matter in hand.'

Mr de Valera's voice was dry, impersonal. Judging by their behaviour, who would have believed how enthusiastically the Chief and Piotr used to speak together whenever they met, arguing happily about nationalism, the collective good and revolution? But then, to look at Nina and herself, who would guess the friendship they had shared?

'That, after all, is why we have all travelled here.'

Now they were strangers. Of all of them, Dev appeared the least changed. Perhaps he had always looked old. 'You are happy with the terms of the original agreement?'

'Certainly.'

'Is there anything further you wish to discuss?'

Nina's half-smile reminded Rita of the cat from Number Twenty. 'I think, Mr de Valera, time for talking with West is all gone.' It always left its spoor on the kitchen doorpost as Rita chased it from the house, then gazed down at her from the wall, pleased, superior, just like that.

The Chief leant forward, his hands joined as if in prayer, gold rims flashing. 'Is that the attitude which vetoed our application to the United Nations?'

Mr Yaramov glared and Nina stopped chuckling. She put her head down and removed some notes from her briefcase. 'Figures for loan.' She scribbled something on a piece of paper and passed it across to the Chief.

'That seems to tally with my calculations.'

'Good. Return, please.'

What Nina did then was quite outrageous, taking the cigarette lighter from Piotr, allowing the flaming paper to drop on to the French polish and burn itself out. Rita cried out in alarm.

Frank stayed her hand. Nina's naked mouth was smiling at her, the mole on her upper lip contemptuous, mocking. A horrible little black mark scarred the mahogany. They were all looking at Rita.

'Go on, woman! Pass them over, so!'

How dare Frank presume to snatch her handbag! Painful enough to be opening the catch and withdrawing the old school shoebag, its background faded now, but her childish chain-stitched animals as bright as ever. From within, the jewels made crunchy noises of protest as she pushed it gently across the table. They must be uncomfortable like that, denied their usual protection of special bags and boxes.

Piotr opened the drawstring and spilled out the contents as if they were so many potatoes. They lay winking and flashing in the hush, exotic sea creatures thrown gasping on to the shore. Then Piotr and Nina began to sort and count them, making untidy heaps and groupings, finally tossing out the ungainly tiara which Rita always thought a touch vulgar and the small one she had worn only once in public, the night of the dinner party which brought Mary and Dermot together.

It meant nothing to Frank. Nor did his eyelids flicker at the sight of her favourite ruby earrings with which she had shared so many important occasions. Indeed, neither he nor Dev seemed interested in any part of what was strewn before them. Frank sat hunched forward in his seat, his hands tightly clasped. Mr de Valera remained bolt upright, his eyes fixed on some point on the ceiling, as if expecting an angel to appear and deliver him from evil.

What hurt most was seeing Nina handle the jewels. She was in a hurry, twisting up the long pearl rope, dragging necklaces and bracelets into piles so that the stones made protesting scratches on the table, sorting small pieces into heaps like so many counters.

The stranger sat and watched, an auctioneer at a cattle mart. Piotr and Nina were like farmers, bundling animals into pens, crowding them into trailers with a disinterest brought on by the knowledge that the creatures they had nurtured were now condemned to die. Did Piotr and Nina not care that everything they held in their hands might be torn apart, reduced to meaningless heaps of gold and silver and stone?

'What will you do with them?'

She hadn't intended to blurt it out.

No answer. She felt Frank shift uneasily beside her and saw Mr Yaramov's nostrils tighten. Her voice must not betray her. 'I mean, it would be silly to break them up, not to keep them as a collection. I'm almost sure that cross is the one worn by the Tsarina in a holiday photograph from the Bosporus.'

Only Piotr met her eyes. He was smiling. He had always smiled too much. 'Such decisions are not in our hands, Comrade O'Fiaich. But I think your husband and Mr de Valera will agree with me, huh? Many things of past is good forgotten, kept in bag?'

They were packing it all away, pushing each piece back into the darkness. It was important to remain calm. This was how it should be, the jewels returned to their homeland, to their own people. Nina's eyes were disturbing.

'So, Ritushka, are glad you lose burden, yes?' In front of everyone, Nina winked at her. 'But I think you not forget everything!' .

The woman might as well have leant across the table and kissed Rita full on the mouth. Did everyone know what she was saying, throwing their love upon the table with about as much contempt as she had shown for the jewels?

She would not cry, she would smile back. It was like the dentist's chair, this pain, concentrating her mind on other things: on whether library books had been returned, the relative cruelties of poison or traps for mice in the kitchen, or, God help her, on the Mysteries of the Cross.

The shoebag was full once more. Mary would have been amused to hear of the adventures of that hated piece of work.

Nina's broad face creased into laughter. Somehow their hands had found one another across the polish, gripping tight, stroking arms and cheek as they laughed and snorted together like children hiding in a broom cupboard.

'Oh Nina, dearest, I have missed you!'

'I also. Even in Western uniform, is funny for me, is strange!'

'It's you who has become the stranger!'

The way Nina rocked about in her chair made it creak. She pounded the table in mirth. 'Is like film stars, this decadence! Is dolls, you know, they not work, they "make home"!'

'What about yourself? When I saw you, I thought of a character out of Pushkin!'

'Am Russian woman! No, I show you, *chérie*, this afternoon, we go to movies like in America. You know this new one, *Oklahoma*? Is full of American dolls, I think?'

'Mrs O'Fiaich regrets she is otherwise engaged.' Frank's voice was chill. They had forgotten the men. Mr Yaramov was glowering at Nina.

'Tonight, perhaps.'

'My wife has an engagement for this evening.' The merriment had gone, a brief fire, quenched. He was so rude, he had always been rude.

The high colour in Nina's face was mottled and lumpy. 'I also, I am having many things to do.'

'Everything is in order, then?' The Chief was like a greyhound straining at the leash.

And then Piotr was passing an attaché case across the table. 'In US dollars, as requested.'

The bowing and hand-kissing and clicking of heels had become another film, an old Chaplin, silent, and moving much too fast. Surely Nina would see that? There was no way of guessing what she thought, slumped in her chair. When Rita came around the table to kiss her, the lips felt deathly cold.

'Can you visit me in Ireland? Wait a year or so and I should be able to entertain you in style!'

Nina laughed bitterly. 'What I want this "style"? What you want, Ritushka, where is dream?'

'You'd love Kerry. We have a cottage there, on the Atlantic.'

'Hah! Is dacha in your country also?'

Piotr was there, trying to lead her away. 'Comrade Nina has not time for vacation.'

For a second Rita feared that Nina might spit in her colleague's eye. As she snarled something at him in Russian, Piotr glanced in fear at the silent member of their party.

'Well, maybe we could meet in Europe sometime? I was saying to Frank on our way over that we should try flying. The airlines are making it so much easier to get about –'

'Rita!' The Irishmen were twitching at the door, wishing the business finished.

'Is last mission, I think, last journey for me.' Her eyes were dull.

'Oh dear, Nina, I wish I could tell you how grateful I am, for the jewels, for so much –'

'So, is fixed, yes? Is finish. Now we forget.'

She was gone, steaming out of the room with her two companions almost running to catch up. And there had been no opportunity to mention girdles.

Over lunch in a dingy Soho restaurant Frank and Mr de Valera chuckled together in Irish. They seemed to refer to Mr Yaramov as 'An Puppet Master', a term for which they did not know the Irish. Then Frank had broken into English. 'But did you ever clap eyes on such an ugly hoor!'

And Mr de Valera roared back. 'Herself? Like the curse of the Phooka!'

Rita knew what they were talking about, she understood their relief at having finished their business and kept their secret. She had expected to feel bereft, but she was surprised to find she did not. When Nina walked away with the jewels, she had somehow set her free. The ropes were cut at last, heavy chains of love and memory and responsibility stripped away in that brief half-hour in a London hotel.

The men were spooning up their puddings. She realized they had removed themselves from her a long time ago; yet she, for some stupid reason, had tried to follow. They sat back, waiting for her to perform some ritual. 'Maybe you'd say the grace for us, Rita, and we'll get the bill?'

Anyone would think Dev was offering her a gift. Frank folded his napkin ponderously while the Chief sat graven faced, head bowed in readiness. She had never liked public displays of piety, and no doubt they'd blow smoke all over her when she finished.

She pushed back her chair. 'Oh, you carry on, Frank. I must go and powder my nose.' She was up and off, leaving the two men gaping after her like a couple of lads at a crossroads.

Evening Shadows

* * *

Sea air made her sleepy, which was why she was in bed at nine-thirty when he crashed in the door. She had come down to Kerry for a rest, unsettled since London, empty. As Frank well knew, she needed to be alone. Now, without any warning, he was in the bedroom, gasping like a man who had run all the way down here without pausing for breath and taking a very high tone. It was like waking into a bad dream. Then the shock as the fears returned, triggered by her husband's surprising, shaming behaviour. Dragging at the bedclothes, pulling her hair, screaming,

'Get up out of it! Get out of that bed you thieving bitch!'

She had never seen him as angry as this, panting with rage, calling her every name, using words you wouldn't hear in the worst slums of Dublin, accusing her of being shallow and stupid and West Brit. Wounding, cruel words. Insults she would find very hard to forgive.

'Stop it, Frank! Do you know what you're doing?'

'Shut up, woman, till you tell me what *you* did!'

Perhaps he *was* mad, fumbling and grunting like an aged badger. He had been drinking, that was it, bored on the long train journey from Dublin, boiling up some grudge. Had someone hurt him, said something unkind about the party? He was always too sensitive to criticism, but never as furious as this.

What *you* did? She had done nothing. All those weeks since they had returned the jewels she had only tried not to fret, stopped the niggling 'What if?' which crept into her mind. It *had* to be all right.

He was pushing her towards the sitting-room, the big

311

hands on her shoulders painfully tight; his face, when she looked round to protest, as dark and sealed off in the shadows of the narrow hall as the faces of coloured people on the streets of America.

'Wait a minute Frank, let me make some tea.' Let this not be what she had most feared.

'Bitch! Liar! *Níl meas madra agam ort anois!*'

'*Madra*'? Had he cursed her? Called her some kind of a dog? He pushed her roughly into a chair by the hearth, fumbling with matches until the lamp lit his face.

'Now.'

Down on his knees, breathing into her face. Whiskey. A man who was always careful with drink, almost teetotal except for the odd special occasion. His father had been too fond of the stuff for his own good, a warning, he used to tell the boys, the best lesson the man ever taught him.

'Tell me what you did with them, you lying, fantastical mare you! I'm not leaving this place till you tell me, explain how you tore the heart out of myself – and the country!'

Please, not this, anything but this horrible, angry hate. And the certain dawning that the worst had happened.

'Are you listening, woman? For once in your bloody life will you answer me straight? *Is tu an bhean is measa agus is fealltaí d'ar casadh orm riamh!*'

Dear God in Heaven, he had called her '*fealltaí*,' deceitful. Was it only Mrs O'Reilly, taking it upon herself to tell him of Rita's occasional dabble in the safe? Well, she could explain that. Had some Nosy Parker mentioned her wearing the odd thing? Or the copies? No, she must not think about the copies.

'Never, in my whole life, a more devious female! Are you going to tell me, or am I going to have to hammer it out of you? Where are those jewels? What did you do with them?'

How much did he know?

'Jewels? Goodness, I've few enough, but they're on my dressing-table in Terenure, aren't they, in Mama's tortoiseshell box?' What if he *had* learned about the copies, could it matter now? The real ones had gone with Nina, without a backward glance.

'Liar!'

Frank's blow across her head was far more shocking than that memory. Yet though she cried out, she hardly felt the fists on her face, her whole body paralysed by a truth from which there was now no escape. It had come. She was finally cornered by this wild, flailing beast who was her husband.

'Stop, Frank, please, stop! Are you mad?'

'Mad? Oh by Jesus, yes, I'm mad, all right, and it's you who's made me!' The face close before her shone with righteous anger. Where was her tight-reined husband, the respected elder statesman? Had she done this to him?

'How can you sit there, you queening cunt of a bitch, you lying thieving hoor you? After what I've learned today!'

'Thieving'? Yes, it was the rubies. God, Mary, Mama, save me, shrive me. He was beating her again, punching her where his clenched fists could reach in the armchair she had covered with a deckchair stripe last summer. The blows were hurting now, as if Frank knew how to hit, to maim, though he had never boxed for sport.

'No blame, Dev tells me, in the circumstances. Always a risk, he says, some cute hoor will try something. Are you listening, bitch? Do you hear what the Chief said? Do you know what you've done?'

She had thought he was really asking, and looked up. A sickening crunch into some echo chamber of her head, and then the warm blood, pints and gallons of it pouring from her nose over her nightdress, staining the good chair. This was no dream. She had become such a woman, beaten by her drunken husband like a common tenement wife. And she deserved it.

Even in the dim light, the bright redness was enough to check him. He sat back on his heels, his voice so thickened with sobs of rage it was hard to catch what he was saying.

'Better forget about that other plan, Dev says, the presidency. You never know who'd have the knife at the ready. Love is blind, he said. Love is blind! Do you know what you have done, woman? Do you understand what the Chief was saying to me?'

Think of this, concentrate on the awful brutality, the sudden haemorrhage of emotion. Seal up the inner chamber, the knowledge of her own transgression and its consequences, far more damaging than his extraordinary loss of control. Only nod. She knew.

'He'll run for it himself, so he will. President de Valera! "Oh yes," he says, "we've had a break in security, got to close ranks, make sure it's one of our best lads in the Park, the country needs that." And do you know who that "best lad" will be? Himself!'

There would be no more beating. To see the way he knelt there in the quiet, pushing his face into her knees, arms pressing on her aching lap, anyone looking through the uncurtained window might think he was praying for forgiveness. Thank goodness there was no one about. Mrs O'Sullivan from the farm would make great hay if she heard even a whisper. From this angle the bald patch on the back of his head looked sore and exposed. He had never been a violent man. This was Mr de Valera's fault. Hadn't he always pushed Frank too far, expected too much of everyone? But would he really do that, take the presidency for himself?

'I'm sorry, Frank. There's been some mistake. I never did any harm.' It hurt to move her jaw. Still, it would be a relief to tell him, to explain her special relationship with the jewels, how she had tried to give them the dignity they were owed. Frank would not understand, she knew that, but surely, if she explained, he would appreciate the way she had dealt with Mary, allowed copies to be made and put a stop to her greedy demands?

He looked exhausted as he got up to sit across the hearth. 'So, tell us how you did it, woman, how you pulled everything down on us.' He was mentally unbal-

anced, that was it, shell-shocked by worry and disappointment. The Chief had promised: Frank *had* to be president.
He needed a rest. Áras an Uachtaráin was to give him
that. So, where to begin? When she looked back on it,
there was no clear story to tell; her life with Frank and the
jewels were a series of images, flickering like those silent
movies the children used to make, picture cards spun
quickly between finger and thumb: Frank and Nina; Frank
in prison and Liam needing to be born; the jewels demanding to be safe; begging to be free. Difficult to think
straight with this numbness slowly creeping over her body
and a sticky congealing warmth. Or was the story more
like the way Mary dealt cards at bridge, deft, neatly
stacked, always falling into a surprising pattern from her
long fingers. Rita wanted to ask Frank that, too. Could he
make sense of it, the sacrifices they had made to end up
here, like this, in an isolated cottage on a Kerry peninsula?
Her lips were thick as car tyres.

'If you mean the Romanov jewels, I did my best to look
after them, you know, often in very trying circumstances.
I don't think I did them any harm.'

'You knew the number of the safe, didn't you?'

'Of course. You were in prison, remember? I told you
afterwards that I had to save the jewels, to make them
safe – no woman would be advised to give birth in her
underwear!'

'Dev wondered was it you switched them. Claimed he'd
had his suspicions for years, said he'd spoken to you.'

'That man would suspect his own grandmother!'

'Well, they're missing some ruby things – earrings, Dev
says, and some class of a ring. They say it's only fakes we
sent.'

God forgive her, the ones Mary hadn't returned until
she came back from England. But Mary was her friend,
she would never play tricks on her, or would she?

'With diamonds and pearls?'

'That sort of thing.'

He was staring at her as if he had never seen her before.

Such a level, clear way of looking, even tonight with drink taken. She had to drop her eyes.

'What have you done with them?'

'I gave them back, honestly, Frank. There's been some awful mistake.'

'Mistake? *Is caimilearaí críochnaithe tú!* Do you understand me? An accomplished crook I'm married to!' He was up again, roaring down at her, the soft bags under his eyes bruised and wet. 'Property put in my protection, stolen from under my nose! I'll tell you what I think there's been, a disaster, that's what! You have destroyed me, so you have! I'm finished, dragged into the gutter with your corrupt civility, your collaborator's ways! To think I believed I could change you! But I'll tell you something, woman, you may have ruined me and my reputation, but you're finished along with myself!'

She hardly heard the back door slam, never asked afterwards where he had gone that night, whether he had taken the mountain track or the back strand, feeling his way through the dark, boggy places she had tried not to imagine for him in the nineteen-twenties.

An agony to reach the lamp, extinguish the flame. She sat on in darkness, listening to the wet sounds of tide and rain, feeling her face swell as the blood flaked and cracked over her skin. Martyrs suffered like this. They whipped and chafed and mortified their own flesh until bad deeds were excised, purified by blood. But her sin would be with her always. It would continue to beat her back, destroy what few feelings they had left for one another, Frank and she. That was her fate. And if she didn't do something fast, maybe it would even shutter her for ever inside red brick on the edge of the city. Frank had behaved like a beast, a vengeful devil. But she was worse. Yes, his words were beginning to sink in, to find their mark.

Making a Confession

* * *

The sitting-room was extraordinary. Like the rest of this little Georgian house, with its view from the slopes of the Hell Fire Mountain to the sea, Mary had done it in the very latest style. Not that it was to Rita's taste. All a touch vulgar, but that was Mary. Who else would want a carpet patterned with skidmarks and whorls, as if the Monte Carlo Rally had driven through a flower market? Who would team it with walls papered in pink and white polka dot and lilac wood?

Difficult to remain seated on the white leather couch. Rita had to cling on for dear life, but she would wait.

The maid had said, 'She'll be down shortly.' What was 'shortly'? And why was it she was no longer welcome in the bedroom, bathroom or wherever Mary happened to be right now? So demeaning to be left like this, like one of Papa's patients.

This must have been how it felt for those poor souls, sitting in the evening gloom of the big drawing-room at Clonkee. Rita used to stumble in there sometimes. Then the men would hunch downwards over their knees and the women give nervous smiles and nods, ready to run like deer if she stepped any closer.

She had never inquired why Papa saw them there each evening, in the house. It was simply the way he did things. The hush in that drawing-room was as intense as here. It used to frighten her. When she was small, she would stand outside the door and listen, wondering whether quiet was a necessary preparation for the shouts and moans which could burst suddenly from her father's study across the hall.

'Sorry, sweetie!'

Tonight Mary was Grace Kelly, the cinched green damask floating a chiffon back panel from coat-hanger shoulders, beige legs stretched into toning high heels.

'Today is impossible. As I said on the phone, I have to meet some people in the Red Bank by seven-thirty!'

Perhaps she honestly did not know what this was about, why ever since Rita returned from Rosbeigh she had phoned and left urgent messages, asking, demanding, finally begging that they should meet? Worse, what if Mary *did* know?

She focused her eyes on a chrome ashtray in Mary's hands, the way it could choke a half-smoked cigarette with one spin of the lid.

'Oh dear, this is very difficult . . .' Her voice was letting her down, reluctant, beseeching. It was all so wrong. 'I don't know how to say this, Mary, and please, don't for a moment think I blame you, but as I said on the phone and in my notes to you, Frank is up the wall – half mad with the worry!'

'How very mysterious! But really I'm much more interested in what happened to your face.'

The hand on her arm was playful, but Mary's eyes were not. The huge blued lids were shuttered against the light.

'Never mind my face. The rubies. He thinks I lost them, you see. I have to know what happened –'

'Hang on! Didn't that silly creature offer you a drink?'

She would have to start again. Wait for Mary to open a drinks cabinet which lit like an organ at a fairground, watch her fussing about with bottles and shakers, slide down again on the couch as Mary rushed off to the kitchen for ice. The pressing dinner engagement seemed forgotten, anyway.

This would have been how it sounded to the patients waiting in the drawing-room, listening to strains of other lives in the house, waiting their turn to speak their mind to Papa, then step out into darkness for the walk across the grounds towards the welcoming lights of the wards.

318

Well, *she* was not a lunatic. She was angry, and the longer Mary fussed about with something strong and chokingly dry the more the aggression grew. The drink helped too. Where in all Dublin had she found green olives?

'Mary.'

'*Sláinte*, darling! Sorry about no lemons. So, you were saying something about old Frank?'

How to tell her of the enormity of what she had done. The atmosphere at home, the awful freezing silence which grew deeper and more chill with every hour Frank spent in the house. Was it really because of the jewels? Because the Russians had nearly created a diplomatic scandal? Because Mr de Valera had come close to being exposed as a one-time communist sympathizer? Because of herself, and Mary.

'Please listen. Do you remember when you borrowed some of my jewellery and had it copied?'

'Now we're going back! God, when I think of how poor we were, that awful flat in Harcourt Street!'

'No, after that, you had the big house in Foxrock for a while. Brighton Road? You *must* remember.'

'That mausoleum!'

'Well anyway, some people have examined the jewels recently, experts, and I'm afraid two of the pieces you brought back have turned out to be copies. Frank is fit to be tied.'

'How dreadful!' The lamplighter eyes were wide and innocent, the way they used to fool the nuns. She had forgotten nothing.

'You had them copied, I know, ruby and diamond earrings and a matching ring? They were my favourites too. You held on to them until the war, and the thing is, you seem to have returned me the fakes. And the originals are extremely valuable.'

Her face was a sphinx. 'I think I need another one of these. It's not every day your best friend walks in with an accusation of theft! That is what you're saying, isn't it, sweetie?'

That lovely house in the Park. Gone. Maybe there was still a chance, if she got the rubies back, she could change Dev's mind. She had planned a new colour scheme for the reception rooms: ivory and white with touches of gold. Now she would be lucky to get in there as a guest. The second drink froze her swollen lips, and gave her courage to go on. 'It would have been the easiest mix-up, of course. I mean, I could never have seen the difference. But as I told you years ago, I was keeping them for someone. I had to give them back.'

'Well, well! Next thing you'll be telling me all that stuff at the coronation was paste! Wouldn't it be a hoot? You'd better get your "expert" to check that too!'

'If you could just get me the originals, I'll take them back and everything will be all right.'

'And where are these "fakes" I'm supposed to have slipped you? I can remember they were quite expensive to have made.'

'They're – well, they're not here. But if you give me what you have, I shall try to recover them.'

'I see, you've lost your jewels and now you want mine?'

If she only knew what she had lost. 'Please don't be mean, Mary! You have no idea the trouble this has caused! Frank's political career –'

'Yes, I'm interested in what you're saying about your dear husband. So he's not exactly the innocent party after all?'

'It's very important, Mary. Please don't tease me like this.'

'Then for God's sake stop fussing! *I* don't want those fuddy-duddy old things. Hardly me, are they? But listen, if you don't want to talk about it, we can leave it for another time. I'm late enough already!'

'We can't leave it! I *have* to know where they are! You've no idea how much this matters.' For a moment she feared that Mary was going to strike her. Drink always made her slightly wild.

The teeth she bared so close to Rita's face had grown

long and yellow as an old horse's. 'No idea? *No* idea? If you must know, Rita Fitzgerald, I have quite a few ideas about those jewels and how you and Frank might have got your lily-white hands on them. I am also aware that my best friend has been keeping that piece of information from me for over thirty years. What you may not appreciate is how much that deceit has hurt me, especially when you consider what Dermot and I have done for you. My God, all the places we've taken you, the people I've introduced! You'd have died of boredom years ago if it hadn't been for Dermot and me!'

How could Mary say these things? How could she forget all the favours Frank had done Dermot, how, despite all his principles, he had backed Dermot's seat with the party, turned a blind eye to all sorts of carry-on? Indeed, Rita had never told Frank about the incident with the butter.

'A few paltry jewels is the least I should expect!'

'They're not mine to give, Mary! They never were. I told you that!'

'Oh for God's sake will you turn off the waterworks! You told me very little, as a matter of fact. But I'll try and get them, on one condition.'

So, she had known. 'What condition?'

'You have to tell me where *exactly* you got them.'

'I can't!'

'OK, no jewels.'

'I can't tell you. I'm absolutely sworn to secrecy!'

'Oh, come on, Rita, how long can anyone be expected to keep a secret in this town? I bet when you do tell me, you'll find I know the whole story already.'

Perhaps she was right. It was unfair the way the Russians had taken so long to end the arrangement. Weren't the jewels returned now, or almost all of them, and the loan repaid? What harm was there in sharing a secret with your friend? For all Rita knew, Dev was dining out on the story all over Dublin. If he ever went out. They said that he and Sinead had hardly addressed a word to one another for years.

'You have to swear to me you won't tell a soul.'

'Honestly, Rita, if you can't trust me after all we've been through!'

She had always known she would tell Mary some day. It would be all right if she kept the story simple: left Nina out of it, didn't mention any figures. 'This is strictly between you and me? Promise?'

'For heaven's sake, go on!'

'It was when we were away, we raised an awful lot of money, you see, far more than we expected.'

'Dermot always said that, said the figures didn't add up. All those Irish bonds and fund-raising rallies. And?' Mary gave her full attention now. She wasn't even smoking, sitting perfectly balanced on the edge of the couch.

'You swear you'll not tell a soul?'

It was fun watching Mary's face when she mentioned the Russians (such monsters now!), describing the jewellery in her underwear, the safe in the kitchen.

'Dermot used to speculate about that, said Frank must have found buried treasure in his terrorist days.'

'Oh, Mary!' How rotten of her to remember those times! Frank had never been a real terrorist. He had fought to liberate Ireland from England's yoke – most of it anyway. And he had been a different man then, doing what had to be done.

'Though Dermot wasn't far wrong when you think of it! Didn't those Reds rob the stuff off the royal family?'

It was how confession used to feel, when she was a child, this growing lightness with each revelation. Her secret had been a folly which she could dismantle brick by brick, so that the worry and guilt dissipated in the changing landscape.

Later, though, when Mary drove her home, she wasn't so sure.

'So how soon can you get me those jewels?'

Mary seemed suddenly in a hurry to be off, revving the big car as she crunched it into reverse.

'Give me a chance! I'll have to talk to Dermot.'

'Mary, you promised! You mustn't tell a soul!'

'OK, OK, but I have to tell Dermot just a little bit. He knows where they are, you see, I don't.'

'Can't you just say I want them back?'

'It's not as easy as that, sweetie. As a matter of fact, I suspect he still has a little loan riding on them. It was what got us going again, before the war. I'll have to explain their importance to him or he'll be offering to give you a racehorse or something instead!'

'But where are they?'

'In England, I suppose. God, he'd laugh if he heard it was the Commies' money set him up!'

'You promised this wouldn't go any further. Frank's reputation, the party image —'

'Don't fuss! God, I'm late. But it's a good thing it's the rubies you want. I sold most of the copies to Mr Basset years ago, to pay off a little debt!'

It was difficult to think clearly through the fug of dry Martinis. Heaven knew, Dermot could afford to repay a loan. Hadn't Rita read in a newspaper only last Sunday that he was a millionaire now, and people were asking how? There weren't many rich TDs in the Dáil. Eamon de Valera still lived like a pauper. There had been a few remarks in the papers about the tiny percentage of sweepstake money which reached the hospitals. Hadn't Dermot helped set that up? Another newspaper had linked him with a rush of planning permissions too.

As she watched the headlights of the car slide around the corner, Rita was suddenly bereft. She had not felt like this for a long time, not since those first months of marriage, with Frank, before the jewels. Then, in all the lonely hotel bedrooms in the big ugly cities they had visited, she had longed for the security of the old kitchen at home. She had known then what she had lost, and been glad; known that by marrying Frank there was no going back.

The cherry tree in Number One was in flower, suddenly beautiful after thirty years of mutilation. Mr Gorman had died last year and his widow did not possess his strength with a saw.

Rewards and Punishments

* * *

She jumped when Frank said, 'What's this about?'

Since he had barely addressed a word to her in six months, his appearance in the kitchen with her note in his hand was surprise enough. She had almost forgotten that angry whisper which he reserved for her alone, so different from the confident public voice. But she hadn't even heard that for ages, not since the horrible night in Rosbeigh when he had swept in out of the blue, quite demented. And not a word of apology since.

Even so, when the bruising and hurt had faded, she had tried to explain. He ignored her. It had become a habit, leaving a room as she entered, eating meals in his study, spending more time than ever out of the house.

Now he held the paper at arm's length as if it were a bomb. So unpleasant having to communicate like this, in writing, in one's own home.

'As I wrote in my note, I have recovered the earrings and the ring which you were worried about. Didn't I promise you I would get them back?'

The silence had deepened after Niamh moved out. She was opening a boarding kennels in Kilternan with her friend, Jane Beauman. Mrs O'Reilly left soon after. Couldn't stand the hush, she said, probably because Frank had fallen silent with her too. Rita suspected that big red nose of hers had picked up the whiff of failure about the place; perhaps the cards had told her there was no glory to be had in dragging her arthritis about for Frank O'Fiaich, retired T D, never the President.

His shoulders sloped in the old red cardigan and there was a burn mark on his tie. He seemed to have grown

324

smaller lately, or maybe it was only the impression he gave, shuffling about the place all day in old slippers, trailing ash and unread newspapers.

'I don't want them.'

'Of course you do! Or at least the Russians want them. They're the originals, you can tell them, the ones that got mislaid.'

The snarl he let out at her – he had no idea of the trouble she had gone to, or the fuss Mary made, even after promising she would fix everything. Then there was the way Dermot looked at Rita now, like a partner in crime. Had Mary told him more than she said?

'Did you not hear what I said, woman? I do not want those things.' The voice, so full of bitterness.

Couldn't he see that she had wanted only to help, to serve a cause he had put higher than his life. If only she could reach out and touch him, smooth away the closed fist of a face to find the young man beneath, the gentle, clever, exciting Frank Fee who had loved her, had captivated her with his politics, his way of life, his children, then stolen away with them all, to leave her quite alone.

'But the Russians want them, you have to send them back. Then everything will be all right. I still say they made the mistake, but even if there was some mix-up, it'll show we were acting in good faith.'

'With that crowd! Anyhow, it doesn't matter, they've decided to forget it.'

'But surely, even if they are only copies, they must have them back, to prove –'

'Why is it I always have to repeat myself in this house?'

'Perhaps because I have got out of practice in listening to you?'

His mouth tightened. He glanced behind him, at the door, as if the hidden listeners might finally burst in and arrest them both. He used to blush when he was angry. The face was red all the time now, tight, bitter, an old priest who had lost his faith. He sighed. 'If you must know, they were on to Dev the other night. Apparently the word's got out. Rumours flying round about this business over there, as well as a few here. They don't like loose talk any more than we do, so they're closing the book on it.'

'Rumours? You mean about the swap, the loan?'

'Dev told them there was no question of leaks from this end, but they weren't bothered. They've come up with their own solution, blaming it all on a member of their team. There'll be a public trial, charges of corruption, the usual penalty. So, that's the end of that.'

'Oh dear, I do hope it's nobody we knew.'

She didn't like the way Frank smiled. For a moment she wondered how much he had been drinking. He took whiskey regularly now, alone in the study at night.

'I'll tell you one thing, there'll be no fellas throwing themselves before the firing squad for that one!'

Papa had enjoyed a drink, but his face had never gone such a colour.

'So what shall I do with the jewellery?'

She had forgotten how blue Frank's eyes were, sapphires on a winter sky.

'Why not shove them where the monkey put the nuts?'

Which was worse, his ugly, cruel words or the hatred in his stare? When he had stamped back up the stairs, she sat down and focused on the knots in the pine table. There was a white, greasy accretion in the grooves, satisfying to dig out with a fork or one's thumbnail. The same as in the kitchen at home, a long time ago.

Her hands had changed. They used to annoy her, the way they had looked so fat and square. 'Workmanlike,' Frank always said when she had complained about them, when he wanted to please her, when he loved her. Now they were thin, the slack skin mottled with irregular freckles. She must buy some rubber gloves. No one had told her how damaging housework could be. No question of replacing the cook. You'd need to be Lady Docker, the money those women wanted. There hadn't been much of a response to her ad for a girl for the rough work either.

Maybe she could manage with a daily woman. Too much money offered to the young these days, big wages in the factories over in England and in the odd one opened up here.

Still, it was nice enough having the kitchen to herself, pleasant to come down after dinner and listen to the tick of the old clock, turn on the BBC Home Service, sit in the carpeted armchair. Mrs O'Reilly had never allowed anything but the Irish station. She felt safe here, the peace rarely interrupted even by neighbours as new faces and young families replaced the aged and dead. Even the telephone didn't ring much now Frank wasn't in demand. Of course, Liam called sometimes from London, full of news about the newspaper and sporting events. He rarely asked about them, about Frank and herself, never appeared interested. Perhaps some children weren't. When Eamonn called, he only inquired about her health, as if she were very old and he a doctor. Funny, like all priests, he steered well clear of inquiries about the state of her soul or her marriage. Only Niamh understood that. She had always seen more than was good for her. Leaving the good job in St Vincent's Hospital had been a terrible blow for Frank. Yet she was so like him, suiting herself. The kennels were an unexpected step. She had never even owned a dog. Rita feared that her friend, Jane, was a trifle domineering.

Yes, one was quite alone now. The realization did not worry her. Digging and digging at the table top, another thought slowly emerged from the bruised scramble of her brain: she had got something she yearned for in all the years of marriage, in the long years when her beloved jewels had languished in darkness, separated from her by husband, servants and children, released only occasionally in stealth and guilt.

Now, at last, this kitchen was hers alone.

The safe felt very empty. Her hand found the little box and pulled it out. She was shaking as she pushed the big ruby on to her finger. It seemed to draw heat from her hand, glowing richly within its ring of icy diamonds, the pearl a spotlight on the summit. The imperfect skin over her knuckles faded and the short, square shape looked longer, narrower. A Romanov hand. She fitted the earrings, watching the cluster of diamonds above the pendant ruby sparkle back at her from the spotted mirror above the old sink.

In the heel of the hunt Mary had said, as if she were doing her a favour, 'By the way, you can keep the copies if you ever get them back. You wouldn't catch me wearing those things!'

Then Frank had said, 'I don't want them.'

So, willy-nilly, they had become completely hers. Her own Russian crown jewels.

She pulled herself straight. The woman in the mirror was older than she remembered, but not old. Fifty-five years old. The mousy hair had gone a touch grey and dry, the lines on her face and neck were etched deep, eyebrows drooping like curtains over grey eyes. Then an earring flashed, and the hand which rose to it sparked lights which fluttered from the mirror to the kitchen walls. The woman smiling at her was suddenly beautiful: ageless, stately. Almost regal.

XII

Widow's Weeds, 1970

* * *

She had gone into town for a hat.

'Darling girl, you do realize you're going to be on the front page of every newspaper in Ireland – not to mention Great Britain and the civilized world?'

'Please, Mary, there's no need to exaggerate!'

The restaurant was crowded and a rude young woman at the next table was openly staring. She had been listening to them ever since they sat down, though what she found of interest in two aged women having coffee together Rita could not imagine. You could only hope she was not a reporter. She was dressed badly enough, and it was imposs-ible to tell who you might meet in Brown Thomas these days. As Rita said to Frank once (in the vain hope of sparking him into conversation), such are the consequences of giving every Tom, Dick and Harry notions of fine living. Freedom was one thing, but putting money in the pockets of the *hoi polloi* was quite another.

'You read the newspapers, don't you, you look at the photographs?' Mary was giving the young reporter plenty to write about. 'And you still say you wouldn't mind being splashed across the front pages as one of those pathetic little women we all laugh at over breakfast?'

'Mary, please, all I need is a hat –'

'Of course you would! A woman in your position has a duty to look right. So don't talk to me about hats!'

She should never have agreed to the coffee. There was something not fitting about going out shopping at a time like this. And thanks to Mary there she was having her private affairs broadcast to every busybody in the Social and Personal Café.

'I beg you, not so loud!'

The huge eyes narrowed and then shut down, great flat lids showing subtle blends of blue and rather clumpy mascara. The silent freeze, as unnerving now as ever it had been. At the next table Miss Big Ears had finished her tea ages ago. Her shoes needed a good clean. Such impertinence, to sit eavesdropping in dirty shoes.

'As I said, I have a perfectly serviceable black coat, thank you very much, and I believe my Donald Davie shirtwaister will look quite adequate if anyone cares to come back to the house.'

'If? If?'

Mary was hooting now. Just for a second she looked like a schoolgirl. The eyes had grown rheumy, though, and the coiled hair on top of her racehorse face had lost any natural blondeness years ago.

'Girl dear.'

But how did she manage to preserve those long red nails which touched Rita's sleeve?

'This is life or death! You cannot appear tomorrow wearing that same dreadful old black coat I've seen you in for years!'

'It is not dreadful! You helped me choose it in Switzer's sale in what, 1966? It is still a very, very good coat.'

'And as your best friend I will not stand by and see you in a marked-down antique on the front pages of the national newspapers!'

Her words crashed between the tables like china. She was glaring, gripping Rita so fiercely their eavesdropper stiffened slightly, as if she might be witness to violence. Rita stayed silent, knowing any arguments would encourage her companion to do worse.

The voice had dropped to a whisper. 'All I want is your agreement. Will you grant me that, for all our sakes?'

At least she was no longer shouting Rita's affairs like a paper-boy.

'What is it?'

'I want you to let me take you in hand for this, that's all. Let me do that, at least?'

'Really, apart from a hat, there is nothing I require. And you know Frank never liked extravagance.'

Mary smiled. 'Rita, my sweet, it is no longer up to Frank, is it? It is in the national interest that you turn out tomorrow looking like the wife of a statesman. God knows what people will make of the rest of the O'Fiaichs – you're not exactly your average first family!'

'This is not the United States, Mary!'

'Just as well or Frank would have been shot dead years ago!'

She could still wound. But what would Mary know of family life? Rita had better manners than to remind her of her barrenness.

'Agreed?'

The proprietor and Mary seemed to know one another rather well.

'Howard, I want you to meet a very old friend of mine! Mrs Rita O'Fiaich, Howard Woolf.'

Mr Woolf's face was all concern. 'Of course, my dear Mrs O'Fiaich, I am honoured that you have come to me at such a time.' He drew her to a little damask couch. 'You'll accept a glass of sherry?' He waved a hand off-stage and as he drifted away towards a mirrored wall, Rita could not decide if it was himself or his shop which smelt so delightful, a scent of roses, thyme, salt and the hot sun on Mediterranean brick; the scent of another age, before Frank.

Memories of a childhood holiday unsteadied her, even before a first sip of fino from a gilded glass.

Mary did not sit down. She was pacing about, her heels sinking sharp tracks in the velvety grey ground. 'We want, we need, Howard, a coat and a hat to meet the occasion which my dear old friend must face tomorrow.'

Mr Woolf did not smile this time. He had a nice face, a smooth, sallow complexion above a pearl-grey suit and rather showy waistcoat. Even in old age Mary had not lost her ability to collect the odd exotic. 'And such an occasion, Mrs O'Fiaich, perhaps the hardest one ever.'

She recognized the long, measured look. It was the scrutiny of a new hairdresser or the rather naïve young artist who had asked to paint her portrait a few years ago, and then, poor boy, attempted to get Frank to buy the picture.

'There aren't many ladies of, forgive me, your age, to whom I would recommend such an absence of colour, but . . .' He touched something in the glassy wall to reveal racks and racks of gleaming fur. 'Yes, for you I think we can bend the rules a little.'

Afterwards she could not remember how she crossed the room, whether it was he or his silent lady assistant who had removed her coat, but there she was, a more amused, aristocratic Rita, staring back at herself in a black mink and matching pillbox. The stranger reminded her of someone she had seen in a book, an old photograph of Tsarina Alexandra, or was it Grand Duchess Xenia, stepping out of a troika in snow.

Mama's furs had felt quite different, stiff and dry and very dead. This one still lived. She wanted to stroke it, to press her face into it, feel its cool balm over her skin, and for just a second she thought of dear Nina again, of that hot, masked look she had when she reached out to touch something she thought beautiful.

It was not Rita's sort of thing at all.

Mary was sitting on the couch, gazing short-sightedly at a dreadful modern painting, bony ankles crossed, arm raised to sip what was probably a second glass of sherry.

'No, I'm terribly sorry, but it's just not me . . .' No, this was far beyond what she had been led to expect. A new coat, perhaps, if Mary insisted, but a *mink*?

She did her best to struggle free, but even as each garment was slipped away another slid gently up her arms to little encouraging cries from Mr Woolf and his accomplice.

Then suddenly, after all the rattling of hangers and *sotto voce* instructions behind her, a silence. There was nothing more to say. The wide lapels upturned to silk her cheeks, the huge covered buttons, and oh, that low-slung half-belt, a richness of black ink flowing out from narrow shoulders to a swaying hemline like the velvet curtains of dreams.

'Perfection!' Mary had stood up at last, holding out her arms to her as Rita struggled across the room.

'It's madness! I can't!' Rita's voice came out in a hiss. She felt curiously breathless, choking for control. They were on a high ledge. She must not look down, should not allow her eyes to stray towards that regal image in the mirrored walls. 'You know full well I haven't got the money for this! Tell him it is quite impossible!'

Mary tossed herself free with that maddening social laugh of hers. She didn't even have the good grace to lower her voice. 'I know no such thing! Don't I know there must be some money coming from Frank's estate – God knows, the way you two lived he'll have racked up a few bob in the bank! Not to mention that hush-hush business in America. Don't you also have a bit left from your parents? Well, now you can have it all – now the screws are off!'

It was paralysing. Modern times or not, there were certain things one did not discuss in front of shopkeepers. Rita turned away, and saw herself again.

'You're captain of your ship, girl, at long last! And you, Howard, are a genius!'

He had been keeping at a discreet distance, but now he rushed to them, happy and eager like someone picked from the crowd to meet a royal visitor. 'Seeing you in that coat, Mrs O'Fiaich, makes sense of my whole life's work. All you need now is a spark of colour – might I suggest a diamond brooch, maybe, or some rubies?'

The lines of hanging fur had disappeared. There were no more coats to be seen, nothing but this softly glowing presence about her body, this reflection of a fascinating eminence who was not Rita O'Fiaich at all. She dragged her eyes away from it and took a deep breath.

One thing she had learned in her long life: if something had to be done, you were better off doing it yourself. 'Oh dear, Mr Woolf, this is so difficult . . .' He tried to hush her, but she bashed on. 'The trouble is, I don't know if you know my daughter, Niamh? She can be very impulsive, you see, involved in the dog world and something to do with animal rights. She may even have picketed your shop . . .'

She might as well have told him her daughter was a drug addict.

'I am so sorry, Mrs O'Fiaich. I had no idea. Children can be very opinionated nowadays. Don't I know, with five of my own.'

'She has mellowed a lot recently, though. I don't think she's as militant as she was.'

Mary gave a snort.

'Ah, the young, Mrs O'Fiaich, they come on a little strong sometimes, but isn't it wonderful to see them exercising their rights. Isn't that what your husband fought for, after all?'

She had not the heart to inform him that Niamh was not as young as she might sound. He probably knew. But he seemed determined to forgive Rita her daughter, and she still had to get out of the coat. 'And another thing, you see, I am not a rich woman.'

He looked pained for the first time, almost insulted. 'Dear lady, please, let us not discuss money at this time. I want you to see this coat as a loan. Wear it tomorrow with my blessing, as my contribution to the life of a great statesman!'

People could be too kind for their own good. She gave herself up to staring at the personage in the mirror. Who would have believed that a short, aged woman with a pigeon chest and stumpy legs could look like this – important, dignified, patrician.

'Oh, Rita, do stop floostering and say yes!' The way

Mary was fussing about now, gathering handbags and scarves and gloves, you'd think they had another more pressing engagement, that they had wasted quite enough of her precious time. And she the one who had drunk all the sherries.

Rita thanked God Frank was not around to see this. All his life he had stood out against patronage, even against the interests of his own wife. Goodness knew there were plenty of perks available if he had only stooped to pick them up.

For his sake, she made one last try. 'That's not to say I don't have some money of my own, but I had never planned to spend it on such an item . . .'

Mr Woolf smiled as if he were hearing a familiar story. 'Please, Mrs O'Fiaich, only wear it tomorrow. Come back to me when you are ready and we will discuss terms. If by then you feel you cannot accommodate such a coat in your life, I will be happy enough that you looked so right, so very beautiful, at such a moment in the history of our nation.'

And so, somehow, there they were out on Grafton Street again with her old coat in a box much too good for it, and Mary waving at a taxi. In such a coat and hat it would have seemed wrong to run for a bus.

Relicts

* * *

Odd to think how many times she had stood at identical
graves, the same Greek chorus of wives, the same party
stalwarts gathered about the draped tricolour. To younger
members like Mr Haughey or Mr Boland, they were
already history, old men and women flickering endlessly
on a screen. Only her generation noticed how with each
exposure their number had dwindled, so that at every
gathering the group became more female, yet somehow
remained the same.

An effort not to look at Niamh. She had not bothered
to wear black, though as far as she was concerned, it was
her mother who was in the wrong. No attempt either to
conceal her greying hair or even control it under a hat.
Not a finger's worth of glove covering the unpolished
nails. There had been no apologies when she pushed into
the limousine that morning, only implying by the way she
arranged her rather large hips that it was Liam and his
family who were taking up the room, that it was an
inconvenience to herself they had made such a huge
detour from Terenure to her awful bungalow in Kilternan.

Rita knew better than to open her mouth. But for a
minute, when Niamh's eyes fastened on the fur, she
couldn't help wondering if a daughter had ever eaten her
own mother.

'For the love of God, Mammy, will you explain to me
what's that on your back?'

Why must she snarl in that common Dublin accent
which all three children had affected?

'Indeed, and I might ask you the very same!'

338

'It's disgusting! My own mother in a fur coat! I can't believe you'd do this to me!'

'Niamh, please, can't you see Mammy is upset enough as it is?'

Liam was trying to help, but why did they all persist in calling her Mammy?

'At least it's black.'

A neat answer, she thought, even if it sparked off a long discussion about bourgeois conformity, with young Aidan defending his earring on the grounds that he had agreed to leave his leather jacket at home in London and his sister complaining about some student party in Sussex she was missing because of Grandad's death.

Best to keep out of it. Tempting, though, to comment that nobody knew how to dress for funerals any more. Niamh's brown skirt was stiff with dog-hairs and her shoes looked like a pack of red setters had trampled over them, which they probably had. Liam hadn't even brought a bowler hat. It was a small mercy he hadn't flown over the whole family. She found their whinging accents strangely foreign, and Sara's flower prints and tinkling Indian jewellery had made a bright enough circus in the cathedral.

She looked out at Dublin Castle, restored at last to a vulgar copy of the place which her parents had enjoyed. Good for tourism, so they said. Christ Church slid by, towering above the site of recently discovered Viking streets over which the Planning Office would build their new offices. Progress: what the politicians called 'bringing Dublin into the twentieth century'. The bridge was wild with plastic bags, blown with the grime and petrol fumes between razed Georgian houses and the blackened façade of the King's Inns. Rita only thanked God that Niamh's heated discussion about the export of live horse-meat kept her off her other favourite hobby-horse: the destruction of the city. Her father would be spared any more attacks from her on that score.

Through the glass partition the driver's ears were burning. You had to be so careful these days. The way the new satirical magazines poked fun at respectable Irish men and women – even dug up unpleasant details about their private lives. There was no respect any more. Well, they would have trouble finding anything to write about her two boys. Was it the blindness of a mother to believe that the underneath of any upturned stone would yield nothing but dry earth? Journalists might do better with their spades around Liam's perfect wife. Make-up an inch thick and the smell of perfume would choke you. Looking down at her daughter-in-law's expensive black suit and patent-leather shoes, Rita wondered if Moira might be the weak link in the upright O'Fiaich front. If so, there was hope for them yet.

Saying Goodbye at Glasnevin

* * *

Even in daylight, the flash of cameras was frightfully bright. She dared not close her eyes, couldn't really, thanks to the mascara on her lashes. At least she was not expected to smile.

Everyone jumped when the soldiers fired into the air. Mary stood firm. Her performance today was worthy of the Abbey Theatre, the way her huge eyes stayed fixed on the flag-draped coffin as it was lowered into the ground, the tragic mask beneath the huge mantilla more convincing somehow than when she had buried her own.

Eamonn had finished his litany at last. He motioned Rita to throw some clay into the pit. It did not feel like the same stuff as the garden, this earth from which Frank and the rest of them were supposed to have come. Glasnevin clay clung cold and wet, a fleshy ball which bounced on the lid with a thin sigh, causing her to wonder had they put Frank in the best casket after all.

Still, this was hardly the time to question the undertaker. The thing looked solid enough, for its purpose.

'I'm sorry, Frank, I only wanted to do what was best.' The mourners might suppose she was saying a prayer.

Niamh stepped up beside her, letting clay trickle messily through her fingers. She appeared to be mesmerized by the grave, an untidy child again as she carelessly wiped her eyes with a muddy hand. Cameras blazed. Frank would not have liked such public display. Then Liam and Eamonn took charge, regrouping them: the family that prays together.

Jack Lynch kissed Rita's cheek, another one for the press. She was so surprised she didn't notice what he said.

341

It must have been the coat; he had paid her the barest civil attentions in the past. Maureen Lynch stepped next in line with her nice smile. 'I'm so sorry. Such a good man!'

Mr Cosgrave barely touched her hand. A cold fish at the best of times.

On and on they came, a long stream of familiar faces and strangers claiming acquaintance; soft country voices, smooth urban tones, an occasional scrape and twang from across the border. This was Frank's life passing before her, clasping her hand, dark men and mismatching women settling upon the family like a swarm of flies on a bone, then drifting away again from that dead place of carved marble and plastic domes.

It was nearly over. The way Eamonn tried to take her arm anyone might think her one of his doddery parishioners. She shrugged him off. After fifty-one years with a public man, she should be allowed a last audience alone. The family looked quite cheerful as they walked away. She was glad to note that Niamh had got herself some black stockings anyway, even if there were a run on the right leg.

It was cold here, but Frank was out of the wind. She peered into the pit again. Perhaps it was old age, but over the last few days it had often slipped her mind he was gone, that her husband of over half a century was down there in a box with brass handles which looked as fake as the wood. But then, she was used to silence, the bitter, unforgiving silence of a man who had refused to address a word to her for sixteen years. She would not feel alone. On the contrary, in this coat she felt cherished again, cosseted in a way she had not enjoyed since those odd times with Nina in America, and later, at home on dark afternoons with the jewels. The wind was from the east. So why the sudden memory of cinnamon, the smell of city streets, the breezy vastness of that country which they had roamed all those years ago? Tastes of hot apple, sweet on the tongue, smells of oil and concrete, senses of a rich, pungent, limitless place where they were young together and anything had seemed possible.

It was Sergei who had brought it all back to her, in death. Standing behind her when she turned from the grave, beaming with the same pure delight as when they had met unexpectedly in the towering cities. Here to collect what was his.

He relaxed his grip on her ringed fingers and stepped back. The space between them as wide as the grave.

'Dear lady.'

'How are you, Sergei? How is Piotr, and Nina?'

'Dead, the two, dead and gone, like much else.'

It was not a shock. She had felt Nina gone from her for a long time past.

He was frowning at her, waiting for a reaction. 'Alas, we are not hard, like jewels, we human peoples. We must, how you say, rot?'

Just like the man, this unsuitable topic introduced to a lady who had just buried her husband. But then, he was Russian, and old. He must be very old. It was hard to tell. Now she really looked at him he was not much changed from the young man she had last seen in 1920.

'Here, of course, we believe the soul has life everlasting.'

He chuckled as if she had said something witty at a cocktail party. Out of the corner of her eye she could see rough fellows with spades waiting to fill the gap in the ground and stifle Frank's angry silence for ever. Further off, the family stood awkwardly by the cars. They would be worrying about the gathering back at the house, but they would just have to wait.

Sergei's false teeth gleamed. 'Is better put faith in precious stones, no? Is immortality, I think.'

Downright blatant. Did he expect that by coming to her now, to this place, he could make her break down, pull the stones from her ears and hand them over just like that, 'All right, Officer, it's a fair cop'? These people were so crude, unforgiving. They did not deserve their treasures. At least in her country peasants like him could be moulded

343

into something more *savant*. Say what you like about the Irish, after so many years in politics she liked to believe that even Frank would never behave like this.

'Yet you have survived, Sergei. I missed you that time in London, in '55.'

'Ah yes, I go away to eastern borders, for long time. Here is last journey, I think.'

'Surely not?'

'I stay now in Moscow, now peoples listen. Because I live long, you know, I remember.'

'And do you tell them everything you can remember?'

His laughter was as inappropriate as a machine-gun, an explosion of noise ripping into retreating backs, causing some to stop in their tracks and look back for a moment at herself and this fat man at the graveside.

'Of course no, dear lady! Is many things, my country-men, like yours, not like to listen. But some day, perhaps. So, I come here, you see, I check memory.'

'I hope you can report that all is in order?'

He kissed her hand then. She had removed her glove to throw clay on the coffin. Earth still clung to her fingers and to the ring on her right hand, soiling the huge ruby. The way he stared, it was as if he were committing it to memory. When he looked up at last, she could have sworn there were tears in his eyes. But then, she had always assumed that Russians cried easily.

'You didn't believe I would honour our obligations, Sergei?' The realization that she was whispering made her blush like a bride. 'That I would guard our memories?'

His voice too was low. 'I know are hard times, comrade, even in West.'

'If you mean what I think you do, Mr Grigoryev, I must remind you that an inheritance such as yours is never for sale. That is something you should have understood years ago.'

'Is sentiment like this one which undermine revolutions.'

'And causes them.'

344

He had the good grace to smile. 'In Soviet Union we have many, many revolutions.'

'It must be very unsettling.'

'Is will of peoples, dialectic. You, I think, are not keeping ideals? You Irish do not want more revolting. Is like concrete, this place. This inspiration to Russian peoples, is corrupt puppet of capitalist West.'

'Surely you're being a touch over-dramatic, Mr Grigoryev?'

'So I ask, Comrade Rita, who inherit this memory?'

His hand was tight on her fingers as his eyes travelled across the graves to the family stamping impatiently beside the limousine. Indeed, they looked less than appropriate beneficiaries. The thought of Niamh ever wearing such things was quite ludicrous; the idea that Rita would leave them for Eamonn to hand over to the Church or to Liam, for that matter, made her shudder. They would most likely to be sold to support a business venture, unless Moira were to get her polished little fingers on them first and have them remodelled into some vulgar modernity. In fact, the very suggestion that she, Rita O'Fiaich, would behave so appallingly was downright insulting. How could men think like that? How like Frank, Mr de Valera and now Sergei and his Kremlin cronies to imagine even a tiny part of that immutable inheritance could be reduced to money; that one chip of those precious stones or ounce of pure metal might be weighed as the currency of an old woman's will.

She wished he would go away, go back to his politicians and plotters, faceless and unimaginative the world over. He did not deserve to be told.

'You insult me.'

'I apologize, dear lady, but –'

Difficult not to weep for the disappearance of friendship, this loss of trust. But such thoughts were foolish. The man was an enemy, a thief of his own past who had stolen the jewels to pretend they never existed.

'I have no claims on these items, I am only their

345

guardian. They belong to your history, which I suppose you, like many politicians here, would prefer to bury. They will be returned to your government on my death. A letter to that effect is in the hands of my solicitor. I should add that I have read accounts of the Soviet Union in the *Reader's Digest* which make me a little nervous. You seem a surprisingly vengeful people. But should anything untoward happen to me, I have given instructions that a more detailed explanation of how the jewels came into my care should be sent to a journalist, a young woman I always enjoy reading in Saturday's *Irish Times*. Of course, if I die a natural death, that memoir will be passed on to the Taoiseach, and, I feel sure, incinerated for the public good, like much else in Ireland's time-honoured tradition.'

His eyes hardly moved, but she could swear the puffy skin around them tightened and grew pale. His breath came in bubbling gasps between pursed lips. 'You know, of course, how this story is looking? You know what peoples are thinking? Silly old woman talking, destroying memory of husband? Destroying how you call it, patriotism for motherland?'

'Perhaps. But it's an interesting story. And by allowing that chance it be told, at least I would have kept faith with our ideals. Remember all that truth and justice we used to talk about?'

'I remember.'

When he shrugged the huge shoulders and smiled she glimpsed again a young Sancho Panza in an upholstered suit. It was not easy to dismiss the friends of youth, to blame them for the way life made them speak with their heads instead of their hearts.

'And I congratulate you.'

There was real warmth in the way he hugged her, pressing her face into the weft of his heavy coat as he kissed each side of her head. 'Goodbye, comrade. I congratulate struggle to hold what you believe. But is wrong, I think. Are not understanding these things, you Irish, not reading Marx or Lenin.'

'I think Frank banned them! But Nina used to say the same about yourself!'

'Hah! You fight good, Rita O'Fiaich. OK, maybe are last true revolutionary!'

With a bow he was gone, a troll with big feet stumbling away between stone angels and Celtic towers.

It seemed a good omen when the sun came out. It caught the line of diamonds on her finger, a blaze around the blood-red stone, the pearl like a cool drop of spittle at their centre. She checked for the earrings (to make sure he had not bitten them off in his embrace) and the feel of their solid presence made her suddenly happy. The past was dead, six feet down in the brown earth. Tomorrow she would buy a gramophone and the music of Rachmaninov and Shostakovich. She would fill her empty house with sounds which Frank would have condemned, like so much else, as English. When she tired of them, she might purchase a couple of airline tickets, take Mary to some place where they could sit together at café tables and feel the sun heat through to their bones. Majorca was very popular these days.

She had already decided about the coat.